THE BITTER SEED
OF MAGIC

Spellcrackers.com

SUZANNE MCLEOD

www.spellcrackers.com
www.orionbooks.co.uk

The right of Suzanne McLeod to be identified as the author
of this work has been asserted by her in accordance with
the Copyright, Designs and Patents Act 1988.

First published in Great Britain in 2011 by
Gollancz
An imprint of the Orion Publishing Group
Orion House, 5 Upper St Martin's Lane,
London WC2H 9EA
An Hachette UK Company

This edition published in Great Britain in 2011 by Gollancz

1 3 5 7 9 10 8 6 4 2

A CIP catalogue record for this book
is available from the British Library

ISBN 978 0 575 08433 9

Typeset by Deltatype Ltd, Birkenhead, Merseyside

Printed and bound Great Britain by
CPI Group (UK) Ltd, Croydon, CR0 4YY

The Orion Publishing Group's policy is to use papers
that are natural, renewable and recyclable products and
made from wood grown in sustainable forests. The logging
and manufacturing processes are expected to conform to
the environmental regulations of the country of origin.

Praise for Suzanne McLeod

'The fast pace of the plot and the fascinating cast of characters will give you a happy little vacation between the covers'
No. 1 *Sunday Times* bestselling author Charlaine Harris

'Refreshingly original ... compelling'   *SciFi Now*

'Funny and charming, with enough action to keep any book junkie entertained: Suzanne McLeod isn't just adept, she's bloody brilliant'   *Myfavouritebooks.blogspot.com*

'Fang-tastic!'   *Lovevampires.com*

For Corrie and Sophie
faithful friends

Prologue

Curse: n. A magical imprecation that brings or causes great trouble or harm.

Curses are never good – and never more so when you end up trapped in the middle of one – like the *droch guidhe*, the curse that started eighty years ago.

Clíona, a powerful sidhe queen – one of the noble fae – fell in love with a human, and she chose to bear him a son. Like all mortal children born of sidhe and human, her son was human and therefore ill-suited for life in the Fair Lands. So although she loved him with all her heart, she left him with his father when she was forced to return to her throne, charging those lesser fae who lived in the humans' world to watch over him and keep him safe.

Only the lesser fae didn't watch him closely enough.

The vampires found him.

And they lured him to his death.

Distraught at losing her son, Clíona cut off the lesser fae from the Fair Lands and *laid* the *droch guidhe* on them, *that they should also know the grief in her heart.*

Faelings – the mortal children of lesser fae and humans – were (and still are) the first victims of the curse: easy pickings for the vampires through no fault of their own. Unwilling to see more of their mortal children die before their time, and hoping to deny the curse its prey, London's lesser fae first chose to stop having children with humans, but as time moved on, it became clear that not only were no faelings being born, but since the curse had been *laid*, no full-blood fae children had been born either.

The curse had blighted the lesser fae's fertility.

And while they might be nearly immortal, while they might be able to heal themselves of most injuries, they are the offspring of the Shining Times, born of magic and nature conjoined, and to survive, they must continually renew their connection to keep it strong, and that means they must procreate. For if the fae don't procreate, then the magic doesn't either, and if the magic *fades*, then it won't be long before the fae follow it.

London's lesser fae are dying – literally – to break the curse.

But now they think they've found another way.

Me.

Chapter One

I stood at the entrance to Dead Man's Hole, the now disused mortuary under Tower Bridge, shivering as the chill March wind sliced through my leather jacket. The wind tossed the distant voices of tourists visiting the bridge with the angry cries of the seagulls, and brought me the wilder scent of the river. Weak sunlight flickered into the mortuary's large cave-like interior, making its Victorian glazed-brick walls and curved ceiling waver with watery reflections. Before me, my shadow stretched thin across the rough concrete floor, only to fade as it reached the large white sand and salt circle *drawn* in the room's centre. Inside the darkness of the circle lay the dead girl I'd come to see.

More than fifty humans a year lose their lives in the River Thames.

I wiped my damp palms down my jeans and walked into the mortuary, nodding at the female police constable standing watch on one side. The astringent scent of sage coated with something sweet and thick caught the back of my throat. I swallowed back a choking cough, and kept walking until I reached the edge of the circle. Flecks of rust-coloured bone and the dried green of shredded yew patterned the sand and salt in intricate swirls like the ritual ashes scattered after a dwarf's funeral pyre. The blood-spattered bone and yew meant the circle was consecrated to stop the dead from rising and hell-born visitors from appearing: standard police practice since the demon attack on London last Hallowe'en. And overkill in

3

my opinion, considering it was now March, not October. But then, my opinion wasn't one the police were usually interested in.

More than fifty humans a year lose their lives in the River Thames; around eighty per cent are suicides.

'Stay outside the circle, Ms Taylor,' the WPC said, her voice echoing the disapproval evident in her expression, her hand tightening around the extendable baton at her side. I quickly lifted my own hand in acknowledgement. She was a witch, and while I was no longer on the Witches' Council's hit list, witches still tend to get a little trigger-happy around me. The last thing I wanted was to give her an excuse to zap me with the Stun spell stored in the baton's jade and silver tip.

Careful not to let my trainers scuff the sand circle I studied the dead girl staring sightlessly up at me from its centre. She was in her late teens, and Mediterranean 'girl next door' pretty: dark brown eyes, blue-black hair still wavy even while wet, and a dusting of freckles over her nose. More freckles dotted the dark skin of her shoulders, but where the spaghetti strap of her flowered sundress had slipped, the line of paler flesh it exposed suggested her colour was a result of sun or a sunbed, and not her natural skin tone.

More than fifty people a year lose their lives in the River Thames.

And none of them fae.

The dead girl didn't look like any sort of fae. The suntan was the obvious giveaway; only human DNA produces melanin. As a sidhe fae, I could lie naked in the middle of the Sahara for a week and the dark-honey shade of my skin would never change, the blood-amber colour of my hair would never lighten, and even the sunburn would be nothing more than a rosy blush thanks to my fast-healing fae metabolism. But Hugh – Detective Sergeant Hugh Munro of the Metropolitan Police's Magic and Murder squad – wouldn't have called

4

me in to look at the body if this was just an ordinary human death.

And the witches wouldn't have put her in a consecrated circle.

So either she wasn't all human, or—

Dread constricted my throat. I didn't want this to be real. I didn't want to think about what this girl's death might herald. The *droch guidhe* that afflicted London's fae had already mutated in the past by blighting their fertility, and now it looked like it might be mutating again. And if it was, was this girl's death my fault? Had I somehow caused it by not doing what the fae wanted – by not having the child they wanted? A child they *thought* would *crack* the curse – despite there being no reason other than I was sidhe. Guilt at my continued refusal stabbed at me, but it was too life-altering a decision to say yes to without some sort of guarantee ... and without knowing the magical consequences for the baby, the one innocent I should protect above all others ...

I touched the gold pentacle where it burned reassuringly against my sternum, then shoved my fears away into the locked box in my mind.

Right now, none of that mattered.

What mattered was finding out if this girl's death was a random death – a *human* death – or not.

I flipped the metaphysical switch inside me and *looked*, checking for magic. The circle glowed like a ring of blood-red neon shot with bright stars, the Stun spell in the WPC's baton winked like an iridescent green firefly in my peripheral vision—

—and the girl's body disappeared beneath a binding of dirty-white ropes. I frowned, narrowing my eyes to get a better *look*. There was nothing neat about the spell trussing her up in a lumpy cocoon; it looked as if someone had gone crazy and sprayed her with a dozen cans of magical silly string. So whoever had tagged the girl was an amateur – or wanted the police to think they were – or they'd been in a hurry …

Whatever the answer, the girl was still dead.

Detached sadness at the waste of life rippled over me. I hadn't known the girl, she wasn't a friend I'd loved and lost … I clutched the gold pentacle – *Grace's gold pentacle* – as the memory of Grace sacrificing herself for me at Hallowe'en rose like some malevolent leviathan, eager to consume me— The box in my mind snapped shut again and the sadness drained away, leaving me numb and empty.

The mortuary and the dead girl came back into focus.

The silly string wrapping the girl's body blurred for a second. I blinked and rubbed my eyes, wondering if I'd imagined it, then crouched and *looked* closer. The string blurred again, near her head, and as I followed the lumpy line of the cocoon towards her hands, it shimmered like hot air in a heatwave. There was another spell—

'Genny.' Hugh's deep voice behind me made me start. I turned as I straightened and looked up at him. At just over seven foot tall – small for a mountain troll; usually they average around eight feet – he towered over my own five foot five. Concern creased his ruddy face, and anxious dust puffed from his head ridge to settle like pink icing sugar on his neatly trimmed black hair and pressed white shirt. Hugh always looked like he was still in uniform, even after four years as a plainclothes detective. Or nearly always. Memory flashed me a disturbing picture of the only time I'd seen him look less than smartly turned out … his rough hewn body nude and gleaming like polished red granite, white silicate blood streaming from the vampire bites in his neck and shoulder. He'd been forced to fight for his life, and for the lives of his friends and colleagues. And for me. He'd won, but it had taken six solid months of being buried and baked in his home earth, in the Cairngorms, to heal his injuries. And his mind.

Trolls are deeply pacifist at heart; killing doesn't come easy to them.

He'd only been back on active duty for a couple of weeks.

'Are you all right, Genny?'

'Yes, why?'

'You're crying,' he rumbled softly.

Was I? I touched my face, frowning as I realised my cheeks were wet, and swiped the tears away. Damn. I hated when that happened; like some part of me was reacting independently to the rest of me. It was occurring more and more often.

Sympathy softened the grey-cloud colour of Hugh's eyes. 'I'm sorry, I should have know this would upset you, finding someone in the river after what happened on All Hallows' Eve—'

'I'm fine.' I blinked and looked up at Hugh. This wasn't the time or place to talk about then … *about Grace.* 'Really, I'm fine,' I said again, firmly. 'Ignore it; I do.'

'I can't ignore it, Genny.' He laid his large hand gently on my shoulder. 'I was wrong to contact you. If the victim's not human, then this should be the fae's business to deal with, not yours.'

'We've been over this, Hugh.' I patted his hand on my shoulder, taking comfort from the warm grittiness of his skin under my palm. 'I have to find a way to *crack* the curse, so there's no way I can walk away from this, even if I wanted to.' Which part of me did: the scared part, that after five months of fruitless searching for an answer – one that didn't involve me getting pregnant – now wanted nothing more than to hide away and pretend I'd never heard of any fertility curse. 'And you were right to call me. The girl's body is *tagged* with some sort of Glamour spell.'

His concerned expression changed to one of disappointment and his fingers twitched with determination before he carefully removed his hand from under mine. Hugh is impervious to magic – actually, trolls are impervious to a lot of things – but the whole 'not affected by magic' also means they can't *see* it or *sense* it either.

'She didn't tell you,' I stated. *She* was Detective Inspector Helen Crane, Hugh's boss – and my own personal nemesis. *She* was also a powerful bitch – sorry, *witch* – so she had to have seen both the spells.

'No, but I suspected as much.' His massive shoulders shifted in a frustrated shrug.

Mentally I winced; looked like the *communication* problem Hugh was having with DI Crane wasn't getting any better, and it probably wasn't helped by his decision to keep me informed about any deaths involving magic; something DI Crane had refused to do. She knew all about the curse, and she had a vested interest in *cracking* it, but she'd decided she'd rather cut her nose off than even try to work with me.

Hugh indicated the dead girl. 'What can you tell me about the Glamour spell?'

'Well … it's smothered beneath the other spell, the one that binds her, and since she's dead and the Glamour is still in operation, I'd say it's probably some sort of Cosmetic or Disguise spell, and not an assumed projection which would've dissipated at the point of unconsciousness.' I pursed my lips. 'Quite what it's hiding though, I won't know until I remove it.'

The WPC made a noise like her broomstick had poked her, reminding me she was listening. 'I can't let Ms Taylor interfere with the evidence, Sarge,' she said. 'You told me you only wanted her to check things out.'

'Ms Taylor being here is my responsibility, not yours, Constable Martin.'

'I know the way things stand, Sarge, but—'

'But I am still your superior officer, Constable,' he rumbled warningly. 'At least, I am right now,' he added, a little ruefully.

'And I want you to stay that way, Sarge,' she said, throwing me a half-disapproving, half-entreating glare.

I gave her my best poker-face back. Hugh might look like he was only a few years older than my own twenty-five – especially since his recent 'bury and bake' session – but he was nearing seventy, and as he'd already pointed out to me on several occasions, he was certainly old enough to make his own career decisions without my advice.

'I want to stay your boss too, Mary,' Hugh told her calmly, as if having me here wasn't going to get him hauled over his boss's witch-fired coals. 'But we have a duty to this poor girl and Ms Taylor can help us do that.' He turned back to me. 'Can you tell what the victim is under the spell?'

'I can definitely tell you she's not fae,' I said, 'otherwise the body would have *faded* after death.'

'I know that, Genny,' he said, thin fissures of exasperation bracketing his mouth. 'Is she faeling?'

I waved a hand in frustration. 'She's been in the Thames, Hugh. Whatever the Glamour spell is, it's bespoke, made-to-measure magic that's survived being in fast-running water, which not only means it's expensive, but that she could be anything from a Beater goblin to a mega-rich "It" girl sneaking out in disguise.' I was crossing my fingers for the latter, going by the out-of-season tan, but something told me I wasn't going to be that lucky.

It wasn't a premonition – I don't get those; just the knowledge that four weeks previously the badly decomposed body of a faeling had been pulled out of the river and an inexplicable *administrative error* had meant the body had ended up languishing in the standard human morgue as a Jane Doe over the weekend before someone had discovered she wasn't fully human, by which time only fragments of some unidentifiable spell remained. Or so I'd been told. I'd never got to see for myself.

Not like now.

Still, if this girl was faeling, at least she didn't appear to have been in the water long. Then I realised what was nagging at me. My own inner radar should've been telling me what species the girl was – it's normally pretty good at that—

I looked up at Hugh. 'I really need to remove the spell to tell what she is.'

'Which Ms Taylor is not authorised to do.' DI Helen Crane's commanding voice cut in loudly before he could reply.

Chapter Two

My heart sank. The Witch-bitch herself had arrived. Just what we didn't need.

I turned to see her striding through the entrance of the mortuary, tall and slender, with her blonde hair pulled back in a severe bun: the fortysomething icon for witches and the police force both. She was beautiful, even with her patrician features harsh with anger. And as usual she was blinged-up like a goblin queen, the spells stored about her jewellery-bedecked person flashing and sparking in my *sight* like fireworks at a trolls' New Moon party.

I briefly closed my eyes to disperse the afterimage burned on my retinas and wondered sourly why she couldn't have turned up half an hour later. Now we were going to have to convince her to let me check out the dead girl, a much tougher proposition than the nice *fait accompli* Hugh and I had been hoping for.

'I gave strict orders to the effect that Ms Taylor's particular talents' – the vitriol in the inspector's voice made it clear it wasn't my talent with magic she was alluding to – 'were not required in this case, Sergeant Munro.' She halted, ramrod-straight, and stood far enough back that she didn't give the impression she had to look up to Hugh; a stance she'd perfected dealing with the trolls who worked for her. 'Please remove her from *my* crime scene before I have her arrested for obstruction.'

'I'm not the one doing the obstructing, though, am I?'

I murmured, annoyed at her attitude, even though I hadn't expected anything more from her.

Hugh moved so he was between us. 'Ma'am, the victim is *tagged* with a Glamour spell; it's possible she may not be human—'

'I am fully aware of that, Sergeant, which is why I have arranged for a full coven chapter to remove the spells without damaging them. They are evidence, after all, and will need to be investigated. If – and I stress the word "if" – the victim is determined "not human" after the safe removal of the spells, then I shall, of course, inform the appropriate persons within the fae communities.'

'The coven won't be able to get here for a good couple of hours, ma'am, and the spells have been in running water,' Hugh said in a neutral tone, glossing over the fact that his boss had just admitted to keeping him out of the picture. 'It's likely that they will deteriorate before the coven arrives. Ms Taylor can remove them now.'

'Sergeant, your concern is noted, but we will follow procedure on this. Please ensure Ms Taylor leaves.'

Angry at the way she was treating Hugh and the dead girl, and determined not to let her get away with stonewalling any longer, whatever her reason – and angry just because she was *her* – I stepped round Hugh and placed myself firmly in front of her, close enough to get into her personal space, close enough to smell her expensive floral perfume and close enough that the spell in her huge sapphire pendant shone like a captive star beneath the pale blue of her blouse, even without using my *sight*. *What the hell* was *the spell she had stored in it?* Oh yeah, something to do with protection from vampires. She had a phobia about them – a phobia that had nearly got me munched on the first time we'd met. Which was the Witch-bitch's standard operating procedure when it came to me.

I held up my company ID card. 'Inspector Crane, I know

we don't see eye to eye' – a hell of a clichéd understatement, despite the fact I was looking right into the Witch-bitch's own cold baby blues – 'but you know I work for Spellcrackers.com. As a company we've done consultancy work for the police before. You yourself have even employed us' – okay so she'd never actually employed *me*, just Finn: *my* boss, *her* ex-husband, and now my sort of … well, Finn's and my relationship is still in a stand-off position, what with the fertility curse hanging round like an over-eager matchmaking mama – 'so maybe *I* should stress that the "following procedure" excuse doesn't wash.'

'Ms Taylor—' She paused, visibly composing herself. 'By the time I get approval to pay your fee, the coven chapter will have been and gone.'

As excuses go, it wasn't even as good as the 'following procedure' one. I flapped my ID card and trotted out a flat version of my usual work spiel: 'Spellcrackers.com ~ *making magic safe* ~ Guaranteed. If you're not satisfied with the results, then don't pay.'

Personally I couldn't care less whether she paid me or not; not only was removing the spells costing me nothing but my own time, since this was my day off, but this wasn't about money. This was about the curse. And if this poor girl's death had anything to do with it, then I wanted— no, I *needed* to know. No way was DI Crane going to sideline me this time.

'You're well aware of the Spellcrackers.com guarantee,' I said. 'Not to mention my time's going to be a lot cheaper than a chapter of coven witches – surely your budget approval people can't complain at that,' I finished sweetly.

'It's too dangerous.' Her lips thinned. 'The body could well be magically booby-trapped.'

I laughed. She was getting desperate now. 'Ple-*ease* don't tell me you're worried about me, Inspector?' I leaned in closer still and lowered my voice. 'You and I both know that there're only the two active spells on the girl's body, but even if we've both missed something ... well, it's not like you've ever been concerned about my wellbeing before' – which was why she'd turned up too late at Hallowe'en, and why Grace was dead— *No, don't think about that now* – 'in fact quite the opposite,' I carried on in the same low voice. 'So I would have thought you'd jump at the chance to leave me in harm's way. Again.'

Consideration flickered in her cool blue eyes and for a moment I thought I'd won. Then her expression smoothed over and she stepped back. 'All very persuasive, Ms Taylor, but it is well known that you are unable to cast the simplest spell. Therefore I find I am not confident in your abilities to consider you as a suitable consultant ... in this case.'

I decided that if she ever did employ me to remove a spell for her, I'd make damn sure she hadn't tampered with it first. But she was right, my spellcasting abilities are nonexistent, despite me being made from magic – the magic's own little joke on me, I guess. Not that I was going to let her use my handicap to her advantage.

'This isn't about casting spells but removing them,' I said, 'and that I can do. I can even offer you a free demonstration.' I held out my hand towards Constable Martin, still standing to one side, her gaze carefully averted as she no doubt wished she was anywhere else but here. I *focused* on the firefly-green of the Stun spell in her baton. I *called* it— Shit! Too fast! The spell barrelled at me like a shining green bullet and I had a moment's panic that I wouldn't be able to catch it before it hit. I gritted my teeth as it skidded to a halt above my palm, millimetres above my skin, and started spinning like a drunken top.

I held it up, hiding a mixture of relief and triumph. 'One Stun spell, Inspector.' I smiled, ignoring the creeping numbness spreading over my palm. 'Now, I can *absorb* it whole' – hopefully without knocking myself out, but hey, I wasn't going to tell *her* that – 'or I can *crack* it' – not an option she'd choose; it was way too expensive a spell to be blasted back into the ether – 'or I can attach it to whatever you want.'

I tossed it lightly in the air, praying I didn't fumble the catch. I tilted my head in question and bared my teeth in a smile. 'So where would you like me to put it?'

Hugh rumbled a cautionary warning behind me.

DI Crane clenched her hands, her multitude of rings – a lesser person might call them substitute knuckle-dusters – clinking in fury. 'That spell is police property, Ms Taylor. Return it to Constable Martin's baton immediately.'

I tossed the spinning spell again, contemplating the tempting little thought that suggested zapping her would be a quick – if extremely stupid – way to end this argument.

As if he'd read my mind, Hugh squeezed my shoulder. 'That's enough now, Genny. Do as the inspector says and return the spell to Constable Martin, please.' He gently pushed me towards the constable, who gave me a disgusted look and held out her baton. I flicked my fingers and sent the Stun spell back into the smooth piece of jade.

'Done,' I said, turning back to Hugh.

'Thank you, Genny.' He looked down at the scowling inspector. 'Ma'am,' he said quietly, 'the press are already outside. If Ms Taylor walks out now while we wait for a coven to arrive, there will be a lot of speculation.'

Crap. The last thing I needed was the papers speculating; I had enough problems being the only sidhe in London without the tabloids taking an interest in me again. But DI Crane didn't need any more bad press where I was concerned either, not after she'd all but publicly accused me of murder not so long ago. I'd heard her superiors hadn't been happy. Of course, they weren't the only ones; I'd been pretty pissed off too.

Hugh lowered his voice further. 'Ma'am, I think you're allowing your personal feelings to cloud your professional judgement in this matter. It might be wise to take a moment to reconsider your decision and allow Ms Taylor to help with this particular situation.'

She flexed her beringed fingers as she turned her back on him and moved stiffly to contemplate the dead girl in the circle. Looked like Hugh's 'good cop' routine was working ... so maybe one last straw would break her.

'Inspector,' I said conversationally, 'if it turns out the dead girl isn't fully human, do you really want the fae community' – and by 'fae community' we both knew I meant Finn – 'to know you delayed matters unnecessarily?'

After a moment she turned, high spots of angry colour staining her cheeks. 'Sergeant, you and Ms Taylor have made your points. If you can assure me of the undamaged retrieval of the spells, then I'll authorise Spellcrackers.com to do so.'

Relief flooded into me. 'Thank you, Inspector.'

'Don't thank me, Ms Taylor. Just remove the spells, and then remove yourself.' She turned on her heel and strode out.

I narrowed my eyes at the circle. After dealing with Witch-bitch Crane, removing the spells was going to be the easy part.

Wasn't it?

Chapter Three

Ten minutes later, the authorisation forms were signed, my fee – hardly worth bothering with, if it weren't for the principle – agreed, and the preparations nearly finished. Once DI Crane had capitulated, she'd gone into whirlwind mode; anyone would think she wanted shot of me!

I watched as she reached inside her briefcase and carefully extracted a large padded velvet bag. Slipping the bag off, she held up an unframed mirror the size of a dinner plate. 'This is a solid silver *casting* mirror, Ms Taylor. I have two of them; one for each of the spells.' She leaned over and gently positioned the mirror on top of its padded pouch inside the circle. 'They are extremely costly. Please try not to damage them.'

I had no intention of even touching them; silver might well be the best way for witches to isolate magic – especially when you want to pick it apart at leisure – but it's not the easiest to use when you're allergic to it. My usual method – *tagging* unwanted spells to a salt block, then *cracking* the salt block along with the spell – was messy but effective, but it wasn't going to leave much to investigate. I could think of other things I'd be more comfortable transferring the spells to, like synthetic spell-crystals, or a lump of wood, even a plastic bucket – after all, magic isn't fussy; with enough *focus*, spells can be attached to *anything* – but the DI was the one running the show, so the silver *casting* mirrors were it.

She stood up and waved a hand at the circle. The thick white candles standing at the five points – air, earth, fire, water and spirit – flickered into life, the red neon magic in the circle glittered like the Milky Way, and the smudge sticks of smouldering sage flared, their herbal smoke twisting up to gather, cloud-like, against the curved brick roof of the mortuary.

'All ready for you, Ms Taylor,' she said with a cheerful edge to her voice.

I stifled a grimace. Never mind the mirrors; I wasn't happy about the rest of the magic show either, something she was well aware of, judging by her sudden change in attitude.

Trouble was, while magic might not be fussy – or something you can talk to or reason with – it definitely has a will of its own; and it tends to be unpredictable and capricious at times, especially around me. Being sidhe, and made of magic, has its disadvantages. Of course, witches are human – or at least their DNA doesn't show the paternal sidhe side of their parentage – and they have their own disadvantage; they need all their textbook rituals in order to manipulate the magic. But, for me, all the DI's extras just meant added complications.

I waved my own hand at the circle. 'Is all the paraphernalia really necessary?'

'Ms Taylor,' she said briskly, 'we're in the centre of London, one of the busiest cities in the world, and I am responsible for its magical Health and Safety, among other things. We have to take precautions against every eventuality, no matter how slight. So yes, "all the paraphernalia", as you so charmingly put it, is necessary.'

Probably true, though I was certain if she could get away with making things more difficult for me, she would. Needing more reassurance, I took stock of my audience. Constable Martin was staring studiously at nothing; she wasn't going to grass up her boss. Hugh watched from near the mortuary's entrance, his huge bulk almost blocking out the sunlight; he was on my side, but magic wasn't his forte. The only other person around was on the opposite side of the circle: Doctor Craig, the doctor on police call.

He was crouched down, scratching his almost unreadable bird-footprint notes on the yellow pad balanced on his tweed-trousered knee. His familiar bald pate, with its halo of grey curls parting over his jug-like ears, gleamed in the candlelight. He looked up, as if suddenly aware I was studying him, gave me a vague smile along with a quick head-to-toe assessment, then returned to his yellow pad. He was famous for his note-taking at HOPE, the Human Other and Preternatural Ethics clinic, where he was doing hands-on research into 3V (vampire venom virus) and where I volunteered, and both his presence and the obsessive, scratchy noise of his pen made me more at ease.

He hit my internal radar as a straight human, though I knew he could *see* and *sense* magic, thanks to a touch of magi-cal blood somewhere in his ancestry. And he'd always made it clear he'd be happier without the consultancy work he did for the police – making life better for the living was his thing – so no way was he in the DI's pocket. And none of her prepara-tions had fazed him.

Thinking about Dr Craig's ethos reminded me why I was here. I looked at the girl; she was dead, but finding out what killed her – whether it was the curse or something else – and stopping it from happening again could make others' lives bet-ter, maybe even save some too. So worrying about DI Crane having it in for me was wasting time. I dug out half a dozen liquorice torpedoes and crunched them quickly: the sugar boost makes it easier to work the magic. I handed my jacket to Hugh for safekeeping, touched Grace's gold pentacle for comfort and offered up a brief prayer for success to whatever gods might be listening.

And stepped inside the circle.

DI Crane muttered something vaguely Latin-sounding

behind me, magic prickled over my skin and the circle sprung up around me with an audible crack, like the jaws of a swamp dragon snapping shut. The dome of magic loomed over me like a giant inside-out multi-mirrored disco ball, reflecting my distorted face back at me, and I saw myself blinking in shock. What the hell had she *drawn* her circle with? This wasn't standard. It should have been a nice clear dome, like a huge soap-bubble blown by a child. I took a deep, calming breath—

—it felt like I was trying to inhale a cactus—

Silver!

She'd put silver dust in the circle.

Fuck! She hadn't just loaded the circle for demons, but for vampires too. My pulse sped up and I looked past the myriad ethereal mirrors to see her watching me with narrowed eyes. Was the silver dust just a normal precaution ... or had she used it deliberately, knowing my father was a vampire?

I shelved the questions. Most of London's fae knew I had a sucker for a father, so it wasn't much of a secret, not now, and I didn't have time to dwell on the Inspector's possible motives. I wasn't even sure I had time to deal with the spells before the silver knocked me unconscious.

Concentrating on slowing my pulse and my breathing to minimise the silver's effect, I knelt on the floor next to the dead girl. I gently took her damp hand in mine, double-checking she didn't have any more than the two spells on her: flesh-to-flesh contact makes it easier to sense the magic. I frowned. Her skin was wrinkled from being in the water, but it was still soft and pliable; either rigor mortis hadn't set in yet, or it had been and gone ... only the body looked too undamaged to have been in the water long enough for rigor to have passed. Still, time and silver weren't waiting for me.

I released her hand and plunged both of mine into the mass of magic binding her, flinching as the dirty-white ropes writhed around my lower arms, feeling like cold slippery eels. Gritting my teeth, I ignored the rest of the circle's distracting magic and *focused* on the rope spell. I *called* it and the ropes pulled away from the body with a nauseating sound like flesh being ripped from bone, and a sweet, rank smell assaulted my nostrils. Shuddering, I gathered the bundle into my arms and tried not to think how they were starting to resemble a mass of rotten intestines; or how the more I pulled at the ropes, the more the girl's body twisted and jerked like a fish struggling to escape a hook.

An urgent gasp almost broke my *focus*. Annoyed, I frowned up at Dr Craig.

'She's bleeding,' he shouted, pointing towards the girl's head.

Bleeding? I froze in shock. She couldn't be bleeding, she was dead!

Wasn't she?

But there was definitely a small puddle of blood spreading out from beneath her head.

'Genny, you need to start resuscitating her,' he ordered. 'Inspector Crane, you need to open the—'

The rest of his words were lost as I yanked at the last of the ropes and slid them down onto the nearest silver *casting* mirror, squashing them on with my hands and my will. A distant part of me registered the stinging burn in my palms, the sharp scrape of silver in my throat as I sucked air deep into my lungs, the brief dilation of the girl's pupils as I leaned over her head, pinching her nose and tipping her chin. I fastened my mouth to hers and forced my own breath into her body. I averted my head, inhaled, then breathed into her mouth again; watching the girl's chest rise—

Why the hell didn't DI *Crane break the circle?*

Another breath; another slight lift of the girl's chest.

The ropes had to be some sort of Stasis spell, trapping the girl at the point of dying, maybe.

Breathe again.

For fuck's sake, get a move on, Inspector.

I clasped my hands together in a fist and raised them over my head, bringing them down on the girl's chest with a hollow-sounding thud.

DI Crane swam into my sight: she was on her knees outside the circle, sweat beading her forehead as she traced glyphs on the outside of the mirrored dome with panicked, jerky movements. Behind her, Constable Martin was gripping the inspector's shoulders, her eyes closed in concentration; and looming behind both of them was Hugh's worried red-dusted face, alongside half a dozen others.

Crap, what the hell was wrong?

I sucked in more air. The copper smell of blood mixed with the rank sweetness and masked the sharp scrape of silver.

'I can't break the circle,' DI Crane shouted, her voice coming as if through a thick wall. 'The silver— blood— sealed ...'

I fastened my mouth back on the girl's as my mind raced to catch up: *Silver to hold a vampire— fresh blood in the circle—* Shit, maybe my vamp half was screwing with the circle's containment magic?

I breathed out.

'You'll have to *crack* it,' she shouted.

I briefly raised my head to take in more air, and *focused* on the magical dome of mirrors and the anxious group of police behind them. No way could I *crack* the dome; the mirrors might not be physical, but the salt and sand and bone in the circle were, and they would turn into enough shrapnel to flay the skin off anyone standing too close. I'd have to *absorb* the magical dome instead. Absorbing magic was never fun; absorbing sharp pieces of mirror, however metaphysical they might be, was going to be a fucking nightmare ...

—I lowered my mouth to the girl's—

She coughcd and retched, filling my mouth with bitter-tasting liquid, and I swallowed reflexively, shock, disbelief and hope coursing through me.

'She's alive,' I yelled.

The circle had to open – now!

I hurriedly but carefully rolled her over into the recovery position, then thrust out my arms, palms up, and *called* the magic. The candles guttered and snuffed out; a wind howled and buffeted my body; the dome of mirrors rattled, glowing red with reflected neon and blood ... Time seemed to stand still as the Glamour spell peeled away from the girl and I saw her true face. No longer human-pretty, she had small, black bead-like eyes, a hooked beak of a nose, thin, almost nonexistent lips and a receding chin: a faeling, and one with corvid blood, going by the black feathers growing from her scalp. The feathers were stringy with blood, and the shape of her head was oddly uneven ... Time started again, and the mirrors exploded into feather-winged flames and flew towards my heart like iron-tipped darts to a magnet.

I had a moment to think, *Oh crap!* before they hit—

—but the pain didn't come—

Instead, some*thing* grabbed me, and yanked me out of the circle.

Chapter Four

After an infinitely long moment of disorientation, the oddly light feeling in my bones told me that I'd been plucked out of the humans' world and was now somewhere in *Between*.

Between is the gap that links the humans' world and the Fair Lands. And unlike those places, *Between* is still malleable enough that with enough power and will, you can mould it into whatever you desire. Of course, depending on the magic's mood, its interpretation of your desires can be unpredictable at best, probably nightmarish at worst.

Much like the owner of the pale gold eyes, with their vertical, cat-like pupils, into which I was looking. I recognised the eyes and their owner, of course – hard not to when she was the only sidhe I'd ever met. Not that recognising her was going to help much. She wasn't exactly the type you could get any meaningful answers from, not being fully *compos mentis*. Which might account for her ... outfit.

Her head was crowned with a corona of yellow and white honeysuckle flowers, and long stems of golden heart-shaped leaves twined through the hip-length curls of her silver-blonde hair. Her dress was a flowing robe of yellow silk which billowed around her like sails in a nonexistent wind. That same wind riffled the feathers on the huge gold wings that spread out from her shoulders and framed her slender form. She looked like the love-child of a Rossetti painting and a Russian icon.

The angelic love-child raised her hands and suddenly we

were standing in brilliant sunshine. Tiny cartoon-like cherubs, complete with rosy cheeks, golden wings and glittering halos, zipped around our heads like sugar-hyped garden fairies, white fluffy clouds nipped our ankles like a litter of playful puppies and the scent of honey, cinnamon and sweetened vanilla fragranced the air. Above us curved a twenty-foot-high dome of magic, painted the sapphire blue of a clear summer sky. Etched into the blue was the smiling image of a benign old man with a long white beard.

I'd been beamed up to Disney Heaven. Lucky me.

The angelic sidhe looked to be in her late teens (although since she was virtually immortal, gauging her physical age by her looks was a guessing game I was never going to win) and she was staring at me with the expectant look of a young child who knows she's done something clever and is eagerly waiting for the pay-off: adult amazement.

I got the hint: I was supposed to do something – only I didn't know what … I flashed back to the last (and only) time I'd met her: I'd been knocked out by magic, and as I'd come round she'd been leaning over me. That time she'd been dressed up like an angel from a colouring book: *Cinderella's Christmas Spectacular*, and so I'd called her 'Angel' when she'd refused to tell me her real name. Obviously the Disney Heaven scene was meant to jog my memory, and it did. It was also starting to scare the crap out of me. I couldn't begin to imagine how much juice it took to make this huge patch of make-believe exist, let alone to bring me here. Nor what an über-powerful sidhe who had the mental age of a five-year-old could do if she decided to throw a tantrum … like the one about to hit any moment now, judging by the speed at which her expression was turning sulky.

'You're supposed to say the magic words.' She stamped her foot. 'You said them last time!'

Last time? I dredged my memory, then crossed my fingers

behind my back. 'Does this mean I'm dead?' I said, hoping the words weren't prophetic.

She gave a delighted giggle and clapped her hands. 'Do you feel dead?' she asked in a conspiratorial whisper.

It was the same answer she'd given before – so we were obviously following a script. Trouble was, my copy was blank. I ad-libbed, 'Not really. But then I didn't feel dead the last few times it happened either.'

Her laugh cut out and she peered closer, a small frown marring her delicate features, then she lifted her hand and poked her finger at my forehead. A jolt of raw power knocked me flat on my butt. 'Bad!' she exclaimed, her bottom lip sticking out in a sullen pout. Then she twirled away, humming tunelessly.

I sat there, winded. 'Nice to see you too, Angel,' I muttered, wondering what the hell she could possibly want with me. Or maybe it wasn't her that wanted me?

Angel was one of Clíona's Ladies. She'd gone AWOL from the Fair Lands last Hallowe'en and ended up in London. Clíona had been desperate to get her back, so in exchange for some information I'd needed, I'd found Angel and returned her safely to Clíona. In gratitude Clíona had granted me a boon: an offer of sanctuary at her court, the offer open for a year and a day, so long as I didn't 'bear a child'. Of course, if I did get pregnant then she'd kill me. Faerie gifts are to die for.

But if it *was* Clíona who wanted me here, why wasn't she putting in an appearance?

'What I really need is a clue,' I said under my breath.

Something brushed against my hand, and when I looked down, the playful clouds were littered with black feathers.

Goosebumps pricked my flesh. I quickly scanned the dome but could see no one other than Angel. Carefully, I gathered a handful of feathers and waved them at her. 'Don't suppose you know anything about these?' I asked, keeping my tone light.

She dashed over, bent down and peered into my face again.

Something old and sly and dangerous shadowed the pale gold of her eyes and I froze, instinct turning my bones liquid with fear. A scream lodged in my throat and I had to force myself not to scuttle away and hide—

Then *It* was gone and I sagged in relief as she squealed with excitement, snatched the feathers and tossed them into the air. They morphed into a murder of black crows and soared up to join the cartoon cherubs in their zipping flight paths. She flexed her long wings, gathered up her yellow robe and skipped away again.

I huddled among the playful clouds, getting my adrenalin-spiked pulse back under control. *Damn.* Angel was little Miss Looney Tunes, but even she was preferable to whoever her hitchhiker was. Still, I'd got my clue, now I just had to decipher—

Something wet dripped down the bridge of my nose and I swiped at it. Blood? I sniffed. It was sweet and coppery, but it didn't carry the liquorice undertone of 3V infection. So not mine then, thankfully.

I wiped my hand on my jeans and squinted up into the light. Slowly circling through the rosy-cheeked cherubs and the glossy blue-black crows like they were part of a gigantic cot mobile was a parade of soft toys: a plush polar bear, a mermaid with a glittering tail, and a fluffy rust-coloured bull passed over me as I watched. I flinched as blood splashed my face again. A beribboned unicorn and a copper-scaled dragon followed. I dodged the next splatter and frowned up as a pair of horses, one silver and one black, trotted before a well-stuffed brown teddy bear ...

The crows were dive-bombing the toys, spearing them with their beaks, making them bleed.

The hair at the back of my neck stood on end.

Was this another clue, or just a gruesome game?

Suddenly Angel shrieked in anger and whirled down

towards me. Heart racing, I jerked my arms up in defence, but before I could stop her, she punched her hand deep into my chest. Her eyes gazed into mine, the molten heat of her sun-bright pupils burning me as her magic seared my soul. Pain detonated in my centre as she ripped something from me and the world turned to grey mist, filled with gaping, hungry mouths and desperate, far-away screams—

—and then I was back in Disney Heaven, staring in shock as she lifted her hand triumphantly to display a squirming tangle of shiny entrails hanging from her fist. I clutched my stomach, convinced she'd gutted me, but as reality trickled through my horror, I realised my body was still whole and undamaged. I looked back at her, and the wriggling intestines resolved themselves into a nest of angry, hissing snakes.

'It is a soul, child,' a voice growled low in my ear, startling me even as I recognised the rank butcher's shop breath accompanying it. 'Not yours, you will be reassured to know.'

I was – but only by the information, not by the speaker. I twisted around to look warily at the large grey dog almost the size of a Great Dane looming at my shoulder. An unworldly glow emanated from its sleek coat like a silver aurora borealis as it regarded me steadily out of eerie grey eyes. The phouka, in her doggy guise, a.k.a. Clíona's bitch.

Crap, this really wasn't turning out to be such a good day.

Chapter Five

'Oh, look,' I said flatly, 'it's Grianne, my faerie dogmother, come to join in the heavenly fun. Why am I not surprised?'

The phouka bared long black fangs a true dog would never have. 'I have asked you before not to refer to me by that ridiculous mortal name. And this is not the time for levity.'

'Damn.' I bared my own teeth in a grin. 'And there was me thinking I was supposed to laugh in the face of death. Got that one wrong, then.'

'I am not here to kill you,' the dog said with evident disappointment. 'You are not with child, and my queen has given you a year and a day to find the answer you seek. Until then, you are safe from me.'

Yeah, like I was going to believe that. Next she'd be telling me that goblins had given up wearing bling.

When I was fourteen and a runaway, Clíona had sent the phouka to terminate me. According to Clíona, my father's vamp DNA taints my gene pool, and makes me an abomination – even though my mother's magical genetics means I'm pure sidhe through and through. No way was Clíona about to let me pass that taint on, curse or no curse. Only back then, things hadn't quite gone the phouka's way. Instead of killing me, she'd run into an opportunist vamp and I'd ended up saving her, which meant she'd ended up obligated to me for her life. So she'd reluctantly given me a reprieve. But if she could find a way for me to end up dead without getting her paws dirty, she would.

I jerked my head, indicating Angel, who was poking at the hissing snakes. 'So whose soul is it?'

'It is the sorcerer's soul. Eating it was not a wise choice, child.'

'I'm not sure "wise" or "choice" came into it at the time,' I said, hiding the relief that washed through me at her words.

Consuming the sorcerer's soul at Hallowe'en had been one of those act-now-and-live-with-the-evil-indigestion-later kind of things. The lack of immediate nasty consequences, together with the desperate need to find a way to *crack* the curse, had pushed it to the bottom of my to-do list, but now it looked like I could cross it off. It also looked like I owed Angel one.

'Chomping the sorcerer's soul was more an instinctive kind of revenge thing,' I said blandly, 'payback for the evil bitch sacrificing me.' *See? I have teeth too, oh dogmother.*

'I have already told you, child. I am not here to kill you.' The phouka's ears twitched in disapproval, the air wavered around her and Grianne took her human form. She sat next to me, dressed in one of her usual silvery-grey Grecian numbers. Her long, sharp features aligned in a haughty frown. 'My responsibility here is only to my charge.'

I gestured at Angel who had ripped off the head of one of the snakes and was busy sniffing it. 'So who is little Miss Bloodthirsty?'

Angel went to pop the snake's head in her mouth—

— and Grianne barked sharply. 'Please do not eat that, Angel.'

Angel?

Angel stopped, a mutinous look in her eyes.

'Why not allow your new creations to dispose of it?' Grianne said, her voice taking on a placatory tone I'd never heard before. 'I believe it would be good quarry for their hunters' instincts.'

Angel's face scrunched as she chewed over the idea, rather

than the snake's head, then she grinned, squealed and flung the head upwards. Between one blink and the next, the tiny cherubs had grown sharp red horns in place of their halos, their wings had turned black and pitchforks had materialised in their fists. One little red devil shot forward, expertly speared the head on its fork and brandished it high, taunting the others, before zooming out of the dome. The rest whirred in an eager, hopeful mob around Angel. As I watched, she tore off another snake's head and threw it up with happy glee.

Devilled sorcerer's soul. Hopefully they were taking it somewhere hot. 'Is Angel her real name?' I asked, curiosity getting the better of me.

'She was first named for Our Mother' – Grianne's grey eyes stayed fixed on her charge – 'but it was not a prudent choice, as the goddess quickly took her for Her own, and to call her by that name is to risk Her answering.'

I suppressed a shudder as I recalled the *something* I'd seen looking out at me from Angel's eyes. Had that been Her – Danu, The Mother? And if Angel was once named for Danu, then why were we in Disney Heaven, with its clichéd image of the Christian God? Somehow that didn't seem overly tactful, or prudent. If I were Angel, I'd be wary of pissing off a goddess who was likely to appear and answer my prayers in person. But then again, if I had Danu hitchhiking in my mind whenever She felt like it, then maybe I wouldn't see Her as a higher – and much scarier – being. It explained a lot, though: the combination of Danu and Grianne was enough to make anyone barking mad.

'Clíona renamed her Rhiannon, but she has not answered to that name for a long while,' Grianne continued, with a long-suffering sigh. 'Now she goes only by those names she chooses herself, and she has been Angel since you returned her to us. It would not be a problem, but she also insists on manifesting wings. At least she has not yet mastered them enough for flight, and we hope this phase will pass before she does. It is difficult enough to keep track of her as it is.'

'So,' I said, pushing away an overly affectionate cloud hovering near my face, 'who is she?'

'Clíona's youngest daughter.'

No wonder Clíona had been so hot for me to find her and send her home! Having her youngest daughter safe was obviously more important than her erstwhile goal to eradicate me and my vamp-tainted blood. I filed the information away; maybe I could use it somehow to make Clíona take back her death promise if I became pregnant (unlikely), or refused her offer of sanctuary (very likely) ...

Grianne rested her chin on her hands. 'She has been watching you since you helped her.'

I snorted. 'You can tell Clíona from me that stalking is illegal.' Not to mention skin-crawlingly creepy.

'It is Angel who watches you. She has conjured your image in every mirror, pool of water or silver surface at court. Sometimes she spends all night observing you sleep.'

'What? So the whole court's spying on me – all the time?'

'They can do so, if they have a mind to.'

Great. I was the star in my very own magical *Big Brother/ Truman Show*. My life was now complete.

'But there are not many who find you entertaining.' Grianne's mouth turned down. 'You work, you eat, you sleep, you read. It appears you lead an uneventful life.'

'"Star" to "has-been" in five seconds flat,' I said drily. 'My ego bleeds.'

'That is, until this morning.' Her lip curled, either in either amusement or disgust; I was never sure with Grianne.

I grimaced. 'Guess a murder always ups the ratings.' Another drop of blood stained my jeans. 'And talking of that, it's been *interesting* catching up, Grianne, but sitting here chatting isn't helping the poor corvid faeling who's just died, so maybe you could get to the point as to why I'm here, or, you know, just send me back?'

'You used to enjoy our talks, child,' she said, sounding unusually wistful, but her gaze was still fixed on Angel. I doubted she was much for listening.

'If by "talks", you mean "lectures"' – *on and on, about all things fae* – 'and by "enjoy", you mean "suffer", then yes, I did. Get to the point, Grianne.'

'Of course,' she said briskly, 'you should know that Clíona came to regret what she had wrought with the *droch guidhe*, so she petitioned Our Mother for a way to undo it. Our Mother decreed there should be a child for a child, and Angel is that child. She was created to break the curse.'

Whoa. I stared at her, questions jamming my mind to a standstill until the important one finally popped out. 'So why isn't the curse broken?'

'Our Mother's decree did not come with any specific commands other than to give birth to the child.'

Of course it didn't. Gods and goddesses don't do instruction leaflets – that would be way too easy. Although *a child for a child* sounded like it meant some sort of …

'Birth is not the only path that Clíona has trodden seeking an end to this,' she said. 'Death has been another.'

… *sacrifice.*

'It did not break the curse either,' she finished in the same brisk tone.

'Do London's fae know about all this?' I demanded.

She briefly turned her eerie eyes on me. 'Have you asked them what they know, child?'

Have I—? Surprise hit me like a stampeding troll. Crap. I hadn't. In fact, the only fae I'd talked to about the curse were Finn and Tavish the kelpie, and if I was honest, they hadn't exactly been long conversations. As for the rest of London's fae, I definitely hadn't tried to talk to them about *anything*; all

I'd done was hole up in my flat with the ton of books they'd collected over the last eighty-odd years in their efforts to find a solution.

Fuck. *Why the hell would I do that?*

'As I have already told you, you lead an uneventful life. This is not what Clíona intended when she gifted you this time to break the *droch guidhe*.'

I really needed to find out what was going on. I jumped up. 'Okay, message received. You can send me back now.'

'I would, but it was not I who brought you here.' She pointed at Angel, who was still humming as she smiled up at the blue-painted sky. All the devil/cherubs and hissing snakes were gone now, but the crows were still attacking the toys. They appeared to be concentrating on some more than others, but with all the bloodstained stuffing flying about, it was difficult to be sure. 'Angel was watching your trials with the faeling and the human police,' Grianne said, 'and as soon as the circle opened, she *called* you to her. I only followed in her wake.'

I narrowed my eyes. '*She* being Angel, or The Mother?'

'I do not know, child.'

Great. I was either here at the whim of Miss Looney Tunes, which could mean I was stuck here, or The Mother, which might be much worse. There was only one way to find out. I took a deep breath, arranged my face in what I hoped was a suitably deferential smile (just in case I was addressing The Mother), and strode over to Angel. 'I really would like to go back now, please,' I said, 'if you could arrange it? Or if there's something you think I should know, then please could you tell me?'

Angel grinned, showing small, white, even teeth, grabbed my hands and twirled us round. Her golden wings beat the air, and a backwash of honey and vanilla-scented wind blew my hair back and the dome blurred as she whirled us round and round, faster and faster … and as our feet left the ground, she let me go—

—and I flew through the air, crash-landed into the side of the dome and slid down into a crumpled heap. The proverbial stars blinded my vision in a rainbow of coloured lights, and as they cleared, I found her leaning over me.

'They are all dying,' she whispered, then danced away from me, the long tips of her golden wings dragging in the fluffy clouds.

'Who's dying?' I croaked.

The wheeling crows cawed loudly, then dropped, their small black bodies plummeting down, morphing back into blood-splattered feathers as they fell. *Right, the faelings.*

'He is killing them,' she shouted.

'He?'

She raised her arms up to the blue-painted heaven. The old man's benign smiling face had changed. And now a sharp-featured caricature of a horned Satan laughed down at us instead.

Someone really needed to buy her a digital camera.

She crouched next to me and I froze as she fixed me with her pale gold gaze. 'She prays for my help.' Shadows shifted in her eyes and she touched her finger to my breastbone. 'Her prayers disturb my thoughts. Put ashes in my mouth. Pierce my flesh. ' Her voice took on a deeper timbre. 'You will stop this. You will answer her pleas. You will break this curse. You will give them a new life.'

I really hoped that didn't mean what I thought. 'What new life?'

Angel blinked, and a wide happy smile bloomed on her face. 'She says to send you back now.'

She flicked her finger against my chest—

And I tumbled into freefall …

Chapter Six

'The sidhe's not *fading* again, is she, satyr?' A male voice: rough, remembered, hated—

Thin ropes snapped tighter around my ankles. Panic raced through my body; instinctively I jerked my legs against the bindings.

'By all the gods, dryad!' Another male voice: angry, worried, and reassuringly familiar. Finn. 'I told you, keep your branches to yourself before I take an iron axe to your tree.'

The ropes slithered away, taking my panic with them. I was back in the humans' world. *Finn* was here. Wherever *here* was. Finn meant safety—

Then my body chimed in with a barrage of complaints, too mixed up for me to work out what part of me was suffering the most – my stomach, my head, or my back, where I was laying on something cold, hard and unyielding; concrete, maybe.

A gentle hand brushed my face. 'C'mon, Gen, you need to wake up now,' Finn said softly.

'Don't want to,' I groaned in a whisper. Opening my eyes was too much effort. 'Everything hurts.'

'Yeah, well, *absorbing* a circle will do that,' he said, exasperation threading through the worry.

Yeah, and getting thrown around by a goddess doesn't help much either. Still, I was alive, if not yet kicking. And thinking of being alive— 'The corvid faeling?' I opened my eyes and stared up at Finn where he crouched beside me; his face was sombre, his usual moss-green eyes dark with sadness.

I sighed. 'She didn't survive, did she?'

He shook his head.

Damn. I didn't think she had, not after seeing all the crows die, but I had to ask.

'Hugh told me the doc isn't sure if her head injury was deliberate, or a result of her being in the river.' Finn's light touch as he brushed away a tear from my cheek told me I was crying again. *Damn stupid tears.* 'You couldn't have done anything, Gen; the doc said even if she'd been on the operating table while you removed the spells, he wouldn't have been able to save her.'

'*They are dying.*' Angel's voice rang in my mind. '*He is killing them.*'

I knew the poor corvid faeling wasn't the first to die, and by the sounds of it she wasn't going to be the last. Whatever was happening was ongoing, and it was down to the curse. Angel – or rather, The Mother – had been clear on that. They – *She* – had also been clear that *I* had to stop it.

And I was with Her one thousand per cent; the sooner faelings stopped dying the better. I just wished She'd given me more than a caricature of a photofit to go on.

I gritted my teeth and sat up. Vaguely, I registered I was outside, sitting on the concrete dock of Dead Man's Hole, not far from the disused mortuary where the dead faeling had been found. There were still police and others milling about, so I couldn't have been out for long ...

My vision blurred, a wave of dizziness hit me and I dropped my head to my knees.

Finn draped my jacket round me. 'Take it slowly, okay?' he said, his voice low with concern as he rubbed my shoulders.

Part of me wanted to melt into that concern. It would be so easy. He was my friend, and more – or at least both of us wanted him to be more. Trouble was, 'more' to me meant going out on a few dates, getting to know each other a *lot* better, and having fun finding out if the attraction between us was as hot and magical as it seemed. But thanks to the curse, Finn's 'more' meant he wanted to court me, to jump the broom with me— To make a baby with me. And that wasn't the only problem with whatever our relationship could be. Magic and fae genetics might make me a full-blood sidhe, but my father was still a vamp. Most fae – the majority – are wary of vamps, and rightly so, but Finn hated vamps with a passion. If it wasn't for the curse, would he still want 'more'? Still want *me*? I wanted to believe he would, but ...

But yearning after him like a Glamour-trapped human wasn't going to get me any answers. Or stop the killer. Or *crack* the curse.

'*You will stop this. You will give them a new life.*'

If I took Danu's command to mean what I thought it meant, and *if* I ignored all the problems that came with me having a child, then me getting pregnant should *crack* the curse and stop any more faelings dying because of it. They were pretty big 'ifs', especially considering the life-altering consequences involved. But even if they turned out to be not so *iffy* in the end, the faeling from three weeks ago and the corvid faeling today would still be dead, and whoever killed them would still be free. The murderer might be motivated by the curse – which wasn't in any way a justification – but that didn't mean once the curse was gone, that he'd stop killing. Odds were he'd find another reason to justify his actions. And faelings could still end up as victims, even without a curse making them easy targets. So before I changed my mind and got all positive about the whole baby-making/curse-breaking business, I needed to find the murderer.

And that meant I needed to talk to the police and tell them about my tête-à-tête with The Mother.

And that meant talking to DI Helen Crane.

Yeah. Like that was going to work. The Witch-bitch wouldn't

give me the time of day, even with Hugh backing me up, so I was going to need help: someone she wouldn't ignore. And that someone was sitting right next to me.

I rested my cheek on my knees so I could look at Finn. 'The faeling's death is to do with the curse,' I said quietly.

His hand on my shoulders stilled. 'How do you know?'

I opened my mouth, but nothing came out – not because I didn't want to tell him, not because he wouldn't believe me, but because The Mother's commands obviously came with a gag clause, one that currently had invisible hands around my throat doing their best to strangle me. Why the hell would she do that? Unless … she didn't want me inadvertently tipping off the murderer.

'Sorry,' I finally gasped, 'can't tell you!'

'"Can't", or "won't"?' Finn was good. He caught on quick.

I reached out, squeezed his knee and shook my head.

A thoughtful frown lined his forehead and I studied him as the invisible hands relaxed their hold on my throat. He was worth studying. With his strong, clean-cut human features, his short bracken-coloured horns standing about an inch above his dark blond wavy hair, his broad shoulders and honed muscular body, he looked like every human's wet dream of a sex god – if their idea of a sex god was dressed in a dark chocolate-coloured business suit, with a cream shirt open enough at the neck to offer a tantalising glimpse of luscious tanned skin sprinkled with sleek sable hair, that is. But the handsome-human look was just that: a look, or rather a Glamour – not a spelled glamour, like the one on the dead faeling, but a true Glamour, made from his own will and self-perception.

Finn's fae self is wilder, more feral, more gorgeous …

At the thought, magic bloomed inside me and lust and longing spread a rising heat through my body, catching me by surprise. A faint sheen of gold rippled over my fingers where they still rested on Finn's knee as the magic reached out to him and I snatched my hand back in horror before he noticed. This so couldn't be happening – not now, not after the magic had been quiet for so long. Crap. The last thing I needed was for *it* to join in and play matchmaker. I screwed my eyes shut, determined to push the feelings away.

It felt like trying to push back an incoming tide.

Trouble was, the magic *liked* Finn; it always had done. Of course, it didn't help that he didn't just *look* like a sex god; he was one, or at least descended from one, since his long-ago satyr ancestors were worshipped as fertility deities – until the archetypal horned god image was relegated to the dark side and characterised as all that was evil.

Oh, and renamed Satan.

Damn it! If The Mother thought I was going to suspect Finn, the ultimate white knight and all-round good guy, of having anything to do with the faelings' deaths, then She was nuttier than Angel.

But there was more than one satyr in London, and Finn's herd, like the rest of London's fae, were desperate to hear the pitter-patter of tiny hooves – so desperate that nine months ago they'd shelled out big-time for the Spellcrackers.com London franchise, and made Finn the boss – *my boss* – as a pre-emptive nuptial gift, to give us time to *get to know each other* (and making Finn their number one prospective curse-cracking daddy in the process). I didn't know how much money was involved, but I knew they were up to their eyes in hock to the Witches' Council. That amounted to a lot of desperation.

I opened my eyes. 'Finn, what's the head count of the herd?'

'Ninety-three.' His gaze sharpened. 'Why?'

Too many suspects. I needed some way to whittle them down. 'Just wondering.'

'Wondering what?'

The invisible hands grabbed my throat. I shook my head again.

He gave my shoulder a reassuring squeeze. 'Okay, then.' He slid his phone open with a quiet click. 'Then if you can't tell me, maybe you can tell Helen.'

Stupid irrational jealousy spiked as he said her name. I wanted him to call her: it was the right thing to do, to tell the DI in charge about a clue that could help solve the faelings' deaths, and maybe prevent more. That was a solution I wanted more than she did, going by her recent stonewalling. The fact that *Helen* was still Finn's number one speed-dial, despite being his ex for however many years, and that she never seemed far from his mind despite him saying it was over between them? Well, actions speak louder …

He snapped his phone shut. 'Helen wants us to meet her at Old Scotland Yard' – the Met's Murder and Magic squad HQ – 'and she needs you to give a statement about today.' He gave me a sympathetic look. 'Do you think you're able to get up yet, Gen?'

'Sodding hell, satyr, stop mollycoddling the bloody sidhe.' The loud, sneering words snapped my head up. 'She's got to be taken care of, and if you're not up to it, then I am.'

Damn. I'd forgotten about the dryad.

Chapter Seven

I glared past Finn's broad shoulders at the tall, thickset dryad. His arms were crossed, and he was smiling down at me with too many bark-stained teeth showing in his mahogany-coloured face for it to be anything but menacing. To be honest, he could've been sitting on the floor crying into the purple bandana wrapped round his clipped scalp and I'd have still felt threatened. Five months ago Bandana and his vicious little dryad gang had tried to kidnap and rape me. He'd used the fertility curse as his *extenuating circumstances.*

I stifled a shudder, determined not to give him the satisfaction of seeing my fear. 'What the hell is he doing here?' I demanded.

'He was here first, Gen.' Finn shot him a scathing look. 'Apparently he walked in and pulled you out of the circle as it imploded.'

Bandana grinned wider. 'You should thank me, sidhe. You tried to swallow too much magic and it was ripping you apart. If it hadn't been for my hold on you, you would have *faded.*' His long ankle-length brown coat split into a cape of thin whip-like willow branches that shifted in the spring breeze. I suppressed another shudder as the sensory memory of his branches tightening around my arms and legs surfaced. My stomach roiled. I pushed Finn away and hunched over, vomiting up a stream of brackish-tasting liquid.

'Oh, and I poured salted river-water down your throat while you were out of it.' I heard Bandana say happily through the noise of my own retching. 'Didn't want the magic to have any nasty lingering after-effects.'

Sadistic bastard.

'You're the only nasty lingering after-effect round here,' I spat out when I could, wishing, not for the first time, that I'd blasted the whole of Bandana into wood shavings when he'd tried to kidnap me, instead of just his appendages.

Finn held out a bottle of water. He'd just *called* it, so it was ice-cold from the fridge. I thanked him, rinsed my mouth and gave it him back – and it disappeared. Clasping his offered hand, I hauled myself up and stood swaying as another bout of dizziness hit.

I shrugged on my jacket, glad of its warmth against the chill breeze, and held on to Finn as I willed the light-headedness away. The Thames rushed past behind us, its waters slapping loudly against the concrete dock, almost blotting out the background buzz of tourists and traffic. A raucous caw drew my attention up to Tower Bridge above us. A large raven perched on one of the parapets, head cocked to one side, watching. Was the bird something to do with the dead faeling? There were ravens at the nearby Tower of London—

The bird dived down and past us and my gaze caught on the high railings fencing off the dock from the public, behind which a snap-happy contingent of paparazzi were clustered, their cameras flashing like a mini electric storm. I froze in panic until I realised the cameras weren't pointed at our little group but at the half-dozen uniforms – Constable Martin among them – gathered by the police cruiser tied up at the dock.

'The dryad *cast* an Unseen spell,' Finn muttered, squeezing my hand reassuringly.

Relief filled me, then Bandana being first on the scene clicked in my mind. His presence wasn't likely to be a coincidence. Ignoring the fear that sliced through my gut, I shot him a disgusted look. 'You've been following me, haven't you?'

'No one ever notices a tree, unless we want them to.' His cape of branches rustled proudly. 'Not even those who stand in our shadow.' He spread his arms out and turned a slow circle, magic dripping from his fingertips like raindrops from twigs. 'Something else you should thank me for, sidhe.'

My attempted rapist was stalking me.

I swallowed, hoping I wasn't going to vomit again. I had to stop him.

Finn let go my hand and took a step forward, his fists clenched. 'You and the rest were to keep your distance until the Summer Solstice, dryad. That was what was agreed.'

I had to get him to leave me alone. Just as soon as I could move without falling over.

'That was before dead faelings started clogging up the river,' Bandana sneered. 'What happens if *she's* next? You might be first in the queue, satyr, but snagging pole position means sod all if the sidhe's dead. We have to protect our future.'

I needed a plan.

'Gen's more than capable of protecting herself most of the time, dryad,' Finn growled, and I mentally cheered him on, 'but if she does need help, you'd be last on her list.'

Bandana wasn't even on *the list.*

I took a steadying breath and nudged Finn's arm, telling him to stay out of it, then, moving slowly, I walked towards the dock's handrail until I was out of sight of the press, not wanting to rely on Bandana and his Unseen spell. I looked down at the river – the tide was in, and the water eddied brown and murky just below the dock – then turned to face Bandana. 'I want you to take a message to Lady Isabella,' I said calmly. Lady Isabella wasn't high on my list of BFFs, but since she was Head Dryad and Bandana's graft-mother, I knew he'd pay attention.

He strode over and stood next to the railing, legs apart,

branches flexing, leering down at me. 'What's the message, sidhe?'

'Tell her I don't want you or any of her other thugs following me.'

He made a noise like branches creaking in the wind: laughing. 'You forget I just saved your life or something, sidhe?'

Talk about bigging himself up! My life hadn't ever been in danger, not that I bothered to tell him that. Instead I *focused* on the group of uniforms by the dock and *called* the Stun spell from Constable Martin's baton. She didn't notice as the green firefly of magic shot towards me. Luckily, I caught it easily this time and held it up between us. 'Now, I can be civilised if you think you can persuade Lady Isabella I'm serious. Or I can leave you here for her to find.' I hit him with a 'just give me an excuse' look. 'I'm easy, so it's your choice.'

'Lady Isabella won't be happy if you do anything to me,' he sneered, the tips of his whip-like branches flaring warily around him.

I shrugged, bouncing the Stun spell on my palm. 'That'll make two of us then, seeing as I'm *so* not happy right now.'

'You'll be even less happy if something happens to you,' he said, keeping a watchful eye on the Stun spell, obviously calculating whether he could dodge it from this close.

'A point I happen to agree with,' I said matter-of-factly, 'which is why there's a more interesting part to my message.'

He stopped watching the spell and frowned at me.

'So here's the deal: I'll agree to the dryads courting me' – his yellow eyes widened, and behind me I heard Finn stifle a groan – 'but I won't accept you or anyone else in your gang who took part in your little "rape the sidhe" excursion. Got it?'

Bandana's expression turned sullen for a moment, then he nodded sharply. 'Got it, sidhe.' He looked over my shoulder at Finn. 'Well, satyr, seeing as the sidhe's all hot for some real wood in her bed, looks like you're missing more than sap in your pencil.' He laughed, and the mocking, creaking sound was repeated by the nearby trees. 'But hey, no hard feelings; drop by sometime and I'll give you some tips on how to get it up.'

Anger and disgust ripped through me. He really wasn't worth the ground he was planted in.

'Try keeping it up like this,' I muttered and before he could react I slapped the spell on his chest. Burned mint scorched the air as green lightning arced around him, shoving him back against the railing as it stunned him. Impulsively, I dropped to a crouch, hooked my hands behind his ankles and used his own momentum to heave him up and over the railing. The splash as he hit the water echoed through the loud buzzing in my head as my legs gave way and I collapsed onto my knees, gasping; the exertion was too much, too soon after being jerked around by The Mother. I knelt there, watching in a satisfied daze as the fast currents of the Thames whisked Bandana's unconscious body away. Lady Isabella would still get my message, just not quite so quickly.

After a few minutes, I realised Finn was again offering me a hand. I looked up to meet his gaze.

'Lady Isabella's not the only one who's not going to be happy,' he said quietly, belying the flash of anger in his eyes.

No, she wasn't. I wrapped my fingers round his and let him help me up. 'He's a willow; a trip down the river isn't going to kill him. Unfortunately.'

'That wasn't what I meant, Gen.'

'I know,' I said, reluctantly pulling my hand from his and stepping back.

'Why, Gen?' A muscle twitched along his jaw, but beneath the anger, I could see the hurt, and remorse pricked at me. 'Why did you do that, why agree to let them near you, when I've done everything in my power to keep them away from you? To keep you safe?'

He had. For the last five months he'd kept a gentlemanly distance from me, while managing to convince the rest of London's fae he was my boyfriend/lover/whatever. He'd also convinced everyone to respect our privacy after the trauma of Hallowe'en and Grace's death – 'privacy' being a nice euphemism for: *no, we weren't going to have sex in the middle of a public fertility rite for all to witness,* no matter how much they all considered that a great idea. I owed him a hell of a lot for that, and I'd find some way to repay him, but—

'I'm sorry, Finn.' I held my hands out. 'I wish things were different, that we could work this out just between us, but two faelings are dead because of the curse. I've got to find out what's happening and stop it. It's time I started talking to the rest of them.' And why the hell I hadn't done that before now was something else I needed to find out.

'Hell's thorns, Gen, they've been desperate to talk to you. The only reason they haven't is because every time I asked you, you said you weren't ready to deal with them yet.'

'I did?' I said, astonished. Damn, there was too much that I seemed *not* to be doing. Almost as if it wasn't me in control ...

'You should've told me you'd changed your mind.' Finn raked his fingers through his hair, his expression troubled. 'We could've organised things, kept it all on a formal basis. But now you're going to have every dryad in London turning up on your doorstep. And they're going to want to do more than talk. Then there's the naiads; they're going to send their own candidates to court you once they hear. I'll talk to the herd Elders, see if ...'

His voice faded as suspicion dragged an elusive memory from a dark hole in my mind. There was something about a ... spell around my wrist? Yeah, that was it. I pushed my jacket sleeves up and *looked* at my arms. The right was clear. The left was patterned with a blood-coloured band of rose-shaped bruises that encircled my wrist like a monochrome tattoo. The 'tattoo' marked me as Malik al-Khan's 'property' and protected me from other vampires. As vamps go, Malik was a good guy … although my recent memories of him were a bit on the hazy side, which was never a good sign around vamps; it probably meant he'd been using his vamp mind-mojo to make me forget what I was only now remembering. But that was a problem for later. As for his mark, well it was a *convenient* thing to have – if I ignored the whole 'he hadn't asked, and I wasn't any sucker's damn property' issue. I'd got so used to it that I never even noticed it now, but as I squinted at it sideways, I found what I was *looking* for: the spell, hidden beneath the rose-shaped bruises. As I *focused*, the spell grew brighter, twisting up my forearm like the stem of a briar rose, its multitude of tiny thorns pricking painlessly into my flesh and vanishing into my body.

A Sleeping Beauty spell.

Anger roiled in my gut. The damn spell was magical Valium, turned you into an emotional zombie. Now I knew why my life had been so *uneventful* since Grace's funeral. I grimaced as the spell's stem disappeared up my jacket sleeve, winding itself tightly around my elbow, the thorns puncturing my skin. Bandana's salt-water emetic must have temporarily neutralised it, but now it was resetting itself.

'Gen.' Finn grasped my shoulders. 'You're not listening to me. This is serious.'

He was right. There were only two people who could've got close enough to me to have *tagged* me with the spell, and one of them was standing in front of me. The other was Tavish, the kelpie. If I was looking for a culprit, Tavish – that scheming, over-protective, arrogant, alluring, charming, centuries-old wylde fae who was also my sort-of ex – won hands down. But if I was looking for someone to be my 'prince' and 'awaken' me, then Finn could easily play the heroic stand-in. But getting that close to him meant the magic's matchmaking got a chance to push my libido into overdrive.

Damn, whatever I did I was screwed (no pun intended), but at least with Finn and the magic I had a chance of being in control.

Decision made, I reached up and cupped Finn's face. His skin was warm and firm under my touch and the magic rose from within me, leaping like golden wildfire between us. His eyes widened in surprise, their moss-green depths flickering emerald, and his hands tightened on my shoulders. I drew him down to me, waiting for him to tell me 'no'. He didn't. Our lips met in a soft kiss that slipped like molten gold into my centre, pooling heat at my core. Gods, he tasted as wonderful as I remembered, like sweet ripe berries. Lust wrapped in longing shivered through me, followed by misgivings that had nothing to do with the magic. I wanted this, *wanted him* – but I didn't want him to think this changed things. Or that kissing him was nothing more than a means to an end.

I pulled back far enough that I could see his face. 'Sorry,' I murmured, dropping my hands. 'I shouldn't have done that.'

'Hey, don't apologise,' he said quietly. Then his mouth quirked and he added, 'Not your fault I'm irresistible.'

Surprise winged through me.

He waggled his brows. 'Sex god here, remember?'

I gaped at him, incredulous. 'Are you flirting with me?'

'Obviously not well enough,' he said wryly, 'if you have to ask.'

Some indefinable barrier I hadn't even realised existed between us fell away and time seemed to roll back to when we first started working together, before everything got serious with vamps and sorcerers and curses, and when his outlook had been more about enjoying what life brought him. An ache closed my throat. I'd missed that Finn. Now it looked like I could have him back.

Lightness lifted my heart and a grin slowly spread across my face. 'Irresistible?' I snorted, poking him in the chest. 'Ha! In your dreams.'

Mischief glinted in his eyes. 'My dreams, my rules. So sex god works for me.'

I laughed. 'Keep working, and maybe you'll get somewhere in another century.'

He slapped a dramatic hand to his chest. 'You do thus grievously impugn my reputation, fair lady. I demand satisfaction.'

'No chance,' I snorted. 'You're really on a losing streak'

He pulled a hopeful hang-dog face. 'Well, I s'pose I could settle for us getting all smoochy again. I think I can fit you in' – he made a show of checking his watch, then grinned, teeth white against his tan – 'in about thirty seconds' time. But it's a one-time special offer, so take me while I'm hot.'

I rolled my eyes at him, then as I felt the spell's thorns prick my shoulder, reality smacked me in the face. I sighed and held my arm up like a kid asking a question. 'Is that offer good for a Sleeping Beauty spell?'

He stilled, his brows meeting in a frown as he took my arm and studied my wrist. A muscle jumped angrily in his jaw, then he blew out a breath and said almost to himself, 'Well, that explains a lot, doesn't it?'

'Yep,' I agreed. 'And a certain kelpie is *so* not going to be a happy water-horse after this. I'm thinking gremlins in his precious computers ... or maybe duck weed in his lake.'

'Ouch.' Finn winced. 'Remind me never to upset you. Hey, but if you need help, then I'm in.'

I grinned. 'Thanks.'

He let go of my wrist and smiled ruefully. 'Guess this means I'm not that irresistible after all.'

'Oh, I don't know.' I tilted my head and smiled playfully.

'You could always try and convince me. Maybe kill two birds with one kiss?'

A sharp gust of river-scented wind sliced between us and he reached out and carefully tucked a stray strand of my hair behind my ear. 'Probably not a good idea, Gen. Tavish must've *tagged* you after the funeral. Those type of spells aren't meant to last for more than a couple of weeks, to help you get over things, so it should've worn off by now, which means he's added his own spin to the spell. If I defuse it instead of him, it could cause problems. Want me to try and pull it apart instead?'

Always the white knight. But much as I appreciated his concern, I couldn't help regretting that reality had brought responsible, serious Finn back. 'Thanks, but I'm not sure there's time.' I jerked my head over at the police still milling round the launch bobbing next to the dock. 'There's my trip to Old Scotland Yard. I have to give a statement, remember? I don't want to delay it, and to be honest, I'd feel happier if the spell's gone before then. That's if you don't mind …'

'Mind? "Tempt not a desperate man",' he said softly, eyes bleak. Then a wicked light eclipsed the bleakness so quickly I thought I'd imagined it. 'Though, talking about tempting' – a grin spread across his face – 'how about a bet? Dinner says the power of my kiss demolishes the spell inside a minute. If it takes longer, then it's my treat.'

I narrowed my eyes. It was a bet he couldn't lose. 'Do you *really* expect me to fall for that?'

'Yep,' he said, much too happily. 'Unless of course, I'm *really* not irresistible.'

Anticipation fluttered in my stomach and I struggled to contain my smile. 'Go on then,' I said, deliberately offhand as I stuck my chin out and puckered up. 'Get it over with.'

All teasing left him as he reached out and clasped my face, mirroring my earlier movements, then bowed his head and rested his forehead against mine. The flutter brushed my heart, turning nervous – in a good way. 'This one's for the spell,' he murmured, his breath warm across my cheeks. He dropped a light kiss on my mouth. My lips tingled, and a pulse of power slipped over my body, pebbling goosebumps on my skin. I felt the thorns pop out of my flesh and the briar stem wither and dissipate back into the ether.

'Wow,' I murmured, warring between being impressed and disappointed that the kiss was over so fast. 'Looks like dinner's on me then.'

He gave a quiet, satisfied laugh.

'Now this one' – he tilted my face up, thumbs caressing my jaw, his eyes dark and solemn – 'is for you alone, Gen.' He pressed his lips to mine, a quick hard kiss that filled me with his magic and stopped my heart for one glorious second, leaving me breathless, wanting and stunned.

Oh boy, now I really was screwed.

Chapter Eight

It's always handy to know you've got a five-hundred-plus-year-old – and therefore *very* powerful – vamp on speed-dial, even if the realisation is one of those good news/bad news things.

The bad news was I'd been arrested.

Not for the kiss (even though the kiss was *so* worth being arrested for, and more) – although seeing it was DI Helen Crane who did the arresting, the kiss was definitely a contributing factor. But on the face of it, the charge was for Misappropriation of Police Property, the police property in question being the Stun spell I'd *misappropriated* from Constable Martin's baton, the one I'd used to knock out Bandana. Talk about irony. Witch-bitch Helen Crane had all but pounced on me with barely hidden glee as soon as Finn and I turned up at Old Scotland Yard.

More bad news: I was locked up in a state-of-the-art silver-lined police cell. The twelve-foot-square room had no windows, a six-inch steel door, a CCTV camera high in each corner, icky plastic facilities, and the ultimate in sleeping luxury: a barely there foam mattress. The cell was designed for keeping vamps and dangerous witches in line. Maybe I should be flattered she thought so much of me? Nah, she was just going for overkill again.

I shifted uncomfortably on the thin mattress and carefully tugged down the sleeves of the snazzy white paper jumpsuit provided by the Met's fashion dept, adjusting them so that the silver-plated 'slave-bracelets' studded with chips of jade (Stun spells) and citrines (Magic Dampening spells) no longer touched my skin. I did the same with the jumpsuit's legs – not that it would make much difference; every time I moved the heavy leg manacles slipped down again, so now I had a nice neat line of silver-burn blisters encircling both ankles.

Yet another helping of bad news: my phone call to Malik – or, to be precise, as it was daylight, my call to Sanguine Lifestyles, the vamps' 24/7 answering/gofer service. The request to make the call had just popped out of my mouth without any conscious decision on my part. That meant Malik had not only used his vamp mojo on me but planted a mind-locked order in my head. No wonder my memories of him were so hazy.

'Damn arrogant vamp,' I muttered. I didn't need to be *ordered* to call him if I needed help.

After all, I wasn't stupid. If the Witch-bitch thought she could make a strong enough case out of my stealing the Stun spell to show I was a danger to humans, I could be taking a one-way trip to the guillotine. It was an extreme possibility, but thanks to fae not having 'human rights', it was still a possibility, and one she'd taken great pleasure in reminding me of during my arrest. Calling Malik, hell, calling *anyone* who could get me out of Clink was a no-brainer. Okay, so it might end up with me paying in blood, but considering the alternative, there really wasn't any contest.

Still, irritation at high-handed vamps aside, at least the woman at Sanguine Lifestyles had been reassuring. 'No problem, Ms Taylor. If you can give me the details, I will have a solicitor there within half an hour.'

It had sounded too good to be true.

Now, eight hours later, of course, I'd discovered it was.

I growled in frustration and frowned at my left arm.

The final bad news was that as well as wearing the pretty police-issue jewellery, I was now also sporting a nifty spell bracelet. I'd uncovered it when I'd been looking for any magical leftovers from the Sleeping Beauty spell. Like that one, the bracelet had been nothing more than a line of shadow hidden beneath Malik's mark. With the citrines in the silver manacles dampening my magic, it had taken me all day to force the bracelet back into its original form.

But hey, time was one thing I had plenty of.

I gave the bracelet an assessing look. Tavish really had gone to town when he'd made it. Even pissed off as I was at the tricky, scheming kelpie, I had to admire his spellcraft. The plait of green-black horsehair tied tightly round my wrist was threaded with twelve glass beads, five clear, and the rest deep red. I hadn't a clue what they did. Interspersed between the beads were seven tiny charms. The first two were detailed replicas of a red telephone box and a red London bus, both made from enamelled gold. The telephone box had been crushed: I guessed to stop me from communicating with anyone outside London. And the bus was missing its wheels: probably to make sure I couldn't leave – or be taken from – the capital. The third charm was a wooden spindle – no guesses needed as to what that did – but at least it was broken, thanks to Finn's kiss. The fourth was an inch-long miniature sword – like some sort of scimitar – so perfectly carved from obsidian that it could only be the work of a Northern dwarf. The fifth and sixth were a gold egg, crackled like old china, and a plain gold cross; again, I hadn't a clue what they did. And the last was a miniature platinum ring set with a black crescent-shaped gem.

Malik's ring.

I knew it was his, not just because I recognised it, but as I touched it the knowledge of who it belonged to, and what it was for – contacting him – was suddenly there in my mind. Damn vamp and his mind-mojo.

'Of course, I should've known the pair of them were in it together,' I told the ring. 'They're as bad as each other when it comes to being scheming, arrogant and over-protective.' And it wouldn't be the first time the pair had joined forces to make my life 'safer' in their opinions. 'Question is, do I try and activate you, or not?'

I tapped my knee thoughtfully. The worst that could happen would be I'd end up knocked out by the Stun spells stored in the fancy silver manacles. The best …

'Hell, there's got to be some good news in all of this,' I muttered.

Focusing, I carefully ran my finger along the edge of the tiny sharp blade, wincing as it sliced cleanly through my flesh.

I stared at the bright bead of blood.

It trembled with magic.

Then before the spells in the silver manacles could kick in, or I changed my mind, I smeared the blood on the ring. It dropped off the bracelet into my palm, growing large enough for me to wear.

'Here goes nothing,' I murmured, and pushed it on my finger.

Chapter Nine

The over-large double doors in front of me were Victorian style, the six panels painted white, the frames a bright sky-blue. The paint looked fresh enough that I gingerly touched it to check it wasn't still wet; and that the doors weren't some magical construct. The paint was dry, and the doors felt as mundane as any other. There were no locks or handles, just steel push-plates. Curious about whether this place was as real as the doors felt, I glanced around. I was on a small, boxy landing. Behind me, a large green arrow pointed down a dimly lit concrete stairwell (which thankfully didn't have the sulphurous nose-wrinkling smell of most such places) but otherwise there was nothing to indicate where I was … except I was now in jeans and, oddly, one of the lime-green hi-vis T-shirts sporting the Spellcrackers.com logo that we wore whenever we worked in a public place. And my feet were bare and half-frozen: the concrete floor was cold.

The knowledge in my mind told me Malik's ring was a way to contact him. I'd sort of expected to get the magical equivalent of a telephone call, to hear his voice with its not-quite-English accent in my head. But as soon as I'd put the ring on, I was just standing here in front of the blue and white doors.

I eyed them speculatively. 'Right, enough of cold feet, let's find out where you lead.'

I pushed the right door open. It swung back easily, if slowly, and without the spooky sound effects I was half-expecting, and left me staring into a long shadowed corridor about ten feet wide. The corridor was made from steel beams, the ones on the walls criss-crossing each other to leave large diamond-shaped gaps that had been fitted with glass. The diamond windows framed a spectacular view of the dying sun searing the cloud-laden sky with golden fire. It reminded me of one of Tavish's Turneresque paintings. I frowned; the corridor was familiar too ... then it clicked: it was one of the high walkways of Tower Bridge.

I'd chased gremlins along every single frustrating step of both the two-hundred-foot-long corridors, five – or was it six? – times, in the last month alone. The little machine-hexing monsters kept getting down and dirty in the bridge's engine rooms, and Spellcrackers had won the contract to evict them ... which was proving to be so much easier said than done. But now, as I scanned the gloomy walkway, it was empty of all life apart from the lone figure about halfway along gazing out over the Thames.

Malik al-Khan.

I headed towards him, bare feet silent (but warming up) on the rough blue carpet. As I came closer, he turned to me, his expression enigmatic. I stopped, stunned at the sight of his pale, perfect face, his dark almond-shaped eyes that showed his part-Asian heritage, the black silk of his hair where it slipped just below the sculptured line of his jaw ... Damn. I'd almost forgotten how beautiful he was. A memory surfaced of him lying still and defenceless during the demon attack, and my heart lurched wildly at the thought that I might have lost him too. Shocked at my reaction, I clutched Grace's pentacle at my throat and scowled, my steps slowing.

Sure, he was eye-candy, and I'd have to be more than dead not to have the hots for him, *and* he'd come to help me when I'd asked, putting himself in danger for me, which gave him not just my unending gratitude, but also a place in my heart. But no way was I going to *fall* for the beautiful, arrogant, infuriating, over-protective vampire. He might be a good guy for a vamp; but vamps don't do partnerships; they go for that whole 'master and slave' type of deal. And while I was sort of okay with all the other vamps thinking I was Malik's 'property', I wasn't interested in being the trophy sidhe/arm-candy for real ... however hot his arms – and the rest of him – might be.

I relaxed my grip on the pentacle and speeded up over the last twenty-odd feet. I stopped just out of touching distance, and ignoring the splinter of regret lodged beneath my ribs, I held up my left hand with his ring on my third finger and waggled it. 'So does this make me a Bride of Dracula? 'Cause if it does, you've got the clothes wrong.'

'Good evening, Genevieve.' Pinpoints of red – *anger*? *Or just power*? – flared in his pupils, then were gone. A warm, calming breeze sprung from nowhere and slipped over me like the barest touch of silk. Power then, since he was using *mesma* to play with my senses. I relaxed despite myself at the small vamp trick. 'The ring is merely a conduit, while your outfit is one I am aware you have recently worn. Wearing clothes that you own and are familiar with assists in grounding your consciousness in the dreamscape.'

Ri-ight. So this was a dream and not a gaol-break, then. Figured.

His own outfit was familiar enough too: a plain black T-shirt and black jeans. The casual clothes showed the lean, hard muscles honed to peak perfection before he had taken the Gift. Of course, physical strength wasn't an issue for him now, not with his vamp powers, and he wasn't going to grow old or lose any of that muscle tone, whatever he did or didn't do – the reason why so many vamp wannabes hit the gym. But all that lean, hard strength made me curious about his past. Having been on the receiving end of his compulsive neat-freak skills a couple of times, I was almost ready to bet he'd been some sort of soldier. I looked down. His feet were bare too.

'What's with the no shoes thing?' I said.

His enigmatic expression didn't change. 'I decided it was easier than choosing an unacceptable option from your own footwear collection.'

Footwear collection? I had about two dozen pairs of shoes, and half again as many boots and trainers; that was a long way off Imelda Marcos territory. And he'd said it with a straight face, so I couldn't tell if his tongue was in his cheek or not, nor did it explain why he wasn't wearing any. And when the hell had he checked out my footwear anyway?

'I take it that "familiarity" also explains why we're here enjoying the view then?' I indicated the walkway, and the bird's-eye panorama it gave over London. The wind-rippled waters of the Thames reflected the blazing clouds, giving the river a metallic sheen, and in the distance the Ferris-wheel silhouette of the London Eye was a dark, nobbly circle against the bright sky. Nearer was the Tower of London, its two outer stone walls guarding the massive castle compound with the mediaeval White Tower dominating the centre. Dusk seemed to swathe the Tower's regimented battlements and the lead-capped turrets in ever-shifting shadows. As I looked the shadows coalesced into a huge amorphous shape that rose high into the heavens, the sound of wings buffeted my ears, and the bridge beneath me turned insubstantial and swayed. Vertigo hit. I shot my arms out for balance—

'Genevieve! Look at me!'

I blinked at the sharp order, and fixed my gaze back on Malik. The bridge solidified. I blew out a relieved breath and lowered my arms.

'The more recognisable the landscape is to you,' he said, 'the less likelihood there is of your subconscious invading the dream. It allows for a continuing illusion of reality.'

Right. No more staring at the view. Unless … 'So, there's

no other reason for being here other than it's somewhere I know?'

'Why do you ask?'

'The faeling who died this morning was found in Dead Man's Hole.' I waved in the direction of the Tower, careful not to look. 'She had corvid blood, possibly raven.'

'Ah. I did not know the faeling's heritage. No, I am sorry, Genevieve. I chose here because it is one of two public places that you frequent on a regular basis, and where you wear your eye-catching outfit.'

I plucked at the T-shirt. 'Trafalgar Square being the other?'

'Yes, but it is normally too populated a place to use as a dreamscape. The lack of people would make your subconscious uneasy, and it would try to compensate. I have no desire for our conversation to be held while you attempt to corral pixies, entertaining as that might be.'

Entertaining for him and everyone else, maybe. And he was right, I chased enough of the mischievous little fiends in my real life job without adding them to my dreams. I sighed and gave Malik a resigned look. 'I suppose I shouldn't really be surprised you've been spying on me.' After all, everyone else was. Maybe I could charge a fee?

'Then you will be surprised.' Amusement glinted in his eyes. 'There were thirty-four videos of your energetic interactions with the pixies on YouTube, last I looked. There are fewer of you dealing with the problems here, but the bridge management are particularly vigilant at updating their blog when it comes to any interruption in service.' He smiled fully, and I caught a glimpse of fang. 'I have no need to spy on you when the general public are happy to do the task for me.'

I *was* surprised – not by the YouTube vids; that was old news – but by Malik being web-savvy. For some reason his enthusiastic acceptance of modern technology hit me as out of character. Then I remembered he and Tavish were friends and co-conspirators. And Tavish is a top geek for hire; rumour has it he even contracts for the Ministry of Defence. Maybe Tavish's geekery was catching, along with his magical expertise.

'And of course, there's this other little surprise.' I held my left arm up again, rattling the charms on my newest accessory. 'I can guess what four of the spells are for; care to enlighten me about the sword, the cross and the egg? Oh, and the beads?'

He inclined his head, an elegant acknowledgement. 'The beads are time, they span a month each. The egg is to contain the sorcerer's soul. The cross is protection from the demon.'

I frowned: twelve beads meant twelve months, which made sense, what with Clíona's year-and-a-day time limit and the fact that five of the beads were clear of magic. The egg had to be why the sorcerer's soul hadn't caused me any problems so far – and now Angel/The Mother had removed the soul, it no longer would, thank the goddess. And that explained why the egg was crackled, like old china. A cross as a shield symbol was pretty standard, although it would have to have been infused with the faith of someone who *believed* for it to work. Not that that was too difficult, as most churches would provide one, for a suitable donation.

'And the sword is to sever your tie with Rosa,' Malik continued, all trace of amusement gone now, 'should she attempt to reactivate the spell you share.'

Shit. I rocked back on my heels at this mini-bombshell. Rosa was a vampire, and the spell we shared linked us together magically. It had allowed me to unwittingly borrow her body whenever I'd used it – *unwittingly*, because I'd thought the spell was a bespoke Glamour spell, one I'd used as a disguise on my 'faeling rescue missions'. It had turned out to be much more. Vamps' souls are magically bound to their bodies as part of the Gift – hence their near-immortality – and it usually takes the removal of the heart or head, or total destruction of the body (usually by fire or daylight, or a combination, depending on how old the vamp is) to kill them and release the soul (which then goes straight to Hell, or its equivalent, according to most human religions; personally, I wouldn't want to guess). But the spell had trapped Rosa's soul, leaving her body functioning but vacant. When I'd found out the truth, I'd resolved never to use the spell again. And then Rosa had been lost in the Thames at Hallowe'en, and the spell tattoo on my body had gradually faded until it was now almost gone. I'd assumed she was too.

Worry tied a knot in my gut. 'Are you saying she could come back?'

'No, not after this length of time,' he said. 'The sword is a precaution only, in case she was found and her soul somehow restored.' He studied the water a hundred and forty-odd feet below us, and a tendril of his grief, twisted with guilt and anger, soured my own euphoric relief. The emotions felt like *mesma*, but he didn't seem to be projecting them intentionally; it was more as if I was picking up an echo. It wasn't something I'd experienced before. I shivered and hugged myself, uneasy. Was it part of the whole conscious dream thing? But I didn't ask, not wanting to intrude.

Finally, the emotional echo died and I moved to him and touched his arm gently. 'I'm sorry,' I said. And I was, for him, not for her. He'd loved Rosa; he'd been the one to give her the Gift. But Rosa was better off gone. I'd inadvertently lived some of her thoughts, her memories and desires, both as a human and a vamp – it wasn't an experience I ever wanted to repeat.

He turned and looked at my hand, staring at it, apparently uncomprehendingly, for a moment, then raised his eyes to meet mine. They were opaque and unreadable. 'Rosa truly died a long time ago,' he said with no inflection in his voice. 'Now her soul will be at peace.'

'Losing someone you love is—' My throat closed. I lifted my hand to Grace's pentacle, but in a movement almost too fast to see, he caught my hand and held it. 'Thank you ...' He paused, then continued, 'Thank you for your sympathy, Genevieve.'

I nodded. 'You're welcome.'

He raised my hand and pressed a kiss to my fingers. A spark of magic ignited, like a golden ember from a smouldering fire, as his lips graced my skin. My pulse leapt and my grief disappeared as my body flooded with anticipation and desire. I swallowed, tasting the sweetness of Turkish Delight, and heat curled inside me. His pale fingers gripped mine, the crushing pain muting to pleasure as his eyes darkened and filled with predatory speculation, and something else I couldn't name. My clothes felt too hot and too tight, my breasts heavy, my nipples aching as they pushed against the thin T-shirt. An insistent need throbbed between my legs, and at the curve of my neck where he'd once bitten me.

He lifted his head, scenting me, his pupils incandescent with fiery hunger, and fear slid adrenalin into my veins, hyping the lust already lacing my blood. I froze, willing my errant pulse to slow, and concentrated on not wresting my hand from his hold. It might be a dream, but it felt real enough, and he was still a vamp. You don't struggle with vamps, it gets them too excited. And right now I was excited enough for both of us.

We stood like statues on the high walkway, the rays of the dying sun turning us golden, and the silence and tension coiled between us until I wanted to scream, to lash out at him— To offer him my body and my throat.

Instead I fell back on my childhood training and counted: one elephant, *two elephants*—

His lips drew back and I stared, transfixed, at his sharp canine fangs. His two needle-like venom incisors were still retracted, which was good, wasn't it? Donating blood was one thing, getting a venom hit at the same time? Well, if that happened I'd be falling a long, long, lo-ooong way off the wagon. And the last thing I'd want to do was struggle.

Five elephants ...

Sweat trickled down my spine.

Seven ele ...

I wanted desperately to drag my eyes from his fangs, to stop imagining the bliss as they pierced my flesh, the delicate pull of his mouth at my throat spiralling pure, dazzling ecstasy into my body ...

Ten ...

A tremor shuddered through him. He leaned closer, his dark spice scent eddying round me, his silky hair brushing my cheek. I angled my head, yielding. His lips pressed against the vulnerable spot under my jaw and my pulse jumped eagerly.

Thirteen ...

He sighed and the tension slipped away like fast-melting ice, leaving me somehow desolate and bereft. His thumb brushed over his ring on my finger. 'Why did you use this, Genevieve?' The words were a bare whisper against my skin.

Really, really *not for the reason you're thinking.* I shrugged, an infinitesimal movement of my shoulders. 'I was getting bored with the entertainment provided by the police.'

Seventeen ...

'You were concerned that your phone call to Sanguine Lifestyles had not reached me?' he asked softly, an odd, indecipherable note in his voice.

'Yeah, that too.'

He pulled back, black eyes opaque as he studied me for a long moment. 'No other reason?'

Like maybe I wanted to lose myself in your power? Feel your body join with mine? Not then. 'No.'

He released my hand.

Chapter Ten

I waited until I was sure my knees were going to hold me, then tucked my hands into my jeans pockets, out of temptation's way. His or mine, I wasn't sure. Talking with him was one thing; touching him looked like it blew my self-imposed 'hands off' policy into orbit. And what the hell had caused me to react like that to a simple kiss? It certainly hadn't been anything he'd done – at least, I didn't think so. I moved to lean against the criss-crossed steel-beam wall of the walkway, putting more space between us.

A deep frown lined his brow and he turned to stare out at the Thames. The sun had disappeared below the horizon and a parade of bright lights had sprung up along the river's banks, reflecting oranges, reds and blues down into the water. I knew the walkway had its own lights, but here in Malik's dreamscape it remained dark, shadows obscuring both its ends.

'You have no need to worry, Genevieve,' he said finally, speaking calmly, as if nothing had happened. 'Your solicitor is at this moment speaking to a judge to facilitate your release.'

Back to business. I relaxed and took a breath. 'Thank you,' I said.

'Details of your arrest have not been notified to the press,' he continued. 'You are apparently helping the police as an outside consultant with the investigation into the faeling found dead this morning.'

Interesting. 'If they're covering up the arrest, then why's it taking so long to spring me?

'Detective Inspector Helen Crane is insisting that you know more than you are revealing to her. It has caused complications.'

'Figured she'd use that against me,' I muttered.

'Do you know more, Genevieve?'

'Yep, and I'd be overjoyed to tell her everything – except I can't.'

'Can't, or won't?' he asked. Finn wasn't the only one who caught on quickly.

'Can't,' I said. 'The info came with a gag clause – a magical one.'

'I see.' He turned to me, his usual impassive expression back in place. 'Perhaps you should tell me all you are able.'

I started talking, beginning with Hugh's early morning phone call, the dead faeling wearing a Glamour spell, the argument with Witch-bitch Helen, right up to the silver-in-the-circle débâcle. He stopped me now and again to ask a quiet clarifying question, then resumed pacing – well, not exactly pacing, but his movements were enough to make me think 'agitated'. But as he kept shooting glances into the shadows gathering around the far-away doorway, I didn't think it was my story making him edgy.

'Now this is where it gets tricky,' I said, shifting in my perch in the V of one of the diamond-shaped windows to a more comfortable position. I started to tell him about my visit to Disney Heaven, expecting the goddess' strangling hands to cut me off any second. To my surprise the gag clause turned positively garrulous, and the words came streaming out in one long, breath-stealing rush: '—and the goddess wants me to answer someone's prayers and stop whoever is killing the faelings because of the curse and ultimately break the damn thing.'

I stopped suddenly, as if released from whatever magical

compulsion had kept me talking, and sank to my knees on the rough carpet, gulping for air. I stayed there, relearning how to breathe, awash with relief that I'd finally managed to tell someone about my heavenly trip.

Malik crouched in front of me, his elegant fingers clasped together. 'And you have not been able to speak about this to anyone but me?'

'Not so far.'

'Which would suggest that those you have not been able to talk to are connected to these deaths in some way?'

He'd reached the same conclusion I had about the Goddess' horned god photofit.

'No,' I said firmly, 'Finn's got nothing to do with this.'

'Genevieve.' Malik tipped my chin up, his expression gentle. 'We all have the capacity to justify unimaginable actions when desperation and a belief in a greater good persuades us that they are the lesser evil.'

I ducked my head and contemplated his bare feet; they were long and elegant too. 'Unimaginable actions' added up to when he'd attacked and left me for dead when I was fourteen. And then there was the other time – *or times? Did the last one count, seeing as I was already dead?* – that he'd killed me. He'd had good reasons, and I'd forgiven him. Hell, I'd *asked* him to kill me that last time, though to judge by the sorrow haunting his words, he hadn't forgiven himself.

I reached out, touched his clasped hands briefly. 'This isn't you we're talking about,' I said quietly.

Regret flickered in his eyes. 'The satyr is no different to any other, Genevieve. And he has shown he has both the will and capability to kill.'

'Finn hasn't killed anyone …' but even as I said it I remembered he *had* once set a trap to kill Malik, and he'd staked a vamp on his horns (the vamp had later vanished, so I didn't think Finn had actually killed him). Both incidents had been to defend me. 'Finn wouldn't kill an innocent, whatever the end result.'

'But you admit the satyr could kill if he thought the death deserved,' Malik said.

There was no hint of accusation in his mild tone, but I didn't like where he was going. I narrowed my eyes. 'Why are you so hot to blame Finn?'

'I am trying to divine the goddess' intentions, this is all. Do you believe She means that you should bear a child to break the curse?'

'Fine, side-step the issue then,' I muttered, not caring if I sounded like a sulky child. Whatever I'd expected him to do after I'd told him about my heavenly trip, this wasn't it.

'Genevieve, it is not I who is side-stepping the issue.'

No, it was me. Not that I knew what I'd expected him to do or say differently. I picked at a snag in the blue carpet as I tried to work out what I wanted.

'Genevieve?'

'Yes!' I ground out, yanking out the thread. 'I think that's what She means.'

'And what would happen if you told the fae about your goddess' command?'

I threw my hands up. 'They'd do what they've been doing all along, of course: try and convince me to have a child.'

He cast a quick look past my shoulder, making my back crawl, then focused back on me. 'Until now you have refused to bear a child because the outcome – breaking the curse – was not a certainty,' he said. 'But if the goddess has provided that certainty, then there is no reason for you to refuse any longer.'

I scowled. 'Got it in one.'

'So why do you not have a child as the fae wish, then this will all be over?' he asked in a perfectly rational and totally aggravating tone.

I jerked my head up. 'And what if I've misread the goddess' commands because I'm so fixated on what the fae want?' Yep, there it was: I wanted him to come up with a different explanation for what She'd told me, one that didn't involve me getting pregnant. 'Or what if the reason I can't tell anyone else is because they'd all jump right into the curse-breaking side of things and no one would look for whoever is murdering the faelings?' *There, side-step that!* 'And even if I did have a kid and break the curse, who's to say the killer wouldn't kill again?'

'The police are already looking for this killer, and they will continue to do so, regardless of the curse.' He studied me, his expression thoughtful. 'Genevieve, do you not want a child?'

Fuck, no! 'I'm only just twenty-five, Malik – I'm too young to be tied up with a kid.'

'Yes, you are young, but the child would be an adult in a few years, and you will still be young. You are sidhe, a near-immortal; you will be young for centuries yet. It is but a small portion of your life to devote to a child, if the end result is one you desire?'

I jumped up, frustration, fury and fear raging through me. 'Listen!' I jabbed a finger at him. 'One: if I were ever to have a child, then there's no way I'd let it fend for itself, just because it was a so-called adult. The child would be my kid for life.' I jabbed at him again, my voice rising. 'Two: do you really think I haven't thought all this out for myself? And three: what the hell do you think you're doing? This has nothing to do with you – you're not fae. And if Tavish has put you up to persuade me, then you can tell him from me: it won't fucking work. I do *not* want a kid, and unless I get something more significant than some iffy photofit and some cryptic clues, then I'm not going to, not now, and not ever. I *will* find another way to break the curse, even if it kills me.'

He rose in one graceful, effortless movement, concern and

bewilderment on his face. 'I understood that this situation was not one you wanted, Genevieve, or were comfortable with, but I did not realise that having a child engendered such fear in you.' He reached out, but I twisted away before he could touch me. 'Why is that?'

'You're asking me?' I clenched my fists, trying to keep from shouting at him. 'When you know what happened between my mother and father? What he did to her? Talk about a bad start in life!' I snorted. 'And it didn't get any better, did it? Hell, my own father married me off to a psychotic, sadistic sucker, then I spent the next ten years being a pawn in some shitty Prohibition game cooked up between the lot of you, a game *I* didn't even know I was playing. Oh, and let's not forget, I've died three— No, wait, that might even be *four* times now. Four times, Malik! I might be sidhe and nearly immortal, but that's pushing it for anyone. Next time my death might stick, my body might actually *fade*, and there will be nothing for me to come back to. *No way* am I bringing a kid into a world like this, not with all the bad luck and tainted blood in my heritage, even if there wasn't the damn fertility curse to deal with.'

He frowned, perplexed. 'I never met your mother, but from what I heard, your father was besotted with her, and Nataliya with him. I do not know that he ever did anything untoward to her—'

'C'mon, Malik – that story about my father finding her at a fertility rite and the pair of them falling head-over-heels and then her tragically dying in childbirth? It's just that: a *story*. One I stopped believing in a long time ago.'

Like I stopped believing in a whole lot of other things, like my father had my best interests at heart, and vamps were just people with pointy teeth, all thanks to the psychotic vamp my father betrothed me to: a.k.a. the Autarch, Britain's Top Dog vamp – and Malik's erstwhile master. I ignored the terrified, sick feeling in my stomach that always accompanied thoughts about my betrothed and glared at Malik.

'It just doesn't stack up.' I smacked one of the steel beams. 'I mean, how the hell did a vamp gatecrash a sidhe fertility rite in the first place, let alone survive long enough to get one pregnant? And then he actually kidnaps her when he escapes? Oh, and not to mention managing to keep her hidden from her queen and court long enough for a child to be born?'

'Ah.' He brushed his hair back where it had fallen forward. 'I understand now. You think your father forced your mother in some way—'

'I know he did!' I yelled. 'No sidhe would willingly have a child with a vamp – it just doesn't happen!'

He stilled. Hot flames flared in his pupils, then snuffed out. The temperature on the walkway dropped about twenty degrees and I shivered in the sudden icy air as my horrified mind caught up with the stupid, thoughtless words my mouth had uttered.

'And you know this how?' he asked, his voice as chilly as the air.

I grimaced, my anger fleeing in the face of an insulted vamp – a powerful, *dangerous*, insulted vamp … a vamp I cared something for, and truly hadn't meant to hurt. *Way to go, Gen!* 'Look, Malik, I'm sorry, that didn't come out—'

'Quiet, Genevieve.'

His order snapped into my mind, and my mouth stopped talking. Shock tripped through me, but before I could protest, he added, 'Sit down and do not speak to anyone but me until you leave here.'

I half collapsed, half sat on the walkway, disbelief coursing through me that he'd sicced me with his mind-mojo.

'Falling at your feet, is she? Lucky you, old chap.'

The loud, jovial voice came from behind me, and snapped me out of my shock. I twisted round to see its owner strolling along the walkway, his long platinum hair blowing out behind him like he was the star in a shampoo ad. The blousy red poet's shirt and tight black trousers he was wearing added a pseudo-romantic flair, as did his dark, hooded eyes. But the manic grin, wide enough that I had no trouble seeing his fangs, spoiled the whole Byronic throwback look.

Tentative relief settled in me as I realised that Malik's chilly rage might not be all about me.

'You are not welcome here,' Malik said, his voice soft with threat. 'I suggest you leave now.'

Blondie threw his arms as wide as his grin. 'Give it your best shot, old boy,' he called, speeding up to a jog. Smoke-like shadows coalesced around us, drawing into spear-like lines of darkness that shot along the walkway to strike the now-sprinting vamp chest-on. He screeched, a high yipping sound, and the shadow spears vanished as he blurred forward and skidded to a halt a few feet away.

'Dreamscapes are such *fun*,' he chuckled, leaping up to hang from the steel rafters like a spider, 'although I did expect the sidhe to be a tad more graceful.' He leered down at me. 'Still, I'm sure the blood makes up for any clumsiness.'

'The sidhe is not your concern.' Malik's tone was back to being icy.

Great, let's all talk about me like I'm some sort of pet.

I narrowed my gaze to peer at the vamp hanging above me. I recognised him. Blondie was the vamp Finn had once 'staked' with his horns, who'd later vanished. He'd kidnapped a human friend of mine to blackmail me into taking his blood-bond. I'd considered him pretty much a low-life opportunist at the time, so I hadn't been too worried when he'd disappeared. Now I wasn't sure quite what he was, but Malik's spike in tension (which, oddly, I was picking up again, like I was some sort of radio receiver) suggested Blondie was definitely dangerous.

Blondie dropped down, smoothed his hair and winked at

me. 'Any chance you'd be up for sharing with an old drinking buddy?'

'Do not even consider it, Maxim,' Malik growled, his voice vibrating harshly next to my ear. I jumped, startled at finding him crouched next to me. 'Give me your hand, Genevieve.' He held out his own, and I placed mine in his, thinking he meant to help me up.

Maxim gave a barking laugh. 'Getting territorial over the sidhe, are you? Good God, that's not going to go down well with His Royal Highness.'

Royal Highness?

Malik's grip tightened on my fingers. I flinched.

'*My apologies, Genevieve.*' Malik's voice was calm in my head. '*I did not intend to hurt you.*'

'Don't you want to know why I'm here, old man?' Maxim asked cheerfully.

'No.' Malik flicked his hand, and the other vamp shot through the bridge's suddenly insubstantial wall. For a second I thought he was gone, but he popped right back in and hunkered down next to us.

'Good one that, old chap – caught me unawares,' he said, still grinning, 'but now you're in the vicinity, as it were, there's something I've been meaning to talk to you about while our esteemed Lord and Master isn't around. A little proposition about the sidhe here.'

'This is not the time, Maxim,' Malik said, glowering down at where he held my hand. Then he added in my mind, '*Genevieve, give me my ring, please.*'

I frowned, adding 'Royal Highness' and 'Lord and Master' together and getting *Autarch*. Terrified panic clutched at me and I grabbed Malik's arm. 'What's this got to do with the Autarch?' I demanded.

'Why, the Turk here is His newest Oligarch … Or should I say "toy"?' Maxim rubbed his hands together with glee.

'How long's it been now, five months? Tell me, is His Royal Brattiness still at the "eviscerating and stringing of guts" stage, or has he moved on yet?' Maxim gave me a sly look. 'The rest of us have been greatly enjoying the holiday.'

I shot Malik a horrified look. 'What the hell is he talking about?'

'*There is nothing to fear, Genevieve.*' Malik's voice came with a heavy push of *mesma* that should have filled me with reassurance. It didn't. '*You will be safe. But now you must go.*' He pulled his ring from my finger—

—my eyes snapped open. I stared up at the white ceiling of the silver-lined police cell, my stomach churning with barely suppressed fear, for me, and for Malik.

Blondie – *Maxim* – had said Malik was the Autarch's new torture toy, and while Malik had looked okay, it had been a dream, and dreams and looks could both be deceiving.

Damn. I'd known Malik was London's new Oligarch, and as Oligarch he would have been forced to swear an Oath of Fealty to the Autarch. I hadn't thought through what that meant until now, no doubt thanks to Malik's mind-mojo, but I was pretty sure I was the reason Malik had taken on the job. After the events last Hallowe'en I'd asked him to extend his protection to all of London's fae and faelings until Clíona's time limit was up, and he'd said yes. But that protection was worthless if all the Autarch had to do was snap his psychotic little fingers and say jump, and Malik would have to say how high.

It seemed to me to be an utterly stupid move on Malik's part.

But stupid was one thing he wasn't.

So what the hell was the beautiful, Machiavellian vamp playing at?

I sat up, my white-paper jumpsuit rustling, and checked out my left wrist. The spell bracelet was still there, half-submerged back into my body. After another few hours it would be totally absorbed. But Malik's ring-charm was gone.

Looked like I'd have to find out the non-magical way, and actually ask him in person. As soon as I got out of gaol.

Chapter Eleven

'Here you go, Genny,' Hugh said, his ruddy face lined with concern, as he offered me the envelope containing my belongings. We were alone in the small cupboard-like custody room. It was a part of Old Scotland Yard I'd never seen before, or ever wanted to again.

'Thanks,' I said, taking the envelope and upending its contents carefully on the counter between us. My phone, Spell-crackers ID, wallet, watch and Grace's gold pentacle all slid out. I picked the pentacle up – a restless, fretful feeling that I hadn't been aware of suddenly calmed: I'd missed it – and fastened it round my neck. Oddly enough, I'd been wearing it in Malik's dreamscape, even though I hadn't been in the cell. I shrugged, but then dreams were like that. I tucked my ID and wallet into my jacket's inner pocket, and stuffed my phone into my clean jeans. My bloodstained clothes from yesterday were being kept as evidence.

'And thanks for getting me the clothes too,' I smiled up at Hugh as I snagged my watch. What I needed now was a long, lo-oong shower, something I'd been fantasising about sitting in that itching, burning cell. I checked the time: it was gone two in the afternoon—

'*She's* had me locked up for nearly thirty hours!' I snapped the watch on in frustrated annoyance. 'And that's *after* I admitted guilt, agreed to pay double what the spell's worth, not to mention the extortionate fine. Dammit, Hugh, if it wasn't for my solicitor's connections' – *thank you, Malik, for choosing a top-notch firm* (although I hadn't expected anything less) – 'she would've left me to rot.'

Hugh pushed a receipt form and one of his over-large troll pens towards me. 'I don't know why the inspector's behaving like this, Genny,' he rumbled worriedly. 'There are rumours the top brass are making noises, and I'd hate to see her career ruined.'

'I wouldn't,' I huffed, signing for my things. 'And if the top brass have any sense, they'll get rid of her and give you a shot at the job.'

'No, she's a good DI. And she's worked hard; she's had to because she's a witch. Having her in the job helps all of us non-humans.' He filed the form somewhere under the counter, then his expression shifted into his 'what I'm going to say is important' look. Inwardly, I sighed, guessing what was coming next.

'I know how you feel about her, Genny' – conciliatory dust puffed from his head ridge, the pink motes glinting in the harsh fluorescent lighting – 'and she's in the wrong, but something needs to be done, and not just for her sake, but for all of us. I've tried talking to her, but she won't listen. Maybe if it came from someone outside the force, someone close to her like Finn, it would hit home more. Will you talk to him, see if there's something he can do?'

I'd rather clean out a swamp-dragon's lair, but this was Hugh. I sighed. 'Okay. But I doubt it'll help. Finn's part of the whole problem; we both know that.'

'Thanks, Genny.' He rounded the counter, then carefully punched the security code into the exit door and held it open. 'I'll be in touch as soon as I can about the faeling's death,' he added in a barely heard murmur.

I walked out into the main Back Hall reception, hearing the door click shut behind me with deep relief as I scanned the long, high-ceilinged room with its drab, utilitarian green décor. Finn wasn't waiting for me, and after that kiss I'd sort of expected he would be. Feeling peeved, and not a little disappointed, I turned my attention to the smart fiftyish woman who *was* waiting: Victoria Harrier, my solicitor, and apparently one of the top criminal defence lawyers in the UK.

She was pacing, her phone clamped to her ear. Everything about her was understated, from her bobbed grey hair, pale pink blouse and maroon suit down to her black leather court shoes, but it was expensive, classy understatement. I had a horrible suspicion that her normal hourly rate was more than my week's pay. Paying her bill was probably going to be one of those never-ending debts. *Damn.* I didn't regret siccing the Stun spell on Bandana and sending him down the river, but it was proving to be a high-priced option; next time I'd settle for buying a chainsaw.

I thumbed my own phone on and rang Sanguine Lifestyles to ask for a direct number for Malik. The response was efficient, polite and frustrating: they didn't have one. Mr al-Khan contacted them at sunset. Partially reassured that he did actually speak to them daily, I left a message for him to call me urgently.

'Ms Taylor.' Victoria Harrier snapped her own phone shut as she saw me finish my call and came briskly towards me, her low-heeled court shoes almost sparking off the green linoleum floor. She halted in front of me, her eyes glinting with the same ruthless competence she'd shown in getting me out of gaol so much quicker than Witch-bitch Crane had wanted. 'Now, just to reiterate the situation, Ms Taylor: you've already pleaded guilty, and paid both the reparation and the fine' – Ms Harrier had actually paid them, and had added them to my no doubt already hefty bill – 'but the judge insisted on both a Conditional Caution and a Restraining Order, and that means you must stay away from Detective Inspector Crane's investigation. You do understand that, don't you?'

'Yes, I understand.' Complying was a different matter entirely.

'Perfect.' A smile as bright as polished steel lit her face. 'Now we still have certain matters to discuss, so I'd like to offer you a lift home, if you have no objection?' Her smile didn't change, but it wasn't a request.

I gave her a considering look. No doubt she wanted to outline exactly what would happen if – or rather, when – I screwed up on the terms of the caution. But while she'd got me out of clink, and quickly, she was a witch, and that had my suspicious antennae twitching like mad. Still, she had one thing in her favour: DI Crane appeared to hate her almost as much as me; a feeling Victoria Harrier reciprocated, if the nearly tangible animosity between the two of them was anything to go by. At one point I'd been expecting broomsticks at dawn, or whatever it was that witches did.

But I had another more curious and perturbing question: why was a witch working for a vampire? Something that just didn't happen, not with the ancient live-and-let-live-but-ne'er-the-twain-shall-meet covenant the two species shared. I didn't have an answer. Yet. But I was going to find out.

'Sure,' I told her. 'A lift would be great, thanks.'

Finn was waiting outside, leaning against the black-painted railings, hands stuck in his pockets, the afternoon sunshine making sharp silhouettes of his horns as he contemplated the pavement. Surprise and pleasure that he *was* waiting flashed through me, then my heart took over, leaping in my chest as the memory of his magic and his kiss stunned me and left me staring at him like some Glamour-struck human. *Damn*, that was *so* not a good reaction. If it kept up, I was going to have problems talking to him without drooling. I forced myself to look past him to the black stretched limo waiting next to the kerb. A uniformed chauffeur was holding the door open

– Victoria Harrier obviously travelled in style – and, feeling cowardly, I wondered if I could make a run for it.

A loud caw distracted me and I looked up at the arched stone entrance at the top of the short cul-de-sac. There was a large raven sitting atop it. The bird cawed again, bobbed its head in acknowledgement, as if it had been waiting for me to appear, then launched itself into the clear blue sky—

'Gen.' Finn's voice snapped my attention back to him as he pushed away from the railings, his smile wide with obvious relief, and came towards me. I tensed as he wrapped his arms round me and pulled me into a hard hug instead of his more usual greeting, a brief touch on my arm. Then as I breathed in his warm berry scent, the tension washed out of me, to be replaced by yearning and need. I forgot everything and hugged him back, succumbing to the heat of his body against mine, the quick thud of his heart, the sharp tug of his magic at my core … *wanting him.*

He buried his face in my hair. 'Gods, Gen, I'm so sorry,' he whispered, his warm breath feathering along my cheek and curling desire deep inside me. My own magic stirred, and the desire fanned hot, turning into lust, and I pressed myself against him, eager to get closer, not caring about anything other than being with him. His arms tightened. 'I'm so sorry. I tried to explain about the dryad and the spell, but Helen—'

Reality crashed over me like a cold shower and I jerked out of his arms, blinking as I stepped back. I stared at the pavement, getting my heart and my libido under control. Shit, what the hell was wrong with me? It was only one kiss! But even as I asked myself, the answer came: it wasn't just the kiss. There was Tavish's Sleeping Beauty spell, and whatever spin he'd added to it. *Damn kelpie.* And who knew what other magics the goddess had sicced on me? Still, looked like Helen Crane was good for something: the mere mention of her name was a sure-fire passion-killer.

I fixed her beautiful patrician face in my mind and carefully lifted my eyes to Finn's, relieved that the urge to throw myself into his arms was nothing more than a bad idea. What was it he'd been saying?

Oh yeah. 'Finn, this isn't about me stealing the spell,' I said, 'or about me using it. For whatever reason, Helen is out of control. And she's abusing the powers of her job.'

'Hell's thorns, Gen' – he ran an agitated hand through his hair – 'don't you think I don't know that?'

'Hugh thinks you could maybe talk to her, make her see sense?' I said tentatively, then promptly forgot everything else as I watched him rub his left horn. My own fingers itched with the need to join his, to see if his horns were as hot and responsive as I remembered …

'Helen's having a rough time just now,' he sighed. 'It's complicated.'

Helen equals passion-killer: check. 'Complicated!' I pulled a 'heard it all before' face.

'Yeah, I know. But this really is.' He hesitated, looking at the police station behind me for a moment, then lowered his voice. 'It's about Helen's son. He turned up a few months ago and it's causing a lot of problems.'

'Helen's got a son?' Confusion filled me. 'When did that happen?'

Finn's perplexed expression told me I should know what he was talking about. Part of me thought maybe I did, but the rest of me was more interested in his broad shoulders, and in him losing the suit jacket, oh, and the moss-green shirt that matched his eyes, and where that might lead …

… and my mind filled with images of a cute baby satyr with green eyes and tiny horns. Though, of course, the baby would only have horns if it was a boy. If we had a girl, she'd be sidhe, like me. Then again, I'd have to make a conscious decision to have a little girl, otherwise the magic would default to the

82

father's – *Finn's* – genes for sex, species and magic. In fact, I'd have to make a conscious decision to become pregnant (unless there were some truly extraordinary circumstances and a fertility rite involved) … So, a baby boy with cute horns, tiny hooves and a fluffy tail, or a baby girl with my own amber-coloured cat-like eyes—

'—and Helen gave him up to the sidhe when he was born, so he's a changeling,' Finn finished. He looked at me like he obviously expected me to comment. When I just stared at him, bemused, he added with a touch of exasperation, 'Hell's thorns, Gen, you want me to talk to Helen, and I'm trying to explain why there's a problem. Helen's having difficulty dealing with it. It's a very emotional time for her, and I know that's not an excuse …' he added quickly, seeing my expression.

No, it's not, I thought, breaking eye contact with him before the broody baby nightmares started up again. I stared at the stone archway at the end of the road. It was safer. So Helen's son was a changeling – not that I was entirely sure what being a changeling changed about a mortal, other than being brought up in the Fair Lands from birth. Briefly I wondered how old he was if he was back and causing problems? Mid to late teens, maybe? But regardless, why was I standing here listening to Finn go on about Helen, his ex, *while thinking about having his baby?* Either I'd turned into a total idiot without noticing – *or someone, like maybe, oh, a certain goddess, or the magic?* – was messing with me.

And why the hell was Finn so concerned about Helen's kid, anyway? After all, he'd told me there was nothing between them any more – *maybe I really was an idiot to believe that?* – and that the baby wasn't his the last time this had all come up … my gut knotted as I suddenly realised he hadn't. He'd clammed up instead.

'Witches always have daughters if the dad is sidhe, don't

they?' I asked, interrupting his not-so-lyrical waxing about Helen.

'What?'

I risked a quick look at him. He was frowning at me like I'd suddenly started spouting pixie.

'That's how you get more witches,' I said, answering his question literally. 'If the dad is human and the kid is a boy, then they're a wizard: if it's a girl, they're a witch's daughter. And if the dad is lesser fae, then they always have a boy: a faeling ...' I trailed off as his frown deepened into understanding.

'Helen's son isn't mine, Gen,' he said, a muscle jumping in his jaw and an odd, indecipherable look crossing his face. 'His father was a human she met before I knew her. If you wanted to know if I had a child, all you had to do was ask.'

I frowned. I should've done ... only for some reason, I'd never thought about it. But then, curiosity about Helen's son, along with a lot of other things I should've been finding out about, had been pushed out of my mind by the Valium effects of the Sleeping Beauty spell Tavish had sicced on me.

'You're right. I should've asked, and I'm sorry I didn't.' I gave him a rueful smile, and considered whether I should say I was sorry about Helen having a bad time, but I couldn't; it would be a lie. But I felt I should make an effort ... 'Well, at least that explains why she's such a—' I stopped myself from saying bitch, and substituted a more politic, 'Why she's such an unhappy person all the time. And why she blings herself up like a Christmas tree with all those spells; she must have lost a lot of her magic when she gave birth to a wizard.'

'She didn't,' Finn said, his expression verging on impatient. 'She got to keep it when she gave him up.'

I gaped at him. 'Really? I didn't know that was possible.'

'Apparently it is.' He held up his hands, signalling an end to the subject. 'Look, I'll talk to Helen again, but she's only one problem. There's the rest of the fae to worry about, and after

84

what happened yesterday with the dryad, it's going to be more difficult keeping you safe.'

I sighed. Looked like flirty Finn had disappeared overnight while I'd been in gaol, leaving serious Finn, with all his white knight tendencies, back in charge.

'Finn, I thought we'd got past this,' I said, keeping my voice neutral. 'I can look after myself, I'm not helpless.'

''Course not, but—' Finn grasped my hands, and green and gold magic sparked between us. He shot a surprised look at it, then appeared to accept it.

I gritted my teeth, chanting *Helen, Helen, Helen* in my head, trying to ignore the thought that kissing him would be so much better than talking.

'Look, Gen, I'm sorry I went on about Helen. I know it looks like I'm thinking more of her than you, but— Hell's thorns, there's things we should talk about, and I know you can look after yourself, but it's not going to be easy dealing with the dryads, or the others. I can help. Why don't we go somewhere quiet, and talk?'

Just as I was about to say an eager, unthinking yes, a loud cough brought my attention back to Victoria Harrier, who was standing next to the limo, not trying to hide either the interested expression on her face, or the fact that she was waiting.

Oops! I'd forgotten about her. Damn magic.

Finn's talk was going to have to wait until later. Much later, like when I'd got hold of something to stop me throwing myself at him. Silently chanting *Helen, Helen,* I did a quick mental calculation. 'Talking sounds good, but let's say my place around nine-ish?' I nodded towards Victoria Harrier. 'I think she has to tell me the dos and don'ts to keep me on the straight and narrow.'

He cast a look at the lawyer, then gave a soft laugh. 'Yeah, like you'll take any notice of her.' His thumbs skimmed over my knuckles and another cascade of magic sparked between us, only to fall flat on Helen's name. 'I've got a better idea. Why don't I follow you, and we can chat once she's gone?'

I shook my head, still chanting desperately, 'Nah, leave it till later. I want a shower' – *boy, did I want a really long, really cold shower* – 'and there's other stuff I need to get out of the way first.'

'Hey, tomorrow's Saturday. It's usually quiet, take the day off.' His grin told me he was trying to make amends. 'I'll swing it with your boss, he's really a nice guy.'

'He is.' I forced out a smile. I was getting heartily sick of chanting Helen's name in my head. 'But I can't put this appointment off' – I pulled my hands from his, the lure of his magic lessened and I sighed, relieved – 'so nine, okay?'

'Appointment?' His grin faded. 'Can't you postpone it?'

'Not really.'

'C'mon, Gen?'

'I have to do this today. I'm sorry, Finn.' I gestured at Victoria Harrier standing patiently next to the idling limo. 'And I have to go, the meter's running, and she's probably more expensive than a taxicab.'

'Have to … ?' Comprehension dawned on his face. 'It's the sucker, isn't it?' He clenched his fists in angry disgust. ''Course it is. And now you're going to see him because he's the one paying for the fancy lawyer and the fancy car—'

'Hang on a minute! *I'm* the one paying for this!'

'Not up front, you're not, Gen.' He shook his head angrily. 'And to get someone like her to drop everything, you'd need to be.'

He was right, even if I was planning on footing the bill in the end (however long it took; a thought that had me wincing) – not that I was going to stand there and argue about it with him. Irate, I pushed past him. 'Look, I'll see you later.'

He caught my wrist and pulled me back. 'Gen, it doesn't

matter what he's told you. All suckers are dangerous.'

I jerked easily from his hold. Turns out anger works as well as chanting Helen's name. 'Right now, Finn, the suckers are the least of my worries. There's no vamp in London who'd even say hello to me – or to any other fae or faeling – without Malik's permission.'

'Hell's thorns, Gen!' Consternation clouded his face. 'There's no way any vamp can guarantee that sort of blanket protection—'

'He's running London, so yes, he can. That's the way vamps work. They either toe the line or their ashes feed the fishes. You know that.'

'Feeding … Gods, I should've realised— *That's* why you started to fade this morning – he's been taking too much blood. Gen, I can't let you do this; it has to stop—'

'You don't know what you're talking about, Finn,' I stated, keeping my voice level. Of course I wasn't feeding Malik – hell, I hadn't even *seen* him until last night. But maybe I had been overdoing it on the donations. It was something to think about later, but— 'And even if you did, it's still none of your business.'

'I'm your boss, Gen, so it *is* my business if you can't do your job because you're too weak.'

Damn. 'It always comes back to that, doesn't it?' I tried to ignore the hurt, furious that I hadn't even seen it coming this time, and dug out my Spellcrackers.com ID card, grabbed his hand and slapped it on his palm. 'I resign,' I said. 'As of now.'

He looked down in shock for a moment, then he held the ID card back out to me. 'I'm sorry, Gen. I shouldn't have said that.'

'No, you shouldn't.' I glared at the ID card. I loved my job.

'I'm worried about you, that's all,' he said, sounding defensive. He grabbed my hand, put the card in my shaking palm. 'Look, take it back.'

I hesitated, wanting to curl my fingers round the thin bit of plastic ... but I didn't want my job held to ransom every time I did something he didn't like.

'Don't do this, Gen,' Finn pleaded, 'not over some sucker. He doesn't care about you; all he's doing is using you.'

No, he isn't – it was them – London's fae, Clíona, the goddess – they were the ones using me, or wanting to anyway, with the damned fertility curse egging them on. But Finn was one of the good guys. My fingers started to curl—

— and something sharp tugged inside me, made me almost scream with pleasure – magic.

I shot a look at Finn, caught a spark of emerald in the deep moss-green of his eyes, and realised he'd done it deliberately. Anger flashed white-hot: I'd had enough of everyone trying to force me to do what they wanted.

I dropped the card, then turned and walked towards the limo, ducked my head and climbed inside.

Victoria Harrier got in after me. 'Are you ready to go?' she asked calmly.

I nodded. The door clicked shut, cutting out Finn's calls to come back. Within seconds the limo was moving, and we were enveloped in quiet, air-conditioned luxury. Outside the tinted windows, London seemed far away. Tears pricked the back of my eyes and I swallowed down the ache in my throat. Time enough for a pity party later.

After the killer was found and the curse was *cracked*.

Chapter Twelve

'**W**as that a good idea, resigning like that, Ms Taylor?' Victoria Harrier asked a few moments later, breaking the silence.

I stopped staring blindly out of the window and finally noticed the inside of the limo. Victoria Harrier sat kitty-corner across from me on the back seat. The usual limo bar area had been replaced with a James Bond-style mobile office: a couple of high-end laptops, a 'does-everything' printer, three telephones on cradles and various other gadgets sat next to neat piles of stationary and files. I *looked*: Buffer spells protected every electrical item. More spell-crystals were stuck to the doors and the opaque smoked-glass screen that partitioned off the driver: no doubt for privacy. It was all just as fancy – and expensive – as Finn suspected.

'If you're worried about your fee, I'm good for it' – sooner or later – 'but since you're Malik al-Khan's lawyer, he's probably already guaranteed it.' I recalled my earlier suspicions. 'Although I am curious about why a witch is working for a vampire – I thought the Witches' Council's ancient tenets forbade it?'

'I'm *your* lawyer, Ms Taylor.' She pressed a button and a table slid out in front of her. She reached for one of the laptops and powered it up. 'I've never worked for Mr al-Khan. I haven't met him, or spoken to him, and I hope I never do. I detest vampires and everything about them.'

I looked at her, amazed. 'Then why did Sanguine Lifestyles hire you?'

'You have my services because I'm one of the best criminal defence lawyers in Britain,' she said briskly. 'I have excellent contacts within the justice establishment, and I have quite some influence within the Witches' Council, something I was able to use to your advantage when it came to dealing with DI Crane.'

'Yeah, I get that,' I said, 'and I never expected you'd be anything less. But then, I thought Malik was paying your bill.'

'Sanguine Lifestyles approached one of my colleagues,' she said, her fingers tapping the keys. 'My colleague is a first-rate lawyer, and he does a tremendous amount of very lucrative work for the vampires. He mentioned the job, and I convinced him to pass it on to me. My reputation is as good – maybe even better – than my colleague's, and once I'd explained the circumstances to him, he was happy to agree.'

'What circumstances?' I asked flatly, wondering whether I should be worried that my lawyer had shanghaied me when she clearly realised I didn't detest vampires quite as much as she did.

She turned the laptop around. The screen showed a smiling family portrait: an attractive man – the father, presumably – in his mid-forties, delicate-looking blonde wife probably in her late twenties or early thirties (going by her kids), although she looked younger. Three boys, I guessed around ten, nine, and eight, all with their dad's brown hair and serious smile, a pale, waif-like girl of about seven with curling blonde hair like her mother's, another child, maybe three years old, with a wild crown of brown curls, and a very obvious bump under Mum's clingy dress. Five and a half kids seemed like half a dozen too many to me, but then, I didn't even want *one*, so who was I to know?

'My son Oliver, his wife Ana and their children: Charles, Edward, Andrea, James and little Henry,' she said fondly. Oliver bore such a distinct resemblance to her that her words were more confirmation than anything else. It also confirmed that as the son of a witch, Oliver was a wizard.

'Nice-looking family,' I said, waiting with apprehension for the tale that obviously went with the picture.

'My daughter-in-law, Ana is a faeling,' she said. 'Her mother was a water fae.'

Damn. The wife was a faeling, which meant the kids were too, and all of them susceptible to the curse. I studied the picture again: there didn't appear to be a pair of gills, a flipper or a fishy eye in sight, so she and the kids seemed to have inherited more human genes than fae. My dread went up another notch as I wondered which one had fallen victim to the vamps.

'When Ana was fourteen,' Victoria Harrier carried on, touching the screen with a gentle fingertip, 'her mother disappeared, on the way home from work one night. She was found in the Thames three weeks later.'

'Vampires,' I said redundantly.

'Yes. I looked up the police report later. It was horrific reading. There were at least six of them; they drained her dry, then tossed her away like an empty drink can.' She looked down, clasping her hands together as she composed herself for a minute, then carried on, 'Ana understandably went a little wild after that, substituting anger for her grief, except—' She stopped, and drew in a calming breath. She smoothed her skirt down over her knees, then resumed talking. 'You know about the curse, Ms Taylor, so you can imagine how well a fourteen-year-old's attempt at fighting back turned out.'

Actually, I could, and I was amazed Ana had not only survived, but had ended up with a husband and a large brood of kids. I'd have bet on her living a short, painful life as some vamp's blood-slave. Maybe she'd been lucky.

'Oliver – my son – found Ana in one of those blood-brothels in Sucker Town.' Her lip curled, although I don't think she realised it. 'Blood-houses, I think they call them. She was sixteen. She'd been there more than two years by then. Oliver's very quixotic in nature. He set out to save this beautiful, sweet, damaged girl; he got her out of Sucker Town, into rehab at the HOPE clinic, and then of course he fell head over heels in love with her. A year later they were married.' She smiled proudly at the laptop screen. 'That was taken not long ago to mark their ninth wedding anniversary.'

'The vamps at the blood-house just let her go?' I exclaimed in astonishment.

'Of course,' she said, closing the laptop with a smug snap. 'Oliver was working with the law firm responsible for updating the licensing laws for vampire premises. He didn't give the owners of the blood-house any choice in the matter.'

'Ri-*ight*,' I said, getting it. Oliver had blackmailed them – and, surprisingly, it had actually worked. Ana had been lucky after all; except something about the story felt off ... I clasped the pentacle at my throat and frowned out the tinted window, absently noting we were driving through Trafalgar Square.

'You were expecting a tragic ending after such an awful beginning.' Victoria Harrier derailed my thoughts. 'So far it hasn't transpired. I intend to see that it never does. For the sake of my daughter-in-law and my grandchildren, I am going to help you to put an end to this terrible curse.' She held out a box of tissues. 'You're crying ...'

'Sorry, didn't realise,' I muttered absently as I grabbed a couple and swiped at my face.

She frowned, then decided to ignore me. 'My aim is to give you any practical help I can.' She picked up a manila folder and pushed it towards me. 'Jane Bird' was printed on the white label stuck on the front. 'I know you're convinced that the faeling found dead this morning is something to do with the curse, so this file contains photocopies of the police reports. The faeling hasn't been identified as yet, but she is thought to be late teens, early twenties. She doesn't match any missing person on the list – I've put a copy of their latest list in for you – but going by "Jane Bird's" appearance, it's possible she is related to the ravens at the Tower of London.'

Her mention of the ravens reminded me of the bird at Tower Bridge this morning, and the one bobbing its head at me from the stone archway outside Old Scotland Yard. He/she/they had to be something to do with 'Jane Bird', it was too much of a coincidence otherwise. But I realised the raven – easier to think of it as only one bird – couldn't be from the Tower: the Tower ravens agreed to have their wings clipped when they took the job and couldn't fly for the duration of their contracts. Although that didn't mean 'Jane Bird' wasn't a relative. Something definitely to look into, I decided, and flipped open the file. The top sheet had Hugh's signature on it.

'That's everything I've been able to obtain so far,' Victoria Harrier said, her efficient tone suggesting that I should find it impressive. It was, sort of, if I hadn't known that Hugh would've given me the same info soon anyway. 'I've also arranged for you to meet with the Raven Master and the ravens tomorrow lunchtime. I will, of course, be with you, to forestall any future problems with your Conditional Caution and DI Crane's own investigation.'

A meeting with the Raven Master? *Nice!* Victoria Harrier's practical help was, well, practical, except ... I tapped the file as I narrowed my eyes at her. 'You have to know that DI Crane doesn't like me' – an understatement, but I was being polite – 'and while I noticed you and she don't get on ... well, to be blunt, you're a witch, and you detest vamps, so how do I know you're not just stitching me up in some way?' Okay, so maybe I wasn't being that polite.

'A valid question, Ms Taylor.' She smiled. 'I hope I can put your mind at rest, if you'll bear with me. I take it you've heard of the Merlin Foundation. But do you know what it does?'

The Merlin Foundation financed the HOPE clinic where

I volunteered, and others like it, plus it was into schools and other things. Its bureaucracy was something you had to experience to believe when it came to asking for funds: the doctors at HOPE were forever complaining about it. 'I've heard it described as a sort of Magical Masonic Society devoted to charitable works,' I said, going for diplomatic.

She laughed. 'I know it's sometimes seen as secretive, but then, it's been around a long time. And you're quite right that it's devoted to a tremendous amount of valuable charitable work, but it is the older, more private side of the Foundation that I want to tell you about.' She smiled, and proceeded to give me a history lesson. 'The Foundation came into being back in the fourteenth century, when the witch persecutions were at their worst. The Witches' Council devised a plan: a select number of witches would marry into the higher echelons of our country's ruling classes and produce sons – more wizards, of course: Great Wizards, who would grow up to occupy positions of influence, able to protect their witch relatives, and who would also marry witches chosen by the Witches' Council, to ensure our magical legacy would continue. That tradition still carries on today, albeit in a somewhat different form.'

I had a vague memory of my old boss, Stella, mentioning the Witches' Council had approached her about marrying a wizard when she'd been younger, and offering to pay her a Bride-Price, a kind of huge reverse dowry, but she hadn't liked the guy – he was a stuffy prig – so she'd said no.

'Now the Foundation is far-reaching, and with its backing, and that of their own families, many of its members occupy positions of power throughout the government, financial and legal sectors.'

'In other words, nepotism rules.'

'Exactly, Ms Taylor,' she said. 'My husband is a wizard, as are my sons. With their connections in the Foundation and my own in both the magical and legal communities, I can assure you that Helen Crane will not cause you any more problems, even if she didn't have her youthful indiscretion to count against her.'

It sounded good, but— '*What* youthful indiscretion?'

Chapter Thirteen

'**H**elen's son, of course,' Victoria Harrier said, 'the one Mr Panos was talking about. Like me, Helen Crane is from a powerful witch family; she was chosen to marry a wizard, but instead she— Well, Helen developed an infatuation with some boy, and in the age-old way she found herself pregnant. The boy apparently took fright at the responsibility, and once Helen's son was born, her family, backed by the Witches' Council and the Foundation, agreed she should give him up to the sidhe.'

I frowned. 'But her son was still a wizard?'

'One with no significant family connections. So you see, she's not looked upon kindly by the Foundation.'

Part of me was starting to feel some reluctant sympathy for the teenage Helen, if not the current one. Another part of me was still trying to assess just what Victoria Harrier's true priorities were.

'I hope that reassures you, Ms Taylor, that I have your best interests at heart when it comes to dealing with any problems you might meet, especially if they pertain to the fertility curse. I have my grandchildren to consider.'

There was still something not quite right about what she was saying; I just couldn't pin down what it was.

'Now,' she said, 'I understand that despite not being able to tell us why, you are convinced that "Jane Bird's" death is to do with the curse?'

'Yes.' Damn goddess and her gag clause.

'And of course, I understand your reluctance to leave the investigation of "Jane Bird's" tragic death to the police, so I will do all I can to help you with it. The sooner her cause of death is discovered and settled, the sooner you'll be free to move onto other more certain solutions to stop the curse.'

The penny finally dropped, with a loud splash. She didn't just want to help; she was a fully paid-up member of the 'get the sidhe pregnant' brigade. And with her daughter-in-law being part water fae …

'Let me guess. Lady Meriel is one of your connections in the magical community?'

She leaned forwards and patted my knee in what I was supposed to believe was motherly concern. 'Lady Meriel appreciates that it is only natural for you to be worried about having a child under the circumstances, and that you are not going to make the decision to become pregnant until you've exhausted all other avenues. If I can help expedite those avenues for you, maybe it will make the final decision easier and quicker for you.'

The limo slowed to a halt and I glanced out the window. Trafalgar Square again. The driver had to be deliberately going in circles so Victoria Harrier could take her time talking to me on Lady Meriel's behalf. Figured. Absently I scowled at the crowd of tourists gathered round one of huge bronze lions. They were roaring with laughter at the pixie pack dancing a jig along the lion's broad back. Automatically, I made a mental note: about a dozen of them. Another week and Trafalgar Square would be overrun and the council would be calling Spellcrackers to banish them. Pixies are sort of ugly-cute, even if they are a pain to catch, and I always got the job— Except this time I wouldn't. Not now I'd resigned. A sick feeling roiled in my stomach. But it wasn't only the loss of my job making me feel ill, it was the goddess' command: *You will give them a new life.*

If the fae knew that, I'd probably end up pregnant within the hour. Now that was a scary thought. But they didn't, and ironically, it was thanks to the goddess' totally wonderful gag clause.

I grimaced and turned back to Victoria Harrier. 'In that case, why don't we start by looking into those other avenues now, seeing as I'm not going anywhere?' I said, drily, and settled back against the seat – it was either that or force my way out of the limo. I was saving that option for later.

'Perfect.' She pulled a notepad and pen towards her, unable to hide the hint of triumph in her eyes. 'Lady Meriel is concerned at the lack of information available to her. I'm told the kelpie, Tavish, who lives in the Thames has been absent since Hallowe'en. The consensus of opinion is that he's gone to the Fair Lands to speak to Queen Clíona on your behalf. Has he had any success?'

'Not that I've heard.'

She made a note. 'I understand that your father is a vampire; have any of the fae commented that this could cause a problem, or made any objections?'

I frowned. 'Why does Lady Meriel want to know that?'

She blinked at me as if surprised I was asking, then tapped her pen and said firmly, 'Please answer the question, Ms Taylor.'

'As far as I know they don't care,' I said slowly, curious as to what was going on.

'Good.' She made another note and underlined it. 'Now, I think we should talk about your 3V infection.' A vaguely familiar gleam lit her eyes for a moment, sending an uneasy tingle down my spine.

'Well, it's not exactly a secret any more, but I'm not sure it's any more relevant than your last question.'

'I believe it's relevant to you, Ms Taylor. You have stated your reasons for not wanting a child are because of possible implications for the child's future, an entirely understandable and commendable concern.' She nodded in approval. 'But as I told you, Ana, my daughter-in-law, also has 3V; she controls it using G-Zav' – the vamp junkies' methadone – 'yet Ana is expecting her sixth child – her sixth *healthy* child – and I can reassure you that all of my grandchildren are completely clear of 3V: there's no sign of V1, V2 or V3 in their blood at all. 3V is not passed on from mother to child in the womb. She'd be delighted to chat to you about it all, and it might help to put your mind at rest.'

'I volunteer at HOPE,' I said, 'and believe me, it's not the physical implications that worry ...' I trailed off as the picture of her happy, smiling, *very* pregnant daughter-in-law came back to me, and several things hit me at once. She had 3V. She was faeling. She was on G-Zav, had been for at least ten years – and while she wouldn't have quite the same problems using G-Zav as a full-blood fae would, that was a major feat in itself. The only place she could get G-Zav was HOPE, and if any faeling was a regular there, I'd know them.

And I didn't know her.

My tingle of unease grew fangs and took a bite out of me. I looked around the plush car at the expensive equipment: wealth and power and magic are as attractive to vamps as blood. This family had it all ... and it was beginning to look like there was a distinct possibility there was a blood-sucking fanged cuckoo squatting in their well-feathered family nest. Not only that: I now realised what had been bothering me about Victoria Harrier and her faeling daughter-in-law. Witches and wizards were fanatical about their magical human lineages. Marrying a faeling would be well out of a wizard's comfort zone.

'Something's worrying you now, isn't it, Ms Taylor?' Victoria Harrier's probing question focused my attention back on her, and on the familiar gleam in her eyes.

'Yes, it is,' I said. As she waited expectantly, I decided to test my theory and *called* my own magic. It uncurled from my centre, up and out into my fingers, dusting them with a golden glow. I reached out and clasped her face, pushing the golden magic into her as soon as our skin touched. She jerked with surprise, then relaxed into smiling compliance, her pupils lighting with pinpricks of gold as she succumbed easily to my Glamour.

Too easily.

Glamouring someone isn't much different from a vamp mind-lock: the aim of both is to control the victim. Vamp mind-locks can be like magical Rohypnol – more humans end up as a quick snatch-and-suck than you'd think; they just don't remember. Add in a side order of vamp *mesma* along with the mind-lock and vamps can play pick and mix with their victims' senses and emotions, making them believe anything for a time. But siccing a mind-lock on a human outside of licensed premises is illegal, and can end in a one-way trip to the guillotine. I sincerely doubted Victoria Harrier, a well-known witch, had ever set foot inside a vamp club, licensed or otherwise.

Of course, Glamouring a human was just as illegal and carried the same sharp-edged consequences.

The hair at my nape rose in an ominous and not-so-subtle reminder of that as I gazed into Victoria's adoring, Glamoured eyes. Tentatively, I checked the tangled net of her mind, dusting it with golden magic, and found just what that familiar gleam in her eyes had told me I would: a looping skein of hard blackness, worn smooth and even like a well-trodden path. No wonder she had succumbed so quickly; she was pre-programmed. Whoever the vamp was, he or she had been reinforcing their commands for years, which wasn't a mind-shattering discovery after hearing the daughter-in-law's history. But trying to remove the command *would* be mind-shattering; it was too deeply embedded. The much simpler option was to remove the vamp, but that was a job for later. For now, though, I just needed to take my Glamour back without disturbing anything.

As I started to retreat, Victoria whimpered in distress and I stopped, fearing that despite being so careful, I'd overloaded her with Glamour. I started to pull back again, slower this time, feathering the magic and letting it trail gently from her mind. She moaned, a low sound of pleasure that echoed inside me, and her pupils expanded into bright orbs of gold. Fascinated, I leaned towards her and placed my lips on hers, tasting the adoration in her exhaled breath, drawing in the sweetness of that devotion, pulling the energy of her adulation into my own body and feeling it hit with a hot jolt of electric bliss that was both more than and less than sexual. I gasped against her mouth, trembling with the urge to pour my magic into her, to fill her until her mind worshipped only me, until her heart beat only for me, to take her and make her mine, and mine alone—

I stilled, my mouth on hers, my hands cupping her face, savouring the delicious sensations as I teetered on the edge of temptation. Some part of me knew this was wrong, very, very wrong, but there was another, deeper part of me that said this was what I needed … I pressed my lips against hers again, sighed, and drew my hands and my magic reluctantly away as I followed the smooth path made by the vampire.

She moaned again, and this time I settled back in my own seat, my eyes fixed on the tinted windows and the world outside, giving her the semblance of privacy as her body surrendered to the commands entrenched in her mind, the ones my own magical invasion had triggered and curiously enhanced.

I caught a glimpse of Nelson's Column in the distance. We were still trundling luxuriously along in the traffic, the driver obliviously going round and round in circles until he was given the signal to take me home.

'So, Ms Taylor, what do you say now you've had time to think about my suggestion?' Victoria Harrier asked.

I turned to find her sitting straight-backed, a slight flush to her cheeks, as calmly as if nothing untoward had happened. Of course, in her mind it hadn't.

'You know,' I said slowly, 'I think you might have a point about my 3V infection. I truly hadn't thought about it in those terms before. Maybe I should speak to your daughter-in-law.'

She gave a pleased smile. 'We can visit Ana now if you like.' She gestured out the limo's window. 'She lives in Trafalgar Square with her grandfather, the fossegrim.'

Ana's grandfather was the fossegrim? Shit – the old water fae was supposed to be totally and utterly insane. I'd been warned to stay away from him when I'd taken my first pixie eviction job for Spellcrackers. He'd come over from Norway with the very first Christmas tree after the Second World War: he'd been in love with the tree's dryad and she'd died fighting in the Resistance. He'd been half-mad with grief, until he met a new lady love – but then he'd lost her too, to the curse. He'd gone on a killing spree in revenge, then holed up in the square's fountains, where he'd been ever since. Ousting a blood-sucking fanged cuckoo out of their family nest was one thing, but no way did I want to run into the fossegrim, not without some sort of magical protection.

I gave Victoria Harrier a wary smile. 'Okay,' I agreed, backpeddling fast, 'but I think we'd better leave the socialising until after we've seen the ravens.' And after I've had chance to check things out and come up with … some sort of plan.

'Perfect,' Victoria Harrier said, with a satisfied expression. 'I'll arrange it for tomorrow. Now how about we get you home, Ms Taylor.'

Chapter Fourteen

'**H**ang on,' I muttered as my phone vibrated. I bumped the door to my flat closed with my hip, careful not to spill the cup of blood I'd just picked up from the Rosy Lea Café. With an annoyed sigh, I reactivated the protection Ward by banging my forehead against the painted wood; the Ward shimmered into life, a faint purple tinge on the white door. I dropped the ten-kilogram bag of salt – also from the Rosy Lea – next to the bucket beside the door and flexed my fingers, working out the cramps from carrying the salt up five flights of stairs. Life would be so much easier if I didn't live in a converted Edwardian attic.

'And life would be much easier if I didn't have jealous witches, scheming fae, Machiavellian vamps, and The Mother of all goddesses to deal with on top of the fertility curse,' I told the door, giving it a frustrated kick. I took a calming breath and muttered, 'Stick to dealing with one problem at a time,' and pulled my phone out.

I had a text from Finn:

I'm sorry. We need to talk. But not 2nite. I'll CU 2morrow.

Short and not so sweet. I stared at the text, puzzled. It wasn't like Finn and his inner white knight to leave me to my own devices, particularly when he knew my plans involved the vamps. Irrational disappointment flashed in me that he wasn't beating my door down, as I'd half-expected him to be, along with morbid curiosity about what he *was* doing ... and whether it had something to do with Helen.

Damn. I snapped my phone shut, put the cup down, hung my jacket up, tucked the police file Victoria Harrier had given me next to the bucket of salt, and mentally shelved Finn and the rest of the day's dilemmas until later. I glanced at the clock: a little over four hours until sunset, so time enough for that long shower, a bite to eat and a bit of research before I headed off to Sucker Town and the vamp side of my problems.

But first things first. I might be home, but that didn't mean I was safe.

I grabbed my drink and a handful of the salt already in the bucket and turned to look – and *look* – at my living room-cum-kitchen.

And at the books.

They were piled in knee-high stacks in my living room floor like a miniature village of tottering skyscrapers made of … well, stacks of books. Not being able to afford any furniture other than floor cushions was a definite advantage when it came to accommodating the fae's curse-*cracking* research library, or at least the latest batch from the thousands of tomes they'd collected over the last sixty-odd years. The books had been arriving and disappearing on rotation ever since Tavish had told me about them and I'd insisted on checking them out for myself. Except *I* hadn't been the one insisting, had I? It was him, or rather him and Malik, the other half of that annoying, over-protective little double act. Between the Sleeping Beauty spell and Malik's mind-mojo, I was surprised they'd stopped at imposing the curse-*cracking* reading on me, and hadn't just wrapped me up in the proverbial cotton wool and kept me under magical house arrest.

It hit me that I didn't need the books any more: the Librarian could have them all back.

I gave a loud whoop and, grinning happily, started to weave my way through the books to the kitchen, glancing through the open bedroom door as I did so. Spring sunshine was cutting bright rectangles on the wooden floor, which was thankfully clear; at least the books hadn't migrated in there again. A lot of them were disturbing, eye-opening and literally nausea-inducing, so definitely not required bedtime reading. In the current piles were everything from an eleventh-century grimoire bound in sorcerer's skin (a major *eew!* to read, even wearing three pairs of salted surgical gloves); a papal leaflet titled *Inquisitional Techniques and Demonic Exorcisms*, printed in 1573; a first edition of *Frankenstein* – author anonymous, of course; a pile of Walt Disney picture books; *Grimm's Fairy Tales* in five different languages; half a dozen new paperback releases with nothing in common other than 'Curse' in the title; and—

A virulent green cover on one of the many unread piles caught my eye: *The Esoteric Practice of Malediction Prophecies* by Michael Nix. I reached out to pick it up— Then snatched my hand away as a flash of magic revealed that the snot seeping out from its spine was real.

'Sneaky,' I muttered. After the first 'WTF?' spell I'd unwittingly triggered – the one that transported me straight to Finn; luckily he'd been working the late shift at Spellcrackers, but even so, naked is *so* not the way to appear anywhere unannounced – I'd taken precautions. I looked up at my chandelier hanging from the vaulted roof and counted another row of blackened beads marring the long strings of amber- and copper-coloured glass drops. The Seek and Reveal spells embedded in the beads had cost me the equivalent of three months' wages, even using my own crystals, but since it had exposed everything they'd sent – so far, at least – it was worth the expense. I narrowed my eyes at the snot-dripping book and scattered the handful of salt over it; it belched musty orange dust and I grabbed a tissue from my jacket pocket as I sneezed.

'I can see you're havin' a fun day, doll.' The amused burr came from the bedroom door behind me.

Startled, I turned too fast, and several book stacks avalanched like mismatched dominoes into a cluttered heap around me.

'Tavish!' I said, and my heart gave a happy little leap at seeing him. The feeling that all would be right now he was here brought a wide beam to my face. 'When did you get back?'

He shot me an answering grin, his sharp-pointed teeth gleaming white against the deep green-black of his skin. As his eyes crinkled, the rim of white surrounding the beautiful, brilliant silver of his pupil-less eyes vanished. The grin softened the angular planes of his long face: Tavish isn't so much handsome – with his Roman nose and pointed chin, his face is a less delicate version of my own, showing the sidhe part of his make-up – but like the kelpie-horse that is his other shape, he is compelling, alluring—

I started to step towards him, then sneezed again, and as I blew my nose, I realised I'd been staring at Tavish like a Charmstruck human. I wiped the silly grin off my face and gave him an irritated glare. 'You're doing it deliberately, aren't you?'

His own grin faded as he placed his hand on his chest. 'Ach, doll, but it sorrows my heart tae lose your smile.'

I stifled the urge to go to him and throw my arms round him. Damn, I'd had enough of this magical attraction stuff with Finn; I didn't need it with Tavish too. Suddenly wary, I clutched at the cup with one hand and balled the tissue in my other, needing something real to hold on to. 'I'll lose more than my smile if I let myself fall for your charms, kelpie,' I said flatly.

He threw his head back with a snorting laugh and I glimpsed the delicate black-lace gills flaring either side of his throat. 'Aye, doll, perhaps – but I wait for the day when you nae longer wish tae resist me, when we shall ride intae the depths together.' He sobered as the turquoise swirling in the depths of his silver eyes lit an answering curl of desire inside me. 'And 'twill be a glorious pleasure for us both, my lady.'

I looked down and nudged a couple of books with the toe of my trainer, willing the desire away. Tavish was wylde fae, a kelpie, a soul-taster, and capricious, like the magic – not to mention dangerous, if he was talking about riding into the depths. But he was also my friend. So was it a warning? Trouble was, asking outright wouldn't get me the answer, just like it was pointless confronting him about the bracelet, or anything else. He could talk round corners for England if he chose to: at my best guess, he'd been doing it for more than a millennium.

'If wishes were horses, we could all ride away on them,' I murmured, recalling one of my father's sayings.

'If wishes were fishes, we'd all cast nets,' he replied cheerfully.

And the fishes would be caught. Hmm.

'You're looking guid, doll,' he said, still showing his teeth.

I shot him a sceptical look. I'd spent the night in a police cell; there was no way I looked 'guid'. Then I realised he wasn't looking at me, or rather my body's shell, but at my soul. And it probably did look all shiny and bright to him now the black tint of the sorcerer's soul was gone. So why wasn't he asking how I'd got rid of it? Unless, of course, I wasn't the only one chatting to Malik in his dreamscapes – was that why Tavish was here now? Had the two of them been plotting again? Not that any of that explained his outfit, which was unusual, even for him.

He was dressed Elizabethan-style, his starched white neckruff a stark contrast to his green-black skin. His dreadlocks were piled into a spiky topknot, and the beads intertwined with the dreads were a brilliant aquamarine, matching the silk lining of his pantaloons.

'Nice outfit.' I raised my brows. 'Did you escape from a fancy dress party or something?'

He twirled his hand in a flourish of lace as he bowed from

the waist, keeping his eyes on mine, and I had the strangest feeling *he* was wary of *me*. 'The queen had hersel' a hankering tae return tae earlier times, and her court has dutifully obliged her.'

'Are you telling me that Queen Clíona can turn back time?' I asked, astonished. 'By several hundred years?'

He straightened and gave me a thoughtful look. 'Am I telling you that? I dinna ken, doll – 'tis always possible, for time is nae fixed in the Fair Lands as 'tis here in the humans' world.' He looked back over his shoulder and I thought I saw the flicker of candlelight instead of sunshine behind him ... then it was gone. 'I returned here tae you at this time as I desired tae do, but who kens where or when in the humans' world I would be if I hadnae made my choice?'

'That doesn't really answer the question, Tavish.'

'Maebe there's nae answer to be had.'

An idea started to form in my mind. Was he just being tricky, or was he telling me something I needed to know that he couldn't divulge? I left the idea to find its own shape and said, 'So, what's Clíona been saying?'

'Her offer of sanctuary is as before, doll, and she's nae telt me of any change.'

She hadn't told *him* of any change, but that didn't mean she wasn't ready to tell someone – *me* – otherwise. Was that why he was here? To arrange for me to see her? Maybe after my trip to Disney Heaven—

'I want to speak to her, Tavish. I want to ask her if there's *anything* she can tell me, however insignificant it might be to her.'

'She willnae allow you tae visit, doll. Once you join her court, you cannae return.'

'Will she come here to speak with me, then?'

'The Ladies Isabella and Meriel willnae open the gates to allow her entrance—'

'Bullshit! You're standing here talking to me, so why can't she do the same?'

'She's a queen, doll. Queens dinna loiter in doorways chatting.'

Damn. If he wasn't here on Clíona's behalf, why was he here? I stared down at the cup, looking for an answer ... and the earlier idea bloomed in my mind. 'Tavish, you said you *chose* to come back to me now, but the queen's taken the court back to the past ...' I tilted my head. 'Does that mean you can choose a particular time to come back to, as it were?'

He dipped his chin, looking curiously at me. ''Tis nae something I've tried before, doll.'

'What if you could go back to when the queen spoke the curse, and persuade her not to?'

He shook his head. ''Twould nae be possible, you cannae undo the time that is already passed betwixt two bodies; the queen's path and mine together are already walked.'

'Okay, so what about me? I've never met the queen, I could go back—'

'It doesnae work that way, doll. The curse doesnae stem from when the queen uttered it and gave it substance, much as a stream doesnae spring from where it gushes out of the earth. It comes into being long before that; even should you happen on its source and change the path it takes, the stream will still exist—'

He broke off suddenly as a thin green arm snaked around his waist; a fine gold chain hung with chinking small keys trailed from the arm's wrinkled but obviously feminine wrist. The distant lilt of music – a *harpsichord*? – sounded, and as Tavish turned his head, his image in the doorway faded as if a sheet of opaque glass had dropped between us.

The glass cleared. 'She wants you to see what is to come,' he whispered, his head bowing in acquiescence, his beads turning as dark as his green-black hair. Beyond him I glimpsed a dark, wood-panelled room, candles burning in wall-sconces, a four-poster bed hung with thick tapestry curtains tied at the corners, the mound of covers turned back. A tall, locust-like creature crouched near the bed, carefully and methodically smoothing the pale sheets with a long-handled brass warming pan.

In the middle of the room stood the green-skinned female. She was as skinny as her arm had suggested, and mostly human-shaped, except for the high, hairless dome of her skull, and the flat holes where her nose should be. She was naked, her skin sagging in wrinkled creases and her breasts hanging like empty, pendulous sacks. Her only adornment was the thin gold chain with the tinkling keys trailing from her wrist. Now, I noticed that the other end of the chain was linked around Tavish's left ankle; rust-coloured stains marred the otherwise pristine whiteness of his hose. She smiled in anticipation – one long tooth protruded from her upper gum – as she lifted the chain and lazily pulled. She might look old, but she was strong, for Tavish jerked and gave a grunt of discomfort, his leg muscles bunching with effort as he fought to hold his position.

Was this Clíona? I tried to ask the question, but found I couldn't speak, couldn't move; I was suddenly trapped in that frozen, frightening place like a child in a nightmare.

The green-skinned female slid in next to Tavish, filling the gap he'd left in my bedroom doorway. She smiled, and a long forked tongue flicked out from between her lips and licked across his eyes. He flinched back, knocking his head against the door jamb, as she turned to face me. She slowly slid her hands down her wrinkled body, the air around her shivering with magic, and I watched, transfixed, as her body changed with time-lapse speed: her wrinkles smoothed out, her waist thickened, her abdomen stretched and swelled, her hanging breasts perked up, growing fuller and heavier, their pale nipples jutting out into large turgid peaks, until she stood panting and sweating, her hands cupping her now-massive pregnant belly. After a few seconds, her gasps subsided and she stroked her palms up over her extended stomach and then grasped her breasts, squeezing and pulling the engorged teats, even as she whimpered in pain, until blood seeped out and fell like dark rubies onto the warm honey colour of her enlarged belly. She cried out, the sound eerily familiar, and I looked up to meet her eyes—

—but instead met my own amber-coloured eyes, saw my own shocked face staring back at me, my sweat-drenched hair flat against my scalp, as if I were looking in a mirror. Blood-tinged tears snaked down my face, dripped off my chin and splattered on my pregnant stomach. My double reached out, the chain chinking on her wrist, and grasped Tavish's hand, pressing it to her blood-smeared belly.

And I felt his touch on my own body. I looked down in stunned disbelief to find myself as naked as my double, my own abdomen swollen in pregnancy, my bladder painful with the pressure between my legs, my breasts aching and lactating blood. Something moved inside me and I stared in mute horror as the skin of my stomach bulged: a hoofed foot kicked low on the left side; a two-fingered clawed hand pushed out high on the right; the point of a sharp horn poked out above my belly button.

'Little sidhe.' The husky voice calling my name jerked my attention back to my pseudo-reflection, who stood with her legs spread wide and her arms outstretched, fingers gripping either side of the doorway, her head thrown back as she grimaced in pain. Tavish's hand was splayed low, dark against the paler colour of her swollen belly, as if he could help support the heavy burden. I stared as smoke spiralled out from between his fingers and the oversweet smell of cinnamon clogged the air. My double writhed and screamed, her mouth opening wide to reveal four needle-sharp vampire fangs. Blood gushed from between her legs and pain, sudden and jagged, sliced inside me. I huddled over, clutching my own stomach and cold, viscous liquid slid down my own legs.

Then Tavish was there, the weight of his hand on my own stomach burning into my skin as I struggled, panting with terror and shock, feeling *it* starting to push out between my legs. I doubled over in agony, scratching at his hand, desperate to get him away from me, desperate to escape—

''Tis this that she wants tae show you, doll,' he whispered, his breath scorching my ear. ''tis *this* that could occur.'

My legs gave way and I fell forward, thudding onto my hands and knees. I screamed again as the molten burn of his hand sank into my flesh, eclipsing even the hot, tearing pain between my legs.

'She would have me rip the babe from your belly and steal both its soul and your ain.'

I had to stop him; I had to save it— *I had to save the baby.*

Sobbing, I groped blindly at his legs, shredding his hose, raking bloody furrows in his calves, anything to make him stop—

'So, 'tis a warning, tae nae let any of them plant their seed in your body.'

Fire blazed in my stomach, licked vicious, all-consuming flames through my body, and he roared in anguish. 'I cannae gainsay her, doll: she has taken my reins, and you are nae tae trust me, for I am nae longer my ain master!'

—my fingers snagged on something cold and hard. *The gold chain.* I grabbed it where it trailed from his ankle, yanking at it with both hands, pulling his leg out from under him, feeling the little gold keys cutting into my palms, feeling his hand slide from my flesh as I collapsed, weeping, into the cold blood spreading beneath me.

'Sidhe,' the soft, husky voice murmured as sharp claws

punctured the soft skin under my jaw and lifted my chin, 'open your eyes and look at me, sidhe.'

I was frozen in the same nightmare state as before and I couldn't refuse her order. I opened my eyes and stared into her acid-yellow ones.

'Losing a child is ... painful. The heart cracks and shatters into sharp, splintered pieces; pieces that are disparaged by the indifference of others.' A curious expression crossed her wrinkled green face, and then her tongue flicked out and delicately licked a hot line across my face. 'You, sidhe, you are not indifferent; you feel my pain in your tears. You will remember.' She brought her face so close to mine that she was nothing more than a blur of green. Our lips met; her tongue slithered into and out of my mouth, leaving behind a taste of something bitter and sad. 'You will remember.'

I swallowed, and the bitterness ran like sour juice down my throat, until it hit my stomach—

And I disappeared into a furnace of remembered pain.

Chapter Fifteen

There was a banging noise in my head; it meant something ... The noise rolled around my mind like waves breaking on a shore, loud and close, then fading away ... A rank butcher's shop smell of spoiled blood wrinkled my nose. And the noise came back, this time shrieking like a storm wind battering through the trees. I half-opened my eyes and peered in confusion at the scattered pile of books next to me, and at my kitchen area beyond them. Why was I lying on the floor in my flat? Quiet footsteps tapped and scuffed on wood ...

Memory caught up with consciousness and hit me like a Beater goblin's baseball bat— *The baby*. I curled into a ball, protectively hugging my stomach, a whimper of terror escaping from my mouth ... then, as I felt my belt buckle dig in at my waist and registered the absence of actual pain, reality began to reassert itself. Pulse leaping with frantic hope, I ran my hands over my body, checking, and finally lay back and stared blindly at my beaded chandelier in heartfelt relief.

I wasn't pregnant, and I hadn't lost a child.

And if there was no child – what the fuck was the whole Ellen Ripley/*Alien* baby show all about?

The quiet footsteps stopped and something white blurred my view of the ceiling.

'Fiddlesticks! Mother's going to snap my twigs off if you're broken,' an annoyed voice muttered.

I squinted at a pair of feet in strappy silver sandals standing in the congealing blood next to my face: one heel was broken and half the pink-painted toenails were chipped. The feminine feet didn't look threatening – but looks aren't what matter; whoever it was had forced their way through my protective Wards, so chipped pink toenails or not, they could probably take me. My gaze skimmed over the shoes, past the thin ankles and up the slim, badly scratched legs that disappeared into white stretchy shorts. I stopped at the tattered edge of a pink and white flowered skirt that tented above me. Something about the way the material flared up was odd … like there should be an up-breeze to go with the movement. Then the skirt's owner flattened the material as she bent down to study me, her bright eyes shining like polished green conkers, her lack of eyebrows giving her face an unfinished look. A scratched pink cycle helmet perched askew on her clipped scalp, the broken strap dangling by her left cheek.

Another dryad – and going by the eyes, I'd say it was Sylvia, Lady Isabella's own daughter. Last time we'd met she'd tried to kidnap me.

This time I suspected her intentions were 'friendlier', as in 'Nominated Go-Between' … I really hoped so; I wasn't sure I was up to dealing with much else right now.

'Are you hurt, Ms Taylor?' she shrieked, giving my shoulder a hard poke.

I winced at the noise – *did she think I was deaf or something?* – and smacked her hand away. 'Not as much as you're going to be if you touch me again. And hel-*lo*' – I pointed at my face – 'eyes open here?'

'Just because your eyes are open doesn't mean you're awake, or even alive.' She straightened, hands keeping the skirt under control.

'I was moving! Dead people don't move.' Not usually anyway.

'You were convulsing,' she stated. 'It's not the same as moving. And you're covered in blood.'

'Lamb's blood,' I muttered, irritatedly eyeing the flattened Rosy Lea Café takeaway cup and my uncomfortable, blood-drenched jeans. Note to self: next time someone sics an *Alien*-inspired illusion spell on you, put the cup of blood down first. 'It was dinner,' I added with a sigh.

She tilted her head enquiringly to one side. 'Are you going to lick it off the floor?'

Eew! 'No!'

'Oh,' she said, sounding disappointed. 'Well, anyway, you should be grateful I was here to save you.'

Save me! What the—? I grimaced; was she channelling her graft-brother Bandana or something? And lying on the floor looking up her skirt was getting old, and as I didn't appear to be suffering any ill-effects of whatever magic Tavish's new mistress – or whoever the hell she was – had treated me to, I got to my feet.

'Listen up, Sylvia' – I poked *her* shoulder, hard enough to rock her back on her broken heel – 'even if you did rush to my rescue, which is debatable, you're a dryad, so you'll have a long wait before I'm indebted to you or any of your pals.'

'Gosh, you really are an ungrateful sort, aren't you?' she pouted, rubbing her shoulder.

'C'mon, drop the injured act, Sylvia. It's really not going to get you anywhere.' I stuck my hands on my hips. 'Ri-*ight*, let's get a few things straight: this is my *home*, and you're an uninvited guest, so you can start off with how you managed to get in, before *I* start snapping off your twigs.' Not that I actually knew where her tree was, but—

'There's no need to be like that.' She made a little moue of disdain and fluffed out her flowery skirt – which I now realised was actually a fifties-style dress, one more suited to a summer heatwave than a cold spring day, since the halter top only just covered her 'Hello, boys!' cleavage. The top also didn't hide the cuts and scratches marking her bare skin, the ones she was now examining intently.

'I'm waiting,' I said.

'Oh, well.' She gave an exaggerated sigh. 'I wanted to see you, but none of your neighbours would buzz me in; they all said I'd have to phone you,' she said, holding out her hand. A small compact mirror appeared in it. She opened the compact and adjusted her helmet. 'I mean, can you *believe* it?'

Actually, I could. My witch neighbours might not be over-joyed to have me still living in the building, but after the events leading up to All Hallows' Eve, they'd beefed up security.

'I tried phoning, but you weren't answering, and I knew you were here because the trees outside told me you'd come home. Then I remembered the old escape ladder at the back of your building that leads to the flat roof.' She waved the compact vaguely at my bedroom. 'I did intend to knock, until I saw you convulsing on the floor.' She snapped the compact shut. 'Your Ward caused me a bit of bother, though. Good thing the win-dow frame is wood and not one of those horrid plastic ones, otherwise I'd never have got in.' She held out her scratched arms and chewed her bottom lip. 'It's going to take a while to mend the damage though.'

I *looked* through my bedroom doorway – now reassuringly back to being the entrance to my own room and not to Tavish's shadowed bedroom in the Fair Lands. The bottom half of the sash window was raised up – so at least Sylvia hadn't broken through the physical window – and still framed in the opening was the sheet of metaphysical blue glass – the Ward – which now had a cartoon starburst of a break in its centre. *Damn.* That was going to cost me. But while I was updating the Ward, I might as well do the sensible thing and get one that denied entry to everyone, since Sylvia, Tavish and Lizard Lady were probably just the start of my uninvited guests. Anxiety con-stricted my chest. Tavish is a centuries-old wylde fae, and let's face it, no one gets to live that long if they're stupid and easily trapped, so the Lizard Lady, whoever she was, had to be über-powerful, which didn't bode well for Tavish. But then again, Tavish could be slippier than a whole nest of eels when he wanted, so his whole 'nae longer my ain master' tip-off might not be as troublesome to him as it appeared. Not that there was anything I could do to help him right now—

'Ooh, have you seen this?' Sylvia flapped a magazine – *Witch Weekly* – in my face. The front cover had a picture of a pretty teenage witch holding a cocktail and sitting in a jacuzzi with half a dozen older guys. The headline read:

SECOND SCHOOLGIRL STAR IN HOT WATER!
IS MORGAN LE FAY COLLEGE CURSED?

'Such a scandal! The Witches' Council are talking about axing the show because of it. Which would be such a shame – I love all those reality TV shows, don't you?'

—not when I had an overly friendly dryad to deal with.

I hitched up my bloodied jeans, trying to make them more comfortable, and pushed the magazine aside. 'I don't have a TV, Sylvia, so no, I don't, and I'm not in a chatty mood, so hurry up and tell me why you wanted to see me, then you can toddle off back to your tree.' I indicated the rest of the scattered books and the puddle of drying blood we were standing in. 'I've got a busy evening ahead being a Domestic Goddess.'

Her helmet fell forward over her forehead as she frowned around at the mess. She pushed it up absently. 'Gosh, I forgot: you can't sort things out with magic, can you? What you need is some help – and I know just the person to provide it.' She gave me a dazzling smile.

Was I going to take the bait – sorry, turn down a free offer of help? Okay, so it wasn't going to be truly 'free', but since I had an idea that being friendly was the starting price—

I nodded, and she held out her hand; this time a pink

iPhone appeared; the small white flower-shaped phone-charm dangling from it glowed with a Buffer spell that made the phone look like it was wrapped in thick, protective plastic. She waggled it, obviously expecting me to comment.

Impressed despite myself, I said, 'Nice bit of magic. I haven't seen a Buffer like that before.' I touched a finger to the spelled charm; it shocked me back.

'It's my own *blend*.' She beamed. 'I add powdered rowan berries. The standard spells don't last long with me *calling* my phone' – she gave a creaking laugh at her pun, and I lifted my lips in a smile to show I got it – 'you really don't want to know how many scrambled SIM cards I ended up with.'

I really didn't.

She thumbed the iPhone's screen and it started ringing on speaker.

Nine rings later someone answered. 'I told you not to phone me at work, Sssylvia. I'm busssy.' The soft, sibilant voice sounded grumpily familiar: the Librarian.

'Libby, darling,' Sylvia said loudly, 'this *is* work. I'm over at the sidhe's place and you can't move for books.'

'Ssshe wanted them.'

'Well, we all know that she's not going to find anything in them, don't we, Libby, so do me a favour and *call* them back, will you?'

I looked down at the scattered piles of books. There was one I wanted … I saw it next to the flattened takeaway cup and gingerly picked it up. Underneath was a small gold key. I picked that up too, then promptly wished I hadn't as it melted into my palm and disappeared. Figured.

'Told you, Sssyl, I'm busssy,' the voice hissed down the phone. 'Cataloguing.'

'Gosh, Libby, then maybe I'll have to get busy and put a "Keep Your Thieving Claws Off" spell on my books,' Sylvia shouted at the phone, then winked at me. 'Now stop being grouchy and *call* the books back.'

A sibilant sigh echoed down the phone, and then my ears popped with the sudden pressure as the piles of books vanished.

'Thanks, Libby.' Sylvia smiled in satisfaction, then whispered, 'The old dragon loves my paranormal romance books; she's just too mean to buy them herself.'

'I've got my hearing aid in, Sssyl,' the voice grumbled.

'I thought you said you didn't need one, Libs,' Sylvia shouted into the phone again, then tapped it, muttered 'amplify' and hung the iPhone on an invisible hook between us. 'Anyway, I bought a couple of new romances yesterday; they're on the table in my dressing room. Oh, and don't forget—'

'Ask her what she knows about Michael Nix's book,' I interrupted, holding up the volume I'd retrieved.

'Michael Nixsss, *The Esssoteric Practice of Malediction Propheciesss*,' the Librarian hissed. 'He is a purveyor of nightmares and future fears. I did not sssend you that one.'

Nice! I dropped the book. I'd salted it, and its magic seemed to be spent, but holding it for too long probably wasn't a great idea. 'Well, someone did,' I said, 'then I think they paid me a visit.'

'What did they look like?'

'She was green, deficient in the tooth area, wrinkled and over-free with the cryptic threats.'

'Gosh, that sounds like one of the *bean nighe,* don't you think, Libby?'

I looked down at my bloodstained jeans. A *bean nighe*? Just my luck.

'A washer woman? Why would a Herald of Death be visiting you, sssidhe?'

Not a question I really wanted an answer for. 'She was wearing a chain of gold keys,' I said. 'Does that mean anything?'

'Ahh … Ssshe was the Phantom Queen then.' The Librarian drew the name out with something approaching reverence. 'Ssshe ofttimes appears as such.'

The name sounded familiar—

'But I thought Clíona imprisoned her years ago, Libby?' Sylvia frowned at the iPhone.

'A sssidhe queen cannot hold a goddess for long. Ssshe may have escaped, or Clíona may have relented, or ssshe may have agreed sssome bargain with the Terror.'

—and my memory clicked in with the answer. 'Are we talking about the Morrígan? The goddess of prophecy, war and death?'

'Ssshe is also Anu, the goddess of sssovereignty, prosperity and fertility,' the Librarian said, her delight and satisfaction evident.

Of course she was the goddess of fertility – after all, that was the theme of my life right now. Not to mention, I must have used up my next ten years' quota of luck, seeing as I now had not one, but two goddesses taking an unhealthy interest in me.

'Gosh, that's right,' Sylvia said, grinning at me with excitement. 'Did she show you one of her prophecies? Was it anything to do with the curse? Do tell.'

Telling them might shed some light on the *Alien* baby bit, but I wasn't sure I was ready to 'chat' about it; for all that it was false, the memory was grief-filled and painful. And I wanted a chance to think it all through. Then there was the fact the Morrígan had chosen to appear as a *bean nighe*. The *bean nighe* were dark fae, changelings taken from those mothers who died in childbirth, whose souls were lost. Whether it was the association, or down to whatever magic the Morrígan had sicced on me with her bitter kiss, flashing in my head like a neon arrow pointing 'victim here' was the picture of Ana, Victoria Harrier's very pregnant daughter-in-law.

Questions started piling up in my mind.

I looked at Sylvia and her phone. The Librarian was the local font of all knowledge, and everyone knew that trees were the original gossip girls.

Chapter Sixteen

'Before I do tell and show,' I said, 'do either of you know a water faeling called Ana?' At Sylvia's puzzled look, I added, 'She's married to a wizard.'

'Oh, you mean Annan,' Sylvia said, adjusting her cycle helmet as it wobbled.

'Why do you assk?' the Librarian said.

'Someone mentioned her, and I thought it was odd she was married to a wizard. They're usually all about their magical lineages, aren't they?'

'Annan is the great-granddaughter of Queen Clíona. The wizard married her because ssshe is descended from sssidhe royalty.'

Wow, Clíona's descendents were popping up all over the place, which could hardly be a coincidence. Or a surprise really, with two goddesses on my case.

There was a tiny chiming sound, and a scroll of buff-coloured vellum appeared in the air in front of me, accompanied by a pungent twist of wood-smoke. Its red silk cord untied and the vellum unrolled itself with a definite flourish. 'This is Annan's lineage,' Sylvia said, sounding slightly awed.

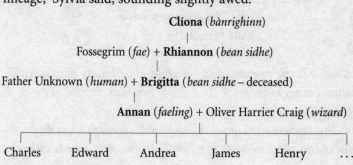

Clíona (*bànrighinn*)
|
Fossegrim (*fae*) + **Rhiannon** (*bean sidhe*)
|
Father Unknown (*human*) + **Brigitta** (*bean sidhe* – deceased)
|
Annan (*faeling*) + Oliver Harrier Craig (*wizard*)

Charles   Edward   Andrea   James   Henry   . . .

I read down the family tree, and immediately recognised Clíona's daughter's name, Rhiannon. That was the name that Grianne, my faerie dogmother, had called Angel. So maybe it was Angel/The Mother who was putting ideas into my head about Ana (her great-granddaughter) being a possible victim?

'Such a tragedy, wasn't it, Libby?' Sylvia said.

I peered at the family tree. 'I take it you don't mean Ana's marriage to the wizard, but about her mother being attacked and killed by the vamps,' I said drily, 'and Ana herself being caught by them.'

Sylvia gave a choked laugh that sounded like leaves rustling. 'Gosh, yes, Brigitta was killed by the suckers, wasn't she? I'd forgotten that. That was a tragedy too. So sad, such a lot of heartbreak in that family, and all because of the curse.'

'Clíona brought it on herssself,' the Librarian grouched. 'If ssshe had not *cast* the *droche guidhe*, it would never have happened.'

'So, what did happen?' I asked.

There was another chime, and a yellowed newspaper popped into the air to hover next to the family tree scroll. For a moment it fluttered in the breeze through the open bedroom window, then Sylvia snapped her fingers and it became as still as a board.

I stepped up to it and began to read:

FAERIE PRINCESS RESCUED FROM THE TOWER.
by 'Thomas the Rhymer'
Our Man in the Fair Lands

A sidhe faerie princess and her child have finally been released after being kidnapped and held prisoner in the Tower of London.

The traumatised princess (age not specified) has been returned to the bosom of her family in the Fair Lands after the ordeal, while her baby daughter (5 months) is being cared for by extended members of the princess' family in London—

A horrified chill crawled down my spine. I narrowed my eyes at Sylvia and her pink iPhone. 'So who's going to explain what that means?'

'Well,' Sylvia's face squinched up like she was in pain, 'you know what Algernon and his friends tried to do to you?'

Algernon had to be Bandana, the dryad. I hadn't known his name, nor had I really wanted to. 'You mean when they tried to kidnap and rape me?' I said flatly, thinking that Sylvia hadn't necessarily been blameless in that nasty incident.

'Fiddlesticks, now I've made you cross.' Her shoulders slumped. 'They weren't supposed to do *that*. If I'd known *that's* what they planned, I'd have told someone.'

'Go on,' I said, giving her a hard stare as I crossed my arms.

'Well, it all happened about forty years ago. The Old Donn, he was the one in charge then, he was desperate to find a way to break the curse. As we all still are.' She gave me a pointed look. 'Anyway, short version, that's when the idea of finding a sidhe willing to have a child came up, only Clíona wasn't prepared to let us court any of her ladies, and none of the other queens wanted anything to do with the curse. So things were at a bit of a stalemate. But then Clíona's daughter Rhiannon was visiting London. When the Old Donn and two of the other wylde fae found out she was here' – she pulled another pained face and pointed at the hovering newspaper – 'well, that's what they did.'

Fuck, so I wasn't the first! They'd already tried the 'kidnap, rape and make the sidhe pregnant' plan in an effort to break the curse with this Rhiannon— except their plan obviously hadn't succeeded, since the curse was still in existence … but looking at the family tree, Rhiannon *had* given birth, to a daughter … and the newspaper had mentioned a baby girl … so—

'Rhiannon wasss visiting the fossssegrim when the Old Donn took her,' the Librarian's voice hissed out of the phone. 'Ssshe was already carrying hisss child.'

Shit. That meant— 'They abducted and raped a pregnant woman!' I said, sickened.

Sylvia cringed. 'Well, technically, yes.'

'They either did, or they didn't!'

'They performed a fertility rite,' the Librarian said. 'Rhiannon agreed to it, but ssshe has never been in her right mind, and ssshe did not understand what it meant. It was a ssstrange ss-situation.'

Rhiannon wasn't in her right mind? Of course, they were talking about Angel – for a moment I'd forgotten Rhiannon and Angel were the same person, and that Angel was Ana's grandmother.

Two more yellowed newspaper articles materialised in front of me with another chime. Their headlines proclaimed: BRUTAL SLAYING AT THE TOWER OF LONDON, and TRAFALGAR SQUARE'S FOUNTAINS TO BE EXORCISED.

I skimmed down the pieces. They detailed the killing spree that the fossegrim had gone on when he'd become unhinged at losing his lady love to the curse, and the fall-out that followed. Neither story carried any mention of Rhiannon, or their daughter. Those details had obviously been kept out of the news.

'The fossssegrim exacted hisss revenge on the Old Donn and the others,' the Librarian said. 'But once the humanss heard about it, they called for him to be removed. An agreement wass finally reached whereby the fountainsss were Warded ssso that the fossegrim was contained for three decadesss. But he wasss unable to care for the child, Brigitta, so ssshe was given into the care of the witches, for her protection. Ssshe grew up with them, and when ssshe gave birth to Ana, the witches cared for her alsso.'

'Obviously not well enough,' I muttered. Damn, poor Ana really was a victim of the curse, in more ways than one. Her grandmother Rhiannon was born to break it, her mother Brigitta was killed by the vamps, and Ana herself had ended up in a blood-house when she was fourteen. And despite her supposed rescue by her wizard husband, Ana was still under the thrall of some vamp, and *still* a victim of the curse. It was a situation I needed to sort out – once I worked out how to bypass the scary fossegrim. 'So,' I said, 'I heard Ana now lives with her grandfather the fossegrim in Trafalgar Square. Is he really as mad as I've been told?'

'Gosh, yes.' Sylvia shuddered. 'I'd stay away from him, if I was you. He likes to drown folk—'

'He hass never hurt a female or a child, Sssylvia,' the Librarian's voice interrupted firmly.

Ah, good to know, since I was going to be visiting his grand-daughter.

Sylvia frowned at the phone. 'But I thought that was why Rhiannon was sent back to the Fair Lands, and why her daughter went to live with the witches?'

'No, Rhiannon wass allowed home because none wanted to incur Clíona's wrath again.'

I snorted. *Allowed home, my arse.* Then something struck me. 'So if Rhiannon went back to the Fair Lands, why did she leave her daughter in the care of the witches?' But even as I asked the question, the answer was there in front of me, on the hovering vellum of the family tree. 'Brigitta was a full-blood sidhe, and you kept her because of the curse. *Damn!* She was going to be your next curse-breaking experiment. You tried to breed from her, didn't you? And Clíona just let you.' Anger welled up in me and I kicked at the book on the floor. It thudded into the wall next to the bathroom door, making Sylvia jump.

'We are not as cruel as you sseem to think, ssidhe,' the

Librarian said in a conciliatory tone. 'We had high hopess that Brigitta would break the curse, ssso like you, ssshe was given her choice of father. And ssshe chose one of the water fae, but when Ana, her daughter, was born, it was evident that the husband was not Ana's father.'

I looked at the family tree again. Ana's father was down as 'unknown', and Ana was a faeling.' I laughed. It wasn't a happy sound. 'Brigitta stiffed you by getting pregnant by a human, didn't she?'

'Yes. Brigitta held usss all guilty for what happened with her mother and the Old Donn. Ssshe took her revenge thuss.'

I didn't know whether to cheer for Brigitta or cry. The fertility curse had really screwed up her life, even before she'd been killed, and now it was screwing up Ana's too. I really hoped I was wrong about a vamp still having his or her fangs in Ana; the poor faeling already had more than enough problems to deal with.

'Sssometimess a fate cannot be changed,' the Librarian said quietly, as if she'd read my thoughts, 'but with forewarning it is posssible. What did the Morrígan ssshow you, sssidhe?'

'Gosh, yes, do tell.' Sylvia gave me an eager look.

'Sorry, no,' I said, and reached over and pressed the 'off' button on her phone. Whatever the Morrígan/*Alien* baby show was about, I wasn't in the mood to discuss it after that sordid little tale. I fixed Sylvia with a look. 'Thanks for getting rid of the books, Sylvia, but what exactly are you doing here?'

Her phone trilled the theme tune from *Dirty Dancing*. She cancelled the call and the phone vanished. Two seconds later the hovering family tree and the newspapers did too. The Librarian obviously didn't want to leave them hanging around (no pun intended). Sylvia smiled coyly. 'Is that, no, you won't tell, or no, the Morrígan didn't show you anything?'

'You first,' I said.

'Fiddlesticks, that's not fair,' she pouted.

'Up to you.' I shrugged and looked down at my bloodstained clothes. 'But if you're not going to talk, then I'm getting cleaned up.' I turned and headed for the bathroom, saying over my shoulder, 'Don't forget to shut the window on your way out.'

'Wait!' she called. 'Wait! I'll tell. You know you said one of us could court you so long as it wasn't one of the Twig Gang. Well, here I am.'

I turned to see her standing with her arms outstretched and a big smile on her face. 'Ta dah!' She grinned. 'Although I'm not as pretty as when I started out, thanks to your Ward.'

'*You've* come to court *me*? Somehow I don't think you're going to be much use in getting me pregnant – not that I *want* to get pregnant,' I finished quickly.

'I'm a dryad, silly,' she giggled. 'Depending on our tree – mine's a cherry, *Prunus avium* – some of us come with a choice of both' – she patted her breasts, then fluffed her skirt – '*accessories*, if you see what I mean. But I prefer to be female, mostly. Especially in the spring. People look at you odd if you're male and dressed in white and pink.'

Like the Barbie pink cycle helmet wouldn't do it? 'You're a hermaphrodite.'

'Actually, I'm cosexual, since I'm a tree.' She gave a delighted laugh and clapped her hands together. 'No one's told you, have they?'

Evidently, it wasn't an aspect of fae life that my faerie dog-mother had decided I needed to know, for whatever reason. And there I'd thought Grianne'd told me everything at least thrice over in her lectures.

'Right, so … you like girls, then?' I said, thinking that having a fluffy-headed cosexual dryad hanging around me was hands-down a better option than Bandana, who came with an excess of sadistic testosterone built in.

'Girls, boys – or both.' Her grin stretched wider. 'It's spring, my sap's rising, and I just *love* sex.'

Oh, goodie. 'What if I don't *love* girls?'

'Oh, but you do! We've all seen the YouTube of you kissing that female vamp last year.' She fanned herself with her hand. 'Gosh, that was hot.'

'That was an act,' I said flatly.

'It was?' Her exuberance visibly deflated as she regarded me doubtfully. 'Um, well, I suppose I could change my appearance. But it's been a long time since I've been male. It'll take me a while.'

I held my hands up. 'It's not an issue, okay? I said I'd let a dryad court me, so fine, we'll court, but courting means exactly that: dating, getting to know each other, finding out if we like each other. Courting does *not* mean jumping into bed together in the next five minutes, or in the next five hours, or whatever. So, y'know, you can just stay as you are.'

'Oh, all right.' Disappointment flickered over her face, then it was gone, replaced by another wide smile. 'So, do you want to go out and get some dinner? It could be our first date? We could chat about what the Morrígan told you.' Her smile turned sly as she glanced down and lifted a foot; a gloop of blood dripped off her silver sandal. 'I could clean this up while you get ready?'

Not exactly what I had planned for my evening, but she didn't need to know that yet. 'Do whatever you like with it,' I said, then added, 'Just as a matter of curiosity, what's Bandana?'

'Bandana? Oh, you mean Algernon? He's a willow, they're dioecious, and he's strictly male.' She sighed. 'He's also a spiteful, bullying cad, though you know that, don't you.'

'Yeah, I do,' I agreed, and closed the bathroom door, wondering how I was going to get rid of her.

Chapter Seventeen

I turned the shower on and stripped my top off, then heard a high-pitched sound. After a couple of seconds I realised Sylvia was whistling while she worked – maybe the Disney books had been hers too; all we needed now were the seven dwarves to show up. I grimaced at my jeans. Better still, a nice Brownie who knew how to get bloodstains out of denim. I carefully unzipped them, peeled them and my briefs down and kicked them away. Then I stared at my stomach.

A black handprint marked my flesh like a brand.

Crap! The uncomfortable feelings hadn't been because my jeans were wet, but because Tavish had *tagged* me with some sort of spell. No wonder his touch had felt like it was burning me. I *looked*, but the handprint didn't change, so whatever the spell was, it wasn't active. Tentatively, I placed my own hand on it. The skin felt leathery and rough, and itchy, as if it were healing; and one finger felt damp. I sniffed it … closed my eyes … sweet, spicy, Christmassy: *cinnamon*.

Which didn't tell me a damn thing.

I slumped to the floor, and sat staring blindly at the tiles. I was *so* not having a good day.

Half an hour later, after the long shower I'd been craving – during which questions had jabbed my mind like carrion crows at a fresh corpse – I wrapped myself in my towelling robe, grabbed a handful of cotton wool balls – the main ingredient of my 'neutralise the cherry tree' plan – and walked out into my living room.

Sylvia was standing under my beaded chandelier with her arms outstretched, eyes closed, mouth partially open, a relaxed, oblivious expression on her face. Her dress flared out like a huge white flower, fully repaired, and all her cuts and scratches were gone. Tiny green buds peaked out from under her pink cycle helmet, and small hair-like roots snaked out from her feet, ankles, even the silver sandals, and trailed through the puddle of blood, which was now much smaller than before.

'I hope you don't mind,' she whispered breathlessly without opening her eyes, 'but blood is such a good fertiliser I couldn't resist.'

''Course not,' I said, opening my hand and launching the cotton wool into the air with a quick push of my will to activate the spells. *Security Stingers ~ the Ultimate Intruder Deterrent.* The spells flew towards Sylvia like small pollen-thirsty bees, buzzing around her and wrapping her face and pink cycle helmet in a mass of fine, sticky, sting-laden threads. She jerked, her eyes opening briefly, then she sighed and they closed again, in sleep this time. Her clothes disappeared, leaving her standing naked, apart from her white shorts and the pink cycling helmet; both were obviously real, not part of her Glamour. She didn't look that different, if you ignored her skin, now greeny-grey bark striated with small brown lenticels, presumably like the trunk of her tree. I waited for her to fall over, aiming to catch her, but she didn't. When I looked down, I realised her roots had embedded themselves in my wooden floorboards and were holding her in place.

I sighed. My landlord wasn't going to be happy about the damage, but at least Sylvia wouldn't hurt herself. I didn't feel right leaving her there naked, so I managed to half-dress her in my robe. 'Thanks for the dinner invite, Sylvia,' I said quietly, even though nothing other than a salt-water drenching would wake her for a good few hours, 'but I've already got plans for later, and they don't include you.'

I dressed in a T-shirt and jeans, both black in preparation for my later plans, snagged the day-old BLT sandwich (last night's snack) and some orange juice from the fridge, then sat cross-legged on the floor in front of my computer and started Googling. Once I'd finished, I picked up the folder Victoria Harrier had given me and took out the police list of missing faelings. It went back a couple of years and it wasn't difficult to see a pattern. The numbers and breakdown of the sexes of the missing faelings had stayed fairly constant until five months ago, when it had changed. Since then, the only faelings reported missing were female. The list noted that most were working girls – a.k.a. girls who were vulnerable and easy prey, the type no one would make much of a fuss about if they vanished. It wasn't vamps. For one, Malik had given his protection to all fae and faelings; and two: for the most part vamps weren't interested in gender when it came to blood or sex. The two dead faelings were just the tip of the iceberg. There were another fifteen missing, and they were just the ones that had been reported.

I chewed my sandwich, staring thoughtfully at the computer screen. Were the others all dead too? Or were they still alive somewhere? I thought back to my trip to Disney Heaven. Angel/The Mother had said: *they are all dying*, not: *they are all dead*, which was sort of hopeful – if the girls could be found before *he* killed them, *he* being the photofit of the horned god, which could either be symbolic – since the horned god was also associated with fertility, and this was all to do with the curse – in which case the photofit wasn't going to help much, or the picture could be literal: the killer had horns – and that, however much I didn't want it to, came down to the satyrs. They were the only horned fae in London.

You will stop this, You will break the curse, and *You will give them a new life.* One and two were no-brainers, the third command … maybe it was just as literal? Maybe I was meant to save the missing faelings, therefore breaking the curse, and give *them* a new life, not actually pop out the next generation of London's fae – or maybe that was just wishful thinking on my part.

Then there was goddess number two, the Morrígan. It didn't take a genius to put together a fertility goddess who had a thing about ravens and who wanted me to remember losing a child, and a dead corvid faeling, to know that she was on the same case as The Mother. Finding and saving the missing girls would be so much easier if the pair of them had talked to each other, and given me more than cryptic clues to go on … still, one good thing about the whole horrific *Alien* baby show and Tavish's dire pronouncements of doom, not to mention whatever nasty spells the pair of them had sicced on me, the Morrígan was adamant I shouldn't get pregnant … as adamant as Clíona was, in fact … so maybe the Morrígan *was* working for Clíona in some way, as Sylvia had guessed?

And then there was Ana, or Annan, Clíona's great-granddaughter, who *was* pregnant, and whose mother Brigitta was dead because of the curse (and the vamps), and whose grandmother, Rhiannon/Angel, had suffered at the hands of London's fae because of it. So when it came to the curse, Ana had 'victim' stamped all her, even without the Morrígan appearing as a *bean nighe*. But that didn't mean she had anything to do with the missing faelings, other than she was a faeling herself. I sipped my juice. Maybe I'd find out more when I visited Ana tomorrow for our little who's-the-vamp chat?

There was nothing more I could do about the missing faelings until tomorrow now, other than email Hugh some questions:

The missing faelings since Hallowe'en – how many have corvid blood, or connections to the Morrígan?
And do any have dealings with any of the satyrs?
Check out Ana (Victoria Harrier's daughter-in-law) – possible future victim.

I went to press send, then stopped and added:

Did any of them worship The Mother?

Someone was annoying Her with their prayers, enough to make Her do something, so it was a clue Hugh needed to know, whether it would lead to anything or not. He was the one really investigating the poor faeling's death, after all. Then recalling another vague suspicion I'd had, I added:

Maybe have someone look at yesterday's circle; I think there was something wrong with the way the yew was laid out ...

I pressed send, and hoped that The Mother's gag clause didn't extend to cyber-space, not that I'd put much in the email. The message disappeared, but whether it would get there ... I sent him a text too, just in case.

I closed the computer down, then padded over to the kitchen and touched the empty cut-glass fruit bowl on the counter. The bowl's diamond-cut facets shimmered with a sudden rainbow of colours, highlighting the engraved glyphs. I dipped my hand in ... and an apple, painted gold, appeared as my fingers passed its edge.

'*Symbol of fertility*,' whispered the bowl. '*The forbidden fruit. The poisoned gift. The healthgiver; an apple a day keeps the vampires away.*'

I sighed, exasperated, and withdrew my hand. 'I've told you,' I muttered, 'I hate apples.' And magical artefacts that had their own snide opinions. The bowl had been a boon from Clíona in return for finding Angel at Hallowe'en. The magical blood-fruit it produced was the equivalent of the humans' G-Zav – faerie methadone for the 3V infection – and while it didn't cure my venom addiction, at least with the blood-fruit, I was the one in control. So long as I didn't let a vamp actually stick their fangs in me.

The bowl gave a small, irritated cough, and the apple was replaced by five gleaming, silver-painted blackberries. '*Sacred fruit of the Goddess. Fruit of the fae. Healer of wounds. Seeds of hope and rebirth—*'

'Yeah, okay, I get it,' I muttered and gathered them up. The blood-fruit burst on my tongue, sweet and tart with the faint liquorice flavour of vamp venom, the juice flowing down my throat like warm blood. My libido went straight to Red Alert – which was why I usually followed the blood-fruit with a cup of cold lamb's blood: it knocked the annoying sexual cravings on the head. But despite Sylvia's obvious enjoyment of the blood, I wasn't prepared to lick it off the floorboards, and the feelings would wear off by the time I got to my evening's appointment.

And as I was running short on daylight, I needed to get a move on.

I whipped my T-shirt off, turned it inside out and put it back on, then tucked my hair into my black baseball cap with its See-Me-Not spell; my standard operating procedure when I wanted to stay below the fae's radar. It appeared to have been working, because even with Bandana following me, no one (including Finn!) had ever mentioned my outings.

I grabbed the padded backpack with the insulated compartment from under the sink, opened the fridge, and carefully transferred the three bags of blood – *my* blood – from the middle shelf. The blood-fruit controlled my venom addiction, but like anyone infected with 3V, my body still produced much more blood than it needed. Bags were way better than leeches (the slimy sort, not the fanged sort) at getting rid of it.

Time to go to Sucker Town, make my weekly donation, and see what insider info I could glean about Malik before the beautiful, over-protective, and maybe still angry vamp got my message at sunset.

Chapter Eighteen

'Sure you want to get out 'ere, luv?' The taxi driver took my money with a morose expression. 'Them vamps, they ain't like regular people. One of me mates, 'is kid got mixed up wiv 'em and 'e ended up in rehab at that 'OPE clinic. An' I gotta tell you too, luv, that you don't get no human cab drivers after dark 'ere in Sucker Town, just them Gold Goblin cabs. Regulations, innit.'

Sucker Town: home to the B-, C- and Scary-list London vamps, venom-junkies and blood-groupies, not to mention the occasional marauding fang-gang. Of course, between the licensing laws, the Beater goblin security force and the local vamps wanting to cash in on the same tourist money the mainstream city centre clubs were raking in, the place isn't as dangerous as it used to be, even six or seven months ago. And thanks to Malik giving me his protection, I was now probably safer in Sucker Town – which the rest of the fae avoid like vamps shun sunlight – than in any other part of London.

I gave the taxi driver a wry smile, tucked my cap in my backpack, and hitched it on my shoulder. 'I'm sure. But thanks for the concern.'

'Suit yerself, luv, yer funeral,' he called even more glumly as he drove off, leaving a fug of exhaust fumes in his wake.

'Everyone's a comedian,' I murmured and turned round to face the entrance of Sucker Town's newest, hottest vampire establishment: the Coffin Club.

I looked up at the sun, half disappeared behind the row of

warehouses, and at the shadows creeping over from the other side of the quiet industrial park, and an anxious itch crawled down my spine. Instead of going in the club, I walked along the side of the building past the life-sized posters advertising the club's vamps until I came to Darius, the vamp I'd come to see. Except he wasn't called Darius any more, not officially, anyway, but William, as in William Wallace. In the poster he was dressed in full kilt and regalia (minus the blue face paint). He looked great, but then, the tall, tawny-haired vamp had always looked like he'd just stepped off the front of a romance novel, even when he'd been a human blood-pet.

Darius and his Moth-girl girlfriend, Sharon, had come to my rescue on All Hallows' Eve during the demon attack. Darius survived, but sadly Sharon didn't – but as she died, she had asked me to watch over him. I owed them both, big time, so it was an unspoken promise I was determined to keep.

Trouble was, watching over him had got complicated – and not in the way I'd thought it would. The first time I'd checked up on him, a couple of weeks after the attack, I'd come loaded up with so many defensive spells that I glowed brighter than the Christmas lights in Regent Street. Malik might have given me his protection, but even so, not taking precautions is just plain stupid. I expected the vamps to stalk me like cats scenting a mouse; instead, every one I came across tripped over their own feet and shoved each other out of the road in their panic to run away. I knew it wasn't the spells scaring them off – vamps can't see magic – which left me curious about exactly what Malik had done.

Darius had filled me in. Turned out, at sunset on Guy Fawkes' Night, Elizabetta, head of the Golden Blade blood, had called together all four of London's blood-families to witness her ascension to Oligarch and Head Fang of London's High Table (I'd killed the last one a month earlier, so the position was vacant). Standing on the dais in the Challenge ring, surrounded by her bladesmen, Elizabetta had held her five-foot-long bronze sword aloft, then shouted for any who would oppose her to come forward. Right at the very end of the required minute's expectant silence, just as she started to smile in triumph, her chest erupted in a spray of blood and bone, leaving a fist-sized empty hole where her heart had been; her head ripped itself from her neck, *Exorcist*-style, zoomed fifty feet straight up into the night sky and vanished; then her body combusted in white-hot flames. Within minutes her burning ashes were scattered by a nonexistent wind.

'No one knows how Malik al-Khan did it,' Darius had told me, wide-eyed with hero worship, 'I mean, he weren't there, and no one saw or felt a thing. Then he does this big appearing act on Tower Hill with her head in one hand and her heart in the other. He took half an hour to walk to the Challenge ring – they had a 'copter up filming him all the way. Elizabetta's head was still screaming at him, right up 'til he stood on the dais and threw her head in the air and it exploded into ashes. 'Course, no one challenged him after that.'

'So why aren't you worried about speaking to me?' I asked, my thoughts swinging between stunned, impressed, and wondering uneasily if Malik's show was all just smoke and mirrors, or if he really was that powerful.

'I'm Blue Heart blood,' Darius said, 'but I'm not part of any blood-family, 'cos Rio gave me the Gift, but she never did the Oath of Fealty part of the ceremony.'

Rio, his sponsor, had given him the Gift for her own nefarious purposes, then dumped him, and since baby vamps are dependent on their masters for top-up feeds to keep their new vamp bodies alive, Darius' immortal future was looking short and bleak – until a sorcerer took a fancy to him and turned him into a fang-pet.

The same sorcerer whose soul I'd eaten.

'So I never swore an Oath then' – he swept a hand through

his tawny hair – 'and I've never swore one to anyone else since, not even the sorcerer. No one owns me now, no one can tell me what to do any more, not even Malik al-Khan, which means I can talk to you, and he can't do anything, 'cos I never swore I wouldn't talk to you.'

Vamp rules and regs: they live and die by them.

'I'm au-ton-o-mous!' He drew the word out proudly. Not only had Darius' stint with the sorcerer resulted in him bypassing the dependant baby vamp stage, it also gave him some backbone. Before that he'd been a 'yes' guy, verging on 'victim'. Now he was proud of standing up to the one vamp everyone else was running scared of, and I was proud of him too. I silently vowed to make sure he didn't lose his head over it like the original William Wallace.

But the next time I checked up on Darius, after Christmas, was when things got complicated. Whatever magic the sorcerer had used to keep Darius' Gift alive had worn off, and with only six months on his vampire clock, he was too young to survive on just human blood, so he'd fallen into bloodlust. Luckily – or unluckily, depending on which way you look at it – the Moth-girls in the blood-house where Darius lived had bound him in heavy chains before he'd attacked anyone. As he wasn't a danger to humans, none of the other vamps could legitimately rescind his Gift, but since he didn't have a master to rescue him, and the Moths couldn't find one to take him on, all that meant was he got the chance to die slowly in agony.

One personal blood donation later, and Darius was almost back to his old self. Turns out, my sidhe blood is as good as a master vamp's, judging by the quick results. So now Darius is my fang-pet, and regular donations of my blood are keeping him alive and well; hence the three bags of blood sloshing around in my backpack, his usual weekly allowance. The irony wasn't lost on me. I've spent eleven years making sure I don't end up a vamp's blood-slave, my will subjugated by 3V to my master's. Now, I might not be the slave, but I was still tied to a vamp by my blood. Having a fang-pet isn't something I want to last for eternity, but so far I haven't found a solution.

And I wasn't going to, standing here worrying about going in to see him – although it wasn't actually Darius I was worried about seeing.

I told myself to stop being a coward, and started walking back down to the Coffin Club entrance.

The club's the only place where curious Joe Public can see vampires in their 'dead as the day is long' state, tackily laid out in all their pseudo-heroic funeral finery, in glass coffins, no less. Whichever vamp came up with the idea had to have a really warped sense of humour, since – despite the myths – vamps have never slept in coffins, glass or otherwise. And back in the eighties they haemorrhaged a hefty fortune on legal expertise and behind-the-scenes manoeuvring in order to regain their 'human' rights by proving they sleep the day away in a sort of light-induced hibernation – as opposed to actually being *dead*.

But thanks to a revival of the classic Hammer Horrors, sleeping in coffins is the new black when it comes to the vamps' money- and blood-spinning industry. And the vamps love a theme, so the coffin shapes outlined on the double entrance doors, the chrome coffin handles and the neon-red coffin-shaped lights were just the start of the *ad nauseam* décor that swamped the club. I'd heard even the toilets had coffin-shaped porcelain loos – not that I'd checked. The only things not coffin-shaped were the small white diamond-shaped bell pushes that decorated the doors like name plaques, which is sort of what they were, since the Coffin Club is run by White Diamond blood.

My father's blood-family.

Predictably, my heart had done the whole 'dropping into my boots' thing when Darius had told me where his new job, and new home were; I *so* didn't need the memories. It had taken me a good ten minutes to put my hand on one of the diamond bell pushes the first time I'd dropped his blood allowance off, even though I hadn't found a single familiar face from the past when I'd checked the club's website. After that, I started making my blood-donation trips at midday. No point tempting fang, is there?

I hitched my backpack higher and with my pulse pounding in my ears, I pressed the bell and looked up into the security camera, waiting until the buzzer sounded and the door clicked open.

Chapter Nineteen

The entrance foyer was done up in twisted funeral-parlour chic: black-panelled wood, thick black carpet, artistically arranged white lilies exuding their overly sweet scent, and plush white velvet seats. A multitude of tiny UV spotlights – the reason why everything I wore, including my underwear, was black – dispelled the gloom slightly and picked out the white velvet ropes that marked a glowing zigzag path to the ticket booth.

A pair of long-haired Irish wolfhounds sat with their ears pricked forwards, pink tongues lolling out the sides of their mouths as they stared at me out of disconcertingly pale blue eyes; the UV spots tinted their grey-white coats silver. I gave the dogs a wide berth. Not that I don't like dogs, but like everyone else, I'd heard the rumours: they were either vamps, or controlled by the vamps. After all, having a load of comatose suckers lying around in glitzy coffins with only humans to defend them is just asking for trouble from some of the more militant pro-humans groups. Even after several visits I still didn't know which of the doggy rumours were true.

I headed into the zigzag ropes, checking out the life-sized coffin-shaped screens for a glimpse of Darius as they flashed pictures of the club's vamps 'lying in state'. He wasn't being featured, which meant he was in his room. I reached the ticket booth – coffin-shaped, of course – to find Gareth, the club's human manager, sitting slumped inside, idly flicking through a magazine: *Bite Monthly*. He was dressed as usual in the club's undertaker uniform, with his black-banded top hat sitting on the shelf behind him. The dour outfit didn't go with his blond surfer-boy good looks.

'Thought you'd be busier at this time,' I said, holding out the entrance fee.

'Members don't turn up 'til the vamps start gettin' lively.' He frowned at the money, but didn't take it. 'It's after five.' He gave me a look almost as disconcerting as the dogs'. 'Only members get in after five, Ms Taylor. Them's the rules.'

'*C'mon*, Gareth. One: I'm not human, so the rules don't apply; and two: you know why I'm here, and I'll be in and out in fifteen minutes tops.'

'Can't do it.' He pointed up at the security cameras. 'Council inspector checks them weekly. We'd lose our tourist licence, and I'd lose my sponsorship.' He opened wide and touched his tongue to his implanted fangs. 'Ain't no chance of gettin' these for real if your sponsor refuses you the Gift. None of the others'll take you on then.' He shut his mouth with a snap. 'You wanna go in now, then you gotta be a member.'

I gripped my backpack strap, frustration pricking me. Getting a vamp to officially sponsor you for the Gift is the Dream Win: the odds-on lottery chance at joining the ranks of the immortal bloodsuckers. Of course, getting the sponsor is less about the lottery as having the right looks, attitude and earning potential that makes a fang-fan an attractive proposition as a future baby bloodsucker. After all, the vamp sponsor and his newly Gifted neophyte will be spending the next fifty to hundred years in co-dependency before the younger vamp gains his autonomy and cuts his bloody apron strings, so no vamp in their right mind is going to offer the Gift to someone who isn't a thousand and ten per cent loyal.

Arguing with Gareth was a waste of time. 'How much for the membership?' I asked flatly.

'Won't cost you nothing but blood.' He pulled out a form

from under his magazine and slid it towards me. 'Just sign on the dotted line.'

Blood might be the price, but it didn't mean I had to pay it. 'Fine, give me two wristbands, then.'

'I'm only supposed to give them to members after they've donated, so the vamps don't take too much.'

'Licensing laws say wristbands are to be given to anyone who asks, Gareth; you know that.'

'Yeah, well. Not many of them ask beforehand.' He hesitated, then pulled out a couple of white silicone wristbands from a large goldfish bowl behind him and tossed them on the form. They glowed under the UV light.

I slipped them on and pulled the form towards me. The details were already filled in; all it needed was the date and my signature. I looked up in surprise.

'Yesterday was your day to visit.' Gareth gave me a pen. 'When you didn't turn up at lunchtime today, I guessed you'd be in to see your boy tonight. And I was bored. It's dead round here just now.'

'Ha, ha,' I muttered, then read down the form. A name next to one section snagged my attention—

Malik al-Khan.

'Owner?' I jabbed the pen in annoyance. 'That is *so* wrong.'

'It can't be.' Gareth frowned. 'I got it off the blood-families' database. It's where I got all your personal info, and it lists Malik al-Khan as your owner.'

Ri-*ight*, a database: well, that clarified everything … and nothing. 'It's not the database that's wrong, it's the concept,' I explained through gritted teeth, although going by Gareth's 'uh-huh' look, it wasn't a concept that bothered him. 'And how the hell did my details get on the database in the first place?'

'Someone put them there,' he said, deadpan.

Yeah, obvious or what? But *who*? Somehow updating a database didn't seem like Malik's sort of thing. Then the hairs on the back of my neck rose as I realised the form was filled out in my *birth* name: Genevieve Nataliya Zakharinova. I gripped the pen, knuckles going white, shocked at seeing it there.

Damn. This visit was a nightmare waiting to happen.

I scratched a signature on the form and shoved it back at Gareth. 'Right, you've got your signature for the camera. Now can I go in?'

'Minnie Mouse?' he spluttered. 'You can't put that—'

'You filled the wrong name out on the form, Gareth, so I can put anything I want—'

A dog growled.

We both turned; one of the dogs from the entrance had moved and now sat not far from the booth. It stared up at us from its disturbing eyes, lips drawn back to display impressive canines, a pair of diamond-encrusted dog-tags swinging on a choke chain round its neck.

'That *is* a dog, isn't it?' I asked, suspicion flaring as I *looked*. A round dish on the counter filled with what looked like water glittered with magic, but the dog still *looked* like a dog, and I still didn't get any vibes suggesting it might be something – or some*one* – else.

''Course he's a dog! Those rumours about them being vamps ain't true, y'know, they're just put around to keep the crazies away.' A puzzled expression crossed Gareth's face as he scanned the entrance behind me. 'Dunno what he's growlin' at though, ain't nothing there.' He waved the dog away. 'Go on, Max, back to the door.' The dog didn't move. Gareth shrugged and turned back to me. 'Anyway, *Ms Mouse*, your *membership* still needs to be sealed for the cameras, then you can go in.' He knocked on the counter top three times. When nothing happened, he sighed and disappeared beneath it, emerging after a few moments holding a tiny Monitor goblin. He wasn't much more than twelve inches high even with the tuft of silver-white hair. The goblin's head lolled as Gareth sat him on the counter between us. His navy-blue workman's boilersuit swamped his tiny frame and made him look like a grey, wrinkled doll dressed in toddler's play clothes. Tiny diamond earrings sparkled in his rabbit-like ears.

'Abraham, new member needs checking out,' Gareth said quietly, then gestured at me. 'Give him your hand so he can do his stuff.'

Goblins, like trolls, are impervious to magic, but unlike trolls, goblins are the ultimate magic detectors; they can spot a vamp mind-lock at twenty paces, and they can sense if someone's under the influence of a vamp's *mesma* with just a brief touch. They're also the ultimate 'letter of the law' followers: once a goblin's agreed a job and been paid, nothing can corrupt them, which is the main reason goblins are so popular with humans who do business with the vamps. And it's why the Monitors act as gatekeepers for the vamp clubs: the law states vamps can't use *mesma* or magical persuasions to force humans to enter any premises licensed for vampiric activities. Being checked out by a Monitor goblin makes the punters feel safe. Of course, there are other ways of persuading people that have nothing to do with *mesma* or magic, which is something the law doesn't account for.

I ran my finger down my nose in the respectful goblin greeting, then held my hand out, palm up. The goblin adjusted his miniature black wraparounds with the precise movements of someone utterly drunk and trying to hide it, then returned my greeting. 'St'early?' he queried to Gareth.

'Abraham, it's not too early, and she ain't human. The vamps can't mind-lock sidhes, so it's just for the cameras anyway.'

'S'okays ...' He belched, his chin falling to his chest, and a sour reek filled the air.

I jerked my hand away, incredulous. 'Are you *mad*? Don't you know how risky it is having a goblin milked up on

148

methane above ground during the day? What if he gets hit by sunlight?'

'Hey, no worries!' Gareth beckoned me to put my hand back. 'Abes ain't gonna explode or nothing: the windows're all specially coated for the vamps. What works for them works for the gobs too.' He gently prodded the goblin, then wrapped the goblin's knobbly fingers round a small wooden seal stick. 'C'mon, Abes, do your stuff.'

'Handmiss,' Abraham slurred.

Frowning, I offered it again and Abraham dipped a finger in the water-dish, reached out and brushed my palm with a butterfly's touch, so light and quick that I almost didn't feel his sharp claw slice my skin. He pressed the seal into my blood, then leaned drunkenly forwards and stamped the form next to my/Minnie's signature.

I stood looking at the neat diamond design he'd cut into my palm, stunned and amazed at how fast he'd been, and at what he'd actually done. 'Okay,' I said slowly, 'since when did you start using *blood* along with magic to seal the forms?'

'One of the vamps thought it'd be a good gimmick, and the members love it,' Gareth said, picking Abraham up and strapping him into a child's high chair next to his own seat. He held up his own hand; a similar diamond shape glowed blue-white on his palm. 'Invisible ink's made from tonic water, the UV lights make it glow, and a spell *tags* it in place. It's like getting your hand stamped with that indelible ink the other clubs use, only some members don't want nobody knowing they've been to a vamp club' – his lip curled with contempt – 'so it suits all round.'

Crap. 'How long does it last for?'

'Long enough, Ms Taylor,' a deep voice said next to me.

I jerked round at the voice, my pulse jumping in my throat, wondering for a mad moment if it was the dog speaking.

A vampire was standing a couple of feet away, an avuncular

smile on his handsome fortysomething face – a fang-free smile, of course, a neat trick the older vamps practise: Fyodor Andreevich Zakharin, head honcho of the White Diamond vamps.

Chapter Twenty

I gave Fyodor a narrow-eyed once-over: long silver-white hair, long-skirted coat covered in military-looking braid sewn with diamonds, waistcoat and breeches tucked into high soft leather boots. His clothes were all white other than his boots, which were gleaming black. His white silk cravat was stuck with a diamond tie-pin so enormous that it would make a goblin queen drool with lust. The white outfit sparkled in the UV lights, giving him a glowing nimbus, like I guessed an aura would, if I could see them. Next to him sat the dog-tagged wolfhound, tongue still lolling, silver-white coat looking not unlike the vamp's silver-white hair.

'Let me guess,' I said, pleased my voice came out calm, 'you're either going to a naff elf-themed wedding, or you're shooting an advert for soap powder that can *really* make your whites sparkle.'

The dog growled low in its throat, and was answered by more rumbling growls. My stomach clenched with apprehension as I flashed a look around me. Gareth was blank-faced, mind-locked – not that he'd be any help, even if he wasn't – and the goblin was snoring softly in his high chair. And half a dozen more huge wolfhounds ringed the entrance hall, standing between me and the exit. *Great, a doggy ambush.*

'Genevieve is our guest, Max,' Fyodor, the sparkling vamp warned, drawing my attention back to him as he patted the dog's head.

I dipped my shoulder and caught my backpack by its handle.

The three bags of blood inside it weren't heavy, but the couple of bricks I kept in it were, and they made it a handy weapon. Malik might've given me protection, but it still pays to stay alert. You never know when some vamp's going to develop a superiority complex, or think he's found a get-out clause that'll let him keep his head attached to his shoulders.

'Guests usually get to leave when they want.' I had a moment's regret that I'd used the last of my Security Stingers on Sylvia the dryad. 'Oh, and there's the other thing: didn't you swear an oath to your liege lord Malik al-Khan not to approach me?'

'Please, Genevieve, put away your fear.' He held his hands out in welcome. 'You have no need of it here. We acknowledge Malik al-Khan's protection over you. We also offer you the hospitality and protection of White Diamond blood while you are with us.'

I relaxed. Slightly. Offers of hospitality and protection were all good, even if I'd rather he hadn't spoken to me in the first place.

'But even were it not for these assurances, you are safe,' he carried on, smiling like he was about to tell me I'd won a prize draw, 'for you are among your true blood-family now.'

I held up my hand. 'Wait just one minute. My father might be White Diamond blood, but I'm not a vampire, and there's no way I'm admitting any connection to you through blood.' Not when I don't know what sort of trouble it could get me into.

'Genevieve, please, I assure you I mean you no harm. Our blood connection is not only through our vampire lineage, but we are also kin through our human bloodlines. Allow me to introduce myself.' He smacked his booted heels together and executed a bow. 'I am Fyodor Andreevich Zakharin. Your father Andrei Yurievich Zakharin honoured me with the Gift, but more than that, he is my patrilineal ancestor: my great-grandfather, to be precise. So you see, we are cousins, Genevieve Nataliya Zakharinova, cousins twice removed. You are indeed among your true family.'

Just what a girl doesn't need: long-lost vampire relatives.

His smile widened, and this time I caught a glimpse of fang. 'I was privileged to be at your christening, although you would not recollect that, but you should recollect meeting me at your betrothal to the Autarch. I asked if you'd be kind enough to call me Cousin Fyodor.'

A flash of him smiling in just the same way, saying just the same words, with my father standing at his side, lit my mind, then it was snuffed out by the gut-churning fear any memory of that night brought me. I stared at him, a voice inside irrationally screaming, *If he was family, why hadn't he helped?* Anger and disbelief that he hadn't – and now he expected me to remember him – burned the fear away. I glared at him. 'Are you trying to be funny or something?'

He frowned in what looked like genuine puzzlement. 'Why would I try and make you laugh?'

'Oh, well, let's see: my wedding night, *that* was when I was paraded like a prize heifer in front of more than a hundred vampires I'd never met before, and then my only faeling friend was tortured and killed by the Autarch, all while *he* happily told me her death was a wedding gift to please *me*. While *all* of you *watched*!' I spat the words out, trying to get rid of the foul taste of bile and terror in my mouth. 'And you ask why I don't remember meeting you!'

A loud growl came from the dog.

'Shh, Max.' Fyodor absently stroked its head, his smile dimming. 'I can understand why you may not value the Autarch's concern for you; these modern times are more lax when it comes to dealing with such insults. But the girl was an upstart.' He waved a conciliatory hand. 'She tried to usurp your place, and the Autarch's authority, Genevieve. What else could he have done?'

'Sack her, send her off with a flea in her ear, maybe? Anything but what he did do.' I clenched my fists, gently swinging the backpack, wanting to smash it over his obtuse, old-fashioned head. The dog gave a warning bark. 'Oh, and just so you know, *Cousin*, his was the insult, not hers: she was *seventeen*, only three years older than me, and he's the prince, the god you all bow to. What was she supposed to do when he started giving her jewels and fucking her? Say no?'

The dog leapt, jaws opening wide, and Fyodor's shout of denial was lost in its loud barking.

I threw myself backwards, jerking the backpack up to shield my throat. I hit the thick-carpeted floor with a thud that knocked the air from my lungs and the rage from my mind. *Stupid*, to let my anger get the better of me! Adrenalin flooded my muscles as the dog snarled, and rough hair brushed my hands as the backpack was wrenched from my grip. The dog gave a series of high-pitched yelps and I brought my knees up, tucked my chin down and rolled back and away, expecting to feel its teeth in my flesh at any moment.

Then Fyodor's deep voice shouted in a language I didn't understand as I rolled into something hard: a wall. My mind raced, trying to figure out a way to escape as I instinctively curled tighter into a defensive ball, bracing myself against the dog's attack. Even if it didn't try to tear me apart, having a hundred and fifty pounds of dog on top of me wasn't going to be fun. The seconds ticked by, and my adrenalin-hyped senses finally caught up with the fact that I didn't have a huge wolfhound trying to rip chunks out of me. I peered out warily from between my arms.

Fyodor had the dog up on its hind legs – the dog was taller than him – and had one arm locked around its chest while his other hand twisted the chain at its throat; choking it as its back paws scrabbled for grip on the carpet. Fyodor made man-handling the animal look easy, but even the newbie vampires can peel the roof off a car like opening a sardine can. The dog was losing. I shot a look towards the entrance. The rest of the dogs were still lying there, blocking my exit, but they appeared unconcerned about their pack mate's plight. I turned back as Fyodor started crooning something in the dog's ear, speaking too softly for me to hear.

Magic prickled against my skin and I shifted uncomfortably. The dog's silver-white coat glowed brightly, as if each hair was a live fibre-optic wire, then its fur receded, pulling back into its flesh like it was being sucked in by a vacuum. The dog's hairless body shone blindingly white for a brief second, and an explosion of magic shattered my *sight*. Then the light dissipated and Fyodor was holding the pale, naked body of a male against him. Long platinum-blond hair hid the male's face. For a second both were silent, unmoving, then the male opened his mouth wide in an ear-splitting shriek, showing all four of his fangs. Fyodor jerked the choke chain, cutting off the vamp's scream, then released him with a disappointed sigh.

Max the dog/vamp slid bonelessly to the floor in a limp tangle of arms and legs.

I sat up cautiously, keeping a wary eye on the other dogs, not sure if Fyodor had just saved me from being Max's doggy dinner, or whether it was all some devious ploy to make me feel obligated. 'So the rumours are true then,' I said. 'Your vamps can turn into dogs.'

'Gareth,' Fyodor ordered, ignoring me, 'please bring Max his cloak.'

The blank-faced Gareth rushed out of his booth with a white velvet cloak which he tenderly tucked around Max, tying the cords in a neat bow around the vamp's throat as if he'd done it a hundred times. He probably had, but was never allowed to remember.

'Genevieve,' Fyodor said, and pointed at the prone vamp, 'this is Maxim Fyodor Zakharin, my son, and your cousin, thrice removed.' He walked towards me and held out his hand. 'May I extend an apology on his behalf and assure you we both regret our lack of hospitality. I am at a loss to explain his behaviour, other than that his hound state is not always easily controlled.'

Maxim? Malik had called the vamp who'd invaded his dreamscape on Tower Bridge Maxim. I glanced at the unconscious blond vamp. Yep, he was the same vamp. I hadn't liked him then, or the previous time I'd come across him, when he'd kidnapped a friend of mine and tried to blackmail me into taking his blood-bond. I liked him much more now he was out for the count.

Ignoring Fyodor's hand, I stood. 'What about them?' I indicated the other dogs.

'Do not be concerned; they are what they appear.' He brushed a couple of hairs from his white frockcoat. 'They are well-trained guard dogs to deter undesirables, and also camouflage, if you will. But to answer your assumption, no, the rumours are not true; my form of the Gift cannot confer the ability to become a hound. Max is the son of my loins, but I did not give him the Gift, and neither did your father.' His face was calm, but his voice held a shadow of regret. 'That honour was bestowed on him by the Autarch himself, a rare occurrence, for he does not share his power lightly. It is his magic that flows through my son's blood.'

I briefly wondered if the Autarch's psychotic tendencies ran through Max's blood too. 'You don't sound too happy about that,' I said, keeping my back firmly against the wall.

'My son owes the Autarch his Oath; it is a situation that causes friction between us. He can be very defensive of any criticism towards his master. It is the only reason I can think to explain his attack, for which I apologise once again; it is unforgivable when we have offered you our hospit—'

The sharp end of a stake appeared in the centre of Fyodor's chest and blood spurted from the wood, splattering my face and clothes. I gave a shocked yelp before I could stop myself. Fyodor's eyes widened with the same shocked surprise as he looked down. He blinked, then grasped the stake with both hands and started to pull it out. For a moment I thought he'd succeed, but then he shuddered, his hands slipped away and he crumpled to the floor, the blood ruining the sparkling whiteness of his outfit.

Maxim stood in his place, white cloak draped around his shoulders, platinum hair drawn back from his widow's peak in a ponytail, his eyes still disturbingly pale blue and hooded. 'Dear Old Dad.' He grinned, flashing all four of his fangs. 'He really does nag on like an old woman at times.'

My stomach clenched uneasily as I glanced at the staked Fyodor: he'd been right when he'd said there was friction between him and his son. I looked back at Mad Max, and decided I positively detested him now I knew he owed his Oath to the Autarch, and was of his psychotic blood, *and* was also standing in front of me looking way too pleased with himself.

'Cat got your tongue, Cousin Sidhe?' He laughed gleefully. 'Now where shall we start—? Gareth, go and get some help and put Dear Old Dad in his coffin.' He nudged Fyodor with his toe. 'Oh, and leave the stake in, it'll make a nice show for the members, and tomorrow we can charge extra for him. And now he's out of the way, Cousin, you and I can have a nice chat' – he made an exaggerated show of checking over his shoulder – 'and look, we're all alone, with no pesky Malik al-Khan around to spoil our fun.'

Not for the first time, I had a fleeting wish for some sort of spellcasting ability, or at least a handy Stun spell. 'What do you want?' I asked, keeping my voice level.

'As I told our esteemed Oligarch, I've got a little proposition for you.' He rubbed his hands together. 'But the Turk's being his usual dog-in-the-manger self.'

'Let me guess,' I said drily. 'You won't kidnap any more of my friends if I go back to the Autarch quietly, so you can get a nice pat on the head?'

'Good God, no!' He gave a theatrical shudder. 'We don't want Him involved, do we? If He knew we were all pally, he'd just demand I hand you over, and I'd have to say *Yes, Sire!* and probably end up as part of the entertainment.' He finger-shot himself in the head. 'Duh! His Brattiness might be a total nutter, but I'm not. Why do you think I put up with Dear Old Dad all the time? It's certainly not for the old man's scintillating company. Malik, on the other hand, will agree to anything to keep you out of the Autarch's clutches.' He beamed, his face lighting up with manic glee, and spread his arms wide, flashing me with more than his fangs. 'Oh, don't you just love it when a plan comes together?'

'It's not my plan,' I said, narrowing my eyes at him, not sure whether his 'happy as Larry' act was for real, 'and I don't appreciate being held hostage for ransom. So no, not loving it so far.'

'Oh, you're not a *hostage*, Cousin.' He held his hands up in mock surrender. 'Far from it! No, all I want is a quick family snap of us together, then you're free to leave whenever you want.'

I raised my brows. 'Okay, now I'm confused. Letting the hostage go before you get the ransom – not that I'm complaining – is one of those cart-before-the-horse things. So: what's the catch?'

'Catch? There's no *catch*, little cousin. All I want is the photo and that's it. Good God, I'm not stupid, you know. The Autarch might have a few screws loose, but he's easily distracted; it's out of sight, out of mind with him. Malik, on the other hand, is like a bleeding elephant. He never forgets if you cross him, and he keeps coming after you until he's managed to stamp you out completely. Look what he did to Elizabetta!' He grabbed his head in both hands with a mock scream of horror. 'Me, I'd prefer to keep my bonce on my shoulders where it belongs.'

I blinked. Personally I'd take Malik over the Autarch any day, but hey, he had a point with the head thing ... and if all Mad Max truly wanted was a picture—

'Fine, where's the camera then?'

'I bet you've got one on your phone, haven't you?' He smiled winningly and fluffed out his velvet cloak. 'I'm a bit short on pockets in this get-up.'

Still suspicious about what he was up to, I pulled out my phone from my jacket pocket and warily held it out.

He took it and examined it as if it were diamond-studded. 'Nice bit of kit! I didn't think this model was out yet.' His thumb moved over the small keyboard, almost faster than I could see. 'I've been waiting to get a shot at one of these from a reviewer I know; she says it doesn't live up to the hype.' His brows lowered in concentration at the phone. 'What do you think?'

'It's a phone. It does what phones do,' I said, trying to calculate if I could make it past the dogs, most of whom were stretched out sleeping now, and out the door before—

'Mind if I take a test pic of Dear Old Dad first?' He looked up enquiringly.

'Knock yourself out.'

He resumed fiddling with the phone, and I started slowly edging away from him and the staked vamp at my feet.

His hand shot out and clamped round my wrist. 'Picture first, Cousin.' He smiled; this time there was nothing *winning* about it.

'Hurry up and take it then.' I jerked my arm away, surprised when he let me go.

'Come and cuddle up here.' He patted his side, his bonhomie back, and indicated I should pose next to him, then held up the phone, camera lens pointed back at himself.

Feeling a bit like I had fallen down the rabbit hole, or was maybe climbing onto the hangman's scaffold, I stepped over the body and angled in next to him.

He clapped his arm round my shoulders with a cheery laugh. I gritted my teeth.

'Okay, now hold your hand up next to your face, the one with the member's diamond on it.' He looked up at the lights and moved us back fractionally. 'Now look at the camera, and— One, two, big cheesy grin, *smile!*' The phone clicked, and the flash blinded me.

I squeezed my eyes tight shut ...

And when I opened them, the scene in the club's foyer had changed.

Chapter Twenty-One

Mad Max, his dear-old-and-bloodily-staked Dad, and even the dogs were gone. The Coffin Club's foyer was empty except for the sleeping goblin in the ticket booth. For a moment I wondered if I'd imagined it all, but my T-shirt was still damp with Fyodor's blood, although someone had creepily cleaned my face and hands. Damn vamp tricks. Looked like the bastard had mind-locked me, something he shouldn't have been able to do. And what the hell game was the mad vamp playing?

Not that I couldn't hazard a guess: he wanted something from me, and while he was leery enough of Malik's retribution not to want to hold *me* hostage, he wasn't above using my possessions as a negotiating tool, since my backpack with its cargo of blood and my phone were also gone. Not to mention there was Darius, my pet-vamp himself, to worry about.

But before I could flush the mad-dog vamp out of wherever he'd disappeared to, a loud Big Ben-type chime rang, the club's front doors swung open, and a crowd of people – *humans* – were laughing, whooping and racing through them.

Suddenly three of them split off and headed for me, their pale grey costumes streaking behind them like delicate wings blown by the wind. I recognised their black-and-white Pierrot faces: they were some of the Moth-girls from the blood-house where Darius used to live. I had a moment to brace myself before all three threw themselves at me, flattening me against the wall, thin arms wrapping around my neck and waist, hands clutching mine, and I was enveloped in a soft mass of rustling silk, satin and lace.

I breathed in the smell of rice-powder mixed with grease-paint as Viola smeared a waxy kiss on my cheek, caught the faint scent of liquorice-scented blood as Rissa's long white hair trailed across my face, and felt the heat of the 3V infection pouring off Lucy's arms around my neck. I laughed, squeezing hands and hugging them all, joining in their enthusiastic greeting—

The present disappeared as a memory speared into my heart.

She looked numbly down at her son where he lay cradled in her arms. The midwife had wrapped him in the blue blanket appliquéd with the red and white train. She'd bought it only two days ago, sure then that her superstitions were unfounded and nothing would go wrong. She touched his tiny, perfect hand … but unlike all those excited day-dreams she'd had, his little fingers didn't curl round her own, but stayed limp and lifeless. That's when she knew he wasn't there, that he was gone.

I clutched Grace's gold pentacle, and looked at the three Moth-girls. They were fanned round me in a semi-circle, almost like they were afraid I'd run away if they let me go. Behind them the crowd of excited, over-eager humans were snaking their way through the white zigzag ropes towards the coffin-shaped ticket booth. A large raven perched on top of the booth watching me. As I looked, it gave a loud caw, then flapped its wings and flew over the oblivious queue and out through the club's open doors, disappearing into the night sky.

I turned back to the Moths.

I *knew* the heart-wrenching memory of the stillborn baby belonged to one of them, just as I *knew* it was the Morrígan's bitter-tasting magic that had drawn the memory out for me to see. But I didn't know which of the girls had lost their child, and none of the three appeared to know she'd shared the painful memory with me. I also didn't know what, if anything, I was supposed to do about it.

'You're crying,' Viola whispered as she slipped her thin arms back round my waist and squeezed. 'Are you all right?'

I nodded, swiped at the tears and the sorrow from the memory dispelled.

'Good,' she said, then pouted prettily. 'Wow, we haven't seen you in ages and ages and ages. We've missed you so much, Genny.'

'Yes, we're so pleased to see you again,' Lucy said, twining her fingers through mine.

''ave you come to see our Darius?' Rissa swiped a tissue along my cheek. 'Lipstick.' She puckered up her own purple-painted mouth, then said, 'It 'ain't bin the same since 'e went and got the job 'ere and you not come any more.'

I smiled apologetically, realising I'd missed them too. 'Sorry, girls. I've been coming here, and without Darius, well, you know ...' I trailed off, and we all stood and looked at each other awkwardly. I hadn't really thought they'd want me visiting – after all, they'd been Darius' little volunteer harem, as well as his breakfast, lunch and dinner most nights. And while we'd all had fun when I was there, I'd sort-of thought it was more because they'd put up with me as Darius' blood benefactor than anything more.

'Yeah, well, it's not the same without him there, but you still could've come, you know.' Viola squeezed my waist again. 'We really, really do miss *you*.'

'Right,' I managed to say past the tightness in my throat. Tears pricked my eyes and I blinked them away. 'Well, I *really* miss you all too.' I smiled. 'So I'll come and see you on your next night off, okay?'

'Yay!' Lucy waved her arms in the air.

'Good.' Rissa sniffed as she smiled. 'Then you will pay up for your poker debt.'

'Ah, now I see it.' I laughed. 'You just want me back 'cos I'm crap at cards.'

'Well, that is another reason,' Lucy teased. 'Oh, it is wonderful to see you again.'

'Hey, you too, girls.' I looked around, suddenly aware that someone was missing. Dread constricted my chest. 'Where's Yana? She's okay, isn't she?'

'She's fine.' Lucy clapped her hands. 'She's got herself a *sponsor*.'

'Really?' I said, surprised.

Lucy nodded. 'It's true. Francine. She's Golden Blade blood. They've been sweet on each other for a while, but the old hag Elizabetta didn't approve. Francine was there when you visited; she used to wait in the rec room at the end of the hallway – long black hair, real sexy-like.'

'Oh yeah, I remember.' Francine was a petite black vamp with a liking for red leather. She'd always hung back, watching from the doorway, but she'd never approached me, for obvious reasons; she wanted to keep her head on her shoulders. 'She okay, this Francine?' I frowned, still concerned about Yana. The vamps who usually frequented the blood-houses were mostly the ones addicted to necking – the dangerous and highly illegal pastime of biting straight into the carotid artery.

'She's a real pussycat,' Lucy shrieked, 'and *hot*,' she added fanning herself. 'But Yana's all right with her, she's one of the house standbys.'

The house standbys were powerful vamps who were experts at controlling a human's heart rate. Without the standbys, the Moths would die the first time anyone necked them, as the blood gushes like a soda fountain, and the standbys make sure the Moths never lose more blood than their bodies can cope with. But even with the standbys a lot of Moths only survive a couple of years at most; their bodies just can't take the abuse.

If Yana had got herself a sponsor, she might still make it to immortality.

'Yana will come later,' Rissa piped up. 'She and Francine are doing, y'know.' She crooked her fingers, and mimed fangs next to the half-dozen bite marks down the left side of her neck.

'Ah.'

'Francine doesn't do necks though, does she?' Viola laughed, and crooked her own fingers down Rissa's cleavage.

'Genny doesn't want to know that!' Lucy squealed, cheeks turning pink with embarrassment.

'Nah, Genny doesn't mind, do you?' Viola smiled with sly invitation.

'Save it for Darius,' I said with a laugh. 'He'll appreciate you more than I will.'

She pouted just as Lucy shouted, 'Hey the booth's opening.' She grabbed my hand, and pulled us into the zigzag of white ropes, cheerfully shoving past everyone until we ended up near the front of the queue, about five back from the ticket booth. Our place had been saved by two couples who were evidently Coffin Club devotees, since they were dressed in undertakers' suits, complete with top hats and funeral wreaths of white roses in their grey-gloved hands. The flowers looked oddly luminous under the UV lights.

'See them?' Lucy whispered as she nudged me, following my gaze. 'Plastic flowers. They paint them with this stuff to make them glow; I seen them do it last week in the loos.'

'Yeah, we're thinking of getting some of that stuff for our faces so they glow like our hands,' Viola said, angling her palm under the lights so her member's diamond glowed white. 'Then we'd stand out more.' She fluffed out her handkerchief-hemmed skirt and pushed up her small breasts under her top.

Her skimpy patchwork of grey lace, silk and satin shone in the gloomy interior. 'We look a bit dingy under these lights, don't you think, Genny?' She eyed me slyly.

'Yep.' I grinned. 'Definitely dingy.'

Lucy jumped up and down with excited impatience. 'Hurry up, hurry up,' she muttered. 'We've been too late to see Darius the last three weeks; someone's always got in before us and booked him up for a private party. That's why we wanted to be first tonight.'

We reached the ticket booth. Abraham the mini-Monitor goblin was still there, his highchair drawn up to the window. He looked perkier now his earlier methane hit was wearing off, but Gareth was gone, replaced by a tall, thin vamp. The hollows under his cut-glass cheekbones gave him a cadaverous appearance that went with his tailed undertaker's suit.

'Hands,' he intoned in a bored voice, waving a UV torch at the Monitor goblin.

I hung back as the Moths all crowded forward and stuck their hands out towards Abraham.

The vamp sighed. 'One at a time, girls.'

The three giggled and shuffled, cooing at Abraham as they got their palms checked, until the vamp waved them past.

I stepped up to the booth and stuck my own hand out. Abraham touched his nose, then my fingers. 'S'okay to enter, Miss,' he said in a soft sing-song.

The vamp waved the torch beam over my palm, lighting up the diamond mark, then stopped and sniffed. He sniffed again, then bent down so he was eye-level with me. 'Oh,' he murmured, his mouth dropping open to show his two sharp canines, 'oh, you're *her*,' he whispered, his nostrils flaring as he sniffed again. '*Sweet.*' His pupils dilated, spreading blackness over his iris and sclera, his top lip curled back and his two needle-thin venom fangs sprang down below his front teeth. A glistening drop of clear venom seeped from the left fang.

His mind-lock brushed weak as mist against my mind, which told me he was probably no more than fifty vamp-years old. And that he was a total idiot if he thought he could catch me in a mind-lock, not to mention the fact that he didn't appear to have got the memo about my protection. I sniffed myself, exasperated. He might be an idiot, but I didn't want his true death on my conscience because he got over-excited and stupidly forgot himself.

I shot my fist out, punching the vamp on the chin, shutting his mouth with a snap. 'Hey, fang-boy, listen up!' I growled. 'Either you stop with the sniffing and go off-line, or your body's going to end up without a head soon.'

Comprehension and fear crossed his face and he scrambled back and grabbed for a plastic sandwich box sitting on the shelf next to the goldfish bowl full of wristbands. He jerked the lid off and buried his face in the box. A faint reek of garlic drifted towards me. Seconds later he came up coughing and spluttering, pink-tinged tears streaking his cheeks.

'Sorry, Ms Taylor,' he whispered, still huddled at the back of the booth. 'You took me by surprise, that's all. I didn't mean anything.'

I rolled my eyes. 'Apology accepted. Now, can I go in?'

He nodded vigorously and I strode through the double doors and into the club's interior. The circular space was empty of Moths – and anyone else, other than the usual human girl sitting stoically at the cloakroom counter next to the door marked 'Office'. As for where the Moths had got to, well, I had a choice of the restrooms, the private rooms behind two doors marked 1–15 and 16–30; the gift shop – DVDs of the vamps lying in their coffins were on special offer! – or the glass double doors opposite me.

The doors led into the Room of Remembrance. The room was set up like a church nave with about twenty glass coffins on top of ornate marble plinths, arranged either side of a wide aisle instead of pews. And a raised stage at the end where the chancel would be. A few vamps, dressed in a variety of military or heroic outfits, were up and milling about among the first few members, so the coffins were empty, but on the stage was another coffin, the blood that smeared its sides glittering in the spotlights. It had to be where the staked Fyodor was stashed. Nobody appeared to be taking much notice, so maybe he wasn't going to be the draw Mad Max hoped.

The Moths descended on me again from out of the gift shop.

'Darius has Room Eleven.' Rissa waved an electronic keycard. 'We 'ave booked him for a private party.'

'We've phoned Yana to let her know, so she's coming over.' Viola gave me a big grin.

'So exciting, isn't it?' Lucy jumped up and down. 'I can't wait to see him.'

'Great,' I smiled, 'but I'm not into the whole, you know—' I did the crooked fingers thing next to my neck. Nor was I up for the mini-orgy Darius and the girls were likely to have to celebrate their reunion. 'So why don't you all go on and I'll join you in a bit?'

'Sure thing, Genny.' Rissa swiped the keycard and the door opened into a long, carpeted corridor indistinguishable from any cookie-cutter hotel. They all ran off, whooping, towards door number eleven.

Now to find Mad Max.

I walked over to the cloakroom. Usually I waited for the security guard to take my bagged blood and give me a receipt, but this time I hopped up on the counter and swung my legs over. I landed with a soft thud behind it and the coat-check girl jumped up in surprise. 'Hey, you can't—'

I reached out and touched her face, entering her mind as easily as driving through an open gate. 'Hi' – I checked her name badge – 'Cheryl. Can I have your keycard, please?'

She reached down, unclipped it from her belt and held it out to me.

'Thanks,' I smiled, taking it. 'That's great. You just forget about me now, and carry on with whatever you were doing.' I reversed out of her mind just as easily and let her go.

She sat back down again.

I swiped the card down the lock and pushed open the 'Office' door. The room inside was a standard security centre doubling as a staffroom. One wall held a row of grey metal lockers; the other wall was banked to the ceiling with TV monitors showing shots of the club above a long bench full of blinking lights and switches. I quickly scanned them: entrance, coffin room, gift shop, the toilets – yep, the loos really were coffin-shaped! – and what had to be the vamps' private rooms. Sitting bolt-upright in front of the TV screens was the human security guard with his eyes fixed intently on the monitors. A cup of tea was steaming on the bench in front of him.

He ignored me.

But of course. Mad Max was expecting me.

I walked past him to the door on the opposite wall, opened it and strolled inside.

'Cousin, how nice to see you again.' Mad Max stood and came round the desk to pull out one of the guest chairs for me. My backpack sat on the other. He gave me a wide beam of a smile and said, 'Please, come and have a seat.'

As offices go it was pretty basic: desk, grey chairs, grey carpet, grey filing cabinet, a flat-screen LCD – currently showing the cloakroom girl – instead of a window. There was nothing to say vampire, or even well-heeled executive about it, other than Mad Max himself. His bright red Hussar jacket, worn over white shirt and blue trousers and with highly polished black boots made him look like he was playing dress-up, which of course he was.

'Thanks,' I said and sat. Of course, there was one thing that said vampire: the three bags of my blood sitting on the desk, one of which was squashed into a clear pint tankard with coffins decorating the outside. A black curly straw was sticking out the top. *Nice – all it needed was a paper umbrella!* Next to the bags of blood was my phone.

'Glamouring a human carries the death penalty, Cousin,' Max said cheerfully, waving at the cloakroom girl on the screen as he sat opposite me. 'Or were you not aware of that particular law?'

Ignoring him, his threat, and my blood, for now, I reached for the phone and called Malik, or rather, Sanguine Lifestyles, his 24/7 answering service. A woman's voice answered with a tentative, 'Ms Taylor?'

'Yes, it's me, and I'm fine,' I reassured her before she could ask, keeping my gaze fixed on Mad Max who was still beaming his hundred-watt smile my way. 'Could you repeat the last message you were given, please?'

'Certainly, Ms Taylor,' she replied efficiently. 'Mr Maxim Andrei Zakharin called, and his message was: "*Genevieve Zakharinova has honoured us by becoming a VIP member of our club. Sadly, the excitement was too much for Dear Old Dad, and I think it might take him three days to recover. Genevieve kindly consented to having a family portrait taken to celebrate our reunion.*"' The woman paused. 'We received the photo of the gentleman and yourself, Ms Taylor, plus the one—'

A beep sounded, and I stopped listening to the woman as Max's beaming smile cut out and was replaced by an almost panicked expression. He produced a remote, pointed it at the flat-screen and the picture of the cloakroom girl switched to one of strange, amorphous red and blue shapes shifting around a dark interior. Two red figures were huddled together in one area, and another red figure was merged with the only blue figure. I frowned, puzzled, until it clicked: I was looking at the new state-of-the-art CCTV monitoring system the vamps were touting on all their websites, supposedly designed to keep the humans safe. It showed a computer overlay of enhanced heat signatures, so basically, the red figures were humans, and the vampires, having a lower core body temperature, showed up as blue.

Max jumped up and rushed out of the office, leaving the door swinging.

'… give Mr al-Khan your message along with the others when he checks in,' the woman's voice was saying in my ear.

Worry tied a knot in my gut. 'Thought you said he checked in at sunset?'

'Normally, yes. Not tonight. Is there anything else I can do for you, Ms Taylor?'

'Thanks, not just now.' I cut her off, and stared at the screen.

Now I knew what I was looking at, the figures looked more like people and less like blobs. The red figures were two up-right humans huddled together. The other human was on the ground, with the vamp on top, and the blue vamp was slowly turning red— It didn't take a genius to work out something was badly wrong. Then I saw the flashing number in the screen's corner.

Room Eleven: Darius' room.

I looked in horror at my blood on the desk.

Surely Mad Max couldn't be stupid enough to take it all? Hadn't he heard what had happened at Christmas, when Darius had gone rabid and fallen into bloodlust?

Fuck! I grabbed the two unopened bags of blood, knocking the tankard over in my haste, but it didn't spill. Oddly, the bag was still unbroken. I grabbed that one too, and stuffed them all back into the padded compartment of my backpack. Then I ran after Mad Max.

Chapter Twenty-Two

The security guard was rattling away into his radio, and either Mad Max's original mind-lock was still in force or he was too busy to worry about me. I grabbed the keycard off the cloakroom girl in passing, vaulted over the counter again and strode towards the vamp who was standing guard in front of doors 1–15. She was dressed in a wide grey crinoline and starched nurse's cap, vaguely circa the Crimean War.

Her eyes widened as she saw me coming.

'Move, or I'll make you,' I warned, knowing I had the unfair advantage. No way was she going to fight back – or even touch me – not with Malik's decapitation threat standing behind me like a looming shadow.

'Sorry, can't do that,' she said. 'Orders.'

I swung the backpack, letting its own momentum carry it and it hit her square on the shoulder. I'm nowhere near as strong as a vamp, but compared to a human of the same weight, I'm a superwoman. Add in the bricks—

The vamp stumbled far enough away from the door for me to swipe the keycard down the lock and lunge through it before she had recovered.

My heart pounding, I raced along the carpeted corridor, past grey steel doors with curious faces peering out from their diamond-shaped windows, towards the group of three figures I could see at the end.

Mad Max held his hands up to stop me as I got closer. 'Cousin, Genevieve,' he called, 'we've sealed the door. There's nothing to be done until morning now. I suggest you go back—'

Bastard! He wasn't supposed to seal the room if there were still humans inside.

This time I didn't give any warning. I hoisted the backpack in front of me and, praying to any gods that might be listening, I launched myself at him, aiming for his chest with the brick-heavy backpack. I caught a glimpse of his eyes rounding with disbelief just before I barrelled into him, knocking him on his back. I landed on top of him and, yelling, I heaved the back-pack up and smashed it down on his head, again and again, like a pile-driver. He shifted beneath me, his hands gripping my thighs, the muscles of his stomach bunching, getting ready to buck me off. Desperate now, I slammed the bag down again, wishing I had something sharper, like a stake, knowing I had to damage him enough that he wasn't going to be getting up anytime soon—

Someone grabbed the back of my jacket and threw me back along the corridor.

I tried to tuck and roll, but the backpack dragged awk-wardly on my arm and instead I landed in an inelegant heap. I scrambled back up to my feet, clutching the backpack, raging with determination and anger. I wasn't going to let—

I stopped, stunned. Mad Max was still lying on the floor, but now a small figure straddled him – a female, if the long curls of black hair were any indication. The other two vamps were rapidly backing up the corridor away from her and Max, their faces contorted with fear. They reached the end and one banged on the steel door, while the other, his brain obviously slightly less panicked, produced a keycard, swiped it and they both fell into the room beyond the moment the door slid open.

As the door closed, the female figure shook herself then, in one fast, sinuous movement, she leapt to her feet and twisted to land perfectly on her red leather six-inch-heeled boots without so much as a wobble. A knife protruded from Mad Max's chest, its bronze handle sticking up like a shiny exclamation point. She put her hands on her curvy hips, took a deep breath she didn't need, and her waist very obviously cinched in even tighter and her breasts mounded even higher above her red leather corset. Then she cocked her head to one side and stared at me, her eyes reflecting yellow like a cat's in the blackness of her face.

I grimaced. Vamps can never resist a flashy entrance.

I recognised her, of course: Yana's new sponsor, Francine, the vampire from Darius' old blood-house. Up close she looked younger than I remembered, more late teens than early twenties, although vamp-wise she had to be at least a couple of hundred years old if she was capable of taking Mad Max. And with her knife sticking out of him, she was either an opportunist, or an ally. I was hoping for the latter.

My hand tightened on the backpack just in case. 'So why did they run?' I jerked my head towards the door the terrified vamps had gone through.

The air wavered round her and for a second a pretty good likeness of Malik stood in her place. Then she was back to being herself again.

'Impressive illusion,' I said, and it was. 'So, are you the new Head of Golden Blade blood?'

'Not yet,' she said, her sultry voice matching her sex-on-legs kick-ass red leather outfit.

Ah, so the position was still up for grabs, which probably meant she needed Malik's backing. Maybe she'd decided assisting me was the best way to get it? I waved towards her and Mad Max. 'You know, the show's wasted if you're not going to help?' I raised my voice in question.

Moving almost too fast for me to see, she was standing in front of me, the sharp end of a bronze knife hovering steadily under my chin. I held my ground, ignoring my hitching pulse, and flicked a finger against the blade. 'Nice toy,' I said.

She smiled, her full lips pulling back to showcase longer-than-normal fangs – another illusion – and the knife flew back and thudded into Mad Max's chest, perfectly aligned next to its twin. He grunted. I looked around her at his face. The bricks had done their job: it was a battered, blood-covered mess, and when he stared back at me from between already swelling lids, surprisingly, he was very much aware, and oddly speculative.

'The bronze knife in the heart,' Francine purred, drawing my attention back to her, 'she paralyse him. Stop his power.'

'Good to know,' I said, stepping past her and over Mad Max to look through the diamond-shaped window in door eleven. It was as bad as I'd hoped it wouldn't be.

The room was square, maybe twenty feet by twenty, and it looked like a hurricane had passed through recently. Broken bits of metal bed and shredded lumps of mattress littered the carpet, a wooden chest was overturned on its side, and the flat-screen on the wall was smashed.

Darius was in the centre, at the eye of the storm.

The eye-candy romance model with the drool-worthy six-pack was gone; instead, his body had shrunk back to bone. His stomach was concave above his jutting pelvis, and only a few wisps of hair straggled from his scalp. A raised map of blue-black veins corded his leathery-looking skin. He looked like he'd been left to starve. As I watched he twisted and turned from side to side in evident confusion, his lips curled back over all four of his fangs, his arms open wide, fingers clutching at empty space. Rissa and Viola were weaving around him in some sort of shifting pattern, their floating grey outfits and long white-grey hair fluttering as if blown by the wind. As I watched, one would flit past him, trailing a bloody wrist and snagging his attention, then as he lunged for her, the other would do the same, distracting him the other way, only they were moving so fast it looked as if there were more than just the two of them …

'You're doing something, aren't you?' I turned to Francine.

'I make the illusion of many Moth. Darius do not think with his brain now, but with this.' She tapped her corseted stomach. 'The Moth, they bait him with the blood. He does not know which to eat next. It is a trick we use sometimes.'

I turned back to the room and came face to face with Lucy, staring at me through the glass. Startled, I jumped back in fear as my old phobia hit; *stupid to still be afraid of ghosts, even now.* I forced myself back to the small window, swiping at my face as I realised I was doing the crying thing again. My chest constricted with sorrow as Lucy turned and walked straight through the others to the far wall, then stood and pointed down at her still body.

Damn, damn, damn. Seeing her ghost didn't necessarily mean Lucy was dead, or at least, not yet. I'd seen Sharon, Darius' now-deceased girlfriend do the same thing. The Moth-girls' ghosts – their souls or whatever you want to call it – can vacate their bodies on demand. It's a sort of defence mechanism against pain, as having a vamp sink fangs into your carotid understandably hurts with a capital H.

Why the Moth-girls sign up for it, rather than the standard venom hit, which is all about pleasure, is a total mystery.

'We need to get in there,' I said, still looking at Lucy's body.

'The door, she is sealed until sunrise,' Francine said at my side. 'She is on the time lock, precaution to stop the bloodlust spreading.'

'Sunrise! Fuck, they'll all be dead by then!'

'Yes. The heart of Lucy is weak. I beat it for her, but I cannot for long. My power, she is lowering.' She spoke calmly, as if the situation wasn't a death sentence for the girls and for Darius – especially Darius, because even if he came back to his senses

176

after draining the Moths, the vampires would rescind his Gift, not in public retribution for killing the girls – it was doubtful any of them had any family, or anyone to worry about them other than the other Moths; their bodies could and probably would just disappear. As would Darius'. No, they'd rescind his Gift because the Moths' deaths would be unsanctioned killing. The vamps can't afford not to control their own.

Even if I did manage to save him now, unless one of them took him on, he was a dead vamp walking. I clenched my fists, desperation and guilt burning in my chest. I shouldn't have encouraged him to stand on his own feet. More than that, I should've kept a closer eye on him.

But crying over spilled milk – or rather, spilled blood – wasn't helping anyone. I had to save the Moths first, and after that I could worry about Darius ... except—

I was all out of ideas.

I looked at Francine. 'So, what's the plan?' I asked.

Chapter Twenty-Three

'The door, I can open her.' Francine stared at me, her odd reflective eyes transparent like glass. 'I make the illusion stay for the escape of the Moth. But Darius, he has the bloodlust, he cannot escape the room. I cannot control him, and I do not like to bring the final death to him.'

Okay, good to know she didn't want to kill him, for all her flat statements. But then, if he wasn't rabid with bloodlust, she wouldn't have to. So she was asking me to feed him – my blood would sate his bloodlust – but getting it into him without ending up as dinner was the problem. Unless ...

He was young enough that I could catch him in my Glamour – I'd done it before, after all. *Once,* muttered my cautionary voice, *and the vamp was already restrained.* I ignored it and asked, 'Will you take his Oath, if the Moths survive?'

'Darius ...' This time some emotion flickered in her gaze, then was gone. 'I will *accept* his Oath, but only if he chooses. The force, she is not right.'

I blinked: a democratic vampire?

'Okay, leave Darius to me,' I said with more confidence than I was feeling.

'Good. Also, I ask the permission for the blood. For the power.'

Of course she needed blood. Well, I was going to be opening a vein anyway, and it was all in a good cause—

I grabbed my backpack and opened it. Miraculously, one of the three bags of blood I'd stuffed in it was still intact and

I held it out to her as blood from the other bags dripped onto the carpet.

Her nostrils flared, her eyes closing briefly, then she shook her head reluctantly. 'Darius, he will need your blood.' She pointed down at Mad Max. 'His blood, I can take. With the permission of my liege.'

Her liege was Malik, but he wasn't here. The worry came back, and I didn't know when – or if – he would arrive. 'He's not here?' I made it a question.

'We are to give you the help if you are in need.' She smiled down at Mad Max, her long canines curving past her bottom lip, her strange, transparent eyes lighting with expectant predatory pleasure.

'Ri-*ight*. I'm in need then.' I waved at Mad Max. 'You've got your liege's permission.'

In a blur almost too fast to see, she whirled into a crouch and fell upon his throat. He roared, his legs jerking uncontrollably, then the sound cut out and harsh slurping noises took its place. Old, dark blood sprayed over the lower walls of the corridor. Judging by her enthusiastic reaction, there was more to her snacking on Mad Max than just getting power.

I shrugged out of my jacket, dropping it next to my backpack, and looked through the window at the Moths dancing round Darius, wondering how long it would take Francine to get her power up to speed – and also wondering how I was going to get close enough to Darius to touch him, let alone Glamour him, without getting my own throat ripped out first.

Long minutes later, and I was still staring anxiously through the diamond-shaped window in the door. I tensed as Darius snagged Rissa's wrist, jerking her out of the weaving dance, but then Viola swiped her own bloody wrist close to his mouth and Rissa slipped from his grasp.

'C'mon, Francine,' I muttered. She'd been slurping on Mad

Max for a good five minutes now. Surely that was enough to get a power hit. 'Hurry it up; he nearly caught her that time.'

A soft hand brushed the hair back from my face, and I turned to find her standing next to me. Her pupils had vanished, leaving her eyes clear as glass and reflecting the overhead lights.

'I am here,' she murmured. Her tongue swiped out like a cat's, catching a drop of blood at the corner of her mouth. She stepped closer, and wobbled on her heels. I grabbed for her, catching her arm and holding her steady. She laughed low and touched her forefinger to the pulse in my throat, sending a shiver of need into my body as the sensation of wings fluttered soft along my skin.

Mesma. Damn vamp was using vamp mind-tricks on me! I knocked her hand away, angry. 'You're drunk,' I said accusingly.

'But yes, of course.' She laughed again, pressed her finger to my chest this time and pushed. I staggered back. She turned to face the door, took a wide-legged stance, then punched her hand straight through the diamond-shaped window. Gripping the edges of the opening with both hands, she braced one boot against the door and pulled downwards. At first nothing happened, then the door groaned, the metal buckled and it fractured from the bottom V of the window opening. She yelled, a deep, guttural sound, and the muscles in her arms and back stood out in relief as she ripped the steel door down and pulled it apart like it was made of cardboard.

'Fuck!' I muttered, impressed.

'The door, she is open.' She doubled over, giggling, then as she tried to straighten, she tottered back and fell on her butt against the corridor wall. I rushed to help her, but she waved me away with both her hands. 'The Moths,' she whispered, then in a louder, crooning voice, she called, 'Come, my pretties, fly to me. Fly, fly, *flyyyy!*'

They came in a blur of grey silk and satin, ducking and

spilling through the ripped steel door, breaking right and rushing past me along the corridor towards the door at the far end, trailing the scent of blood and liquorice and greasepaint behind them.

I quickly crouched and peered into the room. Lucy's ghost was huddled by her limp body while Darius still stumbled around, his hands grasping at the illusions of Moths floating past him. Apprehension prickled down my spine as I gripped the bag of blood in my hand. All I had to do was rush him, shove the bag in his face as a distraction, hopefully piercing it on his fangs, then thrust my magic into him.

My turn to dance.

I bent to duck through the torn door and a sharp pain sliced across my wrist. Flinching, I looked down to see blood welling and dripping from a three-inch cut along my inner arm, right along the vein. Francine swayed on all fours near me, a thin bronze dagger in her hand.

'What the fuck was that for?' I demanded.

'The arm, hold her up in front.' She showed me, clumsily tucking her own arm under her chin, almost toppling over as she did. 'She will keep Darius from the throat.'

I stifled my anger; she was trying to be helpful, even if it was the sort of help I could *really* do without. I swapped the bag of blood to my bleeding hand. Holding the bag and my blood-dripping wrist as a shield across my throat, I ducked into the room before she could think of anything else to *help* me with.

Darius stopped, nostrils flaring, and fixed his gaze eerily on me, no longer interested in the illusionary Moths. Blood flushed the whites of his eyes; his irises and pupils were clouded, like cataracts. He was blinded by bloodlust, all his senses narrowed down to scent alone as he searched for the fresh blood he craved. I felt a tug on my consciousness as he automatically tried to mind-lock me and swatted it aside.

One touch was all I needed to Glamour him. *Skin to skin.* Lucky he was naked; it gave me a lot of skin to choose from.

I flipped the metaphysical switch inside me and let my magic flood out. A golden glow lit the room as if the sun was shining and small tendrils of power sprang like eager vines from my body, questing for someone to latch onto. Still holding the bag up in front of me, I aimed for his ankles – as far away from his fangs as I could get – and lunged towards him—

He snarled and leapt at the same time, smashing me down onto the ground and knocking the air out of my lungs. My head banged off the floor as he pinned me, and pain sliced upwards through my left kidney. I seemed to have all the time in the world to look down and see the broken end of something black and metallic poking out of my diaphragm: a piece of the metal bed. And all the time to look up at Darius as he straddled my hips, to feel the panicked thud of my heart, to smell the honey-scent of my own blood, to see his skeletal face blurring as he yanked my head back and exposed my throat—

But no time to raise my arm and the distracting bag of blood before he struck, his fangs piercing through skin, muscle and the arterial wall of my carotid—

And the world exploded into a pain-filled haze of red and gold.

Chapter Twenty-Four

*H*e held Genny's hand, gazing down at her as she lay sleeping. She was pretty, like sunshine in a jar, as his mum used to say. Happiness and relief filled him. Now Genny was here, everything would be all right; she'd sort it. All he had to do was hold her hand, stop her from leaving, and she'd sort it. He'd done something bad, but he hadn't meant to, he'd just been so hungry. But he was a good boy. He'd always been a good boy . . .

His thoughts stumbled back into his childhood again before he could stop them. He hated lying there night after night, listening for the thump of the front door closing as his mum went off to her night shift. He desperately wanted to shout for her not to go, not to leave him. Then he'd listen as the fridge door slammed, waiting until the second stair from the top creaked, until the landing light under his bedroom door snuffed out. Then he'd hear the click as the handle turned and the hinges whined . . .

'Be a good boy now, Daryl lad,' his step-da would say. 'We don't want to upset yer mum, don't want anythin' to 'appen to 'er, now, do we, lad? So just you be a good boy like yer promised.'

. . . and he'd always been a good boy like he'd promised. He'd promised not to tell then, and he'd promised not to tell now. He always kept his promises.

But now he'd done something bad to Genny. Sadness and loss squeezed his insides, making the hunger come back, then he gazed down at her, at her shining hand in his, and happiness

183

filled him. She'd gone away for a while, but she was back now, and so long as he held her hand she'd wouldn't leave again, and then she'd sort it.

Sunshine in a jar.

The thoughts and memory – Darius' thoughts and memory, I realised after a while – kept going round and round in my head like they were on a children's roundabout, and somewhere I was crying, for the little boy then, and for Darius now. I could feel the tears dripping down my face, but I couldn't see anything past the blinding glow of my magic. I could feel his hand holding mine, except it felt odd, more like I was holding his hand, only that wasn't right either, not when his hand felt small and limp and my much bigger hand enveloped it.

'Darius?'

I looked up as I heard his name and the magic dimmed. Francine ducked through the ripped doorway and came slowly into the room, placing one high-heeled boot in front of the other, watching me with a wary expression.

I felt my mouth smile at her, a wide beam, so happy to see her. She lifted her chin, such a tiny movement, and, oddly, I recognised that she was worried, and scared. I/Darius wanted to tell her it was all right, that now she and Genny were here, everything was going to be all right, but the words got confused with the thoughts in my head.

He loved Francine, she was so small and sexy, and she'd looked after him even before he got the Gift, like Genny looked after him now. If Genny was sunlight in a jar, Francine was dark, dark chocolate. He'd missed her, missed the Moths ... he'd done something bad, but he hadn't meant to, he was a good boy, but he'd just been so hungry ... but she was here now, and Genny was here, they'd sort things out, make things right.

Sunshine and chocolate.

'Darius?' Weirdly Francine sank to her knees in front of me and reached out to cup my face, brushing away my tears.

'I'm holding her hand, just like I promised, Francine.' I felt my lips shape the words, but it wasn't my voice, wasn't my thoughts behind them. The voice and thoughts belonged to Darius ... and so did the mouth, and the eyes I was using. I looked down at my hand where I held his. I squeezed, and Darius' hand squeezed, not mine. I lifted, and Darius' hand lifted mine. *My* hand was the limp one, the one it felt like I was holding.

Shit! I was in Darius' body.

I sand-bagged a rising tide of panic. *This wasn't so strange, was it? After all, I'd been in someone else's body before. All I had to do was stay calm, work out how this had happened, and find a way back to my own body ...*

Which hadn't been in too good a condition last I saw. I squinted past the blinding golden glow of magic and saw myself: the jagged end of the pole was sticking out of my upper stomach, and the wet, gory mess of my throat looked like a wild animal – or a rabid vamp – had chowed down on it ...

'Oh crap. That doesn't look good, does it?' I muttered.

Francine turned my/Darius' face away. 'The sidhe, she is not lost yet. Her heart, you are still beating it, as I told you.' Her words conjured the steady *da-dum, da-dum* of a heartbeat pulsing against my/Darius' palm; it echoed up my/his arm and thrummed in my/his ears. A fainter echo sounded from within my unconscious, injured body. I/He nodded and gripped my limp hand harder, determined to not let go.

'This is good, Darius.' Francine leaned forward and kissed us ...

She watched as Maxim led the blonde child away, trying to shut her ears to the child's loud, hysterical sobs, and her imploring face, knowing her own face didn't show her sorrow, fear, and rage. She'd never had a child of her body, and with the Gift she never would, but she'd made up for it with all her pretty Moths, and it shattered her heart every time she lost one of them. But this child was special, she'd hidden her, kept her safe, loved her, but now Maxim had claimed her. She would repay the bastard. One day.

… Francine broke the kiss, and I was on my own again in Darius' head, trying to come to terms with the loss and pain of another memory shown me by the Morrígan.

Then Darius' own thoughts started chiming in, like a bizarre background track, and I suddenly realised I wasn't *alone* but co-habiting. Darius was here with me – or I was with him – and he was very happy about it, delighted, euphoric even, in a strange, fuzzy sort of way. He was happy both of us were here, me and Francine. We looked at Francine, who was now bending over my still body, and panic bubbled up inside me until a knowing, satisfied thought from Darius squashed my fear. She was healing the wound at my throat by licking it.

Francine would love my blood; it tasted so good, so sweet and thick. Hunger tightened our stomach, and something twitched between our legs … we looked down and grinned—

'You've got to be kidding me!' I said out loud as I grabbed for a nearby piece of mattress and stuffed it between our/Darius' legs, then wished I hadn't as his pain nearly doubled us over. Darius choked back the lump in our throat, and his thoughts disappeared into a jumble of unintelligible expletives.

Crap! The sooner I got out of him, the better … but I didn't even know how the hell I'd ended up inside him in the first place, let alone how I was supposed to get back into my own body. My mind kept chasing the thoughts, looking for answers that weren't there. And there was something else, something important. Worriedly, I looked around the room littered with bits of bed and mattress and tried to *think* …

Finally it came to me: what had happened to Lucy, the Moth whose ghost I'd seen?

Darius gingerly resurfaced. '*Francine took her away.*' The words formed in my mind, along with his self-guilt and worry. '*She said the other Moths would look after her.*'

'*She's not dead then?*' I asked hopefully.

'*No,*' he said, almost overwhelming me with self-blame, '*Francine said she'd be okay.*'

Darius had only attacked the Moths because he'd been lost in bloodlust, and he'd only been lost in bloodlust because Mad Max had stolen my blood. '*It wasn't your fault—*'

'*He didn't steal the blood, Genny.*' Shame and regret curdled inside us. '*I said he could have one bag out of three.*'

'*Why?*'

His mind fuzzed for a second, then he said, '*So he'd give me the job; it was to pay the blood-tithe.*' It wasn't a lie, but there was something else there, something he didn't want me to know. '*I'm sorry, I didn't think I'd need it, not with all the groupies, and I didn't want to give him my Oath, or anyone else, but I kept getting booked for private parties, and then my head started going funny—*'

Images of his childhood mixed up with more recent ones of the private parties, or more precisely, the 'anything goes' orgies, flickered like a movie in my mind, telling me that Mad Max was effectively running a vamp brothel, letting humans into the rooms before the vamps woke up so they could prod and poke and—

Rage and disgust made me want to go and stick another knife in the bastard's chest.

Darius shook our head emphatically. '*It's not like that, Genny. All the vamps love it; you get plenty of blood waking up like that. I did too, sort of, at the beginning.*'

I felt the desperate need in him to be honest with me and got another quick image that I could've done without: Darius *really* enjoying himself at what looked like a 'Bride of Dracula' hen party, if the outfits were anything to go by.

'*But then I started getting confused about where I was,*' he carried on, '*and what was going on – I'm sorry, Genny, I'm really sorry.*'

More tears dripped down our face as recriminations filled us: his, for not asking for help, and mine for not checking up on him sooner. But now what mattered was getting back into my own body and sorting this whole mess out. I tried to piece together my thoughts … Only now we weren't speaking, the background track of his thoughts grew louder and more in-trusive, and my own thoughts kept getting lost in a fuzzy haze. He was relieved and happy that both Francine and I were here; he really loved both of us, and he really wanted us to like each other. We looked down at where she was bent over my body, and at the way the red leather moulded to her—

Darius was getting entirely too happy about things again.

I gingerly tapped the lumpy bit of mattress between his/our legs to distract him and mentally pulled myself away from his thoughts until he was just a muted whisper. My own mind cleared and I realised the 'fuzzy hyped' feeling had come from Darius; he was still high, from drinking my blood and getting hit by my Glamour.

I looked at Francine, still bent over my throat, and at the jagged metal sticking out of my stomach. I was sidhe fae, I was still here; I could survive that, couldn't I? So long as someone took it out soon? Except I was injured and stuck in a vamp (who was keeping me alive by holding my hand), in the middle of a vamp club, with only Francine to help; it wasn't a win-win situation. How the hell was I going to get out of this? Another bubble of panic threatened to burst— then I remembered I had my very own personal Angel watching over me. An Angel with a hotline to The Mother. It was unlikely She'd let me truly die, at least not until after I'd completed her commands. And then there was the Morrígan too. Maybe if I prayed—

'Genevieve?'

My name was both a question and a *call*, and my heart stuttered in thankfulness.

'Malik al-Khan.'

As I spoke, Darius rushed back in alarm and we looked up. A monstrous figure loomed over us, half-obscured by writhing, angry shadows. Flaming eyes blazing bright stared out of a thin, harsh face, its pale skin laced with an ominous map of hungry blue veins, its lips drawn back over sharp white fangs. Hot fingers of *mesma*-induced fear lashed down our spine and Darius screamed in terror. Then, before I could grab our thoughts, we were spinning away in a fiery maelstrom of panic.

Chapter Twenty-Five

I fought my way out of the maelstrom, leaving Darius tucked away in the hidden corner of himself, and looked out of his eyes again.

Francine was kneeling between us and Malik, who had dropped the fanged monster look; maybe he'd just used it to frighten the natives, although Francine could've told him he didn't need all the flashy dramatics.

'—blame is not his, my liege.' Francine's words suddenly registered. 'I beg you to not kill him. Wait, and listen to the sidhe when she wakes.'

Yeah, listen to her: killing him is so not a good idea – for either of us.

'The sidhe lies behind you and is near death, Francine,' Malik said in his calm, not-quite-English accent. 'What makes you think she will live to plead for Darius to keep his Gift?'

As Francine started to talk in a soft, anxious monotone, I shot a quick assessing look at my throat: the wound in my neck was now a puckered mess of scabbed-over skin.

Thank you, Francine! It wasn't pretty, but maybe my body wasn't as close to death as Malik's words suggested, particularly as he didn't appear to be overly worried. I narrowed my eyes at him. Now I wasn't seeing him through Darius' less-than-rosy blood- and fear-coloured glasses, he looked more like his usual beautiful self – other than his hair, which no longer curled like black silk over his coat collar but had instead been buzz-cut close to his scalp. It made him look harder, more dangerous, and at the same time oddly vulnerable. I frowned, concerned, remembering Mad Max's comments about Malik being the Autarch's newest torture toy … was it only his hair that was different … or was there a slight stiffness in the way he held himself?

Uneasy, I studied him further. He was dressed as his übergoth persona: black leather trousers and a muscle-hugging T-shirt topped off with a long leather coat that flared and snapped in a nonexistent wind – a standard vamp trick, which, for some bizarre reason, was impressing the hell out of me right now, and filling me with envy …

Until I realised it wasn't *me* being envious but Darius, who was metaphysically huddled behind me. He couldn't do tricks like that, not yet. Darius' gaze slid admiringly over the muscles under Malik's T-shirt. He also looked good enough to eat …

… and our memories collided as we both remembered sinking our fangs into Malik, recalling the powerful, buzzing taste of his blood … our mouth watered, lust and hunger burned inside us, and something sprang to attention between our legs again, jolting me out of Darius' reverie.

'*Okay, now that is so, so weird, and so, so wrong,*' I muttered in my head.

'*Not wrong.*' Our mouth stretched as Darius grinned lop-sidedly, happily hyped-up again by the memory. '*He's fed us both, so it's, like, normal that stuff happens.*'

'*Normal for vamps maybe,*' I spluttered, 'not *for me.*'

'*Yeah, but you're in me now, and the blood and sex bits get all mixed up.*' A certain part of our anatomy did its weird, excited flex again. '*Even more right now, 'cos you really, really want to get into his pants.*'

'*That. Is. None. Of. Your. Business!*'

'*Hey, it's not like I can miss what you're feeling.*' He gave a sly laugh. '*And it's not like he wouldn't know you were hot for him anyway; he'd smell it if he wanted to. We vamps got supersenses, y'know.'*

'*Okay, eew! And really,* so *not helping.'*

'*Want me to hitch you up with him?*' Our face muscles contorted as I tried to wipe our grin away and he wouldn't let me. '*I could, like, ask him if he's got the hots for you too.*'

'*No! Just, no! And, please, go away. I need to think—*'

'Darius?' Malik crouched in front of us and I vaguely registered that Francine had gone. 'Do you know what you have done here? What the penalty is for causing harm to the sidhe?'

His attention accomplished what I couldn't, and Darius' teasing grin disappeared in the blink of one of Malik's fire-filled eyes, and then Darius himself disappeared into some dark corner of his mind, leaving me on my own in his body.

'Yep, he knows who you are all right,' I grimaced, keeping my hand on the lumpy bit of mattress in my lap, even though things in that department had deflated rapidly. 'But what I want to know is, do you think this counts as death number five, or number six?'

He stilled, then reached out and tipped my chin up with his finger. 'Your eyes glow gold with sidhe Glamour. I knew you could trap some of us in this manner, Genevieve, but I did not know you could possess another's body this way?'

'Yep, it's a new one on me too,' I sighed, relieved that he'd caught on quick, and Darius wasn't going to lose his head just yet. 'Look, I'm a bit hazy on the specifics of how I ended up inside Darius' body, and I'd really like to get back to my own. Don't suppose you've heard of anything like this before?'

'Not without a demon or black magic being involved?' He raised his voice in question.

'No, no demon, nor anything like that this time,' I said quickly, with a shudder.

He tilted my/Darius' head up further, peering closer into

my/his eyes, and his dark spice scent twisted a curl of desire inside us. 'And you are sure you did nothing to cause this, Genevieve?'

'Nope,' I said, pressing down on the bit of mattress, seriously hoping Darius didn't choose this moment to do anything stupid. 'One minute I'm hitting the painful high point of being necked on, then the next I'm hearing voices – or rather, hearing thoughts and memories in my head, only now it's not *my* head …' I trailed off.

'You have thought of something?' His expression turned quizzical.

'I had a visit from the Morrígan earlier today …' I frowned, thinking it through as I spoke. 'She sicced some kind of memory spell on me. Darius triggered the spell – it seems to be triggered by touch; his isn't the first memory I've picked up on – but maybe with me pushing my Glamour into him, the spell had some sort of drastic side-effect?'

'What are these memories?'

'Sad ones,' I said, softly, 'from their pasts. And the spell is still working, even though I'm in Darius' body,' I added, recalling the memory of Francine's, the one of Mad Max dragging away the blonde girl (who was vaguely familiar from somewhere) when Francine had kissed me – or rather, Darius.

'I see,' he said, releasing my/Darius' chin with something like apprehension. And I wondered what memory he didn't want me to know. 'We will discuss this later, Genevieve. For now, we should concentrate on healing your body and restoring you to it safely. I will examine your injuries to see what can be done.'

'Works for me,' I said, more than happy to let Malik use his handy healing powers on my body.

He moved closer to my body and carefully tore my T-shirt. Watching him gently probing my injury was surreal enough to make my/Darius' stomach churn squeamishly, so instead I fixed my gaze on the ripped-up doorway, and thought about the Morrígan and the memories instead. Was I just picking up any memory to do with grief and childhood, or were the memories clues to the dying faelings and, therefore to the curse? And if so, what did they mean, and what was I meant to do with them? And where had I seen the girl in Francine's—

Francine herself reappeared from wherever she'd been, and derailed my thoughts. She wasn't alone. She was dragging a groaning Mad Max behind her, like a child trailing a gigantic rag doll.

'My liege.' She dipped her head at Malik. 'Maxim, he is the only possibility. Fyodor, he is staked. There is none other here above fifty.'

Malik eyed the groaning Maxim for a moment, then stood and moved to one side. 'Maxim will be sufficient.'

Francine kicked and shoved Mad Max – she *really* didn't like him – until he was lying alongside my body. With her two bronze blades still jutting out of his chest, and the metal pole in my stomach, we looked like a couple of gruesome extras in a low-budget horror flick.

I leaned over and poked him suspiciously. 'What's Mad Max sufficient for?' I asked as he fixed me with a malevolent glare from the one blue eye which wasn't quite swollen shut.

'Mad Max?' Francine's mouth fell open, her eyes widened and she backed up, crossing herself in panic until she was plastered against the wall. 'You are *not* Darius! What voodoo is this?'

'It's not voodoo, Francine,' I said, 'just a side-effect of the magic.'

'Voodoo is *evil*.' She crossed herself again, sweat beading on her forehead.

'Be calm, Francine.' Malik's pupils flared with tiny flames and her face smoothed over. 'Darius is not harmed; he has allowed Genevieve to share his body for now.'

'As you wish, my liege,' she replied blandly.

'Did you just mind-lock her?' I asked, curious.

'No,' Malik and Francine said in unison.

I waited for Malik to say more. He didn't, and I realised that was all the answer I was getting. 'Trust me, Francine, I'd much rather be in my own body' – I looked down at it – 'well, maybe not quite this minute, but as soon as Malik's healed me.'

'I believe you should return to your body before it is healed further, Genevieve.' Malik started to brush a hand over his forehead, his 'I'm considering' gesture I recognised from when his hair was longer, then hesitated before running a palm over his new buzz-cut. 'It is possible that with the blood connection between you and Darius, and your attempt to control his mind, that your spirit slipped out to avoid the pain, much as the Moths do.'

That sort of made sense: except the Moths usually vacated their bodies as temporary ghosts, not as squatting tenants.

'I do not understand how they return to their bodies,' he carried on. 'Francine can only tell me that they fly when their blood sings to them, but she tells me their spirits are less susceptible to losing themselves if they return before their bodies are fully healed. She also tells me that those Moths who are able to perform this trick have some fae magic in their blood.'

The Moths were fae, or at least had an ancestor who was fae? Interesting – and reassuring, given I was just about to try the same trick. 'Okay,' I said, looking from him to Francine, 'so how do we make my blood sing to me?'

Francine drew her lips back and her tiny venom fangs sprang down. 'The vampire, he make the blood sing,' she murmured.

Lovely. I – or rather, my body – was going to get a shot of the real stuff. I'd really fall off the blood-fruit wagon after that—

'*Umm, I think maybe I already venom-stuck you, Genny,*'

Darius' apologetic voice interrupted my own internal thoughts. *'Y'know, when I—'*

'It wasn't your fault,' I muttered, scowling at Mad Max who was still giving me the evil eye from the floor, and feeling that same fuzz in Darius' mind again. There was something there he didn't want me to know ... about my blood ... and someone called Andy ... he'd made a promise not to tell—

'Genevieve?' Malik touched my/Darius' face and the thoughts scattered. I blinked and looked up at him. Compassion softened his expression. 'You have no need to worry,' he said softly. 'I will find a way if this does not succeed. But first we shall try this?'

I didn't tell him I wasn't worried, or rather, I hadn't been until I caught a glimpse of his own anxiety beneath the compassion. My heart gave a happy little lurch that he cared, and I flashed him a smile big enough to reassure both of us. 'Hey, I'm hard to kill, remember? Not to mention I've got two goddesses on my case, so no doubt one of them is watching over me.'

He gave me a long, pensive look, then nodded. 'Good, then Francine will finish her preparations.'

Francine stepped forward, jumped up and grabbed something hanging above. The *something* dropped down with a great clanking noise and turned out to be a thick, heavy chain with an odd leather-belt contraption on its end. The chain was attached to a pulley bolted into the ceiling.

I started to wonder what on earth it was for, but almost immediately images flashed in my mind of naked bodies dangling down, the leather belt-thing strapped tightly around their ankles, then the images were quickly replaced by a wide expanse of blank white wall, and the knowledge that Darius was embarrassed and trying not to think about anything else.

'Tell me you haven't killed anyone with that,' I demanded.

'No!' His answer blasted through me with enough shock

and horror, along with a flash of something very definitely to do with sex, that I had absolutely no trouble believing him.

Francine hunkered down at Mad Max's feet and efficiently buckled the leather contraption – '*Ankle cuffs*,' Darius murmured from behind his white wall – around Mad Max's legs, and started hoisting him up.

'What's she preparing him for?' I asked, sincerely doubting Mad Max was being strung up for the usual reasons.

'Your body is too depleted of blood for your heart to beat on its own,' Malik explained. 'You need a transfusion before you can be fully healed. Maxim is a suitable donor, but with his heart stopped by the knives, we will need gravity to aid the transfer.'

I frowned, not thrilled about having Mad Max's blood in my body. 'Why can't I have your blood at the same time as you heal me, like you did before?'

'You need more blood than I can safely give you, Genevieve. Such quantity as you require would risk afflicting you with my curse.'

'Okay,' I said, puzzled, and not entirely understanding his worry. 'But I'm not human, I'm sidhe. Your curse can't affect me, because I can't become a vampire. The magic doesn't work that way.'

'That would be true if you were full-blood sidhe,' he said quietly, 'but your father is a vampire.'

'No, my father being a vampire is irrelevant,' I said firmly. 'Sidhe reproduction is different, so I *am* a full-blood sidhe – I'm like a clone of my mother; that's how it works.'

'I am not willing to take that gamble,' Malik insisted, 'not when his blood will suffice.' He waved at Mad Max, now swaying gently above my actual body. His arms and long silver hair were just inches above my body's face and I wrinkled my/ Darius' face in disgust as I clicked exactly how I was going to get Mad Max's blood: I just knew he was going to taste bad.

'Fine,' I agreed. Getting back in my body was the priority, not worrying about whose blood I was going to get. 'So what's next?'

'Darius should feed now,' Malik said, an edge of displeasure in his voice. 'Sparingly,' he added.

'Okay, let's do it,' I said, then as Darius stopped hovering unobtrusively behind his white wall and leaned us eagerly towards my body's neck, I added; *From the wrist.* Ignoring his vague disappointment, I/Darius lifted up my limp hand, the one we were still clutching, and we sniffed the sweet honey scent that pulsed just under the skin. Hunger cramped our stomach, and we struck—

—thick viscous, honey-tasting blood burst into our mouth—

Cold, *so* cold … every beat of my heart hurt, as if a large hand were gripping it and squeezing, the fingers digging in painfully, then a brief second of respite before the hand gripped and squeezed all over again, like some torturous mechanical pump. I screamed, desperate to get away from the unbearable agony …

'*Drink, Genevieve,*' Malik's voice commanded in my mind, and as Mad Max's metallic, sour-tasting blood touched my lips, I opened my mouth and let it flood in, swallowing convulsively as it hit the back of my throat—

He watched as the boy slid down the slide squealing with pure joy. The security lights flooded the playground in a bright white light that kept the night at bay, and turned the boy's blond curls silver. He wanted to pick him up, lift him and swing him round, and tell him he could fly. Tell him he loved him. It was something the old man had done when he'd been the boy's age: a small, happy thing in among the ever-constant fear. But he hugged the want to himself, tucked it away in his heart. She'd never allow it. It had taken five years from the boy's birth until now for her to grudge him this one brief glimpse from a distance. And he didn't want to give the bitch the satisfaction of seeing his need. Or his pain.

Chapter Twenty-Six

I came awake in an instant, fully aware of where I was: in my own bed, in my PJs, covered by a cool cotton sheet, and aware of who was with me: Malik. The moonlight filtering in through the window left the corners of the room in shadow, turned the wardrobe and chest to dark, silent sentinels and muted the white-painted walls to grey, the same greyness that clung like mist to my mind. As I pushed into the mist, so pieces of events came back to me: the vibration of a vehicle, the hot splash of a shower, and Malik's constant caring presence.

I ran my hand over my stomach, tentatively investigating it – magic sparked as I brushed over Tavish's handprint spell – and found my injury healed—

'The metal is removed, Genevieve.' Malik's voice was soft; a brief push of *mesma* giving the words a soothing note.

'Thank you,' I said quietly, deeply grateful.

The soothing touch of his *mesma* and his presence in my head withdrew. I turned to look at him.

He lay on his side, his head propped on his hand, watching me out of his dark, exotic eyes. The moonlight glinted off the black stone in his left earlobe, played over the pale, gleaming skin of his shoulder and along the muscled contours of his arm, but left his bare chest in shadow. My gaze followed his arm down to where his hand rested on his leather-clad thigh— and stopped. Part of me – the part that was all instinct and lust and heat – was disappointed, even frustrated that he was still half-dressed. The rest of me was intrigued, albeit slightly wary.

I shifted onto my side, mirroring his position, and pasted an enquiring look on my face. 'Should I expect to be seduced any moment now, or am I getting the wrong message?'

His eyes lit with amusement. 'You still have a distinct lack of furniture, Genevieve. I see no reason to sit on the floor when you have a perfectly comfortable bed.'

Damn. I *was* getting the wrong message. 'Ri-*ight*, so we're just being practical here,' I said drily.

'Also,' he smiled, giving me a glimpse of fang, 'you appear to have a dryad tree growing in your living room.'

Sylvia! Oops, I'd completely forgotten about her. 'Back in a min,' I said, and jumped out of bed to check on her.

She was still asleep, still smiling blissfully, and her roots were still digging into my wooden floorboards, but the blood was gone. The buds on her fingers and scalp had grown into long, delicate branches covered with pink and white cherry blossom, and their subtle fragrance filled the room with the scent of springtime. As I stood there, she made a small sound, a sort of hiccoughing snore, and the flowers shivered. A mini-snowfall of petals drifted down to decorate her rooted feet.

Sylvia was fine – out of it, but fine.

I smiled, my anxiety gone. I didn't care about the holes in my floor; she was far too pretty and she looked way too happy for them to matter.

Now to sort out the beautiful vampire.

But first—

I needed a drink. I suddenly realised my mouth felt like I'd swallowed a bucket of sand. I headed for the kitchen, downed two glasses of water, then grabbed the bottle of vodka from the fridge and knocked back a generous shot. The alcohol burned an ice-cold path down my throat into my stomach, where it set up a nice warm glow. Carrying the bottle and two glasses, I walked back into the bedroom and bumped the door closed with my hip.

Malik had moved. He was lying on his back, propped against the pillows with his eyes closed and his hands tucked behind his head. I frowned. Something about the relaxed pose didn't quite ring true ...

My attention caught on the silky triangle of hair that graced his chest. Mesmerised, I followed the arrow of black silk down to where it disappeared tantalisingly beneath the low-slung waist of his leather trousers, and then my eyes were drawn to the rose-shaped scar below his left rib. I'd stabbed him there. I'd also bitten him there once; and tasted his blood in all its sweet, glittering glory. My mouth watered as need tightened my body, and lust and thirst vied inside me. I took a step towards the bed, not sure if I wanted to bite him or—

The vodka bottle bounced with a dull thud on the wooden floor, and it hit me that I'd been practically drooling over him. I scowled at the bottle, absently noticing a yellowing bruise on my left ankle. What the hell was the matter with me? Sure, he was eye-candy, and well worth ogling, but no way should I be lost in lust at the sight of him like that, desperate to taste him, desperate to sink my fangs in him—

Except I didn't have fangs.

But he did. Damn. The vamp was still in my head and I was picking up on his desires. I frowned. I'd picked upon his emotions on Tower Bridge, in the dreamscape, but they felt stronger now, almost as if it was *me* inside *his* head. Curious, I closed my eyes, and tried to wade my way through his feelings. Thirst, hunger, lust, need and something indefinable swirled round me like crossing currents of breaking waves, pulling me first one way then another, and the notion that only indecision was stopping him from giving in to any one impulse chilled my skin. Then I dipped below the waves and found the flat, glassy surface of a vast black sea, old and controlled, and I realised the waves were nothing to worry about. But beneath the sea's still surface something simmered in the dark depths, a memory that called to me, and I pushed down towards it—

And ended up on my butt on my bedroom floor, my head spinning like I'd taken a trip on a roller-coaster.

'I would prefer that you stay out of my mind, Genevieve.' Malik's calm voice floated down from the bed above me.

'Yeah?' I scowled at the bottle of vodka, which was now nestled under the bed among the messy pile of my shoes and boots. 'How about you stay out of mine then?'

'As you wish.'

Something snapped in my head, and a barrage of aches and pains pulled a groan from me, and when I looked down, I saw it wasn't just my ankle that was bruised, but the rest of me too. The bruises carried on up both legs, going from fading yellow to puke-coloured green as they disappeared under my sleep shorts and – I lifted up my strappy vest – darkening to a mottled purple mass over my diaphragm. More bruises tracked down both my arms like blue fingerprints, and the soreness in my back no doubt meant it was as colourful as my stomach.

I pressed my lips together, grabbed the vodka and shakily knocked back another shot in a futile attempt to fool my body that I hadn't gone ten rounds with a starved vamp lost in bloodlust.

Trouble was, my sidhe metabolism meant I'd have to drink the whole bottle – not to mention the two others in my fridge – before I even started to feel the effects. At least the alcohol rinsed away the sour-apple taste of Mad Max's blood. I gently prodded the spreading bruise colouring my midriff: either Mad Max wasn't as good at healing as Malik, or he hadn't put enough effort into it. I was betting on the latter.

And thinking about Mad Max, it was time for the beautiful vamp in front of me to come up with some answers.

Chapter Twenty-Seven

I pitched the vodka bottle and the glasses onto the bed, then, mindful of my aches and pains, I snagged a couple of pillows and made myself comfortable against the bed end. Malik was still lying in his supposedly relaxed pose … a pose that showed off the flex of his biceps, and the lean, hard muscles of his pecs … and I had a sudden urge to flick my tongue over his dark nipples, to feel them come alive under my mouth … desire spiralled deep inside me and my own breasts tightened in anticipation. Damn, even with all my aches and pains, my libido was doing the happy dance about having a moonlit half-naked Malik lying in my bed, and this time the thoughts were all mine. An errant part of me wondered what would happen if I made a move on His Fanged Hotness. Reluctantly, I nixed that idea. Even if I was sure he'd be interested – which I wasn't – there were too many other complications, most of them to do with the curse. Not to mention sex isn't always the first thing on a hungry vamp's mind. Maybe the second …

I stifled a sigh, gave my libido a mental cold shower, and got my own mind back on track.

'Okay,' I said, piecing together the later events at the Coffin Club in my mind, 'so I've got this hazy memory that you agreed *not* to kill Darius for attacking me, and that the Moth-girls, including Lucy, are all on the mend?'

'There is no need for you to be concerned about your friends, Genevieve,' he said, without opening his eyes. 'They are all safe.'

'Thank you,' I said, grateful. If he said they were safe, then I knew they would be. 'But what about you?'

'You do not need to be concerned about me either. I can control my thirst sufficiently that you are not in danger.'

'That wasn't what I meant.' I smoothed my hand over the sheet. Now I was looking at him with more concern (and slightly less lust), the shorn hair emphasising the sculptured planes of his face still suggested vulnerability to me, but even though I'd felt his deep thirst, there wasn't the slightest shadow of blue veins mapping his skin (always a sign of a vamp's hunger). How that was possible was a mystery, but— 'I meant; are *you* okay? You seemed … *edgy* earlier when you arrived. And not just from the situation.'

He opened his eyes, looking at me with his usual enigmatic expression. 'Tell me about these memories that the Morrígan has given you.'

Okay, so he didn't want to talk about himself … yet. Determination settled in me; he would later. For now, I told him about the first sad, sad memory belonging to one of the Moth-girls, and the dreadful memory from Darius' childhood. 'But I don't think they're connected to what the Morrígan wants me to know about the missing faelings,' I said thoughtfully. 'It feels more like her spell was all-encompassing than specific.' Then I described Mad Max's memory of the child on the slide. 'I'm pretty sure that that one is connected, just not how.'

Malik frowned and crossed his arms over his chest. 'What makes you think that?'

'Not sure.' I tapped my glass. 'Instinct, or a prod from the Morrígan, maybe. I got the impression the boy was Maxim's son, but I couldn't pinpoint any clue in the memory as to when it had been. Do you know how long ago Maxim took the Gift?'

'He has not yet reached his first century.'

205

So, not that long ago, but not very specific either, which wasn't because Malik didn't know: he'd answered way too quick. 'Do you know if Maxim had a son, either when he was human or since he's taken the Gift?'

'I have not heard him talk of a son, but that does not mean he does not have one. Many who took the Gift in the past isolated themselves from their human families.' A fleeting bleakness in his eyes made me wonder for a moment if Malik himself had done just that.

'Don't suppose you know when they first invented children's slides, do you?' I smiled hopefully.

Amusement flickered on his face. 'I am sorry, Genevieve, no. It is always possible that Google will be able to answer your question.'

I grinned. 'So you're not the font of all knowledge then?'

He sat up, resting his forearm on his bent knee. 'Is that all the memories?'

'No, I got one from Francine too. Hers is much more informative,' I said, and told him about the hysterical blonde girl Mad Max had been dragging away. And that I'd finally remembered where I'd seen her before.

'She's a faeling called Ana,' I said, thinking that it really couldn't be a coincidence that Ana kept popping up, 'and she's also the great-granddaughter of Clíona.' I filled him in on the whole story, from Ana's loss of her fae mother, her two years in a blood-house in Sucker Town – it didn't take a genius to work out it must have been Francine's – and her 'escape' and marriage to Victoria Harrier's wizard son. 'Ana and her family have been victims of the curse more than once, but I'm not sure how she fits in now. But I am sure there's a vamp hanging round her. Maxim.'

'I can see why you think that Maxim might be intimate with this family' – he brushed a hand over his buzz-cut head – 'but I do not know this is the situation. If he is, then it would be something almost impossible to hide from his master. But I will investigate the matter and if the situation is as you suspect, then I will see that it ends.'

I narrowed my gaze at him. Like fae, vamps don't lie. It's not that they magically can't, unlike us fae, but the old ones in particular are all about their honour. Malik was both old and honourable. If he said he didn't know, then he didn't. Although as he was London's Head Fang, he *should* know ... 'That was a very careful answer,' I said, 'so what is it you're not telling me?'

'There are some things that it is safer that you do not know, Genevieve. One is what Maxim wants from me. I have refused him, but he is persistent, and so when the opportunity presented itself to him in the shape of Darius, he set a trap for you. It is what he does. He prefers to put himself in a position of strength before any possible negotiation. He planned to use your concern for Darius' welfare as a leverage point with me.'

'Yeah, I worked that out.' I sipped my drink, thinking Malik was still being much too careful about what he said. 'What about what he did to the Moths?'

'Maxim has a penchant for playing games, and he does not worry overmuch if he has to sacrifice someone whom he considers a pawn. Although I understand that their part in his ill-conceived plan was an unfortunate error, which Maxim then decided to use to his advantage.'

'Okay, so why did Mad Max stake Fyodor, his Dear Old Dad?'

'You would have to ask Maxim, Genevieve. I do not want to guess at his motives where his father is concerned.'

Another evasion. 'Okay, then I'll guess. Let's say Mad Max staked Fyodor to shut him up, or keep him out of the way, so he didn't spoil Mad Max's blackmail plot to get you to agree to whatever it is he wants. So there's a fifty/fifty chance Fyodor knows what it's all about,' I said pointedly. *See, oh,*

uninformative one, there are other ways of getting information.
'But is what Mad Max wants just to do with your usual vamp stuff, or is it to do with the curse and the missing faelings? With everything else, I'm leaning towards the latter. Especially with Francine's memory connecting Mad Max to Ana, and Ana connecting to the curse, and the missing faelings. That whole degrees-of-separation thing. So, if I take a leap here, Mad Max could connect to the missing faelings' – I stopped and gave the beautiful, and still annoyingly closed-mouthed vamp reclining on my bed an enquiring look – 'unless of course you can tell me something different?'

'I am sorry, Genevieve, but I cannot tell you anything about the missing faelings.' He turned the platinum ring on his thumb – the ring he'd given me, then taken back in the dreamscape. 'If I do discover anything about their plight, then I would as a matter of urgency inform the police and do whatever was in my power to help them.'

Damn. Whatever Mad Max wanted, Malik didn't think it was anything to do with the missing faelings. Or he didn't know if it was. But I still wanted the information so I could judge for myself.

I tilted my head at Malik. 'Did you know Mad Max and Fyodor are my relatives?'

'Yes.'

Finally a straight answer, even if it was monosyllabic, and didn't give me any sort of clue. Maybe if I tried another hook? 'Maxim's been taking my blood from Darius as some sort of tithe,' I said, 'but I don't think that's the only reason. But I couldn't prise the info out of Darius' head, because he's promised to keep it a secret. And Mad Max wanted me to think he was the one drinking my blood, but he isn't, is he?'

'I do not have an answer for you, Genevieve.'

Definite stonewalling now. 'Darius was thinking about a name,' I said, not giving up. 'He tried to hide it from me, but I'm pretty sure it was Andy. Does that ring any bells with you?'

Malik tensed in interest, so maybe he really wasn't the font of all knowledge, and I'd hit on something he didn't know. 'Did you receive any impression of who Andy might be?' he asked.

'Another vampire, maybe?'

'It is possible.' A frown lined his forehead. 'But if he has been giving your blood to this "Andy", I would like to know who he is – if only to ensure neither Maxim nor he are a threat to you any longer.'

'Can't you just order him to tell you who Andy is?' I said, shifting uncomfortably. My aches and pains were heading for the major complaints department, even with the pillows at my back.

'I have no way of forcing Maxim's obedience, Genevieve,' he said. 'He owes his Oath to the Autarch.'

My instinctive terror at the Autarch's name threatened to surface; I swallowed it back. Time to dig in a different direction. 'So now we're on the subject of the Autarch and Oaths,' I said, the calm sound of my own voice surprising me, 'want to tell me what that means for me?'

'You need not be concerned about the Autarch, Genevieve.'

'Easy enough for you to say,' I said, keeping my tone reasonable, 'but I don't know what's going on. And if the general consensus is that I'm your property, and you owe the Autarch your Oath again, then he can demand you give me to him. So I was wondering what my options are if the Autarch comes calling.'

'I have given you my protection,' he said dismissively. 'It is not necessary for you to worry.'

Looked like I was getting the brush-off again, which meant it was time to discuss a few ground rules about whatever our *relationship* was, or wasn't.

I gave him a bright smile. 'You do know I'm not fourteen any more, don't you?'

'I had noticed,' he said, giving me an amused once-over.

'Good,' I said, ignoring the twist of desire inside me. There hadn't been enough heat in his eyes for it to affect me like it did. 'Well then, much as I'm grateful for all your past protection, and your help, you should also know that you can't keep leaving me out of the loop or doing your mind-mojo thing whenever you feel like it.'

An odd, indecipherable expression crossed his face. 'No?'

'No,' I said firmly.

'How do you propose to stop me, Genevieve?' he said softly.

That wasn't the answer I'd expected, and it certainly wasn't what I wanted to hear. I stared at him, a part of me wondering if he was joking. 'What do you mean?'

'You gave me your blood of your own free will.' His eyes were cool, contemplative. 'Not only does it allow me an open invitation into your home, but into your mind. I can make you think or feel whatever I choose to, whenever I choose to.'

'But you won't,' I stated, in spite of the unease crawling down my spine.

His shoulders lifted in an elegant shrug. 'Why not?'

Because you're supposed to be one of the Good Guys. 'Look, Malik, I spent the last five months sleep-walking through my life because you and Tavish got over-protective and sicced the Sleeping Beauty spell on me – I mean, I get that you were both worried about me after everything that happened, but I'm fine now. And the pair of you can't keep leaving me out of the loop. You need to talk to me, to tell me what's going on, to stop hiding things from me. It's my life, after all.'

'I have given my word I will keep you safe, Genevieve.' He paused. 'Even from yourself, if necessary.'

I tightened my hand on the glass, exasperated. 'C'mon, Malik, I can look after myself.'

He raised his brows. 'As you did so successfully tonight.'

'Fine, okay, most of the time,' I admitted. 'Tonight was an exception.'

'No, it was not an exception.' A thread of anger laced his voice. 'You are continually reckless with your own safety.'

My exasperation exploded into frustration. 'I *had* to help them – they're my *friends*, and it was because of me they were getting hurt. If I hadn't, one or more of them might have died.'

'It is possible,' he agreed. 'People die all the time. It is sad, and sometimes regrettable. But their lives are not as valuable to me as yours. You wear my mark, you are my property, and as such I will take care of you. In the future you will not visit Sucker Town without my permission.'

I felt the *order* sink into my mind.

I stared at him in shock. 'You can't do that.'

Chapter Twenty-Eight

'**Y**ou have given me your blood, Genevieve,' Malik said, his eyes black and opaque, 'so I have no need to indulge you, or negotiate with you, or discuss anything. If and when I want anything from you, then I will mould your mind and body into agreement, and I will take it.'

My shock turned to confusion, then to gut-churning betrayal. I poured another drink, almost on autopilot, and knocked it back, concentrating on the clean taste of the alcohol. The urge to smash the bottle over his head erupted inside me, but as quickly as it arrived the anger was gone, replaced by a sick feeling of inevitability. Hadn't I always known it would come to this: that one day I'd end up at the mercy – or otherwise – of a vampire? And despite, or maybe because of Malik's high-handed over-protective habits, I'd believed he thought I was a person in my own right – that he cared about *me*. And I'd trusted that he'd never abuse the power he held over me. But evidently I was wrong, since he thought it okay to mess around with my mind, to make me do whatever *he* wanted without any discussion. Obviously I was nothing more than valuable property – his trophy sidhe.

I stared into my empty glass, not wanting to let him see how much that hurt. I gritted my teeth, tears stinging my eyes at my own stupidity ... Automatically I raised my hand to my neck, seeking solace in the touch of Grace's pentacle—

It was gone.

A quick flash of memory showed me my body in Darius'

room: my throat was a bloody mess … and there was no pentacle. I'd lost it while Darius had been necking me.

Panic, and the overwhelming need to find it overrode everything else, flooding adrenalin through my veins. I jerked up—

—and Malik's hand fastened round my left wrist, holding me in place. 'The necklace is safe, Genevieve,' he said softly, indicating the bedside table, 'but the chain is broken.'

My heart thudded in relief at the sight of the pentacle and the little pile of coiled chain, both glinting gold against the dark wood of the table top. I pulled away from his hold and started to reach out, but stopped. Oddly, my need to touch it had dissipated now I knew where it was. Briefly I wondered why I hadn't felt the loss of it earlier, then that thought was banished by another.

He'd not only found Grace's pentacle and brought it back safely, he'd noticed it was missing in the first place. Okay, so he could just be observant, hard not to be when you were as old as he was, but my gut told me it was more than that. After all, he'd killed me more than once in his efforts to protect me, so his 'I am the master, you will do as I say' pronouncement was just more of the same. But if I needed more convincing … Well, I was damned sure no other vamp would be keeping his fangs to himself when he was thirsty enough to drink an ocean of blood while he watched me drinking vodka … especially since he'd once told me he'd coveted me since I was four. But that didn't mean he wouldn't happily turn me into his cosseted, pampered blood-pet and leave me to twiddle my thumbs in some ivory tower if he thought it best for me. And it didn't tell me why he was playing the big bad vamp in an attempt to distract me from whatever was going on.

And it didn't make me any less angry.

Time to go fishing.

I looked up and met his dark, enigmatic eyes. 'So,' I said,

letting the fury simmering inside me bleed into my words, 'I'm *valuable property*, a possession you need to keep safe. But I'm curious as to what happens now: is this going to be an exclusive arrangement, or am I going to have to earn my keep?' I leaned forward, spitting the words out: 'Are you the only one I'm going to be forced to feed and fuck, or will you be offering my blood and my body around? After all, there's no point wasting me, not now you've got me, is there?'

His pupils lit with pinpricks of rage, then snuffed out almost as quickly. He studied me in silence for a moment, then, talking as if to a recalcitrant child, said, 'There are times when not utilising an asset can better maintain its worth. Your own father was careful to protect you, and to ensure both your blood and body were untouched, so as not to lessen your value.'

'Ri-*ight*,' I snorted. 'And we both know how well that turned out for him – the Autarch *killed* him. Not to mention the fact that my "untouched" value doesn't exist any more – after all, you're the one who infected my blood with 3V, and it's been a while since I was a virgin. So as far as I can see, I'm hardly worth having any more.'

He treated me to another long, silent gaze. 'Your value now lies in you being alive and uninjured, and not in the possession of a vampire. By agreeing to keep you that way, Genevieve, I gain a powerful ally in the kelpie.'

Surprise winged through me. I knew why Tavish wanted me safe – hard not to, with the fertility curse hanging over my head like a phallic Sword of Damocles – and I knew the pair of them were plotting *whatever* together, but I didn't know what Tavish could offer Malik, that had the vamp passing up my supposed coveted sidhe blood. I cast another lure.

'Tavish?' I exclaimed, deliberately injecting disbelief into my voice. 'You're doing all this just so you can stay friends with *Tavish*?'

He settled back against the pillows, crossing his arms loosely over his chest. 'Tavish is an ally, not a friend. His alliance is important to me.'

'Well, somehow I don't think Tavish is going to be the wonderful ally you think he is, so good luck with that,' I said, saluting him with my drink.

My glass went flying, and Malik was just suddenly holding my wrist, kneeling on the bed, his face close to mine. My pulse tripped, even though I'd sort of expected his reaction. 'Explain,' he said, the order sinking into my mind. I didn't try and resist it; I was *happy* to explain, whether he ordered me or not.

I jerked my head at the silver ring banding his thumb. 'I'm not the only one you talk to in your dreamscapes, am I?' I smiled, showing my teeth. 'You told Tavish about my visit with The Mother, which is why he turned up the very next day with his new pal the Morrígan.' And why Tavish hadn't asked me how I'd got rid of the sorcerer's soul. And why Malik hadn't been surprised when I'd first mentioned the Morrígan to him at the Coffin Club. 'But I hope whatever deal he cut with her is worth it, because she's got him chained up as her new slave.' His hand tensed around my wrist. 'There appears to be a lot of slavery going around, though, so maybe it's not something that worries you.' I looked pointedly down at where he gripped my arm.

He didn't let go. He was silent for a moment, his face unreadable, then some decision passed through his eyes. 'You are still suffering from your injuries. Come, and I will heal you.'

I felt a buzz in my mind, not quite an order, more of a suggestion. I pushed it away frustrated. Crap, he'd decided to clam up. Now I wouldn't get anything else out of him. 'No, thanks. I'm not interested, not unless you're prepared to talk to me.'

'Genevieve, you are in pain.'

'And I prefer to stay that way,' I snapped.

'I prefer to heal you.' His dark spice scent swirled round me with a touch of soothing *mesma*.

'No,' I said flatly, trying hard not to breathe, and failing miserably. 'I don't want anything from you, Malik. I'm sidhe, and I heal up well enough on my own, thank you.' I mentally batted away another, stronger suggestion, and tried to yank my wrist from him. 'And don't bother trying to force me: you'll only end up damaging the goods.'

'I do not intend to force you.' He dropped his hand. 'Instead, I would point out that you are in pain, and you have the fae to deal with tomorrow. Would you rather waste time in unnecessary convalescence over the next few days out of unconsidered anger, or accept my offer?'

He had a point, but it made no difference; if I hurt that much I could always buy a healing spell from the Witches' Market. Not to mention—

'I hardly think my anger is unconsidered,' I said, not bothering to disguise the disgust in my voice.

'Would it help if I apologised?' he said quietly, fixing me with a steady gaze.

I blinked. 'What for? Taking over my life and treating me like a possession? Don't bother. If you were really sorry, you wouldn't have done it in the first place.' I waved at the window: the stars were twinkling happily away in the night sky. *Bastards!* 'It's time for you to leave.'

He brushed a hand over his forehead, hesitated, then smoothed it over his buzz-cut. A stupid errant part of me wanted to know why he'd cut it— I growled at it to shut up.

'No,' he said, 'I have told you I will keep you safe, so I will leave at dawn when it is no longer possible for another vampire to gain entry to your home.'

I snorted. 'You're the only sucker who's got an invite, remember, so don't bother—'

'You have been giving your blood to Darius,' he interrupted, a flare of anger lighting in his dark pupils, 'therefore, you have also given him an open invitation. He is young and easily manipulated; and you have already seen how one more powerful has made use of him to gain access to you.'

I laughed – it wasn't a happy sound – and pulled open the bedside drawer. I grabbed one of the empty blood bags and slapped it down on the bed between us. 'This is how Darius gets my blood, and he pays for every single bag – a token amount, admittedly, but it's the principle that counts – and what's more, he's in credit for the next six months. Blood paid for or stolen can't be used against you: I learned that lesson from you. Now get out.'

He settled back against the pillows again. 'I will leave at dawn, Genevieve. Not before. The bed is big enough for both of us to lie comfortably.'

I glared at him, my hands clenched in anger and frustration. London wasn't big enough right now, never mind my bed! But there was no way I could physically throw him out. I wanted to scream, to shove a sharp blade through his cold, arrogant, currently unbeating heart, and then I wanted to empty the other two bottles of vodka in my fridge until I couldn't remember his name, let alone his pale, perfect face ...

I dumped the bottle on the floor, swung my legs off the side and stood, immediately regretting moving so quickly as my battered body objected. I grabbed my pillows and thought about sleeping in the living room, but damn it, this was *my* bed, and *I* was lying in it, whether he was there or not. Carefully, I crawled under the sheet, giving him my back and keeping as far away from him as possible. As my head sank into the soft pillows, I couldn't hold back a relieved sigh.

'Genevieve, I can heal you ...'

'No,' I said, not caring if I sounded sulky or sullen, 'I don't want to be healed. So don't touch me, or speak to me, or use your mind-mojo on me, and I'd be prefer it if you didn't breathe either.' Not that it would make much difference to him whether he did or not. 'I don't want you here.'

'I am truly sorry, Genevieve,' he said, regret slipping round me like a gentle summer breeze.

'If you were truly sorry,' I said, forcing the words past the anger, and yes, hurt, constricting my throat, 'you'd tell me why you're hooked up with Tavish, why I'm such a valuable asset, and what's going on with Tavish, and with Mad Max, and what it's all got to do with the curse. Oh, and you'd tell me what's up with you and the Autarch too.'

I stared fixedly at my bedroom's blank white wall until it went out of focus, waiting for an answer that didn't come, nursing my anger. Malik might think I was a valuable asset now, but he wasn't going to for much longer. I fell asleep determined to find a way to stop him running my life. Whatever it took.

Chapter Twenty-Nine

Tap, tap. Tap, tap. Tap, tap.

The noise beat insistently inside my head and I turned over, trying to get away from it. Instead, I came face to face with Malik's dark, staring eyes.

I blinked, then realised three things almost simultaneously:

Malik had somehow missed leaving before dawn, and was now in his 'dead for the day' state.

A thin sliver of sunlight was hitting the bed like a laser-beam, and it was inches from his bare foot.

And something huge and black was perched outside my window, tapping on the glass with a very large and very sharp beak.

My pulse speeding with apprehension, I leapt up—

—and a *swooshing* sound thundered in my ears as the black thing flew through the window, knocked me flying, and crash-landed almost on top of me.

Feathers.

My mouth was full of feathers. I spluttered and spat them out, scrabbling at my mouth with my hands while something cawed loudly and indignantly next to my ear. There was a pan-icked flapping of wings as it moved, and a huge raven stared down at me from alien blue eyes, its long, grey, very sharp beak only inches away from my throat.

Was it the Morrígan?

The raven started to grow, and within seconds the monstrous bird was looming over me, blocking any escape. Keeping a wary eye on that beak, I scrambled backwards and wedged myself in between the bedside table and the wall.

The raven gave another loud caw—

—and exploded in a snow-storm of black feathers that spun and fell through the air, dissipating into the ether before they reached the wooden floor. Instead of a raven, there stood a naked man. His mouth opened as he let out one last impassioned *caw*, then he collapsed, shaking, onto his hands and knees, his head hanging down, his wheat-gold hair feathering out over the floor.

'Goddess,' he gasped hoarsely, 'that hurt.' Then he curled into a ball, moaning.

Okay. So not the Morrígan.

And not much of a threat either, judging by the moaning, which sounded a bit excessive, like he was putting it on. I unwedged myself from my corner, hauled myself up and ignored the moaning naked guy in favour of Malik.

The sunlight might be weak, but if it hit him, it could cause a serious problem. I kept a wary eye on Mr Moaning Raven as I skirted past him and yanked open the wardrobe. Malik's long leather coat was hanging neatly next to my own leather jacket, just as I'd known it would be. At least the neat-freak vamp was predictable in that area anyway. I grabbed them both, and flung the coat over Malik's top half and my jacket over his feet. It wasn't perfect, but I was pretty sure he was old enough that it would protect him for now.

Then I turned to give my newest uninvited visitor the once-over.

His back view was well worth looking at: broad shoulders narrowing to a taut butt, long, lean-muscled legs, and all covered in tanned skin sprinkled with fine golden hairs that glinted in the weak morning light. A twining tattoo encircled his left ankle, climbed up his calf and twisted around his thigh. It was a complicated pattern of stylised feathers and glyphs, none of which I recognised. The tattoo itself was etched in gold ink that was barely noticeable against his skin tone. A scattering of small diamonds were sprinkled along the tattoo and melded into his skin. When I *looked*, the tattoo and gems glowed with enough power to fill the room with golden magic, hotter than the summer sun.

I'd bet my last liquorice torpedo that the naked man in my bedroom was the raven who'd been following me: but was he a messenger from the Morrígan, or something to do with the dead raven faeling, or both?

Not that he was looking particularly competent for a messenger.

Of course, there was another reason he could be here. I could've snagged myself another hopeful suitor like Sylvia. Damn fertility curse.

'You know,' I said, raising my voice slightly to be heard over his moans, and prodding his shoulder with my toe, 'turning up naked in a girl's bedroom isn't the relationship starter it's cracked up to be. Not to mention that the naiads have already tried it … unsuccessfully, I might add. Oh, and if you're thinking of it as a fast track to courting me, you can think again. It takes more than pretty looks to get me into bed.'

He stopped moaning and lifted his head to peer at me over his bent arm. He looked about my own age. His face was every bit as pretty as the rest of him: high, angled cheekbones, sharp jaw, straight patrician nose and large indigo eyes with slitted cat-like pupils that gleamed more red than black as they twinkled at me.

I stared at him, shocked. He was sidhe.

'I think you're maligning my good character here, my lady.' He rested his chin on his arm, regarding me quizzically. 'After all, I did just rescue you. But I'm prepared to forgive you for' – he grinned – 'a drink. Don't suppose you'd care to pass me the vodka there, would you?'

I blinked at him. 'What?'

'Saving damsels in distress from going up in flames with unconscious vamps is thirsty work. There's the shifting, that takes its toll, even without flying through your window while not physically breaking it. Then I did have to stretch your Ward a bit, but seeing as it was already partially *cracked*, I didn't think you'd mind. I think I deserve a drink after all that, don't you?' He winked mischievously, his grin widening to show straight white human teeth. 'Oh, and pass me a pillow, will you? I can't quite manage clothes yet, and I'd hate to stun you speechless with the rest of my pretty looks.'

'It's not your looks,' I said slowly, tossing a pillow at him in bemusement. 'It's your eyes.'

'Ah, I forgot.' He closed them, muttered something under his breath, then opened them. The indigo irises were the same, but the pupils were now round black and human. 'Is that better?'

Oddly, it was. 'Um ... yes. Who are you?'

He sprang to his feet, clutching the pillow strategically in front of him, then did an odd bird-like hop towards me. He stopped and shook his head in irritation. 'Sorry, takes a while to get rid of the mannerisms. The name's Jack, my lady. Pleased to meet you, at last.' He held out his hand, an expectant look on his face, as if I should know *who* he was even if I didn't know *him*.

'At last?' I echoed questioningly.

'Ah, she hasn't told you.' He dipped his head, his cheeks flushing with embarrassment, which made him look a good few years younger than the mid-twenties I'd originally guessed. 'Well, that puts the hawk among the pigeons, doesn't it? About that drink ...'

Not a suitor, then: a messenger, as I'd previously thought.

I handed him the vodka bottle from the bedside table. It was still a third full. 'Who hasn't told me what?' I offered him a glass.

He did a little dancing jiggle with the vodka and the pillow, managed to get the top off without losing his modesty, then, ignoring the glass, he tipped the bottle up, his Adam's apple bobbing as he drank, and he continued drinking until the bottle was empty.

'Good stuff, this' – he checked the label – 'Cristall. I'll have to get some. Thanks, my lady.'

'No problem,' I said, giving him an expectant look. 'Okay, Dutch courage time over, Jack, back to the question: who hasn't told—?'

A loud knock on my bedroom door and a voice interrupted us. 'Genny?' Sylvia called. 'Are you all right in there? I can hear talking—'

Damn. I'd forgotten about her. Again. 'I'm fine, Sylvia—'

The door opened.

'Ah, look, I've really got to go.' Jack shoved the pillow and empty bottle at me, catching me by surprise and knocking me back onto the bed. I rolled onto my side out of his way as he launched himself at the window. His body concertinaed, folding back in on itself as he sprouted glossy black feathers and *shifted* into the huge raven. The bird flapped his wings once, the backdraught blowing my hair back from my face, then he flew straight through the glass as if it wasn't there and soared away into the sky.

'Gosh! Nice arse!' Sylvia exclaimed from the doorway. She smiled at me. 'Whoever was that?'

'That was Jack, apparently.' I pressed my lips together, frustrated he'd got away before he'd given me an answer to my question. *Who was she – the Morrigan? – and what hadn't she told me?*

Chapter Thirty

'So where did Jack fly in from then?' Sylvia gave me a teasing grin, then peered round me at the leather-coat-covered Malik lying on the bed. 'Gosh, you look like you've had an interesting night.'

'Something like that,' I said wryly. 'Sorry, but I'm not really in the mood to talk about it, though.'

'Okay,' she agreed cheerfully, 'if you change your mind, I'm here.'

I blinked at her easy acceptance, then feeling a prick of guilt, I also apologised for siccing her with the *Security Stingers* and running out on her offer of dinner.

But she surprised me again, accepting my apology with another smile, just as easily as she'd taken Malik's presence in my bed. I guessed her night spent sucking up the blood from my floorboards hadn't only repaired her Glamour – her white fifties-style dress and silver sandals were positively glowing – but left her as happy as— well, as a dryad who'd spent the night sucking up blood.

'Don't supposed you've heard of, or met Jack the raven before now, have you?' I asked. 'When he first appeared his eyes were like mine.' I waved a hand at my face. 'Except his were this indigo colour.'

'He was one of the sidhe?' She clapped her hands and did a little twirl. 'How exciting!'

'So you don't know him, then?' I asked again, hoping that since Jack could change his eyes, that there was always the possibility she'd know him as something different from a sidhe.

'Umm …' She tapped her cycle helmet, her nails making a little drumming tune as she stared into space. 'No, sorry, Jack the raven doesn't ring any bells.' She gave me a wide smile, then said, 'Now, I bet you're hungry, Genny. How about breakfast? I'll just borrow your mirror first – a girl's got to look after herself, hasn't she?'

'Works for me,' I said, hiding my disappointment she didn't know Jack and stepping out the way so she could use the long mirror on my wardrobe.

She whistled and rustled as she pruned her scalp, vanished her excess twigs, *called* a fluffy pink mohair cardigan and repaired the broken strap on her pink cycle helmet. Then she cleaned up her snowfall of petals, repaired the holes in my floorboards by blowing them a kiss, and declared herself ready for breakfast. After a quick look at the contents of my fridge – two bottles of Cristall and nothing else – she cheerfully agreed to go to the Rosy Lea Café to get it. Even more amazingly, she equally cheerfully helped me move my heavy wardrobe in front of my bedroom window, a feat I'd never have managed on my own. I might be stronger than a normal human, but Sylvia had the edge on me. The wardrobe was oak, and as soon as she grasped one side and flattened her 'Hello, boys!' cleavage against it, the wardrobe almost moved itself.

I didn't ask.

I just thanked her gratefully, and told her breakfast was my treat.

After Sylvia had gone, I looked thoughtfully down at Malik where he lay on the bed, his black eyes staring sightlessly upwards. In spite of my temporary shielding measures, the narrow beam of sun had caught Malik's right foot and a diagonal wound now striped his flesh. The wound wasn't bleeding; it looked more like someone had branded him with a red-hot poker, burning down to the bone, leaving the sides charred and crispy.

Maybe I'd missed an opportunity there.

Throwing the coats over him had been one of those instinctive things: *vampire plus sun equals needs protection*. But protecting him wasn't going to stop him running my life. Maybe what I should've done, instead of covering him up, was had Sylvia help me throw him out onto the flat roof outside the window and left him to fry for the day. And I could've chopped his head from his body while I was at it, chopping him irrevocably out of my life.

Damn tyrannical vamp.

But however dictatorial, annoying – and let's not forget secretive – Malik was, I couldn't do it, my conscience and my heart wouldn't let me. Not only that, it wasn't the practical option: without him as Oligarch there'd be no one to protect London's fae and faelings from the rest of the vamps. We'd end up with Open-Fang Night on anyone fae, and the results wouldn't be pretty.

'So, I need to find a way to neutralise you, without actually dragging your oh-so-gorgeous, damned arrogant arse out to be barbecued,' I told him through gritted teeth. 'But for now, I think you'd be better somewhere less flammable.'

I dragged in the thick silk rug that usually covered my living room floor, then leaning over him, I grasped his arm and pulled him towards me. He rolled easily and limply, and with a quick tug I had him off the bed. He landed with a heavy thud on the rug.

'Sorry,' I muttered unrepentantly as I straightened his arms and legs and tugged the rug over him. Grunting with exertion, I managed to roll him up, Cleopatra-style, then I sat on the floor, bracing myself against the wall, and shoved the rug with my feet until it was tucked under the bed.

I hauled myself up, wiped my sweaty forehead and grimaced.

The rug was added insurance against the daylight. If he got a few bruises along the way, well, it was only what he deserved.

'Right.' I dusted off my hands. 'Annoying vamp temporarily disposed off: check. Time for a shower and clothes before Sylvia gets back.'

I tugged off my vest top and sleep shorts and caught my reflection in the wardrobe mirror. Not a pretty sight. The mass of purple bruising centred on my midriff didn't look – or feel – any better, nor did the rest of the multicoloured patches that decorated my arms and legs. But while I might be bruised and battered, I had things to do. I needed to buy a new Ward – Malik couldn't be left unprotected, however much the angry part of me might want to – but I couldn't afford a Ward and a Healing spell. I decided a couple of aspirins and a handful of blood-fruit to up my venom levels – I had a brief relieved thought that even after Darius' attack last night, when he'd venom-stuck me, I didn't seem to be suffering any ill-effects – and I'd live for another day.

I *looked*, and ran my fingers over Tavish's handprint spell where it sat low down on my stomach; it hadn't changed. It was obviously to do with the fertility curse – but hey, right now *everything and anything* was to do with the fertility curse – but since it wasn't active yet, that didn't tell me what it was going to do. Maybe Finn would know, once we got round to talking today. I wondered again what had been so important that he hadn't wanted to chat last night, although with what had happened, Finn *not* being around had turned out for the best. If he'd been here when Malik had brought me home injured, he'd probably have tried to stake – or rather, stick his horns in – the arrogant vamp. But Tavish's spell gave me a good enough excuse to phone Finn and hurry up our chat. Plus, there was my job, or lack of it, at Spellcrackers, and our relationship, whatever it was, to sort out. I fished my phone from my jacket, hesitated, and took the coward's way out and texted him instead.

Can we meet soon, please?

I stared as the little envelope symbol winged off on its way, then stared some more as if that would get me an immediate reply, before telling myself to get on with more sensible things, like checking my emails … which consisted of a load of the usual '*no, I really don't want whatever it is you're selling*' spam, and one from Hugh saying he'd was looking into my queries about the missing faelings, the Morrígan, Ana and the other stuff, and he'd get back to me.

'At least someone's trying to help me,' I said loudly, nudging the carpeted Malik with my foot (not that I thought he could hear me, but it made me feel better). I picked up Grace's pentacle from my bedside table, found another chain in one of the drawers to replace the broken one, and clasped it round my neck as I went over my day's to-visit list.

There was the chat with Finn, hopefully. There was the visit Victoria Harrier, my lawyer, had arranged with the ravens at the Tower of London. And then there was the other visit Victoria had arranged, with her very pregnant daughter-in-law, Ana, to chat about babies and 3V and vamps and curses. I wasn't looking forward to it, as even without Ana being a past, and possibly present and future, victim of the curse, the whole idea of talking to a faeling whose grandmother was a royal sidhe princess (which Angel was, however nutty she also was), and whose great-grandmother was a sidhe queen, filled my stomach with oddly nervous butterflies.

And that gave me another more immediate problem: what on earth was I supposed to wear that would be suitable for a meeting with the ravens, a faeling who had royal sidhe blood, and a serious chat with my ex-boss to sort out both the personal and working sides of our relationship, all the while trying to deal with matchmaking magic. In the end I decided on smart, but casual, with just a slight touch of sexy: a green top of silk and lace, black velvet jeans and killer-heel boots.

'And then tonight,' I said, bending down and giving the evil eye to Malik in the rolled-up carpet under my bed, 'I'm going back to Sucker Town and find out what's going on with Fyodor, Mad Max, Darius and my blood, and what they all have to do with the curse, and you are *not* going to stop me.'

Chapter Thirty-One

Sylvia turned up with breakfast. Only she wasn't alone.
Johnny Depp was with her.

My mouth dropped open.

'Ta da!' She spread her arms wide. 'Look who I found.'

Johnny Depp was with her! And he was dressed in his Captain Jack Sparrow pirate costume!

'Hello, luv.' He chucked me under the chin and made a high clicking noise. 'How's your ship sailing?'

I narrowed my eyes. That clicking was familiar. Damn, he wasn't Johnny Depp but Fishface, a naiad – and the clicking was just him laughing.

'Don't tell me,' I said, trying to remember his real name, 'you're here to court me.'

'Got it in one, luv.' He strolled in trailing the scent of ozone, and stood in the centre of my living room under my amber-and copper-beaded chandelier. He did a three-sixty as he admired the place – not that there was much to admire, but hey, he grinned and looked captivated enough that I almost wondered if he were thinking of moving in—

Half a dozen of the chandelier's glass beads popped above him. His grinning mouth split into a yawn, his cheeks spread until thick fluted fins flared out to either side, his long pirate dreads morphed into a tall, spiny headcrest that tangled with the lower beads, and his costume disappeared, leaving him standing naked in all his scaly pale grey *double* glory.

I blinked. A six-foot-tall-in-his-webbed-clawed-feet naked

naiad wasn't the sort of sight you wanted to see before breakfast. Or brunch. Or anytime, really.

'He really knows how to use both of them,' Sylvia whispered in my ear. 'He's a virtual god once you get him between the sheets.' She squeezed my arm. 'Don't mention I said so, though, his head's big enough as it is.' She patted my butt. 'I love your outfit too, Genny. You look *fabulous*.'

'Ri-*ight*,' I said, wondering whether she'd just given me a personal recommendation, an invitation, or a 'keep off my property' warning.

A large folded towel appeared in Sylvia's hand and she walked up to him and slapped it affectionately on his chest. 'You still haven't got the hang of Glamour yet, have you, Ricou?' She gave me a look that said 'he's a lovable idiot really', and sashayed into the kitchen area where she deposited a large takeaway bag and started unpacking it.

Ricou. Fishface's real name was Ricou.

Ricou gave the towel a disgruntled look – it was bright pink and decorated with white cherry-tree blossoms – then wrapped it round his waist and secured it with the end of his whip-like tail. He stuck his webbed clawed hands on his hips and looked up at the beads. The membrane flickered over the black orbs of his eyes. 'Nice Reveal spells, luv, you get them off old Gillie on the market?'

'No,' I said, pushing the door closed, 'Bernie Mittle made them.'

'Bernie does great work, but you might want to try old Gillie next time. She's just as good, but she's cheaper.'

'You should listen to him, Genny.' Sylvia gave a rustling laugh. 'London's expert on Which Witch for Which Spell, he is.'

'Thanks,' I said, then remembered about my *cracked* Ward and the rug-wrapped fanged occupant of my bedroom. 'So who's the best for good, cheap Wards?'

'Fiddlesticks,' Sylvia said, unpacking what looked like enough food to feed a whole forest of dryads, never mind the three of us. 'I forgot about that. I meant to get you one when I was out. You could always use a blood-Ward for today and I'll pick one up later. Ricky will tell you how, won't you, babe?'

'Sure thing, Blossom.' He steepled his claws together and tapped his lipless mouth. 'Blood-Wards are a tad primitive, but easy-peasy enough. Just draw a line in blood across all entrances and add your will to it. It'll stop anyone crossing. 'Course, the real disadvantage is you have to give them a top-up before they run out, which could be anywhere from a few hours to a couple of days, so you can't just go off and forget about them. Then there's the physical side – there's only so much blood and magic a body can offer up before it starts to run on empty.' He did a wide grin-yawn of a smile. 'But they're handy for a quick, free fix.'

It did sound easy. 'Okay, a couple of questions: do I have to stay inside the blood-Ward for it to work, and what about anyone else inside it; can they leave if they want to?'

'Hmm.' His headcrest quivered. 'You can set the blood-Ward up so *you* can walk through it without breaking it, but it's a bit more complicated the other way. 'Course, if you do set it up so's they can walk out, then it'll break when they cross it.'

'That's great, thanks,' I said. It would work. I could leave, Malik would be protected, and when he woke up at sunset, or whenever, he could walk out … or I could trap him— which had its own possibilities.

'Told you he was the best, didn't I?' Sylvia beamed proudly.

I got the subtext as I looked from one to the other: Sylvia pretending to be Carefree Caterer and Ricou doing his impression of Professor of Spells. To be honest, it was hard to miss: they had a thing going on, and Sylvia had very definitely been warning me off. Which made me wonder what the hell the pair of them were doing here supposedly courting me?

'Look,' I said, 'nice as this little breakfast club is, I've got places to go, people to meet' – *and no way do I want to play gooseberry* – 'so you'll both have to amuse yourselves without me today.'

'Gosh, don't worry about us, Genny. We're both happy to do whatever.'

'Yeah, luv.' Ricou thumped his clawed fist proudly on his chest. 'Ricou here will be honoured to escort you two ladies on the town.'

'Now then, breakfast is served,' Sylvia said brightly. 'We've got some more blood' – she tapped a couple of the large cups – 'and pancakes with extra maple syrup – they're mine, but I'm happy to share; a couple of bacon butties, because the waitress said they were your favourite, and some sashimi tuna and whole sardines for the waterbaby there.' She waved at the half-dozen other cups and containers. 'We also have coffee, tea, orange juice, custard doughnuts and a selection of vegetable crudities.'

I eyed the carrot and celery sticks sitting neatly alongside the broccoli and cauliflower florets, all complete with a sprinkling of sesame seed. *Eew!* That was the sort of rabbit food only Finn ate. And thinking of him … *why hadn't he returned my text?* I left the raw stuff and picked up one of the bacon butties.

'You can drop the act,' I said, waving it to indicate the two of them, 'and you can tell me what you're doing courting me.' I took a bite.

Ricou's membranes flickered over his eyes nervously. Sylvia's dress quivered, and a lone white petal fell to land next to her silver-sandalled feet.

'Well,' I said, after I'd swallowed, 'who wants to go first?'

'Ricou here won you in a poker game.' He flexed his head-crest to free it from the beads, making them jangle. 'Told you that, the last time we met, luv.' He wandered over to the kitchen, snagged a sardine and threw it in the air, snapping his jaws with a loud smacking noise as he caught it.

'He means he fixed it so he won.' Sylvia dribbled the sickly syrup in a criss-cross pattern over her pancakes.

'She's a harsh one,' Ricou said to his next sardine. 'At least Ricou's name was on the list.'

I choked on a mouthful of bacon butty. *There was a list?*

Sylvia absently thumped me on the back. 'Gosh, but then Ricou here didn't remove his name, did he?'

'Ricou was told not to by the Lady Meriel, wasn't he?' He snapped at another sardine.

'Fiddlesticks.' She crushed her empty syrup packet and tossed it into the large takeaway bag. 'Ricou's a hundred and sixty-three, not three. He should be able to stand up for himself by now.'

What list?' I gasped out in between coughs.

'Ricou doesn't see you standing up for yourself much, Blossom. You're here, aren't you? So it looks like Lady Isabella still has you tied to her stake.'

'She does not!' She jabbed her plastic fork at him. 'I haven't been staked since I was fifty!'

'What list?' I yelled.

Sylvia turned to me in surprise. 'The list of who's allowed to court you, of course.'

'Only Blossom here isn't on it.' Ricou's face-fins flared. He was either sulking or annoyed, or maybe both. 'So *she* shouldn't be here.'

'*She* is here because Genny didn't want anything to do with Algernon's Twig Gang,' Sylvia's dress lost a whole shower of petals. 'And I don't blame her, not after they did their usual. Nasty bunch of sticks they are.'

Their usual?

Ricou dropped his fish and flung a scaly arm round Sylvia's

shoulders. He tapped her cycle helmet gently with his webby-clawed hand. 'Aww, Blossom, don't start shedding. I told them I'd strip their water if they tried their grab and grind tricks on you again and I meant it.'

Grab and grind? They'd tried to rape me to get me pregnant; I'd thought they'd done it because of the fertility curse. Now it sounded like it was more a nasty habitual perversion.

'My hero.' Sylvia sniffed and patted his chest. Then she poked him hard. 'But if you want to stay that way, then you'll have to tell your mother to take you off the list, right?'

'Nobody's mother is taking anyone off the list,' I dumped my bacon butty on the counter, too angry to eat, 'because there is no list, not any more.'

'What?' they said in unison, turning to me.

I grabbed a napkin and wiped my hands, fixing them both with a quelling look. 'If I decide to have a child, then it will be with willing, *single* partners only. I'm not getting together with someone who's already dating. This is about *cracking* a curse, not breaking up people's relationships. Whoever thought either of you'd be good candidates was wrong.'

Ricou's headcrest zipped upright in alarm. 'But the curse *has* to be broken. It's not just the fae, there's all the faelings too. I've got six halfling pups, and—'

'You've got six kids?' I interrupted, aghast.

'Everyone on the list has children,' Sylvia said flatly, 'or faelings, anyway. It was one of the criteria, which was why I wasn't on it. I've never sprouted any seedlings.'

There were criteria? 'What are the others?' I demanded.

'Gosh, there's only the two. They had to be under two hundred years old, and have to have at least one faeling, so that they have someone to fight for and they're proven fertile.' She pursed her lips. 'I think there were about fifty-odd on the initial list, but by the time Tavish had finished there was only about a dozen left.'

'Tavish organised the list?' I asked sharply – although why that should surprise me was a mystery. Damn, interfering, *arrogant* kelpie.

''Course he did, luv.' Ricou's eye membranes flickered nervously again. 'Tavish always organises everything. He's the one who said who got to court you, and in what order. Him first, of course. The Ladies Meriel and Isabella wanted it done by lots or something, but he said no. And no one messes with Tavish.'

I frowned. Tavish seemed to be pulling everyone's strings in an effort to be Daddy Number One ... except Tavish had done a disappearing act even before the Morrígan had caught him. Why would he do that if he was first in line? And then there was the *list* he'd organised. If Ricou's facts were right, everyone on it was under two hundred years old – *except Tavish*. Everyone had at least one faeling kid – *except Tavish* ... or at least as far as I knew, but then obviously I'd been on a need-to-know-nothing basis since the very beginning ... my eyes fixed on the wilting carrot sticks—

Everyone on the list had to have proven their fertility.

'Here.' Sylvia wrapped my hands round a cup. 'Have some tea, Genny. It'll perk you up.'

'I don't drink tea,' I said slowly, looking at them both. Ricou's eye membranes were fully down over his black orbs and his headcrest was flat to his head. Sylvia was fluffing out her skirt, refusing to meet my gaze. It didn't take a genius to work out which path my thoughts were following. Finn's and my relationship might not be exactly what London's fae thought it was, but there was a relationship, and it wasn't a secret.

'Finn's got a faeling child?' I asked, surprised my voice came out normal when inside I wanted to scream.

Sylvia took the cup from my unresisting hand, sympathy clouding her glossy green eyes. 'Yes.'

When the hell had he planned on telling me? I didn't need to
ask who the mother was, but I did, and Sylvia told me.

'Helen Crane.'

Chapter Thirty-Two

'*Finn's waiting for you downstairs,*' Sylvia had said.

The echoing noise my boots made pounding down the five flights of stairs to the front door of my building seemed to mark angry time with my shocked, thudding heart. And as I exited onto the street, Ricou and Sylvia hovering attentively on my heels, the church bells of St Paul's Church in Covent Garden joined in with a knowing, mocking clamour.

Finn and Helen had a child together.

A child was a big, *big* secret to keep from someone you intended to marry and expected to have another child with. Okay, so Finn and I weren't getting married, but with the fertility curse 'arranging' things, it was what everyone, including him, expected us to do, even if the reason was less to do with yards of white satin and lace, the damn church bells and death do us part and everything to do with jumping the broom, the patter of tiny satyr hooves, and the fucking curse.

Marry in haste, repent at leisure.

Finn *was* waiting for me outside. My heart did a stupid little jump. It obviously hadn't heard the latest newsflash about him being a *bastard*. But looking at Finn's anxious face, he had – in fact, he looked like he'd bypassed the whole marrying bit and gone straight on to repentance. *Good.*

Except that Finn wasn't the only person waiting for me.

'Ms Taylor,' Victoria Harrier, my solicitor called, hurrying up to me and beaming her polished steel smile that was the opposite of Finn's anxiety. 'I was just about to phone you. Our appointment with the Raven Master is at noon and we don't want to be late. Traffic can be horrendous sometimes.'

'Gen?' Finn shot an unhappy look at Victoria Harrier, then said, 'We really need to talk.'

Victoria Harrier held up a brown envelope. 'Ms Taylor, I have the autopsy report on the dead faeling here.' She indicated her black limo idling at the kerb and the uniformed chauffeur holding open the back door. 'I thought we might look over it on the way.'

I could read an autopsy report, or find out about my supposed friend-and-almost-lover's secret child. Choices. Choices.

I smiled at Victoria Harrier, took the envelope and touched my hand to her cheek and sent a careful order into her mind. 'Would you mind travelling in the front with your chauffeur, Ms Harrier, while I talk to Mr Panos in the back? We need to talk about the curse and our relationship. You're very happy about that.'

Her eyes glazed slightly, then she smiled back happily. 'Of course, Ms Taylor.'

'Thank you,' I said, 'oh, and if we get there, and we're not finished chatting, please don't disturb us.' She nodded and trotted cheerfully off to the limo. Guilt pricked me, but the knowledge that she was in the pro get-the-sidhe-pregnant camp trimmed my remorse to an acceptable level.

I turned to Ricou and Sylvia, still hovering attentively on my heels. Sylvia was making a show of adjusting her pink cycle helmet and pointedly ignoring what I'd just done. Ricou, a.k.a. Professor of Spells, was now wearing a slightly rumpled Johnny Depp Glamour, one with a loud-checked jacket, dark glasses and a trilby – Sylvia's current favourite, apparently, from among the multitude of Glamour spell tattoos that decorated the insides of both his scaly arms. He was also watching me over the top of the sunglasses with an assessing expression.

Was he going to be a problem? 'Look, why don't you two … hang out together for a bit or something?'

'Gosh, what a good idea.' Sylvia grabbed Ricou's hand. 'Come on, lover boy, I know just the place. See you later, Genny.'

I looked at Finn and indicated the car. 'You want to talk, don't you?' *Because I was damn sure I did.*

He nodded sharply and we got in. I touched the chauffeur's hand and (surprisingly easily) gave him the same orders as Victoria Harrier, then the limo door shut with a soft clunk, cutting off the noise, bustle and bells of Covent Garden and enclosing us in the cosseted smell of leather and luxury. The limo looked similar to the previous day's, with its L-shaped seat, the blacked-out screen between us and the driver and the half-dozen Privacy-spell crystals dotted around, except this one still had the bar installed instead of the James Bond-type office. Briefly I wondered if maybe I'd fried some of her equipment in the other limo, then put it from my mind. Finn had taken the back seat, and if my little mind-control party piece had Ricou reassessing me, it had etched the worry lines deeper into Finn's face.

'Hell's thorns, Gen, what are you playing at? The woman's a witch! Using magic like that could get you the death sentence.'

As the limo moved quietly into the busy traffic I flattened my palms on the leather seat and studied him, to give my anger and hurt a chance to cool down. He was in his usual human-looking Glamour, and he looked good. His dark blond hair waved to his shoulders, his sharp, triangular horns were tight to his head and almost hidden. His brown suit was dark enough that it was verging on black. The suit looked dressier than usual, and fitted his athletic, muscular body like it was hand-tailored. His fine cotton shirt was open at his throat, the soft cream contrasting nicely with the darker tan of his skin.

It dawned on me he looked more than good: he always looked great, but today he'd made an extra effort … maybe the bastard thought it would gain him points. My hands curled into tight fists in anger. It didn't.

'When were you going to tell me about your child, Finn?' I said, forcing my voice into calmness. 'The one you fathered with Helen? After all, it's not like we've known each other very long, right? I mean it's only been – what? Ten fucking months?' Okay, so maybe I wasn't as calm as I could be. 'And it's not like we don't work together on a daily basis or anything, is it, Finn? Or that we didn't talk about you having kids with Helen only yesterday, *did we*?'

He let out a breath and pushed his hands through his hair, his moss-green eyes sombre and, oddly, filled with something that looked more like relief than guilt at being caught out.

'I'm sorry, Gen. I really didn't want you to find out from someone else,' he said quietly.

'Then why didn't you tell me yourself?' I demanded. 'Or did you think maybe you'd just wait until I gave birth before introducing me to my future child's brother?'

'Sister,' he said.

'*What?*'

'Helen and I have a daughter. Her name is Nicola.'

I stared at him in disbelief, my anger momentarily forgotten in the face of something that went against everything about fae 'facts of life' I'd had drummed into me by Grianne. 'That's just not possible. Witches *always* have sons – faelings – if the dad is a lesser fae. That's the way the magic works.'

'Why do you think I was chosen to court you, Gen?' Finn said, an old note of resignation in his voice. 'My daughter might be faeling, but she's the nearest to a full-blood fae born in the last century. If I didn't know different, even I'd say she was satyr, and that Helen couldn't possibly be her mother. But I know she is. I watched Nicky being born. I know it's not supposed to happen. Hell's thorns, Helen shouldn't have been able to get pregnant anyway! Most ninth-generation witches never have more than one child, and we weren't even taking part in the fertility rite proper; we just ended up fooling around nearby.' Faint colour stained his angular cheekbones. 'The witches' rites get a bit wild at times,' he said more quietly. 'You know how it is.'

I didn't, never having been to one. I wasn't sure I wanted to, either.

'Of course, once we both realised, we were thrilled. We jumped the broom.' He paused. 'We broke up when Nicky was nine, but we've always stayed friends.' *Because of Nicky.* He didn't say it, but it was as obvious as the worried look on his face. And, of course he was too much of a good guy *not* to stay friends with his daughter's mother— *that explained why Helen was his number one speed-dial.* My heart did its little leap again. Even if his comment about 'fooling around' meant Nicky's advent hadn't been planned. Although, if it wasn't for what he'd said about Helen being a ninth-generation witch, I'd have bet money she'd trapped him. The thoughts kept a lid on my anger.

'Why didn't you tell me about Nicky?' I asked.

He gave me a rueful look. 'I couldn't, Gen.' He shook his head as he saw my questioning look. 'No, not a magical gag, but I gave my word to Helen that I wouldn't speak of Nicky to you unless you specifically asked me if she and I had kids. This was before I met you.'

He'd given his word. Fae don't give or break their word lightly; the magic demands too great a price. My anger redirected itself at Helen. She'd been determined to put a spoke in mine and Finn's relationship wheel from the beginning … except she hadn't known me.

I frowned at him. 'Why would she make you promise something like that?'

'Helen's always been … *conflicted* about the sidhe,' he said, leaning forwards. 'It stems from a problem with her father. For some reason he visited. Most of them don't.'

Right. Witches were the ultimate single parents by necessity. Sidhe dads don't stick around much after the fertility rites, which isn't such a wonderful endorsement for the male of my species, but it's not like the covens haven't been encouraging the sidhe to keep coming back for centuries, so it wasn't all one-sided. But it sounded like Helen's sidhe father was an exception and, sadly, not a good one. I sighed. I so didn't want to start feeling sorry for her again.

'She had a good relationship with him,' Finn said, as if he'd heard my thoughts, 'but then when Helen was eight, her mother fostered a little girl: a relative of her father's.' He paused. 'A sidhe. The two girls were the same age and became great friends, even thought of each other as sisters most of the time, except whenever Helen's father visited after that, he was more concerned with the sidhe, and' – his mouth tightened with disgust – 'he virtually ignored Helen, his own daughter.'

I stared at him, remembering the family tree and the horrific story the Librarian and Sylvia had told me, and pieces of the puzzle dropped into the bigger picture. 'Helen's foster sister was Brigitta, wasn't she? The one whose mother' – Angel – 'was kidnapped and raped by the Old Donn? And you all insisted on keeping Brigitta in London when her mother was sent back to the Fair Lands because you all wanted to breed from her to break the curse, just like you do me,' I added accusingly. 'Brigitta's father was the fossegrim. Her daughter is a faeling called Ana' – I waved at the privacy screen between us and the front of the limo – 'and she's married to my solicitor's son.'

He stilled, and scrubbed a hand over his face. 'Yeah, that's her, but I didn't think you knew the story.'

I laughed: it wasn't happy. 'Seems like everyone I talk to just now has something new to tell me about the curse.'

'But then, you haven't really talked to anyone about it before, have you, Gen?' he said, a hint of reproach in his words. 'So it's only natural now you're asking, that you're going to hear about all the sordid stuff that no one usually mentions.'

He could say that again. I pursed my lips. 'So Helen doesn't like any sidhe because her father ignored her when she was a kid, and I'm the one who ends up as her whipping girl.'

'It wasn't just that. The sidhe took Helen's son for a changeling, remember. When that happened, her feelings understandably worsened. Then things got difficult when Tavish's list came out. When Nicky found out that I was going to be courting you, she got really excited and was desperate to meet you. Helen was ... well, she got very upset about it all. I think she was frightened that after the sidhe took her son, you would try and steal her other child from her.'

I had this vision of a miniature Helen, only with cute little horns and pigtails, jumping up and down on her tiny hooves, then being sent to her room. Poor Nicky. It didn't sound like having Helen as a mum was much fun. But then, maybe I was biased. Not to mention, 'very upset' sounded more like paranoia.

'I know it's irrational,' Finn said, again in tune with my own thoughts, 'but Helen can be very insecure at times. So in the end I promised not to tell you anything about Nicky unless you asked. I always thought you would, but you never did.'

It had never crossed my mind ... which in itself was kind of odd, now I thought about it, but then other people's family were hard to chat about when you were trying to keep your own family a secret. I stared blindly at the rest of the traffic inching along out of the blacked-out window. Finn had given his word, so he couldn't have broken it, but there were ways round that (now I thought about it, Ricou and Sylvia's little act in my kitchen had been exactly that). But having met Helen and been on the sharp end of her jealousy, and now knowing her background, I could see why Finn had kept his daughter a secret – well, not so much a secret, just not mentioned her up until now. My initial anger and shock was dampened by a mix of reluctant pity and sadness for Helen, and sympathy for both Finn and his daughter.

I looked back at Finn, and realised he was waiting for me to say something. Suddenly the situation felt awkward. Finding out my sort-of boyfriend had a secret kid wasn't exactly a conversation-starter once the details were out the way. *So, you've got a daughter.* Um, let's state the obvious, why don't we? In the end, I settled for curiosity. 'So, does Nicky live with you or Helen?'

He gave an odd laugh. 'Gods, no – Nicky is very independent. She's doing a Media and Arts degree. I wanted her to stay with her mother, or with the herd, but she insisted on moving out. She and three of her mates share this tiny two-bedroomed house. I'm lucky if she remembers to return my calls more than a couple of times a week.'

I blinked. 'Just how old is Nicky?'

'Nineteen.' He grinned proudly. 'Last December.'

'Shit, Finn! She's only six years younger than me.'

His grin faltered. 'Why's that a surprise?'

'I don't know,' I said, stumped. I'd never really considered his age. I'd always thought of him as not much older than me, and I'd so never imagined he'd have a grown-up kid. Of course, he only *looked* my age – not that youthful looks meant much, with most fae being long-lived to nearly immortal – but most of the time he didn't act much older either. 'It just is,' I finished lamely.

He rubbed behind his left horn. 'I keep forgetting you've been brought up by humans. I'm a hundred and ten, Gen, but I've only got the one kid. Some fae my age have a lot more.'

'Yeah … Ricou said he's got six pups.'

'Ricou's also got about thirty-odd halfling grandkids and

great-grandkids,' he said drily. 'If I remember right, his youngest is in her fifties and she's got two grandkids herself.'

Oh.

Finn leaned forward, resting his forearms on his thighs.
'Look,' he said earnestly, 'I know something happened yesterday, something to do with the curse that you can't tell me, but
I don't want this to put you off *us*. Nicky's old enough that she
wouldn't be part of our day-to-day life, so— Look, how about
I organise for you to meet her?' He smiled hopefully. 'I can
phone her now. She'd be over the moon.'

Chapter Thirty-Three

Now? *Meet his kid now?* What if she didn't like me? For all that Finn had said she was excited, she was Helen's daughter, after all. And I had enough on my emotional plate just now. 'I don't know, Finn. I sort of feel like I'm standing on quicksand and with everything that's going on, the ground keeps disappearing beneath me. I think I need a couple of days to get used to the idea.'

'Okay, you just let me know when,' he said, reaching out to give my arm a reassuring squeeze. Then he frowned. 'So, want to tell me what's been happening?'

I told him everything about Tavish, the Morrígan, my visit to Sucker Town (leaving out the gory details), the sad memories I kept picking up, Tavish having some sort of deal with Malik (mentioning Malik's name brought a scowl to his face) and, lastly, about Jack the raven's mysterious visit. 'So I think it's all to do with the curse, but I can't work out what, and how it all fits together? Any ideas?'

He tapped the limo's leather seat thoughtfully for a few moments, then clasped his hands together and gave me a frank look. 'Clíona's daughter and granddaughter, and Ana and the dreadful things that happened to them, they're everything to do with the curse, Gen. And to be honest, yes, one of us probably should have told you before, but it's not a story that any of us are proud of, especially after the dryads tried to do something similar to you. We need you to help us, and telling you about all the terrible things that we fae have done in the past to other sidhe isn't the best way to make you feel sympathetic, is it?'

He'd got that spot-on.

'As for the Morrígan and the memories she's shown you … well, they seem to be relevant to Ana and her time with the vamps. It could be that this Maxim – or the other suckers – are a threat to Ana again, and the Morrígan is using you to make sure she is safe.'

'Okay,' I said, frowning, 'but why would she do that?'

'Guilt's one reason. The Old Donn was the Morrígan's son—'

'He was her *son*?' Damn, she'd lost her own son! No wonder she'd told me, '*Losing a child is painful.*'

'Anyway,' Finn carried on, 'the way we heard it, Clíona imprisoned the Morrígan in retaliation for what he did to her daughter. It could be the Morrígan's now trying to make amends by helping Ana through you, possibly because you're the only one she can reach, or because of your connections with the suckers.' He scowled again. 'Or she could just have come to some arrangement with Clíona.'

'So she's got Tavish chained up just so she can talk to me?' I asked, incredulous.

He laughed, but there wasn't much mirth in the sound. 'Don't start feeling responsible, Gen. The Morrígan's been after Tavish for years. If he'd so much as breathed in her direction she'd have nabbed him. It was him, with the help of the fossegrim, who killed the Old Donn and his pals.'

Tavish had *killed* the Morrígan's son? Crap, he really was in trouble, and despite him being interfering and arrogant and over-protective, he was still my friend. He'd helped me when I needed it, and I wanted to do the same for him. If I could just work out how …

'But surely if the Old Donn was in the wrong, the Morrígan can't hold Tavish?' I asked, hearing the worry in my voice.

'Doesn't stop her being upset that her son is dead or

wanting revenge, does it?' Finn said. 'Look, Gen, Tavish is old and tricky enough to look after himself. Don't forget he virtually killed three wylde fae on his own, the fossegrim's not all there apparently. So Tavish will find a way out of whatever problem he's in with the Morrígan sooner or later. I wouldn't waste too much sleep over him, if I were you. And as for the rest, I haven't a clue what the suckers are up to, other than it probably has to do with the usual: blood. Or who this Jack the raven is or what he's after either.' He reached out and took my hands, his fingers were warm and gentle. 'I know you want to find another way to *crack* the curse, Gen, and that it's a big step to take having a child, but—' He stopped and rolled his shoulders like he was getting ready to deliver bad news. 'I know all this info is new to you, and you want to believe that it means there is another way to *crack* the curse, but I don't think anyone's trying to tell you anything different here. I think it's more that they're all using you for their own ends.'

Of course, my own magical gag clause was still in effect, so I still couldn't tell Finn about my visit to Disney Heaven. I pondered on how to convince him, and finally picked up the brown autopsy envelope and told him about all the missing faelings instead.

'They do have something to do with the curse,' I said firmly.

'I believe you, but the police are dealing with it,' he said, then frowned. 'They've been questioning the herd, for some strange reason' – he shook his head in bewilderment, while The Mother's gag clause stopped me telling him about the 'clue' I'd sent Hugh in my email – 'but whatever it's about, it's the coppers' job to deal with it, not yours.'

Which was what Malik had said to me. But The Mother had told *me* to stop whoever was killing the faelings, and when it came down to it, I wasn't going to piss off The Mother Goddess by ignoring her, and that meant no way was I going to leave

249

the police to deal with it. I was going to do all I could to help them – or rather, Hugh, since Witch-bitch Helen wouldn't have anything to do with me. I was still going to visit the ravens, and I'd do anything else it took. But it didn't look like Finn was buying into that, and it was pointless arguing with him about it, not when I couldn't use what The Mother had told me to convince him. I decided to change the subject to something I could tell him about.

Tavish's handprint spell on my stomach.

'Can you show me?' he asked, frowning in concern.

'Yep,' I said, and undid my jeans, leaned back along the bench seat and managed to reveal most of the black handprint without losing too much modesty.

Finn's green eyes filled with alarm and ... anger. He moved closer and gently pushed up my top to uncover the mass of purple bruising. 'You've been injured, Gen?'

'Ah.' I pulled a face. 'I ran into a bit of a problem last night.'

'A *bit* of a problem?'

'You should see the other guy,' I quipped, thinking that while Mad Max hadn't personally injured me, he was ultimately responsible. I was pretty sure that despite being a vamp he looked worse than me right now. 'Hey, and painkillers work wonders.'

'What other guy?' A muscle in Finn's jaw twitched in anger. 'It's that sucker, isn't it? Did *he* do this?'

So much for keeping things light. 'No.' I pulled my top down over my unzipped jeans. 'He helped' – mostly – 'and I'm fine.' I caught his hand. Time for a truth he didn't want to hear – and one I hated to admit. 'Finn, the vamps – Malik al-Khan, at any rate – they're probably always going to be a part of my life. Whatever happens. I can't change that, so it's pointless getting all worked up over it, okay?'

He gave me a long, considering look, then pulled his hand

from mine. 'I'm sorry, Gen, but I'm not sure it is okay. I need to know what "being part of your life" means. I'm not prepared to share, so you need to know that. And if that's not what you want, then there isn't any future for us, curse or no curse.'

My heart stalled, then thumped fast in sudden fear. I swallowed, my hands curling against my thighs. Did he mean he'd walk away? I suddenly realised how much I didn't want to lose him, both as a friend, or maybe more. 'I don't know what to tell you,' I said, the words catching in my throat.

'Are you sleeping with him?'

'No.' I paused, then a niggle of magic made me add, 'Not in the way you mean.'

'Gen—'

'Finn,' I said earnestly, 'I can't lie, you know that. I'm not even going to try and prevaricate, but if you want straight answers, you need to ask straight questions.' I smoothed my suddenly sweaty hands down my thighs before I remembered I was wearing my velvet jeans. 'I'm not having sexual intercourse with him, but yes, I did sleep in the same bed as him last night.' Then I took a deep breath and explained how I'd freely given Malik my blood, and what sort of power it gave him over me: that even without the 3V disadvantage, if he wanted something, all he needed to do was order me and I couldn't refuse.

Finn was staring out of the limo window by the time I finished. After a long silence where I glowered at the glossy wood of the limo's bar (a couple of whorls in particular resembled a Rorschach of a dead bat, and I didn't need a psychiatrist to tell me what that meant), he turned back to me and said flatly, 'What if he didn't order you? Would you want to have sexual intercourse with him then?'

Straight questions are so overrated. I made myself meet his eyes. 'I don't know, Finn. I'm attracted to him physically, but ...' *He confuses me, he's arrogant, I don't trust him, I haven't a clue*

what he wants, and part of me never wants to see him again,
but— 'It wouldn't be something I'd choose, if I were already in a relationship.'

He blinked, then a slow smile appeared on his face. 'Good.'

'Good?' I questioned.

'Yeah.' His smile widened, a hint of mischief glinting in his eyes. 'Now how about I check out your new spell?'

Relief bubbled up inside me, making me light-headed. I gave him a cautious smile back. 'I'm not sure that's a good idea.' It sounded more like playing with fire to me. 'What if the magic decides to take a hand in things?'

'Up to you, Gen,' he said, momentarily serious again. 'But I want to know what spell Tavish and the Morrígan have *tagged* you with, even if you don't.'

I did. 'Okay, then yes.'

'Here and now's as good a place as any.' He waved at the limo's plush interior. 'The car's private, and after your little mind trick on your solicitor, we're not likely to be disturbed.'

I checked my watch: there was still plenty of time before I was supposed to meet the ravens, and the limo *was* private. I narrowed my eyes at him in mock suspicion. 'Just what sort of checking out did you have in mind, Mr Panos?'

A wicked glint lit his eyes. 'I think the spell needs a thorough examination, don't you, Ms Taylor?'

Oh boy.

'If you'd like to take your jacket off, my lady, it'll make the ... examination easier.'

Air in the car suddenly seemed in short supply. I looked down at the long leather bench seat and back up at Finn. He raised his brows expectantly. I hesitated, then ... Damn, I was tired of being sensible, and this was Finn, I trusted him, so what harm could it do? I lost the jacket and my boots and swung my legs up.

Leaning back I propped myself on my elbows and batted

my eyelashes at him. 'How's this for easier?' I said in my best husky voice.

'Much better, but ...' He stripped out of his own jacket, and folded it inside out behind me. Holding his hands up, he waggled his fingers and flashed me a leering grin. 'Why don't you lie back, and let me work my sex-god magic on you, my lady?'

'Your lines don't get any better, do they?' I teased.

He gently pushed me back and gave me a quelling look. 'I think you'll find you'll appreciate my mouth a lot more' – he leaned down and nipped my earlobe hard enough to make me yelp – 'once I really get down to things, my lady.'

'Promises, promises,' I said, more breathlessly than I'd intended, then stifled the urge to turn my face into the jacket's silky lining as his scent of warm berries and woodsy male enveloped me.

He knelt next to the seat and stroked a finger over my hip. 'I like the velvet, Gen,' he murmured, then his grin was back. 'But the jeans are tight enough, that you'll need to lift up and wriggle a bit.' I stuck my tongue out at him and wriggled, sliding them all the way off, and the appreciative look on Finn's face made me thankful I'd somehow managed to go for black and sexy underwear when I'd dressed. He plucked at the hem of my lacy silk top with another suggestive look. 'Think this might get in the way, don't you?' One second later and I had it off and out the way, to another even more appreciative look. I lay back again, anticipation fizzing through my veins. He skimmed a teasing finger over the lace edge of my bra, and then down until he came to the spell. He traced its outline, and I gasped as he lowered and licked a lingering line across the handprint. A quiver fluttered in my stomach as he licked another hot line, trailing wet heat up my body to place butterfly kisses between my breasts. He raised his eyes to look up at me, his breath a warm weight along my skin.

'Tell me what you're feeling, Gen,' he murmured.

Feeling? I was feeling ...? I frowned. Finn was getting all sex god with me, and yeah, he was hot, and yeah, I sort of wanted him – but there was something missing. Lying here half-naked, cocooned from the rest of the world, with the soft leather seat and the low purr of the luxury car rumbling beneath me ... and Finn's mouth on my flesh ... I should be a shuddering mess of lust and hormones.

I wasn't.

'Hmm. Maybe not quite as turned on as I could be?' I said ruefully.

'I thought so,' he murmured. 'Let's try this.' He clasped my face and gently pressed his mouth to mine. As he kissed me his lips were everything I wanted: firm and warm and with a hint of demand, and when I slipped my tongue into his heated mouth, he tasted like sweet, ripe berries. His fingers slid under my hair to rest at my nape as he took the kiss deeper ... and we kissed, and kissed, and the feel of his lips on mine, our tongues exploring each other's mouths was enjoyable, and satisfying, and ... not at all heart-stopping, not like the quick, hard, glorious kiss he'd given me before.

He pulled away. 'Not quite the same as it's been in the past, is it?' he said with a wry look.

'No.' I pursed my lips. 'I feel relaxed, and satisfied with just a kiss, almost as if we've already had sex ... and now we're enjoying the peaceful aftermath; but not quite.' I slipped a button on his shirt, then pressed my hand over his heart, feeling its steady, unexcited thud beneath my palm, and saw his horns were still almost hidden by his hair. Definitely a sign he wasn't feeling the sex-god vibes. 'That's how you feel too, isn't it?'

'Yeah.' He cast a pensive look at the spell, then met my eyes. His were now dark and serious. 'I think it's some sort of Chastity spell.'

'Chastity—? Fuck, that's ...' Speechless, I glared down at the handprint branded on my stomach. I wasn't some sort of medi-aeval chattel, and I sure as hell wasn't going to have anyone else decide my love-life for me, whether it was the Morrígan, Tavish, the magic or whoever, no matter what their reasons were. 'Can you get rid of it?'

'I can try, but it might hurt. Will you trust me, Gen?'

'Yes,' I said, not hesitating.

'Thank you.' He gave me a brief smile, then emerald chips lit in his eyes. He fitted his hand over the spell and I gasped as a sharp pulse of magic hooked deep in my belly. It didn't hurt. It felt good, and I wanted more of it. The inside of the car sparked with green fireflies of magic – but as they dissipated, so did the good feeling.

'Okay?' he asked, a line creasing his brows.

'Oh yeah.' I gave him a breathless smile. 'You can do that again whenever you want.'

His expression turned dark and knowing. He shifted his hand and a remnant of the good feeling echoed inside me. Another sharper pulse of magic hit my core, and I moaned as desire coiled tight inside me then flashed lightning-quick through my body. Green stars bloomed inside the car, and as they faded, the feeling faded with it. I sighed, part disappointment, part need.

'Third time's the charm, Gen,' he murmured.

He took a deep breath, his chest expanding, and pressed his hand hard into my stomach and the spell. He thrust a larger, hotter ball of magic into me, and I screamed at the promise of ecstasy, my spine arching, my back lifting from the seat. Liquid warmth filled my body as green light blinded my vision. I collapsed back, panting, and reached out to fist my hand in the soft cotton of his shirt, my pulse jumping in my throat, wanting him—

—scorching fire ripped through my belly—

—and as I screamed again, this time in excruciating pain,

I heard a deeper, agonised yell echo mine. I convulsed into a ball, desperate to make the pain stop. Hands grabbed my shoulders, burning like silver against my skin—

And I disappeared in a blaze of white-hot flames.

Chapter Thirty-Four

'She'll come round in a minute.' Ricou's familiar voice said.

A breeze of chill air shivered over my skin. The pain seemed to have gone, but just in case, I pulled my jacket closer and stayed curled up on the grass … *Why was I lying on grass?* Confused, I slitted my eyes open.

Finn sat on a low stone wall nearby, his tanned face ashen, hugging himself like he was cold, or hurt. Johnny Depp a.k.a. Ricou crouched halfway between us, and behind him I could see Sylvia. She stood with her eyes closed, a focused expression on her face and her arms stretched wide. Her pink cycle helmet was badly dented and sitting askew on her head. The grey stone outer wall of the Tower of London rose up behind her.

'What happened?' I said, surprised my voice didn't croak.

Ricou looked over his black glasses. 'A fertility fae trying to remove a Chastity spell with a bit of the old slippy slippy, that's what happened. Are the pair of you *insane*? You could've killed each other. Luckily it knocked you both out before you really got down and wet.'

That didn't sound good, but I was still trying to work out how I'd got here from the limo.

'Also luckily,' Ricou said, 'Blossom's got more curiosity than a whole forest of silver birch, otherwise we wouldn't have been following you, and then where would you be?'

I sat up, still bemused. We were on the grassy moat bit

257

outside the Tower. There were tourists everywhere; four lads were rearranging backpacks not five feet away, a smartly dressed Japanese family were pointing cameras at each other, and a group of school kids were gathered around a couple of teachers, the kids at the back patently ignoring them ... just as everyone appeared to be ignoring us, which was a good thing, seeing as all I had on was my leather jacket over my underwear. I *looked* and saw a ten-foot-high wall of slightly creased cling film encircling us, hiding us all from view.

'Sylvia's cast an Unseen spell.' Finn's voice *did* croak. He pointed a shaky hand at me. 'Your clothes are there.'

'Thanks.' I grabbed my velvet jeans and started pulling them on, looking from him to Ricou for an explanation. 'How did we end up here?'

'Well, as I said, luv,' Ricou said, 'Blossom here thought we should follow you, so we did. Once the fancy car got here, it stopped right over there.' He pointed to a private entrance. 'The chauffeur rolled down his window and stared out down at the river while the witch just nattered away on her phone. Me and Blossom were waiting for you two to surface, then all the magic started kicking off inside the car – like Fireworks Night, it was – Blossom thought we should check on you.' He shrugged. 'Then it all quietened down, so we didn't. After ten minutes, the chauffeur chap, he gunned the engine, and yonder gate opened. Then Blossom thought she saw a veil lift and clicked the gate wasn't opening into the Tower, but some-where in *Between*. So we set up a rescue mission.' He grinned and tipped his trilby. 'All part of the service, luv.'

'They think she was trying to kidnap you,' Finn said, his voice still hoarse.

'Kidnap me?' I said, taken aback. 'Why the hell would my *lawyer* want to do that?'

'Dunno, luv,' Ricou said cheerfully. 'She's a witch; they're always a bit odd.'

'Did you see anything?' I frowned at Finn.

He shook his head. 'Sorry, I was out of it too.'

'I know I'm right, Genny,' Sylvia's voice was soft, as if she was far away. 'I saw one of the ravens fly through the gate and vanish with a pop.'

'There's been no *Between* in the Tower for the last forty-odd years, not since MacCúailnge, the Old Donn, was killed,' Ricou said, *sotto voce*, and jerked his head towards Sylvia. 'She says you were talking about him yesterday, so it probably jogged her mind ... she does have a bit of an imagination at times.'

'I heard that!' Sylvia bristled. 'And I know what I saw.'

I checked my watch. I was supposed to be seeing the Raven Master now. Maybe Victoria Harrier would turn round and come back when she discovered I was missing. Trouble was, after my little mind-order, Victoria Harrier would probably sit there for ages, waiting for me to get out of the car – or until someone insisted she check.

'How long has the car been gone?' I asked, shooting a frustrated look at the closed gate.

'Five, ten minutes at the most,' Ricou said.

Which probably wasn't enough time for anyone to have discovered that I wasn't in the car. But as my mind started catching up with what they were saying, I decided maybe I should figure out if Victoria Harrier really had been trying to kidnap me before she did discover I was missing. She was Malik's layer, but he hadn't picked her, nor had Sanguine Lifestyles, she'd chosen to represent me herself because of the curse and—

'My lawyer said she was working for the Lady Meriel,' I said, shooting Ricou a questioning look.

He rocked back on his heels. 'Nah, she's having you on. The Lady wouldn't work with a witch. She thinks they're incompetent. Not only that: if she wanted to snatch you, then I'd be the one doing it.'

'Which isn't exactly a resounding vote of confidence in you,' I pointed out.

'He's right, Gen,' Finn said tiredly. 'None of the water fae would get a witch to do anything for them.'

'But, Ana, her daughter-in-law, she's a water faeling,' I said, still doubtful.

Ricou gave his high clicking laugh. 'Ana hates all of London's fae. She'd have no more to do with any of us than those religious nuts, the Soulers. Blossom told you what the Old Donn did to her grandmother, didn't she? Well, Ana's mother would've loved to've blasted us all to the bottom of the sea if she could. She held everyone to blame. Ana's just the same. She'd be delighted to stick a spear in our guts just for a bit of fun.'

'Exactly,' Sylvia huffed. 'I bet she's resurrected the Tower's *Between* just to spit on the Old Donn's remains.'

'But if she's faeling that's not possible, is it?' I asked. 'She wouldn't have enough power.'

'Gosh, Genny!' Sylvia pulled a 'don't you know anything?' look. Evidently I didn't. 'It's not just about power, but how much the magic likes you. And she's got royal blood.' She gave an exaggerated pout. 'Anyway, I told you what I saw, but see if I care if you don't believe me. After all I've just saved you twice in two days, so what do I know?'

'Sorry, Sylvia,' I said, 'I really am grateful, but after what Bandana – sorry, Algernon – tried to do, you can't blame me for being a bit wary.'

'Mother ordered them all back into their trees after yesterday,' she sniffed, and stuck her chin in the air, only slightly mollified.

Relief ran through me: they definitely wouldn't be lurking around me any more. 'So, let's say Victoria Harrier is up to something, and that it doesn't involve the fae, or at least no fae other than her daughter-in-law.' I stripped off my jacket and snagged my top. 'Anybody got any ideas—'

Finn doubled over, groaning in pain.

I leapt up to go to him, but Ricou grabbed me round the waist, stopping me. 'Might be better if you leave him be, luv.'

'But he's hurt,' I said.

'Well, it's his own bloomin' fault,' Ricou said, without much sympathy. 'He should've kept his horns under wraps.'

'I was trying to break the Chastity spell,' Finn said straightening up slowly, like he was still hurting.

Ricou gave his high clicking laugh. 'With a bit of slippy slippy? Pull the other one, mate.'

'Sex is how you break the spell,' Finn muttered.

'Yeah, but only if you're the one keyed to the spell,' Ricou corrected him.

'I'm sorry, Gen.' Finn grimaced. 'Since Tavish *tagged* you with the spell, I thought that with the curse, and because I was on his list, it would be okay.'

'Obviously not, mate,' Ricou said in a reproving tone.

I gaped at them both, stunned, then anger at Tavish and the Morrígan took over. I pulled away from Ricou, yanked my top back on and stuck my hands on my hips. 'So, what you're saying is this: the only way I can lose the spell is to have sex, and with someone specific, and the only person who knows who that is – well, that would be either Tavish or the Morrígan, depending on whose fucking stupid idea it was.'

'That's about right, luv,' Ricou said. ''Course, if whoever it is dies, then the spell'll disappear on its own.'

I ground my teeth. If I found out who was keyed to the Chastity spell, then their dying was going to be a serious option. And if it was Tavish's idea and not the Morrígan's ... his precious computers were toast.

Ricou tapped my shoulder. 'Mind if I have a butcher's?' He

looked over his dark glasses and winked at me. 'Professional interest, of course.'

'What?' I said still furious.

'The spell. I want to look at it.'

'Sure, why not,' I snapped and yanked my top up. Finn groaned and closed his eyes.

'Don't mind him,' Ricou said as he bent and peered at my stomach. 'It's the after-effects of the spell; a nasty reminder to keep his … *hands* to himself whenever he looks at you. It'll wear off in a while.'

I frowned sceptically at Finn, who was sitting still with his eyes closed. 'I feel fine.'

'He's the one who tried getting happy with it.' Ricou licked his finger and touched it to the handprint, making me flinch. He stuck his finger in his mouth, then nodded. 'Thought so. Cinnamon's been added to the spell. I'd have picked up on it this morning if it hadn't been for Blossom's maple syrup.'

'Enlighten me,' I said flatly.

'You add cinnamon oil to Chastity spells to stop any baby buns cooking in your oven.' He eyed the handprint narrowly. 'It makes you temporarily barren.'

'Hell's thorns,' Finn muttered, his shock matching my own.

A rustling noise like a high wind through the trees whistled around us and Sylvia's eyes snapped open. 'Genny,' she said urgently, 'the police are on their way. I think it's because of you. I'm going to drop the Unseen spell.'

I jerked round to find three of the large high-top police vans the trolls used driving down the road, sirens off, but their blue lights flashing, drawing the attention of the crowd. The vans stopped, the back doors opened and Detective Sergeant Hugh Munro of the Metropolitan Police's Magic and Murder squad jumped nimbly out of the first. Behind him were two female police constables, both witches. Eight more uniformed police constables – all trolls – jumped out of the second and third vans and all of them strode towards us.

The hair at the nape of my neck prickled with prescience – not that I have any precognition skills, but I watch the movies occasionally. This looked too much like where the police corner the bad guys and catch them. I stifled the urge to run. We weren't the bad guys.

'Genny.' Hugh towered over me, his ruddy face creased into worried fissures. 'I'm sorry, but I'd like you to come with us, please.'

'Why?' I said, suddenly wary. 'I'm not under arrest again, am I?'

'No, but I need you to come with us.' He gestured to the van. 'Now, please.'

Chapter Thirty-Five

I sat in the back of the police van, gripping onto the edges of the hard seat, the lap-style seatbelt digging uncomfortably into my bruised and be-spelled stomach. The painkillers were wearing off, as was the shock over the Chastity spell. I'd find a way to get rid of it, but as I really didn't want any buns in my oven either, I shoved it to the bottom of my to-do list.

Hugh was sitting stoically across from me, despite the anxious red dust puffing from his head ridge and settling on his black hair and massive shoulders.

'So what's up, Hugh?' I asked.

He didn't answer, but held up one large finger to silence me: the uniformed witch next to him was casting some sort of spell. I nodded and settled back in the seat. The van smelled of sage, urine and rotten meat, a distinctly unpleasant combination. I wrinkled my nose and gazed out of the window, wishing I could open it.

After a look at Finn, and a quick, lurid explanation from Ricou, Hugh had split us up. I ended up in the first van with Hugh and the WPC. Finn was in the second van, and somehow a charming Ricou and a blushing Sylvia had ended up in the third. My guess was that Hugh was in a hurry and didn't want the hassle of leaving them behind. We'd all made quite the spectacle as it was, the event immortalised for avid speculation on the news by the hundreds of mobile phones held up and pointed our way until we'd all disappeared inside the vans and the protection of the one-way glass.

More tourists cast curious looks our way as we drove past Tower Hill, where they used to carry out public executions – a cheerful thought while riding in the back of a police van. Of course, nowadays executions are carried out in the remote wilds of Dartmoor, with random members of the public invited to attend. As we passed by the War Memorial, a large raven perched on one corner caught my eye. Was it Jack? And if it was, was Jack the same raven Sylvia had seen flying through the Tower entrance; the one she'd thought had flown into *Between*? Hard to know really, as one raven looks pretty much like another from thirty feet away.

Then there was the other mystery: if the gate *had* opened into *Between*, had Victoria Harrier really been trying to kidnap me? And if she had, then why? And there was Sylvia's other strange comment, about Ana spitting on the Old Donn's remains. Why would Sylvia say that when fae don't have remains? We *fade*, literally: our bodies disappear when we die. Was Sylvia just being metaphorical, or was the Old Donn not as dead as everyone kept telling me? And what did it all have to do with the curse?

Magic tingled over my skin as the WPC finished up whatever spell she was casting. I turned round and studied her: black hair in a neat bun, attractive face and full, plump lips that looked like they'd just been kissed, in spite of the determined way she kept them pressed together. After a moment I recognised her: Constable Martin, the WPC who'd been guarding the crime scene yesterday, at Dead Man's Hole, the disused mortuary under Tower Bridge, where the dead raven faeling had been found.

She had a small glass globe about the size of a tangerine cradled in both hands. It swirled pink, shot through with fainter threads of red. I *looked*, checking out the globe's magic, but the colours didn't change, so whatever spell was inside, it was keyed for anyone to use, an advantage for trolls with their lack of magical abilities. As we all watched, the colour drained out of the globe, leaving it full of misty grey clouds. 'Okay, Sarge.' Constable Martin tucked the globe away. 'We're clear.' She caught my eye and gave me a suggestion of a smile. 'Anti-Surveillance Ball. It monitors for Remote Listening spells. You just can't trust the press nowadays.'

'Neat,' I said, impressed, then looked at Hugh. 'So, what's with the dramatic police pick-up then?'

'We had an anonymous tip, that you were in danger,' Hugh said quietly.

I narrowed my eyes. 'What sort of danger was I supposed to be in?'

'They weren't specific,' Hugh said.

'Who are *they*?'

'The tip was *anonymous*, Genny.'

'C'mon, Hugh, I'm not stupid! Anonymous tips don't have you turning out half the force' – okay, a bit of an exaggeration, but *three* vans? – 'otherwise you'd be spending all your time chasing your own tails.'

'Our source *was* anonymous,' Hugh rebuked me quietly; 'we're not even sure if it's male or female. But whoever it is, is a trusted informant in another case – the one involving the dead faeling yesterday. But, before we get into that, Genny, I want to know what you were doing at the Tower.'

'Going to visit the Raven Master and the ravens, to see what I could find out about the dead faeling,' I said, giving him an odd look. 'Like who she was, for a start.'

Hugh frowned, deep fissures creasing his forehead. 'We already know who she was: Sally Redman.' He fished his notebook out and flipped a couple of pages. 'She was nineteen last August, her mother is the landlady of the Rose and Punchbowl, a pub in Whitechapel. The father's name is Grog. He left the Tower back in 1981, took up residence at the pub, but disappeared a few years after Sally was born. The ravens at the Tower haven't seen or heard from Sally for at least three years, nor do they want to. She's been working in various clubs in Soho and they disapprove. All that information was in the report your solicitor *removed* from my desk.'

'It wasn't in the report I saw,' I said drily, thinking Hugh was being uncommonly free with his info in front of his WPC sidekick. I gave him my own news. 'Sylvia thinks my lawyer just tried to kidnap me, and Finn too.' I paused, considering, 'Although Finn wasn't supposed to be in the car with me, so he was possibly just in the wrong place at the wrong time.'

Hugh just nodded as if I'd confirmed something, but Constable Martin leaned forward, excitement animating her face. 'Are you saying *Victoria Harrier* tried to kidnap you?'

'According to the others, yes.'

'Check into it, will you, Constable?' Hugh said. 'See if there is any connection.'

'Yes, Sarge.' She dug out her phone and started tapping the screen.

I was beginning to feel like I was majorly out of the loop. 'Connection to what?' I asked.

Hugh's mouth flattened into a hard line. 'Another girl has been found dead, Genny. The circumstances are similar to yesterday. I'd appreciate it if you could take a look and tell me what you can.'

Damn. 'Another faeling?'

'We're there now,' he said, looking out through the van's windscreen, 'so you can see for yourself.'

The van braked, juddering to a halt and I looked past Hugh's bulk to see where we were. Back at Dead Man's Hole.

Chapter Thirty-Six

Dead Man's Hole, the old disused mortuary under Tower Bridge, was seeing way more use than anyone wanted. The place wasn't much changed from my last visit. The river slapped against the dock outside, and cast watery reflections over the Victorian glazed-brick interior. Half a dozen uniforms – all witches – stood around the walls of the large cave-like room, and in between them were fat white candles that flickered and cast them into shadow. Spirals of thick smoke rose up to collect under the dome of the curved ceiling. My nostrils flared; underneath the heavy, waxy candle smell and the astringent scent of sage, I caught that same sweet, thick and slightly rotten smell from my previous visit. Then I realised it wasn't just nudging my memory from before, but was also reminding me of the maple syrup on Sylvia's breakfast pancakes. Strange, but then I'd never liked the stuff. And with a mounting sense of déjà vu, I followed Hugh to the large white sand and salt circle *drawn* in the centre of the cave-like room.

In the centre of the circle was the new victim. Unlike Sally Redman, the dead raven faeling, this girl was lying spread-eagled on her back, and naked. She also looked younger, maybe fifteen or sixteen years old. I wanted to cover her up and give her back her dignity, but that wouldn't help find who'd done this to her. It wouldn't make them pay. I pressed my lips together and studied her. Inside the circle *drawn* by the police was another one, marked out in red chalk, and inside that was a red chalk pentagram. She'd been laid out with some precision on top of the pentagram, her head to one of the five points, her limbs spread out towards the other four. Around the inner pentagon formed by the crossing of the lines were more red chalkmarks, half-obscured by her body: a joined chain of five rings. My heart lurched with dismay as I made them out, and instinctively I touched Grace's pentacle at my throat.

I looked up at Hugh and murmured, 'The pentacle drawn underneath her matches mine.'

He nodded. 'I recognised the design, Genny. It could be a coincidence, but I doubt it. Someone wants you involved – or implicated.'

I swiped away a couple of tears. *Damn it,* I really needed to find out why I kept crying and sort it – soon. 'Is it possible someone's using the girls to try and *crack* the curse? Or that they want you to think that I am?'

'It appears sensible to think there's some connection, Genny,' he agreed, 'but it's not necessarily anything metaphysical.'

'Why?'

'The pentagram looks to be ritualistic,' Hugh rumbled, 'but Constable Martin assures me it isn't. The points don't face in any direction that could call power, and the design has enough confidence in its execution that she doesn't think it's sloppy work. We both feel that the pentagram is there to draw our attention to the curse and to you.'

'Well, if someone's trying to implicate me, then there's always your boss,' I muttered, looking around. 'Speaking of DI Crane, shouldn't she be here trying to remove me from her crime scene?'

'Detective Inspector Crane is ... no longer in charge of this case,' he rumbled, his voice almost too low for me to hear.

'Really?' I gave him a surprised look. 'What happened?'

'She's taking time off to deal with some personal problems.'

I wondered if the 'time off' was entirely her decision. But

why Witch-bitch Helen Crane wasn't here didn't matter; not having her breathing down my neck was good news for me. But even without my own evil witch nemesis around, the other witchy occupants of the cave-like mortuary were still watching me closely enough to send wary chills down my spine. Not to mention that while we'd been talking, Constable Martin with her neat bun and just-kissed lips had walked round to stand on the opposite side of the circle. With her was another, older witch. She was giving me the once-over with sharp hazel eyes, and was too flamboyantly dressed in flowing fortune-teller chic (the fringes of small silver coins on her skirt and shawl were full-moon bright with spells) to be police. And since her *presence* had been shouting 'power' at my inner radar from the moment she'd come in, I was betting she was from the Witches' Council.

Ignoring her, and the rest of the witchy crew, I turned to Hugh. 'So, do you want me to check this victim to see if she's *tagged* with any spells?'

'Please, Genny.'

I *looked*. It was almost an anticlimax to see the same two spells as before: the dirty-white silly-string spell which cocooned the girl's body, and underneath it, the faint out-of-focus waver of a Glamour spell.

'Looks like the same spells that were on Sally the raven faeling,' I said.

'That's what Constable Martin thought, but I wanted your opinion too.' Hugh laid a gentle hand on my shoulder. 'Do you think you can you remove the spells intact, Genny?'

I *looked* at the salt and sand circle. It was for containment, plain and simple, with no added extras.

'Yeah,' I said, 'so long as I can do things my way, and I don't have to worry about anyone mixing silver or anything else in the circle under the pretext of Health and Safety.'

'That won't be a problem,' Hugh said reassuringly. 'What do you need?'

'The main spell seems to be some sort of preservative/stasis effort. The raven faeling's injuries didn't appear until after I removed it yesterday; it was only then she started to bleed. So the first thing's a doctor.' The poor girl needed someone better than me to resuscitate her if she turned out to be not as dead as she looked.

Hugh indicated the flamboyant hazel-eyed witch. 'Witch Juliet Martin here is our official doctor on call. She has both the necessary medical and magical expertise.'

Witch Martin came around the circle and held out her hand to me. 'Please, call me Juliet.'

I hesitated a moment – most folk with magical ability don't do skin-to-skin contact, for fear of being inadvertently (or otherwise) *tagged* with a spell – then took her hand. Her shake was firm. 'Genny Taylor,' I said redundantly, since she obviously knew who I was. I looked enquiringly across the circle at Constable Martin.

'My daughter, Mary,' Juliet confirmed with a warm smile.

Nice to know we were keeping it all in the family.

I narrowed my eyes at Juliet. Time to test just how accommodating she was going to be. 'Can you cope if I put the spell in a plastic bucket?'

She gave me another warm smile. 'Indeed I can, Ms Taylor.' She sent one of the WPCs off to fetch one.

Now for the important part.

I took a deep breath, stepped into the circle and crouched near the girl's head. Her blue eyes stared sightlessly up, for a moment reminding me of Malik, wrapped in the rug under my bed, and I briefly wondered what I was going to do about him and his *orders*, then I dismissed him. Time enough to deal with the beautiful vampire when he woke up for the night; right now I needed to concentrate on the beautiful, blue-eyed blonde in front of me, who looked much too young to die. Of course, that could just be her Glamour spell; underneath that she was probably something else entirely. But like Sally, the dead raven faeling, I couldn't tell. However the Glamour spell had been *stirred*, it had some way of camouflaging her essence as well as her physical appearance.

The more I stared at her, the more she looked oddly familiar. I frowned, trying to place where I'd seen her—

'She's in the reality show filmed at Morgan Le Fay College,' Juliet said as she joined me in the circle. She put down her doctor's bag, then carefully tucked her flouncy skirt underneath her and crouched on the other side of the girl's body. 'Her name is Miranda Wheater. She's in the sixth form.'

I clicked where I'd seen Miranda before: on the front of the glossy magazine Sylvia had shown me before the Librarian had taken back the fae's curse-*cracking* books. The girl – or witch – had been in a jacuzzi, complete with a fancy cocktail and half a dozen older men, and the headline had shouted something about a curse, which was obviously why the fae had added the magazine to their collection.

I looked from Juliet to Hugh. 'I take it someone's checked on Miranda's whereabouts?'

'Miranda is thankfully alive and well and at the college,' Juliet assured me. 'This child is someone else. There has been a spate of this type of appearance-altering spell, where the wearer has chosen a figure in the public eye who hasn't given their consent to any doppelgänger spells. The Witches' Council has received a number of complaints about them. While it is not as important as finding out who is responsible for this poor girl's death, finding which witch has been *casting* the spells might provide us with some valuable information in both cases.'

'Which witch for which' spell made me think of Ricou and his Johnny Depp Glamour. I filled Hugh in, and suggested

Ricou might be able to help. The WPC returned with my plastic bucket, and Hugh sent her back out to fetch him.

'How do you intend to do this, Genny?' Juliet asked.

'Can you see what looks like thick silly-string all over her?' I asked, lifting a strand. She nodded, which was a small relief; not everyone saw the magic the same way. 'Then it's probably easier if you just watch.'

I touched the edge of the circle with my finger and activated it with my magic. It sprang easily up into a clear dome above us, luckily with no nasty surprises. The knot in my stomach eased slightly. I *focused* on the silly-string, then plunged my hands into the spell and *called* the magic.

Ten minutes later I wrestled the last of the silly-string off the girl and into the bucket. I wiped my hand over my forehead, then wished I hadn't as the slimy residue of the magic stuck to me like the slug-slime the goblins use in their hair gel.

I gave an involuntary shudder, and anxiously checked the girl. Thankfully, even with the removal of the Preservative/Stasis spell she hadn't developed any obvious injuries, or started bleeding from head wounds, or suddenly taken a last gasp at life as the dead raven faeling had. The knot in my stomach eased some more in relief.

Remembering Ricou's small spell tattoos on his inner arms, I slowly ran my fingers up the girl's smooth, pale skin, stifling another shudder at the lifeless feel of it. Nothing on the left. I leaned over and started on the right, hitting pay-dirt – or rather, *spell*-dirt – just above her inner elbow. I *focused*, and let a tiny trickle of power drip into the spell sparking under my forefinger. The Glamour peeled away from her like a banana shedding its skin.

The beautiful blue-eyed, blonde fifteen-year-old was gone, and in her place was a green-eyed, green-haired, green-skinned female of around forty with deep bracketed lines running from her small nose to her pinched mouth. Huge drooping breasts and a roll of excess flesh around her waist and hips made her look as if she'd lost a lot of weight quickly. For a moment I thought she was a *bean nighe*, one of the dark fae, but then I realised she couldn't be, because her body hadn't *faded* after death. I brushed the dead faeling's hair away from her ears to find they ended in a definite point. Not a *bean nighe* then.

'Oh,' Juliet gasped softly, as she placed her stethoscope over the female's heart, 'she's a leprechaun faeling, isn't she? I've never seen one before.'

I hadn't either, but I had once seen a full-blood leprechaun: Juliet was right. I sat back on my heels as she checked the leprechaun faeling over, hoping that whatever had killed her had been quick and painless, and wondering who she was.

'Her name's Aoife,' Ricou said, startling me.

I looked up to see him standing outside the circle. I hadn't noticed him arrive, but the rest of the WPCs had, and they weren't bothering to hide their stares. He was still in his Johnny Depp guise, but he'd taken his trilby off and was holding it against his chest, sadness etching his face.

'Her father is a full-blood leprechaun,' he continued, then turned to Hugh. 'He came over from Ireland in the sixties and hitched up with a girl from Dagenham. They split when Aoife was still a kid. Her mum's passed now, but her dad's back over there. This will cut him up.' He paused. 'Aoife means *beauty*. She was beautiful too, when she was younger ...' He crushed his hat.

'Is she anything to do with the Morrígan?' I asked.

'Her father's from *Rath Cruachán*.' Ricou frowned. 'That's in County Roscommon. Which is where the MacCúailnge, the Old Donn, hailed from, so she could be.'

Chapter Thirty-Seven

I leaned on the railing surrounding the mortuary dock and stared out over the Thames. The brisk wind blew my hair back and brought me the ozone scent of the river; rain was on the way. Ricou's information about Aoife's likely connection to the Morrígan had sent Hugh into detective sergeant mode and next thing I knew, we were all giving statements. I'd told Hugh everything about the Morrígan, the dreams, the Coffin Club and the vamps, and anything else I could think of (that The Mother's gag clause would let me) that could possibly help. Then he'd asked me to wait while he checked a few things out.

I'd spent my waiting time dredging the Internet via my phone for info about *Rath Cruachán*. Google hits on the name brought up the *Táin Bó Cúailnge* – the Cattle Raid of Cooley – apparently fought over the ownership of Donn Cúailnge, a stud bull, who had once been fae. And Donn Cúailnge was linked to the Morrígan romantically (although 'romance' and 'stud bull' didn't necessarily go together in my mind) and their romance had obviously borne fruit in the person of the Old Donn. Which meant the Old Donn was a horned wylde fae, and a prime candidate for The Mother's photofit of the villain of the piece. If it wasn't for everyone telling me he was dead, I'd have been pretty sure I'd found the faelings' killer. Now I was back to thinking the photofit was symbolic, which wasn't helping much in the whole killer identification stakes.

I turned at the sound of heavy footsteps to find Hugh

approaching, carrying two takeaway cups. 'So any chance you're going to let me in on your evidence?' I asked. Then I added, 'The deaths are to do with the fertility curse, and the latest one does sort of implicate—'

'If you will give me a chance, Genny.' He smiled, his pink granite teeth gleaming in his ruddy face, and handed me one of the cups: hot chocolate. 'From everyone's statements and our own investigations, it appears that whoever is killing the faelings has resurrected the *Between* that is attached to the Tower of London.'

'Which is where Victoria Harrier was trying to take me.' I wrapped my hands around the hot cup, sending mental thanks to Sylvia that Victoria Harrier's plans hadn't succeeded.

'Yes, Victoria Harrier does appear to be the lynchpin in all this,' Hugh said. 'She's on the Board of Directors of a TV production company – Adonis Films – which is making a series of historical documentaries at the Tower. That is how she's gained access, we think. There have also been rumours on the streets about "short-term work contracts", aimed particularly at faelings, which lead back to Adonis. Who of course deny all knowledge.'

'And that's how they're finding the girls,' I said.

'Yes,' Hugh agreed. 'Adonis is also the company that make the reality TV show at Morgan Le Fay College – where Victoria Harrier is one of the board of governors. The college appears to be where the Doppelgänger spells originate from.'

'Wow, so she's really smack in the middle of it all!'

Hugh nodded. 'Adonis Films and the college are both subsidiaries of the Merlin Foundation, which is the wizards' ruling body. Victoria Harrier is a director of the foundation, so we're looking into it as well.'

'Yeah, she mentioned the Merlin Foundation; she's a big fan.' I took a sip of chocolate. 'Except— Somehow I don't see Victoria Harrier as a criminal mastermind. I mean she's obviously intelligent enough, but why faelings? And what's it got to do with the curse?' A possibility hit me. 'Unless it's all down to the vamp who's got his fangs in the Harrier family?'

He drank his tea, a frown creasing his ruddy face. 'The vamp angle is one we'll consider along with everything else, Genny, but I don't want to draw any conclusions yet, not until we've questioned Victoria Harrier.'

'Right,' I said, shivering as a chill wind gusted over the river. 'But then even if it is a vamp, Victoria Harrier can't be working on her own, can she? I mean, there're at least fifteen faelings missing, and if the vamp has got his fangs into her, then the rest of the Harrier family are possible victims too. Are you checking them out?'

'Of course.' Hugh gave me a look that plainly said I was trying to teach a troll how to break rocks here. 'Ana, the daughter-in-law, is a bit of a recluse. She spends most of her time in the fossegrim's *Between* in Trafalgar Square. It makes it difficult to pin her down. So it's unclear yet whether she is involved, or by how much. Her husband has been in America for the last six months with his work, and Dr Craig—'

'Dr Craig! What's he got to do with it?'

'—and Dr Craig, who is Victoria Harrier's other son, has been estranged from his whole family for the last ten years,' Hugh carried on, ignoring my interruption. 'Apparently he didn't approve of his brother marrying a faeling. And until we're able to talk to them all, we can't be certain of anything.'

My astonishment at Dr Craig's parentage turned to puzzle-ment. 'But that means Dr Craig is a wizard. I knew he could sense a bit of magic, but it's odd I never picked up on it when I worked with him at HOPE. And odd that he never actually mentioned it, don't you think?'

'People will always surprise us, Genny, even when we think we know them well. Like DI Helen Crane. After your email yesterday, I had the crime scene photos of the circle that she *drew* around Sally Redman double-checked. You were right; there was something wrong with the yew.'

I suppressed an *I knew it!* grin along with the urge to pump my arm in the air in vindication. *Helen the Witch-bitch* was *a crooked cop.* It wasn't just my biased imagination. Now I could legitimately hate her as 'my evil witch nemesis' without feeling guilty. 'She laid the spell the wrong way round, didn't she?'

'Yes,' Hugh answered, 'the faeling's death was suspicious, so the yew was supposed to temporarily hold the victim's spirit, in the hope that a necromancer would be able to talk to her, but instead the yew was *laid* to speed the victim's spirit on its way. Which is what the—'

'—dwarves do with their ritual ashes,' I finished. 'I thought the pattern looked familiar, but it didn't click with me what it meant until later.'

Of course, the fact I'd been beamed up to Disney Heaven was another big hint, especially after I'd uncovered Tavish's spell bracelet and found the London bus charm minus its wheels. After that, I realised the only way Angel/The Mother had been able to pull me out of London was in spirit form, a.k.a. dead. Bandana the dryad had been right: I had started to *fade* – not that I was going to say thank you. He still didn't deserve it, and The Mother wouldn't have let me truly die anyway.

And Helen Crane, the Witch-bitch, deserved everything she got too. She had to know who killed the faelings, because reversing the Soul-holding spell like that meant she had to be covering up for the killer. So maybe all that animosity between her and Victoria Harrier had been an act, and they were really in league together? I looked up at Hugh. 'So does this mean Helen Crane is helping you with your enquires?' I asked, hiding my glee under mild interest. 'And spilling lots of juicy clues now she's been caught out?' Okay, so not hiding it that well.

Hugh's expression turned grim. 'Not as yet.'

In other words, he wasn't going to tell me, even if she was. Figured.

'Genny,' Hugh said, his tone tentative, 'there's something else I need to ask of you.'

'Ah, this is where you tell me why you're letting me in on all your secret police stuff, isn't it?' I smiled encouragingly. 'Fire away. I'm all ears.'

'I want to follow up on Victoria Harrier,' he said, 'and I think the quickest way to find out what she's up to, and to locate the missing faelings, is to let her carry out her plans to kidnap you.'

Um ... did I really want to be the sacrificial victim in all this? Still, it was to find the faelings, and this was Hugh asking; I trusted him absolutely.

'It won't be you making the contact, though, Genny,' he carried on, to my surprise. 'It will be an undercover police officer wearing a Doppelgänger spell to look like you. Witch Martin thinks she can replicate the ones the dead faelings used, so that the officer doesn't raise any alarm bells. Then as soon as our undercover operative is snatched, I'll have enough evidence for the warrants we need. All the spell needs is a small blood donation.'

I tapped my cup, thinking about his plan; something about it set my skin itching.

'Of course,' Hugh added, 'if you're worried about the Doppelgänger spell, once the police operation is over, then you can remove the spell from the WPC yourself.'

'It's not the spell.' I frowned. 'I'm worried about someone else ending up abducted instead of me. What happens if the undercover officer gets taken and you can't persuade Victoria Harrier to tell you where she is, or she does a disappearing act? The officer could end up in a lot of danger. Or dead.'

'It's Constable Martin, Witch Martin's daughter, who will be taking your place, Genny. She's got a rather unique ability.

She has a link with her mother; they can speak to each other in their minds, no matter where they are. Once Constable Martin is taken, she should be able to relay the information needed for us to mount a rescue operation for her and the faelings.'

It sounded like a practical solution, albeit still a dangerous one for Constable Martin. Thinking of that, another query popped into my head. 'Do you know how Sally the corvid faeling and Aoife actually died?'

Hugh handed me his cup and pulled out his notebook. 'Cause of death for Sally Redman initially looks like cardiac arrest, but she was young and her heart was healthy. The toxicology report's not back yet, so it's always possible they were given something like digitalis. But if you discount the head wound – which was nasty, but wasn't a death blow – neither of them had any obvious injuries. For Aoife's cause of death, we'll need to wait until the autopsy has been done.'

'So, no fang marks, or any way to know what's killing them?'

'No, not yet.'

'There's something else bugging me,' I said, remembering The Mother's photofit of the horned god. 'The *Between* in the Tower belonged to the Old Donn, who's supposed to be dead. But Sylvia mentioned something about his remains. Could you find out if he's really dead?'

'Why do you want to know?'

'Can't say,' I gasped as The Mother's gag clause strangled me.

Hugh took out one of his large troll pens, made a note, then snapped his notebook closed. 'I'll check into it and—'

'Sergeant Munro!' A shout from the direction of the police vans interrupted him.

He waved an acknowledgement, then said, 'I'll be back in a few minutes.'

I dropped the cups into a rubbish bag and stared out at the

wind-rippled Thames, that uneasy feeling still pricking at me. Hugh's doppelgänger plan was good, but before he and his boys in blue – although they'd be mostly witches, of course, so he and his *girls* in blue – could rush in, apprehend the baddies and hopefully rescue all the faelings, he needed evidence and warrants. With London's fae as back-up I could put Hugh's plan into action myself without the hassle and delay of all the judicial red tape.

But as I gave it serious thought, I came up with a fatal flaw: *Between* is out of this world, a place created by will and magic. And even knowing there *was* a patch of *Between*, and knowing where its entrance was, didn't mean you could just waltz right on in, not unless its creator wanted you to. Hell, even if you had the magical key, and you got it to work, you'd only end up some place else (I know, I tried it at Tavish's once, which is how I discovered what a swamp-dragon's cave smells like; *never* again!). And *cracking* the entrance from the outside was a non-starter. But *cracking* the entrance open from the inside would be … well, *difficult*, but definitely doable in the right circumstances.

So I needed to be on the inside.

But not as a kidnapped victim. Another plan started to form in my mind …

Hugh rejoined me. 'DI Crane is now officially missing,' he announced with a troubled expression.

'She's disappeared?' I said, stunned, then asked, 'Do you mean she's done a runner, or that you think someone's *made* her disappear?'

'We're still working on that, Genny,' he said.

Crap. I might not like the witch – okay, I was pretty sure I *hated* her – but I didn't want her disappeared involuntarily. I had a sudden image of Helen Crane being the next one to be pulled out of the Thames, and what that would mean to Finn and their daughter. 'Has anyone told Finn?' I started to head towards the vans—

Hugh placed a restraining hand on my shoulder. 'Constable Martin is with him just now, Genny. She's taking a statement, to see whether he knows anything that can help. Let her do her job, and then you can speak to him.' He held out an opened note in a sealed plastic evidence bag. 'This was found at DI Crane's home, Genny. It's addressed to a G.N. Zakharinova, care of Spellcrackers.com. Finn doesn't know who that is; what about you?'

The hair rose on the back of my neck. How the hell did Helen know my real name, when only the vamps knew it? Helen was a witch; they all avoided vamps like the plague, and the vamps reciprocated in kind. Plus Helen in particular had a phobia about them. Not to mention, why the hell was she sending *me* notes? She had to be desperate or devious.

After a few moments I held out my hand. 'It's *me*,' I said. 'I'm G. N. Zakharinova. It's my birth name.'

Hugh nodded and handed me the letter. 'You'd better read it, Genny. Then we'll talk.'

I read it through the evidence bag.

To G. N. Zakharinova,

Your uncle Maxim contacted me regarding his Irish wolfhound. He was concerned about the safety of the dog's offspring. Unfortunately this is no longer something I can guarantee. As I will not be able to speak to him through the usual channels, please ensure you contact him <u>immediately</u> with this information.

Helen Crane

Damn. So Helen had been guaranteeing – or rather, covering up for – 'the dog's offspring'. And now she couldn't, because she'd been found out, and had disappeared (willingly or not). But whether the note was a clue for the police, a cry for help or a warning she'd thought I'd take to Mad Max, I didn't know. One thing I did know—

We had a suspect for the mastermind behind the faeling's deaths. Mad Max's son, whoever he was.

Chapter Thirty-Eight

Hugh's 'talk' about the note was in fact another round of statement-taking in one of the police vans, complete with a laptop-wielding WPC. We went over the memories the Morrígan had given me again, especially the one I'd had of the little blond-haired boy sliding down the slide in the playpark.

'I'm pretty sure he's Maxim's son,' I said, 'and the "offspring" Helen Crane is talking about. But I don't know who the boy is, or even how old he is. I meant to look up when kiddies' slides were invented to see if that would give me a clue.'

'I think I can help with that.' The WPC looked up from her laptop. 'From your description, Genny, my best guess is that the boy is in his mid-twenties to early thirties now.' She smiled at me. 'The slide wasn't a clue – they've been around a lot longer – but the description of the lights was. I'm pretty sure they were halogens, which narrows it down.'

'Mid-twenties to . . .?' I frowned. 'I bet Mad Max would want to keep his son near him, if he got him back.' I flipped through the faces I knew at the Coffin Club and hit on one immediately. 'Gareth Wilson,' I exclaimed, 'the human manager at the club – he's about the right age, and he's definitely a natural blond like Maxim.'

'Check the records, Constable,' Hugh said, 'but I don't want any contact with the club until I say so. I know it's still five hours until sunset, but Maxim appears to be able to move around during the day in his dog shape.' Hugh contemplated his large troll pen as if it had all the answers, then lifted serious grey eyes to me. 'Maxim is unlikely to be very cooperative if it's his son who is killing the faelings, Genny. I think it would be better if we approach the Oligarch privately first, to avoid any possibility of tipping Maxim and his son off and having both of them disappear on us.' He gave me a quizzical look. 'I know we haven't really discussed your association with Malik al-Khan' – we definitely hadn't, not when it was an association Hugh worried over like a mother hen – 'but do you have a way to contact him without me having to go through the normal channels?'

'I've got something even better,' I said, pulling a face as I told him about Malik being trapped in my bedroom. And Hugh was right. The logical way to get Mad Max to talk was to ask Malik as Oligarch to make Mad Max 'cooperate'. But Malik's own cooperation wasn't necessarily a done deal.

For one, Mad Max didn't owe Malik his Oath, and two: if there were no external humans involved, the vamps policed themselves. And if Mad Max (a vamp) and Helen (a witch) had something going on between them, it went against the centuries' old détente between the two species. And then there was the third fact, that Malik had given his protection to London's fae and faelings. Even if Mad Max's son was a human, if Mad Max was part of what was going on, that would be a challenge to Malik's own power-base as Head Fang. So in order to preempt any problems with either the Witches' Council or the rest of the vamp families, Malik could justifiably rescind Mad Max's Gift (a.k.a. rip his head off and burn him to ashes) and declare that an end to it.

Then there was the fact that Malik hadn't exactly been forthcoming during our post-Coffin Club bedtime chat and had made it quite clear that he didn't want me involved, so *asking* him to help wasn't going to work. But finding some way of *forcing* him should ... not only that, the situation gave me an idea of how to sort out my own problems with the beautiful, dictatorial vamp.

'I think I can persuade Malik to cooperate,' I told Hugh, 'but I'll need your help.' Then I explained to him what I wanted, and about the flaw in his doppelgänger scheme, and how it could be fixed. And after a lot of concerned dust-puffing on Hugh's part, we came up with a master plan: one that ensured Malik, as Oligarch, would assist the police; and meant that Hugh's doppelgänger idea would work with or without the judicial red-tape; and as a bonus, also clubbed Malik's 'I Vampire, you Blood-Pet' declaration on his arrogant buzz-cut head.

Then I let Juliet Martin take a syringe full of my blood as I chatted to Ricou, so she and Ricou could *stir* the Doppelgänger spell, and in place of the payment she offered, I asked her to write me a couple of letters on behalf of the Witches' Council. Juliet finished up, and they both made a dash for the disused mortuary just as the rainstorm came.

I sat in the van mentally going over the plans, looking for any last-minute hitches in them, as huge raindrops ricocheted off the roof like bullets, and the leaden afternoon turned dark as night. Thunder rumbled and rolled ominously above me and the air charged with nature's power ... then as lightning struck silver fire across the heavens—

Finn was suddenly there, standing between the van's open back doors and backlit by the storm like an avenging god out of Greek legend.

He'd lost his handsome human Glamour. Now he was taller, shoulders and chest broader and more heavily muscled, the angles of his face hard and feral, his horns curving up almost a foot above his head, their points lethal and sharp. My heart thudded – he was gorgeous, and terrifying, and awe-inspiring ... and with the rain now sheeting down, it took me a stunned moment to realise that despite his eyes blazing emerald with rage, tears were streaming silently down his face.

Chapter Thirty-Nine

'**H**ugh tells me Helen's note was addressed to you,' Finn said, his voice holding an edge of brittleness. 'That you're going to see that sucker about it.'

'Yes,' I said quietly, my heart thudding for a different reason, as disappointment threaded with sadness rocked through me. I'd expected him to be upset that Helen was missing, but ... he'd lost his Glamour, too overcome to hold it, and he was standing there with so much pain and grief radiating off him that it was as if someone had ripped his whole world apart.

'Helen hates the suckers,' he said.

'I know.' Or I thought I had, but obviously we were both wrong. I held my hands out to him, wanting to offer him comfort.

He looked at them, then turned to stare out at the river. I pressed my palms against my thighs, unsure whether to go to him or not. But the tenseness of his shoulders under the drenched suit – which I noted absently still fitted like it was made for him, even without his Glamour – told me to wait.

When he turned back his horns were back to their usual height, his eyes were dry, and the rage in them was gone, replaced by disbelief and something that looked like ... betrayal? He climbed into the van and sunk into the seat opposite, rain dripping off him in rivulets.

'Helen *hates* the suckers,' he repeated, as if he was trying to convince himself, 'so why would she have anything to do with one? Why would she have anything to do with *any* of this? She's a police officer; she loves her job – why would she cover up a murder? Why would she—?' He stopped, a muscle jerking in his jaw, and dropped his face into his hands.

The Helen I knew didn't have any reservations about using her police powers to suit her own purposes if she thought she could get away with it. Somehow I'd always thought Finn had known that, but maybe he hadn't, not until now. Or maybe he hadn't wanted to see that part of her. But I didn't say anything. He didn't need to hear it.

'Nicky's gone, Gen,' he whispered.

'*What?*' I exclaimed, not sure I'd heard right.

'Nicky's gone.' He almost shouted it at me as he lifted his gaze to mine. His eyes were dark with fear. 'She's taken Nicky with her.'

She's taken Nicky— A sick dread roiled in my gut. Helen had taken his daughter. His *faeling* daughter. Fuck. No wonder he was devastated. Tears pricked my own eyes. I didn't care about Helen, but I *did* care about Finn. I sank to my knees and wrapped my arms round him. 'We'll find her, Finn,' I murmured, feeling the panicked thud of his heart beneath my cheek. 'We'll get Nicky back.'

'A sucker's got her, Gen,' he said, in the same low tone, his arms tightening painfully around me. Again I didn't tell him Mad Max's son might still be human; it didn't matter if he was, he was still a killer. 'He's had her for four days—' He stopped, shaking, and I knew he was remembering the time he'd been tortured by an ambitious vamp – and he'd been a captive for less than a day. That vamp was dead; Hugh had crushed her skull like a sledgehammer crushing an egg. My heart broke for Finn, and for Nicky, and I resolved to do whatever it took to save her and the other faelings.

'*Four* days! Gods, I should've made her stay with the herd, I should've—' He stopped, terror, and guilt, that he hadn't protected his child thickening his voice.

I hugged him harder. 'It's not your fault, Finn,' I murmured.

'I'm sorry, Gen.' He moved to meet my gaze, his face drawn and desolate. 'I should tell you not to have anything to do with the suckers. Instead I'm going to ask you … no, *beg* you, please: do *whatever* it takes to find Nicky.'

My throat constricted. 'I will, I promise.'

'Whatever it takes, whatever they want, Gen,' he whispered fiercely. 'I'll do it. Just save Nicky.'

I headed home. Hugh gave me an escort of two uniformed police trolls: Constable Taegrin, his polished black face glinting cheerfully with specs of gold, and Constable Lamber, whose mottled beige headridge was rough and cracked with age. Trolls, like goblins, are impervious to vamp mind-tricks, although unlike goblins they can't sense any magic. But I didn't need them to. Magic wasn't going to be the problem.

In a way, I didn't think Malik was going to be either, or at least not how Hugh envisaged he might be.

'You'll be careful, won't you, Genny?' Hugh had said, doing his father-figure bit. 'A bit of advice: I know you're upset about Finn and his daughter, but put all that out of your mind.'

I told him I would.

'It's going to be sunset before everything else is ready, so don't rush, and remember to keep your wits about you. Don't let Malik al-Khan make you do anything you don't want.'

I knew what he meant. He thought Malik would want blood and sex, because that was what vamps did. Me, I wasn't so sure, Malik hadn't exactly taken me up on any offers in the past, in fact he'd been at pains not to. Now I thought that might have something to do with his deal with Tavish, whatever it was. But unlike Hugh, I wasn't worried if it came down to blood or sex, or both. After all when I'd accepted his protection, I'd sort of expected they'd probably be part of the deal at some point, and it wasn't like I was totally averse – in fact, part of me, the non-thinking part, would be … enthusiastically ecstatic about it all. Not to mention I was going to do whatever it took to make the plans happen. Which started with climbing up five flights of stairs.

'I'm fine, thanks,' I gasped in answer to Constable Taegrin's solicitous question as I doubled over and leaned against my front door, trying to catch my breath.

Taegrin gave me a look that said he didn't think I was (both trolls had taken the stairs like pros, but then, they hadn't been half-killed by a rabid vamp last night). But once I was breathing easy again, Taegrin nodded, and he and Lamber followed me into my living-room-cum-kitchen.

A stiff breeze barrelled through the bedroom door, telling me the window in the room was wide open. I'd left it closed, with the heavy oak wardrobe in front of it. Malik was obviously awake, despite sunset being four hours away. Tension knotted my stomach, and I stopped a good couple of feet away from the bedroom door, with the two constables hovering attentively at my back.

The rug I'd left Malik wrapped in, Cleopatra-style, was now rolled up tight and sitting neatly on the floor at the end of the bed. Beneath the bed my shoes and boots were (creepily) lined up in what looked like style, heel height and colour, and the heavy wardrobe was back in its original position.

I *looked*. The blood-Ward still drifted above the threshold. When I'd *drawn* the Ward, it had sprung up like a golden fog; now it was as thin and insubstantial as a summer's mist. But it *was* still working. Relief slipped through me; with the Ward trapping Malik as well as the daylight, I had a better chance of pulling this off. I stepped further to my left to get a better view of the room.

Malik was on the bed, propped up against the headboard, looking relaxed and unconcerned, with his leather-clad legs stretched out and crossed at the ankles. His chest was still bare, and his pale skin gleamed almost unnaturally in the dim room.

His pale, perfect face was set in his usual enigmatic expression, and his part-Asian eyes were black and unreadable as they met mine. Damn, but he was pretty – maybe even more so with his shorn hair.

'Genevieve, I am delighted to see you.' His not-quite-English accent was mocking. His gaze raked over the two trolls. 'And to make the acquaintance of your ... friends.'

Showtime.

Chapter Forty

I lifted my lips in an equally sardonic smile. 'I hope you're enjoying my hospitality?'

'I believe I would enjoy it even more if you were to make it less restricting.' Pinpricks of power flared for a second in his dark eyes and I had to stifle the urge to go to him.

'That's not something I'm prepared to do just yet,' I said, in a reasonable tone, ignoring the nervous itch pricking down my spine. 'First, I want to negotiate a deal.'

His lips quirked. 'What if I do not wish to negotiate?'

'Do you remember what I once said to you if you refused?

'Yes.' The word slipped like cool silk over my skin. *Mesma.* My pulse sped.

'Same thing still applies, Malik: if you're not willing to negotiate, then I will kill you.' Always supposing I can, I added silently.

'How could I forget such a promise, Genevieve?' he said softly. 'In truth, I was surprised to wake and discover myself not only undamaged, but also somewhat protected.'

My eyes flickered to his foot. The burn wound was gone. Briefly I wondered how he'd healed it without blood. And how hungry he might be. Still, not my problem – yet.

He carried on, 'Threats lose their force if one does not intend to carry them through to their logical conclusion, Genevieve.'

'Your death wasn't the most logical conclusion ... this time,' I said in a flat voice, then added with a cheerful note, 'Nothing personal, of course.'

'No, I imagine it was not.' He smiled, flashing fang. 'Of course, with me gone there would be none to stand between the vampires and the fae.'

'That was a consideration,' I said drily. 'But there'll come a time when the fae no longer need your protection, Malik. Then I *will* make it personal.'

'Ah, but then there would also be none to stand between your sweet blood and the Autarch.'

I strangled my instinctive terror before it could take hold. 'I'll take my chances.'

Something dangerous surfaced in the dark depths of his eyes. 'Do not fool yourself that because the Autarch ignores you now he has forgotten you.'

'Don't worry, I hold no illusions about the Autarch,' I said, 'just as I no longer hold any illusions about you.'

He arched a brow. 'I could order you to take down the Ward, Genevieve.'

'You could, but to do that, I'd have to physically pass through it.' I lifted my hands to indicate the silent, watchful trolls either side of me. 'My friends here have been *ordered* not to let me.'

'It seems I am destined to stay here in your bed then.' He stretched, raising his hands above his head, and a darkness of a different kind swam in his eyes.

I stared, transfixed, as lean, hard muscle moved under his pale, perfect skin. Lust coiled in my stomach, need throbbed between my legs and images flashed in my mind about how pleasurable 'staying in my bed' could be. I curled my fingers into fists, digging my nails into my palms, and used the brief pain to drive him out of my head.

He sighed, the sound lancing like sharp sorrow into my heart. 'Despite your assertion that you do not want me here.'

I wanted him, needed him, needed to go to him—

Two weighty hands descended on my shoulders, holding

me in place. I blinked and took a shaky breath. I scrubbed my hands over my face. Damn vamp nearly had me that time. I let the two constables know that it was okay to let me go.

'Maybe you should be more concerned about what you want than about what I don't,' I said, struggling to keep my voice level. 'Now let's see, what was it? Oh yes, "My value lies in being alive, uninjured, and not in the possession of a vampire".' I quoted his words back at him. '"By agreeing to keep me that way, you gain a powerful ally in the kelpie".' I smiled, baring my teeth. 'Where do you suppose Tavish stands on me being in the possession of a witch?'

He stilled. 'Why?'

'One of them tried to kidnap me today.'

'The attempt was not successful.'

'Obviously not. But the next one will be. I've made sure of it.'

He moved, too fast to see, and was standing in the doorway, hands braced against the wooden jamb, staring at me, his gaze intense.

I took half a step back before I could stop myself, then gritted my teeth and put my foot where it had been. I stared back at him.

'Explain, Genevieve.'

The order clamped round my mind like a steel trap and it took everything I had not to babble uncontrollably. Instead I forced myself to calmly tell him the whole story, along with Hugh's proposal to flush Victoria Harrier out to get answers and enough evidence to get a search warrant to find the missing faelings. I left out one, small pertinent detail: that it wasn't going to be me as the sacrificial kidnap victim, but my doppelgänger.

'Of course,' I said finally, 'you could order me not to get kidnapped, but …' I looked to the two troll constables standing stoically either side of me. 'I've already agreed to the plan.

It will go ahead with or without my cooperation. So you see, it's going to be difficult for you to keep your *valuable property* safe when that happens. Especially if you're still stuck in my bed.'

Malik folded his arms nonchalantly across his chest. 'If you have already agreed to the plan, why are you here?'

'Two reasons. The first is this.' I held up Helen Crane's note, or rather, the copy Hugh had given me.

Malik read it, then gave me his usual impassive stare. 'Continue, Genevieve.'

'Agree to help me with this, and I will give you my word that I won't let the police use me as bait for Victoria Harrier. I will also give you my word I won't try and kill you for a period of one year, or until the fertility curse is *cracked*, whichever comes first.'

'An incentive to sweeten the deal.' His mouth lifted in amusement. 'How interesting. I could, of course, order you not to kill me.'

I folded the note and tucked it back in my jacket. 'It's always an option, but even if you did, sooner or later I'd find a way to get round it, or any other order you give me. Just like today,' I finished pointedly.

'It appears we have reached an impasse then, Genevieve.' His expression closed off. 'This is witch business. The Ancient Tenets agreed between the vampires and the witches prohibit me from becoming involved.'

'Which brings me to the second reason.' I held up another, longer letter, one of the ones I'd asked Juliet Martin to give me in exchange for my blood. 'Dispensation from the Witches' Council.'

He read it, then said, 'It states that you as my proxy have agreed to your blood, of which I am named as owner, to be used in three specified spells. In return there will be no retribution for any action I have taken, or may take in the future in any endeavour involving witches that is deemed by the police to be beneficial to either their enquiries, or to the public good.' He gave a half-smile. '"Actions I have taken" of course refers to the affair involving Mr October.'

I nodded.

Six months ago, one of the hot celebrity calendar vamps – Mr October – had been accused of murdering his girlfriend. His human dad had asked me to prove his son's innocence. By the time the ashes had settled – the ashes being the remains of two ambitious vamps, one who had tortured Finn, and a rogue witch who'd been instrumental in causing the girlfriend's death – Mr October had been cleared of all charges, and the case closed.

Only the girl's real murderer was standing in front of me.

Malik had killed her to protect all the parties concerned, and he knew I could prove it. Human law doesn't allow for extenuating circumstances when vamps murder humans, and the witches would be charging up their broomsticks for attack if they discovered they'd burned one of their own at the stake – never mind she'd richly deserved it – for a crime a vamp had actually committed.

Now if I wanted him dead, I didn't need to do it myself, or worry he'd find some way to stop me. I could just do the whistle-blowing thing, and it would be the police, a.k.a. Hugh and his trusted, incorruptible colleagues, who would hold Malik's life in their hands.

Malik looked at the two uniformed trolls, then inclined his head. 'This is both dispensation and threat. I commend you, Genevieve.'

'Thank you,' I said. 'DS Hugh Munro has the relevant "in the event of my death" letter, although at this point my death or otherwise is not part of the deal. If you agree to help, he will leave the letter unopened for one year. If you don't, then these two constables will wait until dawn, then take you into custody, at which point DS Munro will open the letter and act accordingly.'

'A year,' he said, considering.

'Yes.'

He nodded, shifting back slightly. 'And how do you intend I should help you, Genevieve?'

'Information, using your clout with Maxim to get him to talk, and back-up.' I leaned towards him, baiting the trap, and breathed in his dark spice scent, certain now he would agree. 'I'm open to all and any ideas so long as it helps find out what's going on, and puts an end to it, hopefully with none of the good guys being badly injured or dead.'

'Then it might be advisable not to waste any more time.' He shot a hand out through the Ward, yanked me into the bedroom, kicked the door shut and slammed me against the wall in the same motion. He buried his face in the curve of my neck and inhaled deeply.

Chapter Forty-One

Heart pounding, I shoved at Malik, surprised when he backed off. 'How the hell did you break through the Ward?'

He smiled, flashing fang. 'You used a blood-Ward against a vampire you have freely given your blood to. The Ward holds me in place, but it also stretches with me.'

Which was exactly the warning Ricou had given me when I set the Ward: it was designed for protection, and that meant anyone inside it with a blood connection could do what Malik had done and stretch it; with enough will and time, they could even break it. And the Wards completely lose their effectiveness on your kids once they hit puberty, Ricou'd said in disgust – not that Malik needed to know I knew any of that.

'You came too close,' he said, placing a hand flat against the wall on one side of my head and leaning into me, 'now, tell me what it is you require from me, Genevieve.'

Constable Taegrin's voice called through the door. 'Genny! Are you all right?'

'I'm fine, and he's agreed,' I shouted, so they'd leave us alone. I narrowed my eyes at Malik. 'Haven't you?'

'I have agreed to continue the game you have started. Notes and letters, or should I say, insubstantial carrots and sticks? If you were truly going to "allow" yourself to be abducted, you would have done so without giving me the opportunity to oppose it.' He leaned closer, almost close enough to kiss, and breathed his next words against my mouth. 'What is it you want, Genevieve?'

I put my hand on his chest. His heart wasn't beating, and oddly, it reminded me of Finn's heart thudding against my cheek, and why I was here. I pushed Malik back so I could look him in the eyes, then dropped my hand. 'Helen Crane's been tampering with evidence to cover the murderer's tracks – but Helen's disappeared. That note says she can no longer protect Maxim's son, which means that his son is almost certainly the murderer. I want you to use your Oligarch powers and make Maxim talk to the police, and get him to tell them everything he knows.'

'This is what you have deduced from Helen Crane's note.' He picked up a strand of my hair, twisting it through his fingers.

'Well, from that and other things, like Francine's and Maxim's memories that the Morrígan showed me,' I said, trying not to notice the way my scalp tingled.

'And who do you think is Maxim's son?'

'I'm not sure, but I think it might be the manager at the Coffin Club: Gareth Wilson. He's the right age and colouring…' I trailed off at the mildly interested look on Malik's face. My gut twisted in frustration. 'He's not, is he?'

'No.'

Damn. Sometimes a straight answer isn't all it's cracked up to be. I didn't bother asking him how he knew; if he had any doubts, he would've been more evasive.

'Who is Maxim's son, then?' I asked.

'I do not know.'

Another frustratingly straight answer. 'But he does have a son?'

'It is something I can neither confirm nor deny.'

I sighed. He was holding out on me again. Shame the ordering bit only worked one way. And disappointing as it was that my suspicions about the murderer had been a leap in the wrong direction, it wasn't necessary information. All I had to do to stop the killer and save Nicky and the other faelings was to put our master plan into action. Simple. Now I just had to convince the aggravating, much-too-beautiful vamp whose elegant fingers were still playing with my hair and still sending tantalising little tremors over my skin, to help me.

'The police are mounting an undercover operation,' I told him, and revealed the one pertinent detail of my supposed abduction that I'd omitted first time around: Constable Martin and the Doppelgänger spell.

'She is a police officer,' he said indifferently as he ran a hand down the sleeve of my leather jacket. His touch seemed to burn against my bare skin – *mesma* – and I studiously ignored it. 'She would not do this unless both she and her superiors felt she were capable,' he finished.

'Yeah, I know. But while she's pretending she's me, I could make use of the distraction.' I took a deep breath and mentally crossed my fingers. 'I want to sneak into the Tower, locate the entrance they're using, then *crack* the magic holding it closed. At which point London's finest can swarm in and sort it all out.'

He clasped my left wrist, his skin cool against my more heated flesh. My pulse jumped like it was trying to escape my skin. I concentrated on calming it.

'You still do not tell me what you want of me, Genevieve,' he murmured, giving me a sleepy look that was as much invitation as innuendo.

Bastard was playing with me. Okay, admittedly I'd started it, but if he thought coming on to me was going to make me back down, he could think again.

'I want you to come with me,' I said brightly, 'as back-up.'

His hand round my wrist tightened for a second, then relaxed. His eyes half-closed as he considered me. 'You wish me to play rescuing hero with you?'

'Yes.'

'Why?'

'Despite what you think, I'm not reckless, I don't want to get injured, and if I go in there on my own, it could be tantamount to suicide. Plus you're the best vamp for the job. Once I get us inside, you can do your vanishing-into-the-shadows trick and keep us both hidden while I search for the entrance, and at the same time you can keep me safe.' I smiled expectantly, hoping he'd see it as a done deal. 'Simple.'

He gave me a lazy smile back, and I caught a glimpse of fang as his thumb rubbed over my pulse, the touch sending shivers through my blood. 'And what if I do not wish to accompany you?'

Did I go for straight for Plan B, or take the (definitely interesting) hand he was dealing and see how the cards fell? Choices, choices.

I flattened my palms on his chest, pushing him back again, and this time I left them there, relishing the cool silk of his skin against my own venom-heated flesh. 'Maybe I could persuade you,' I said, giving it my best seductive voice.

He traced a finger down my throat. My pulse there started up a rapid tattoo, even with the venom hit my day's ration of blood-fruit had already given me. 'What had you in mind, Genevieve?' he murmured.

I swallowed, my mouth dry, recalling the images he'd dropped in my head not ten minutes ago, and looked past him at the bed. 'You're the one with the imagination, you tell me.'

He clasped my wrists and lifted them slowly above my head, as if he expected me to protest, and a spiral of anticipation and need twisted inside me. I lifted my chin in silent offering. After all, he was hungry, and with 3V and the blood-fruit turbo-boosting my blood production, I had plenty to spare. He captured my wrists in one hand and pinned them, amused heat lighting his eyes. 'My imagination informs me it has a plan.'

I licked my lips, nervous in a good way. 'And what does this plan involve?'

He traced a tingling line down the lace V of my silk top.

Desire shot through my veins like high-voltage electricity, leaving me quivering.

'It involves' – his fingers grazed the swell of my left breast – 'staying here.'

My nipples tightened, pushing against the lace of my bra.

'Where I can' – he cupped my breast through the silk of my top – 'protect you.' His thumb brushed over the stiff, sensitive peak. I gasped, arching into his palm. 'Yes, I like this plan better,' he said, sounding entirely too pleased with himself.

'Seducing me isn't protecting me, Malik,' I breathed, wondering if this was going where I thought, or if he was going to do his usual, and stop before things really got hot—

He stopped – and I almost whimpered in frustration … until he moved to give the same teasing attention to my other breast. Then I couldn't help but whimper.

'Ah,' he said, his eyes deep pools of drowning darkness, 'but who is seducing whom, Genevieve?'

'I'm the one with my hands above my head.' Mentally, I willed my melting legs to hold me.

'Yet you are not struggling, and see how your body responds to my touch,' he said softly, continuing his light, barely there caresses. 'I find it … intriguing, how much you want this. I wonder what other liberties will you allow me in the hope I will accede to your needs?'

Needs? I closed my eyes and tipped my head back against the wall. *I needed his mouth on my throat, his hands on my body, and him deep inside me.* Were they my thoughts, or his? It didn't matter. I wanted this, and not just to persuade him to help me. I was tired of always being the kid outside the sweet shop with her nose pressed against the glass, tired of sex being about breaking curses, about commitment, of about anything other than pleasure and fun. Life was too short not to enjoy it – maybe a cliché, but it was true. If it wasn't for Sylvia and luck, I could be suffering the same fate in the Tower as the poor missing faelings. I wanted this, wanted Malik, just – well, just *because*. Even if that was selfish, while others might be dying … except until the rest of the plans came together, there wasn't anything else I could do right now. And he did need persuading.

I looked at him from under my lashes. 'What other liberties have you in mind?'

Chapter Forty-Two

'I am uncertain.' He skimmed his hand down my body, slipping it beneath the hem of my top and resting his cool palm at my waist. 'You see, Genevieve, there is really nothing you can give me that I cannot already have for the taking, if I so wished. It removes an element of delicious excitement, knowing you will not resist me.'

Bastard. Play hard to get, why don't you?

'Is that what you want, Malik? Resistance?' I twisted my wrists in his grip, pushing up against him, feeling him hard and ready. 'Do you want me struggling beneath you, screaming for you to stop as you take me by force?'

He continued to gaze at me, his dark, enigmatic eyes giving nothing away.

'Or is it that you want me willing?' His fingers trembled against my side and I knew that was it. I pressed my lips to his throat, tasted salt and spice, and nipped under his jaw. 'Then you can have me, Malik,' I whispered, 'I'm willing.'

He released me and stepped back, his expression suddenly grim. 'Do not lie to me, Genevieve,' he said, his voice harsh.

Surprise winged through me and the air in my lungs seemed to whoosh out, leaving me shaky and unsteady. My heart jackhammered in my chest, then it settled. We weren't playing games any more. This was real. And for some reason he was angry. Angry vamps are never good news.

'I'm sidhe, Malik, we *can't* lie.' I pressed my back against the wall, keeping my eyes on his, wary.

He braced his hands against the wall to either side of my head, and leaned into me. I froze as his anger chilled the air and my breath trailed between us like a malevolent fog. Dread slicked down my spine, and I fought the instinctive urge to curl into a tight ball, to hide. *Mesma.* Nothing more. Just good old vamp *mesma.* I lifted my chin and stared into the opaque darkness of his eyes ... *and was buffeted by a confusing tornado of emotions: intense desire, rabid hunger, unending guilt, and an incandescent rage. All of them tempered and held in check by an implacable will ...*

'Why is having my back-up so important to you that you would do this to obtain it, Genevieve?'

... the emotions swirled around me, and then vanished, leaving me alone in the wind-blasted desolation of a vast barren plain.

'Genevieve?'

I blinked. His feelings had come and gone so quickly that if it weren't for the icy quiet they'd left in their wake, I'd have thought I'd imagined them. I was suddenly aware that maybe I'd misread him. Or he me. Or the situation. 'This isn't just about back-up,' I said slowly. 'I thought you wanted me, and I wanted you too.'

He regarded me for a long moment, then his expression smoothed back to its usual enigmatic blankness. A warm breeze sprung from nowhere, carrying with it a soothing scent of spice and liquorice, and something else, some fragile emotion I couldn't quite catch ... *yearning?*

'Tell me what is so important, Genevieve.'

I sighed, bereft as the feeling dissipated, and the order slipped into my mind. 'I told you, finding the killer, saving the missing faelings, and ultimately breaking the curse.'

'You would sacrifice yourself to me for this?'

I half-laughed, incredulous. 'Malik, offering you blood and sex doesn't even come close to being a sacrifice.' My gaze skimmed over the lean perfection of his chest, followed the dark silky hair there as it arrowed down to disappear enticingly beneath his low-slung leather trousers and I only just managed not to drool. 'It's not like I'm being a martyr here or anything.'

'You have just told me you cannot lie, Genevieve, but I wonder. Last night you did not want me to touch you, today you remind me that you would prefer to kill me rather than succumb to me, and now you expect me to believe that you want me willingly?'

'Wow, for someone who's got five centuries behind them you're a bit dense, aren't you? Last night, I was furious, and damn right, I didn't want you to touch me. And no, I'm not going to be yours or any other vamp's mindless little blood-slave, or your over-protected, pampered blood-pet either. And I'll do whatever it takes so I don't end up like that. But that wasn't what I thought was on the table here. Sex and blood I'm more than happy to indulge in.'

'You say that, and yet you feed Darius by way of a plastic bag.' His mouth curled in distaste.

'*What?*'

'If you are happy to indulge in sex and blood, then what purpose do the bags hold?'

'C'mon, Malik,' I said, exasperated, 'that's got nothing to do with anything.'

'Tell me, Genevieve.'

'Fine. I'm not interested in going to Sucker Town every other night. It's not the highlight of my social life, and not only that, I've got my job' – *or I did have*. I shoved the thought away; it wasn't something to worry about now – 'and other things' – like reading curse-*cracking* books. *Yep, my life is that exciting.* Of course, I could always do with a little less excitement right now – 'so the bags are convenient,' I finished with a scowl.

'Are you telling me you only indulge in blood and sex with Darius once a week?'

I stared at him in disbelief. Was he not listening to me or something? Or was this some sort of vamp pride thing? Or was he jealous? Nah, that was just wishful thinking – not that I wanted him jealous; his over-protectiveness was already difficult enough to deal with.

'What is your problem with Darius?' I demanded.

'Answer me, Genevieve.'

'No, I don't only indulge in blood and sex with Darius once a week.' There, chew on that nicely ambiguous answer, your Fanged Hotness.

A pinprick of rage flickered in his pupils, then it was gone. 'How many times a week?'

Damn orders. 'None,' I growled.

Astonishment flashed over his face. 'Why not, if you are happy to indulge so with me?'

Was he really that stupid? I narrowed my eyes. 'What the hell's with the twenty questions?' And why the hell was he asking them? He was Head Fang: he had his spies all over Sucker Town … I could understand him not knowing about Mad Max's secrets, but surely he had to know about me?

A perplexed line creased between his brows. 'I am trying to understand why you are offering yourself to me, Genevieve.'

'Fuck, Malik!' I threw my hands in the air. 'I want you. I desire you. I lust after you. My idiotic libido sits up and pants when you're around. And it's not like I can hide it: you're a vamp, you've got super-senses, so you must have noticed.'

'I am aware of how you react to me physically, Genevieve.' His frown deepened. 'But you care enough for Darius to take responsibility for his existence, and to put yourself in danger in order to save him. He is by all accounts very … talented, and yet you say you have not taken him as your lover. You have not taken any lovers among the fae either, and this suggests that you do not give yourself lightly, therefore the only conclusion I can come to is that despite your evident physical desire for me, you are not truly willing. I do not wish to take advantage of you.'

My mouth dropped open in shock. 'Okay, this is just way too strange. One: no way am I going to take a lover from the fae, not with a fertility curse hanging over my head, and two: this *seduction* was all your idea. You started it, I just went along for the ride' – *ha, ha,* and wasn't that a Freudian slip? Not that I was getting one – 'I did *not* come here to seduce you. I mean, why would I even think I could? It's not like you've ever had a problem resisting either my body or my blood before. Or now.'

He opened his mouth—

—and I slapped my hand over it, wishing I'd done the same to my own a few seconds ago. 'Oh no.' I shook my head. 'We are so not doing this any more. And don't you dare think about giving me any orders. You're the one blowing hot and cold and playing games, so this conversation is over.'

I ducked out beneath his arms, stalked to the wardrobe and threw the doors open. I stared blindly into the dark interior, wondering if I could just crawl in there and hide as the adrenalin high of anger and arousal dissolved into embarrassment. Did I really have to tell him exactly how I felt? And what was that crack about Darius being talented? And what the hell just happened? Other than he'd rejected me – *again.* And, *hello,* why was I even hot and bothered about that? It's not like I really wanted any sort of actual relationship with him … did I? Shit, I should have gone straight to Plan B instead of giving into a stupid impulse.

Well, I was damn well putting Plan B in action now. I shrugged off my jacket and glanced over my shoulder. He was standing there, arms crossed, a pensive look on his face. I flipped my hand, indicating he should turn round. He didn't.

Bastard. 'I want to change, Malik,' I said sharply, flipping my hand again.

'I wish to see how your injuries are healing, Genevieve,' he answered coolly, as if nothing had happened, 'and I have seen you without your clothes before.'

'Not by my choice,' I huffed, 'and you just lost your chance at that ever again, so either turn round' – I grabbed a long-sleeved T-shirt and flapped it at the window – 'or I'll change outside on the roof.'

His nostrils flared and I tensed, then he turned and gave me his back.

I swapped the silk top for the T-shirt. Damn irritating vamp. I tugged off my high-heeled boots and kicked them under the bed in annoyance. They knocked over the tidy rows he'd left with a thud and I saw his shoulders flinch. Score one for me. I dropped my velvet jeans and caught sight of the Chastity handprint spell on my stomach. Crap, I'd forgotten all about it – weird that the spell hadn't kicked in when things started getting all steamy with Malik. I grimaced and pulled on a pair of black denims.

'It was truly not your intention to seduce me, Genevieve?' Oddly his question sounded … regretful? Or maybe that was my stupid, wishful imagination. *And did the damn vamp* never *give up?*

'I came here with a plan,' I said through gritted teeth, 'and a half-assed idea that you could help me. But I knew you wouldn't just say yes, that would be way too easy; you're a vamp, after all, so I brought my insubstantial carrots and sticks. But then you decided to change the game, and for one stupid, idiotic moment of total insanity, I thought, why the hell not?' I blew out an indignant breath. 'I should've known better. Oh, and you can stop communing with the wall now. I'm decent.'

He turned, his brow lined in a frown. 'Why are you chang-ing?'

'These are my best jeans' – I shook the velvet jeans out and hung them in the wardrobe – 'and so far they haven't got any blood on them. I'm hoping to keep it that way.' I bent and fished under the bed for some more practical footwear. I slumped on the bed and shoved my feet into the flat ankle boots.

He sat next to me. 'I am sorry, Genevieve.' He touched my cheek, a brief, gentle trail of his cool fingers. 'But I cannot let you leave on this suicide mission.' His dark spice and leather scent curled round me consoling and remorseful. 'I have given my word to protect you.'

'I know. You've told me. More than once. But that's between you and Tavish and whatever the two of you've got going on together, it's got nothing to do with me.' I stood. Time to leave. 'Unless of course, you're prepared to tell me what that is?' I paused, but he didn't enlighten me. Figured. 'Fine, I'll see you around then. Maybe.' I took the couple of steps to the door and reached for the handle—

—and, vamp-fast, he was standing between me and the door. 'Do not force me to do this, Genevieve.'

'I'm not forcing you to do anything,' I said flatly. 'You can come with me and protect me, or not. Your choice.'

'It is too dangerous.' Pinpricks of power lit in the depths of his dark eyes. 'You will not go.'

I winced as the order slammed into my mind. Time to let the beautiful vamp in on the limitations.

'Malik, even if I appreciated the whole macho-vamp-protection thing, you can't keep ordering me about. It's not enough to do the job. Your protection only works when it comes to vamps, and it's not going to make one iota of difference to anyone else who is determined to come after me. Like, if the two trolls out there came in and took me bodily away, even if the Ward wasn't there, you couldn't do anything until after sunset. Come dawn tomorrow you are going to be defenceless, and about as much use as a bodyguard as a leaky boat on the Thames. You're daylight-challenged, and you always will be.'

Frustration flared in his eyes.

I carried on, 'Once the killer and Victoria Harrier find out they have a substitute, what do you think they're going to do? They're going to dump my doppelgänger and come after who they really want: me. London's only sidhe. It's only common sense to stop them before they decide to do that.'

'This is a matter better left to the police, Genevieve. I will not agree to your participation.'

I laughed: it wasn't happy. 'You still don't get it, do you? This isn't about you agreeing or not agreeing. You were just my first choice. You're not the only vamp in town, and if you're not prepared to go with me, then I know a vamp that will.'

'Darius is too young and too weak to aid you, Genevieve,' he said dismissively.

'I'm not talking about Darius, *my liege.*' I stuck my hands on my hips and gave him a 'so-there' look. Childish, I know, but hey— 'I'm talking about Francine. All I have to do is ask for her help in your name and she'll give it me. And she's a kick-ass lady who does a mean line in illusions. Not to mention she hates Maxim, so she'll be thrilled to coax him into telling the police and me whatever we want to know. Then let's not forget Cousin Fyodor, and whatever stories he's got to tell.' I mimed pulling out a stake. 'He's old enough that it won't take long to get him back into talking order again. Oh, and don't think your little order about staying out of Sucker Town will make any difference; the police can take me there by force if need be.'

'No.'

I shot him an impatient glare. 'What does "No" mean?'

He brushed a hand over his shorn head. 'No, you do not need to ask Francine for her help,' he said, conceding with obvious reluctance. 'I will accompany you, and I will do all in my power to assist you. On two conditions.'

'Which are?'

'One: your safety is my prime concern,' he said firmly. 'And two: if you are putting yourself in danger, then you should be better prepared physically. You will allow me to heal your injuries first.'

Take his blood? My pulse quickened in anticipation. I wanted to say it wasn't a good idea, except it was, and we both knew it.

'Agreed,' I said, adding, 'Just being practical,' at his surprised look. Reaching down to the threshold, I wiped away some of the dried blood and broke the Ward, then opened the door. I nodded at the two trolls standing to attention. 'We're going with Plan A,' I said.

'Right-o, Genny,' Constable Lamber said.

'Plan A, Genevieve?' Malik raised an elegant, enquiring brow. 'You are aware that I had ordered you not to leave, and therefore these two gentlemen would not have been able to pass your blood-Ward to retrieve you until it dissipated?'

'Not true, sir.' Taegrin held out his hand to me.

'Plan B,' I said, taking the red jellybean from his palm, and the green one that Lamber gave me and showed them to Malik. 'Ward-Key spells.' I'd had a lo-oong chat with Ricou about blood-Wards. 'A drop of my blood and will in the sweets means they can cross the Ward without breaking it, in the same way I can.' I tossed the sweeties in my mouth and ate them and their magic with a smug smile. 'Therefore rendering them able to retrieve me while still leaving you trapped.'

'Bravo, Genevieve.' He inclined his head in acknowledge-ment. 'Speaking of practicalities, how do you intend to take us inside the Tower?'

I pursed my lips. 'Actually, that's the difficult bit of the plan.

I know someone who can help, but I'm not sure if they will.'
Or what it was going to cost me. I gave Malik a sideways look.
'We'll leave off the healing bit until after they've agreed.'

Chapter Forty-Three

I hunkered down in my seat and contemplated the vampire daylight travelling kit, a.k.a the zipped body bag provided by the police. It was made from leather, not the more usual thick plastic. Apparently leather stops vamps from being more than just victims of fashion. The bag – or rather, Malik – was stretched out on the floor between the two rows of seats in the back of the police van.

Malik and the two constables had treated the whole 'getting into the bag and being carried out to the van' project like it was something they did half a dozen times a day. The tourists in Covent Garden hadn't been so laid-back. The mobile phone/camera brigade had been out in force. I'd cringed and hurried, head down, into the van; I just knew I was going to end up with the media hounding me again after all this. Still, better that than dead. And at least I hadn't blown up any bridges this time. Not yet anyway.

A half-heard voice made me look up.

The headlights of the passing traffic glinted on the specks of gold in Constable Taegrin's polished black skin. He was sitting with his feet propped up on the opposite seat, as I was, to leave room for the bag. Had he said something? But he caught me looking and just winked. I smiled back, thinking I must've imagined it. And that my life would be so much easier if I could just unzip Malik and force him to tell me whatever it was he and Tavish had going on, and what it was the pair of them were hiding. Yep, like that was ever going to happen. But the main thing was, I'd got Malik to agree to what we wanted, which was a big relief. I closed my eyes, hoping Hugh and his crew had been just as successful with the rest of our master plan preparations—

'—understand you have a son, Maxim.' Malik's distant not-quite-English voice popped into my head.

There was a short silence, then Maxim's voice muttered, 'Bleeding sidhe. Knew nothing good would come of her slurping up my blood.'

I briefly wondered how I was picking up their conversation – *Mad Max's blood maybe?* – and how they were managing to have it; then scrunched my eyes tight shut and concentrated on listening.

'Where is the boy, Maxim?'

Hmm, why isn't he asking who *he is? Does that mean he knows, or that he doesn't think it's important?*

'Haven't a clue, old chap,' came the breezy answer.

'This is not the time for your games.' Malik's tone was impatient. 'If it is he who is behind these disappearances, then he needs to be stopped, and if it is not him, then he could be in danger.'

'All that ruckus with the faelings is the fae's problem, especially now you've stopped us sticking our fangs in,' Maxim said bitterly. 'And my son's safe enough without your help. So bleeding safe I haven't seen him for twenty years. That bitch won't let me.'

'Ah.' Malik's voice was soft. 'So you do have another child.'

Mad Max has two *kids?* There was another, longer silence. I waited with Malik for Mad Max to answer.

Finally Malik gave up and said, 'The witch has left a note, Maxim, saying she cannot protect your dog's *offspring* any longer. If she is not protecting your son, then you must have other offspring. The witch has now vanished.'

'I saw the new hairdo, old chap,' Maxim said cheerfully

and seemingly at random, 'so I take it His Brattiness has been enjoying himself at your painful expense again. Still on the old eviscerating kick, is he? Or is it the old starvation diet? Must be hard when you can't snack on any passing pigeon and have to rely on His Princely Benevolence. Bet his little royal heart jumped for joy when you made yourself Oligarch and dropped yourself back in his bloody little hands again.'

Terror rolled through me at the mention of the Autarch, and the thought of Malik being in his clutches. I clutched Grace's pentacle at my throat, and swallowed the fear back. Was that why Malik was so hungry – he could only feed off other vamps and the Autarch wasn't letting him? I shuddered and tuned back in.

'—nothing to fear, Maxim. I will not give up your secrets,' Malik was saying calmly.

'No, you bleeding won't,' he replied angrily, 'because you're not getting to know them.'

'Maxim, this situation is as a result of the curse; it could be what we have all—'

'No! Not my problem any more,' Mad Max interrupted sharply. 'I've washed my hands of the whole sodding business. I've lost too much already *assisting* you and your horsey friend. I told you both, don't ask me again.'

We? Who did he mean by we? *And what had Malik and Tavish asked Mad Max to help with?*

'I understand,' Malik said gently after a moment's silence, then added briskly, 'There is another concern. Genevieve knows about the faeling, the one you took from Francine.'

'So what? The little bitch is under the protection of the witches now.'

'But it appears there is a vampire interfering with the family. This was not what we agreed.'

'You're not laying that one on me, mate. Oh, no, nothing

to do with me. I haven't been near the little cow, not since she took a fancy to that pipsqueak of a wizard.'

'Francine?'

'Your butt-licking little illusionist? Doubt it; she's too busy playing with the girls she's still got.'

'Fyodor?'

'The old man?' Maxim gave a barking laugh. 'Good God, you've got to be joking. He's so trussed up in all his promises to everyone and her dog, he has trouble managing a nibble without checking what night it is.'

'Who then?'

'I'm not a bleeding oracle, old chum. If you're all fired up about it, ask my nutter of a cousin to sleuth for you. She's the one who's pally with the fae. But then, you're not her type, are you?' His voice took on a taunting tone. 'She likes them a good bit younger and a good bit more impressionable, like our yummy Darius. Quite a feat that: jumping bodies. Old Francine's got the heebie-jeebies about it, not surprising, really, but it makes you wonder just what my cousin and her pet-fang have been up to, doesn't it?' He lowered his voice conspiratorially. 'I suspect they're a tad closer, if you know what I mean, than we all thought. Not that I'd want to get that close to her; the apple hasn't fallen far from the tree with that one, my bleeding face still hurts like the devil—'

'Maxim, who is Andy?'

My ears perked up: Andy was the name Darius had been thinking of when I'd wanted to know why Mad Max was taking my bagged blood.

'Maxim?' Malik's voice came again, but however they were communicating, Mad Max had obviously gone offline.

After a few more minutes of silence, I opened my eyes. We were driving past the Gothic towers of Tower Bridge, its brightly lit walkways flashing colour into the heavy grey sky. Not far now. I frowned down at Malik in his bag, resisted the urge to kick him and ask what the hell he wasn't telling me, and tried to work out what I'd learned by eavesdropping. That Mad Max had *two* kids was the obvious one, not that the info got me any closer to finding out how Mad Max and his kids were involved with Helen and the missing faelings. The only thing I did know was that Mad Max was afraid of the Autarch finding out – not that I blamed him – which suggested Max wasn't quite as mad as he seemed. Then Malik had asked about the fanged cuckoo nesting in with Ana's family, and while Mad Max had denied having anything to do with Ana, hadn't in fact appeared to like her much, he hadn't seemed surprised, so I was betting he knew who the vamp was—

The van braked, and I winced as Malik's body bag slid into the back doors with a soft thud.

I looked up to see we'd arrived at our destination: the War Memorial at Tower Hill.

Hugh was waiting on the pavement outside, in front of the long stone-built corridor with its Greek-looking columns and huge engraved bronze wall plaques. I grinned as an idea hit me. Maybe Hugh could get Malik to reveal his secrets – after all, the annoying vamp was going to have to do something while he was waiting for me to collect our 'Tour the Tower' entry tickets. I jumped out, thankful that the rain had stopped. We said our hellos, then Hugh silently watched as the two constables carried the bagged-up vampire through the gate and into the vaulted building.

Finally he said, 'I see you managed to convince Mr al-Khan to cooperate.' His ruddy face creased into a concerned frown. 'I hope he didn't cause you any problems?'

'Nothing I couldn't handle,' I said, keeping the grimace off my face as he gave me a searching look. Hugh doesn't have a sense of humour when it comes to vamps. 'Any news on Finn's daughter?' I asked anxiously.

'Sorry, Genny, no.' He gave my shoulder a gentle consoling

pat. 'Finn's out with a couple of WPCs, canvassing all of Nicola's friends to see if they can come up with any helpful information. He should be along shortly.'

I sighed, worried about how Finn was coping, then asked, 'What about the doppelgänger plan?'

'That one's not going too well.' Dust puffed from Hugh's headridge and settled on his black hair. It was beginning to look like someone had emptied a bag of red flour over him. 'Constable Martin spent half an hour talking to the Raven Master and six of the ravens, all of whom claim they know nothing whatsoever about the dead faelings, nor are they interested.' He ushered me through the gate and we walked down towards the Memorial Garden. 'She is currently chatting with Victoria Harrier and her daughter-in-law, Ana, about the antics of Ana's large brood of children over tea and cakes in the café in Trafalgar Square.'

'Damn. So Victoria Harrier didn't buy the switch.'

'Or she is as she seems, and her connections with everything are entirely coincidental.'

'She can't be,' I said, 'unless the vamp's got her so locked up she hasn't a clue what she's doing.'

'It's possible, Genny, but unless I have proof otherwise, the judge won't issue a warrant. My hands are tied.'

Which meant everything rested on my part of the master plan. 'No pressure then,' I said, determined to make it work.

'Once Victoria Harrier and Ana have finished their chat with Constable Martin,' Hugh said, 'if nothing develops, then we'll bring them in for questioning. We've already had Ana's husband picked up in New York, and we've got Dr Craig down at Old Scotland Yard.'

'Don't suppose he's spilled any interesting beans yet?'

'Until we finish talking to him, Genny, I can't be certain, but so far he is exactly what he appears to be: a workaholic doctor who spends more time at his job than there are hours

319

in the day. Unless that changes, he's not going to be of help.'

'What about the Old Donn?' I asked, hoping that one lead might pay out and give us something helpful. 'Did you find out if he's really dead, or not?'

Chapter Forty-Four

'The Old Donn's definitely dead,' Hugh stated, deflating my hope. 'I've had it confirmed by the Lady Meriel. After the incident with the sidhe he was executed, along with two other wylde fae, Hallbjörn the White and Arthur Ursa.'

Executed! Well, executed sounded pretty dead to me, but— 'What about Sylvia mentioning his remains?'

'The three were decapitated, then burned, and their ashes were mixed with salt on Tower Green. Apparently a spell was *cast* to stop them from *fading* until after the execution had been carried out.' Hugh's ruddy face paled. 'The Lady Meriel chose to explain it in detail for me.'

I patted his hand; his skin felt dry and gritty, a sure sign he was disturbed by what he'd been told. But then, Hugh was a softy at heart. No wonder the Librarian's old newspapers had called their deaths a 'Brutal Slaying'. The execution sounded a bit barbaric, but personally, I thought it was well deserved.

'Good to know the Old Donn is a dead end then,' I said brightly. Hugh rumbled, and I gave him another pat to cheer him up. 'You know I couldn't resist.'

'Hmph.' Hugh gave me one of his patented looks that was meant to have me shaking in my boots. I grinned wider; the last time it had worked I'd been sixteen. He sighed, and pointed towards the garden. 'It's not long until sunset, so you need to get going. Ricou has organised everything. Good chap, that.' Hugh nodded approvingly, then hit me with his 'concerned' look. 'Are you sure calling up the Morrígan for help is the right thing to do, Genny? Goddesses can be dangerous to deal with.'

'She's been giving me pointers all along, and she's had her messenger stalking me, so I'm pretty sure the Tower is where she wants me to go.' Of course, typically, she was now making me do things the hard way, since I hadn't seen a single black feather of Jack the raven, her messenger, once I'd decided the Morrígan was my back-door way into the Tower's *Between*. But hey, that's goddesses for you. Not to mention she probably wanted something, so making me ask, instead of offering, was just standard negotiating tactics.

Not that I told Hugh that. Instead I reassured him I'd be fine, and quickly filled him in on the conversation I'd overheard between Malik and Mad Max. Then I followed the path and went down the steps into the sunken garden.

Last time I'd been in the garden I'd been on Spellcrackers business. It had been high summer, and I'd had to remove a flight of garden fairies attracted by the sunbathing tourists and their picnic lunches. The place had been full of life and noise. Now it was full of hundreds of small jasmine-scented tea-lights placed around the base of the high stone walls that enclosed the garden. The candlelight cast an eerie glow over the tall bronze panels inscribed with the names of those merchant seamen who lost their lives in the two World Wars. And in the darker corners, frail shadows shifted independently of the evening wind, drawn by the promise of ritual magic, shadows I tried not to look too closely at, for fear they'd take on more substantial ghostly forms. I shuddered; ghosts are so not my favourite things.

Sylvia was sitting on one of the benches in the better lit section of the garden. Her pink and white dress and pink cycle helmet shone brightly in the last throes of dusk. She waggled her fingers at me, but didn't get up, just gestured towards the centre of the garden.

I walked towards the middle, careful to step over the collection of weapons that was laid out in a circle around the edge of the grassy area. The weaponry circle was large, around twenty feet in diameter, and consisted of swords, daggers, poles, axes, a metal breastplate, a pair of armoured boots and a black-plumed helmet. It looked like someone had raided a mediaeval armoury.

Next to the small bronze pool – the centrepiece of the garden – Ricou was waiting for me in his true form. His blue-grey scaly skin shimmered in the candlelight, his spiny headcrest was flat to his head, his fluted fins flared out either side of his face, and his long whip-like tail was wrapped round his waist, securing what looked like a Union Jack flag in place. As I reached him I realised it was another towel.

'Ricou here's not sure this is such a good idea, luv,' he said, his membranes flickering nervously over his black orb eyes. 'Calling up a goddess isn't going to make her feel too charitable towards you.'

'I think she's sort of expecting me to call,' I said wryly.

'Oh, well, on your head be it.' His headcrest snapped up, then down again. 'Everything's been done as per the Librarian's instructions. She provided the bull's horn herself.' He pointed a clawed finger at where the aforementioned bull's horn, longer than my arm, lay next to the bronze pool. It was curved like a scimitar and the pointed end looked sharp, but the head end was hollowed out enough that my fist could've fitted inside. I had a brief thankful thought that it wasn't the Old Donn's, since I was calling on his mother. Beside the horn was a short silver knife, a bottle of Jameson's whisky, a crystal tumbler, some milk and a pile of clothes – the same clothes that had been found pillowed under Aoife's head when she'd been discovered in Dead Man's Hole this morning.

'The milk's in a carton,' I said, frowning.

'How many cow farms do you think there are in London?'

He did a yawn-grin and thumped his chest. 'Not only that, as soon as Ricou here mentioned "goddess" all they heard was sacrifice. Anyway, it's organic.'

'Oh, good,' I said, not sure if it was. I raked my hand through my hair, suddenly nervous. Crap, I didn't have a clue. I peered down at the whitish liquid in the tumbler. 'What's in the glass?'

His headcrest rose. 'She's a goddess of fertility. What do you think's in the glass?'

Okaay! I decided not to ask who'd made the personal donation. 'Didn't the Librarian say something about ears of wheat?' I asked sceptically.

Ricou's face-fins quivered. 'It's spring; ears of wheat are a bit scarce just now.'

Ri-ight. 'What about the raven feathers?'

'The ones at the Tower all refused, and I couldn't find your feathered friend. But I got you this.' His tail swished out over the bronze pool and a gaping mouth with sharp teeth similar to Ricou's own snapped at it. The mouth belonged to a five-foot-long eel thicker than my arm, twisting sinuously round and round in the shallow water. 'She's female.' Ricou made a clicking sound as he laughed. 'I've checked, so watch your fingers.' He handed me a piece of rice paper. 'Here's the glyph to close the circle, luv.' He sniffed the air. 'You've got about five minutes until sunset now. Good luck.'

'Thanks, Ricou,' I said, then I undid Grace's pentacle from round my neck – I didn't want to lose it in *Between* – and handed it him along with my jacket. 'Can you give these to Sylvia to look after for me?'

'Sure, luv.' He took them, hooking the pentacle carefully over a claw, then he hopped out of the circle of weapons and joined Sylvia on her seat.

Left alone in the circle, I crunched on a couple of liquorice torpedoes and looked round. I'd gained an audience while we'd been talking and the garden was now full. There were a dozen witches, their dark WPC uniforms all merging together. Constables Lamber and Taegrin had been joined by four other trolls. Hugh was standing with Malik, the pair of them almost hidden under the shelter of the memorial building, and sitting next to them was a large silvery-grey Irish wolfhound; looked like Mad Max had turned up in his doggy persona. Hopefully Hugh would get some useful info out of him.

And all of them were here to see the show. Lucky me.

Still, once the circle went up, the show would be pretty much over from their point of view, since they'd stay in this world while the circle, with me in it, would be in *Between* – if I *cast* it right, of course – apparently neutral ground was needed when calling on a goddess.

I wiped my suddenly sweaty hands down my jeans, decided not to send any prayers in case the wrong god heard me, and picked up the silver knife. It burned against my fingers. I walked to the edge of the circle. Holding the rice paper glyph in my left palm, I took a deep breath, *focused*, and sliced the knife through it and my flesh. Pain hit a second later and I stifled a gasp. Then my blood welled, bright and viscous, and the scent of honey and copper and magic filled the air. Hunger – *not mine* – cramped my stomach, nearly doubling me over, a hot, spiced wind blew my hair back from my face, and I looked around to find Malik, now standing inches from me on the outside of the circle, his hands clenched at his sides.

'Set the circle quickly, Genevieve.' His eyes were dark, bottomless holes. I glimpsed all four of his fangs as he spoke. 'The scent of your blood is ... tempting.'

Tempting? A perverse moment of retaliation sparked in me.

I held his gaze, taunting him as I extended my hand and let the blood fall. I felt, rather than saw, the first drop splash on an iron axe-head. It sizzled. His nostrils flared. The second drop hit the tip of the broadsword touching the axe. The tendons in his neck stood out with effort. Time slowed as the third drop splattered on to the black-plumed helmet eating the sword. He snarled and leaped—

The magic ripped out of me and I fell to my knees, screaming as it rushed round the weapons like wildfire and closed the circle. Above me rose a translucent dome of swirling, liquid blood.

I lay there getting my breath back, my eyes closed. *Hell, I'd never felt a circle, not even a blood one, close like that before.* But then, I'd never closed a circle into *Between* before. When I thought my legs would hold me, I struggled up to my feet. Worryingly, I could still see the garden and its occupants. Malik now stood a couple of feet back, watching with his usual enigmatic expression, and I wondered if I'd imagined him leaping for me. But the silvery-grey Irish wolfhound was standing in front of him, and the dog's disconcertingly blue eyes twinkled at me as he wagged his long upright tail. His mouth was clamped round Malik's wrist.

Behind them both was Hugh, the disapproving crevices that etched his face clearly saying, *'Goading vampires is juvenile and stupid and wasting time, Genny.'*

And satisfying, I added silently. But Hugh was right. I sighed, and gave him an apologetic shrug—

Only he wasn't there to see it.

The garden had disappeared. Outside the dome was … emptiness: not fog, not sky, nor space or anything, just rolling emptiness.

Horror crawled down my spine.

I turned my back on it, strode back to the bronze pool and dropped to my knees. Before I could give myself time to think, I thrust my bleeding hand and Aoife's clothes into the water.

'By my blood, and the blood of her child, in this sacred place of war and death, I call upon the Morrígan,' I shouted. 'Hear me, Morrígan, and answer my call.'

Chapter Forty-Five

The water bubbled, the bronze beneath it turning it into molten gold. The eel reared up, and up, its body long and sinuous, then it twisted down and round and snapped sharp teeth in my face. Adrenalin-laced fear shot through me, but I forced myself not to move, to keep my hands in the water. Magic shivered over the eel's skin, turning it a pale, luminous green. Its bald head flared, eyes growing large and glinting acid-yellow, skin splitting into holes where her nostrils should be, her slash of a mouth plumping until her lips puckered into a blood-filled pout. Below the face, bumps sprouted into rounded shoulders, extended into long, lithe arms and ended in elegant hands with thin, claw-tipped fingers that clutched and grasped at the air. Under the arms, the eel's body thickened, morphing into a slender torso with high, full breasts, and then swept down to a narrow waist which tapered into the eel's dark writhing body. The thin gold chain of tinkling keys was fastened around her left wrist and twisted tightly round her human-shaped half, continuing round the eel's like a golden vine winding around a willowy tree until it disappeared into the bubbling golden water below.

'Little sidhe,' she said huskily, looking down at me and smiling. The smile was a predatory pucker of her blood-plumped lips that framed her one protruding tooth. 'I have long waited for your call. I do not appreciate those who are tardy, or casual with my tasks. It will cost you dear.'

My stomach tied itself in knots. Damn goddesses and their

timekeeping – just because time travels differently in the Fair Lands and she'd spent however many days, weeks or years waiting, it didn't mean it was my fault. Not to mention that *tasks* was taking it a bit far. 'You visited me yesterday, Morrígan.' I lifted my chin. 'I'd hardly call that a long time.'

Her forked tongue flicked out, swiping across my mouth. I tensed, managing not to flinch. 'You taste of truth,' she murmured, then she clasped my face, her clawed fingers digging sharp into my skull. 'I will excuse you this transgression,' and she lowered her mouth to mine, pressing a hard kiss against my lips. 'But I fear others will not be as forgiving as I.' She jerked the gold chain up.

The water boiled up like a well-spring, crashing over me. The force knocked me flying and I landed flat on my back. I swiped my wet hair out of my face in time to see the sleek green-black shape of the kelpie horse erupt out of the pool. He reared up above me, front legs flailing in anger, and I froze, not daring to move as he dropped back to all fours, front hooves thudding to the ground inches from my shoulders. He tossed his head, his tangled, beaded mane spraying water droplets in high arcs, then pushed his soft muzzle into my face and snorted. Hot whisky-peat breath seared my cheeks.

'Hello, Tavish,' I murmured, breathing in his scent, and before I could stop it, his magic. A glorious liquid languor spread through my body, drawing an expectant sigh from my mouth, washing all thoughts but him from my mind and raising my own Glamour. Honeysuckle fragranced the air, my skin glowed gold, and my magic spilled out and rippled over the kelpie horse like a stream in full flow—

And Tavish in his human form was on his hands and knees above me. He stared down at me, his silver-coloured eyes swirling, his bead-tipped dreads hanging like a curtain around our faces, hiding us from view.

'Hello, doll,' he said quietly. He grinned, his sharp-pointed teeth white against his green-black skin. ''Tis guid to see you, though you took your ain sweet time coming for me. The Morrígan's been riding me ragged.'

I grinned back, struck by his Charm, and his magic eddied inside me, sending longing swimming through my veins. I reached up and traced the sharp, angular planes of his alluring face, his long, straight nose, his pointed chin, then stroked the delicate black-lace gills at his throat. His eyes closed, a shudder running through his sleek muscular body, as he murmured softly in encouragement. I looked down between us to see him in all his naked glory. 'Not that ragged,' I whispered, my stomach contracting in anticipation. *Oh boy …* Then his words penetrated my mind, and I frowned. This was wrong. I wasn't here for this, but for—

A loud screech rent the air, and Tavish disappeared from above me.

The Morrígan's anger-etched features replaced him as I stared up at her, stunned into immobility.

Her eyes bored like lasers into mine as her body writhed inches above my own. 'You are as addled as the rest of your cursed blood, little sidhe.' Her husky voice was filled with vitriol. 'One look and you are prepared to cast all aside for love and beauty.'

One look? Tavish had hit me with a gut-load of kelpie Charm, and she knew it.

She reared up and lifted her face up to the heavens and shouted, 'Clíona, my sister, see what wretched misery you have wrought! My children are dying and your blood lies here, as weak now as it has always been.' A double-edged dagger appeared in her clawed hand. 'I will gouge her heart from her body, and destroy your cursed blood, and make an end to this.'

She raised the knife above her head, started it on its downward curve …

330

Fucking goddesses and their tests. And what the hell was she talking about Clíona's blood for?

I jack-knifed my knees up to my chest and kicked out and up, catching her in her midriff just above where her human-shaped body joined to the eel's. She flew backwards with another ear-splitting screech and I scrambled up to find her swinging back towards me, like a snake dancing to the charmer's whistle, tooth bared, knife in hand. I rolled to the side, feeling the knife slice through the skin of my shoulder like— Well, like a sharp knife through flesh. The pain barely registered.

Desperately I grabbed the nearest thing: the long scimitar-shaped bull's horn; it was lighter than I expected. Gripping it with both hands, the point curving upwards, I thrust it towards her on her next swing past, but I missed again and stumbled as her blade nicked a stinging line across the front of my throat. I backed up, feeling my blood trickle over my clavicle. I needed to put some space between us, but the Morrígan's damned eel body kept growing longer and longer, stretching out in zig-zags behind her as she slithered menacingly across the grass towards me.

I reached the edge of the circle, my pulse thundering in my ears and my shoulders buzzing against the static of blood magic. My gut clenched in fear as I wiped my hand over my throat and it came away painted in blood. The honey-copper scent was slightly nauseating. How the hell was I going to get out of this? *Plenty of sharp implements at my feet—* But grabbing one of them meant breaking the circle, and losing myself in the emptiness outside the circle wasn't part of the master plan. But then, neither was fighting a goddess. Trouble was, not fighting wasn't an option, unless I wanted my heart cut out.

I gripped the thick end of the bull's horn, calculating her approach, then swayed – and realised, almost too late, that all her shifting about was making me dizzy. She smiled, acid-yellow eyes glinting maliciously as she rose up, twenty-odd feet above me until her pale green bald head brushed the inside of the translucent blood-dome. She angled the knife in her hand, and my legs shook as she gave another gut-wrenching shriek and dived at me. I held my breath, waiting until the last possible moment, then I flung myself forward, turned and stabbed the bull's horn through the eel part of her body and into the ground below—

A heart-hollowing bellow rent the air as I scrambled onto my hands and knees, expecting to feel her knife plunging into my back at any moment. I half-crawled, half-ran until I hit the opposite side of the circle, where I collapsed into a panting heap.

The Morrígan was swaying about, five feet above the grass, and looking down, apparently nonplussed, at the bull's horn pinning her eel body to the ground.

Shit. All she had to do was pluck it out.

I needed another weapon. I looked towards the bronze pool, thinking of the little silver knife with which I'd cut my hand and wondering if I could get to it before the Morrígan did the obvious—

Tavish was lying next to the pond, his head propped on his bent arm, idly flipping the knife through his fingers. Next to him was the bottle of Jameson's, now half-empty. Looked like he'd been enjoying the entertainment.

'Telt you nae tae trust me, doll.' He grinned, but his eyes were pewter-dark with suppressed anger. 'Telt you, I'm nae longer my own master, but you didnae listen.'

Chapter Forty-Six

Tavish was right: he had told me not to trust him, but that didn't mean he wasn't on my side. The Morrígan might be using him to test me, or sic spells on me or whatever, but she was still holding him captive, and Tavish wasn't the sort to just roll over and play slave. He was also tricky enough to give me a clue – which, hopefully, was what he was doing now.

'Don't worry,' I muttered. 'I don't trust you or your fangy friend, or whatever it is the pair of you are plotting.'

He sat up, and rested his chin on his bent knee. Fixing me with a look, he dragged the silver knife along the gold chain clamped round his ankle. The knife made a faint metal-on-metal sound as it disturbed the tiny keys, setting my teeth on edge. He smiled, a quick baring of his own teeth, then pulled a long length of chain from the bronze pool, coiled it round and stabbed the knife through one of its links. He'd pinned himself to the ground, much as I'd done to the Morrígan.

Great clue, Tavish – not!

But his clue, whatever it meant, would have to wait. First, I needed to convince the Morrígan to give me what I came for: two tickets to the Tower of London.

I frowned at her. She was still contemplating the bull's horn, bending over so she could peer at it from just a couple of inches away. She seemed to find it fascinating. Hopefully she'd stay that way, since fighting her wasn't going to work; there was no way I could win against a goddess, not in the long run, so I needed to think of something else, and fast. I pushed myself to my feet, blinking as my head swam and the scene in front of me went fuzzy. I looked down to find my T-shirt and jeans were soaked with blood. Crap, I was wearing my last clean pair too. I touched my hand to my throat and stared uncomprehendingly at my blood-drenched fingers. Then I got it: she'd nicked a vein when she'd sliced me, and if it didn't heal soon, fighting would be the last thing I needed to worry about.

What I really needed was Tavish's fangy friend right now. Still at least this way, when Malik healed me, I'd end up with a two-for-one deal.

I tore the sleeve off my T-shirt and tied it round my neck in a makeshift bandage, then checked my shoulder, but compared to my throat, that was a scratch. I staggered over to the bronze pool, picked up the carton of milk and the crystal tumbler, but left the silver knife. Taking it would've put me within grabbing distance of Tavish and never mind anything else, he *was* still tied to the Morrígan. I continued my stagger until I was a couple of feet away from the Morrígan – not that the distance made much difference, not when the eel part of her body could keep extending, and extending …

She moved again, this time so her upper body was upright. 'You have spirit, little sidhe,' she said haughtily, 'and more than I expected.'

'You want something from me, Morrígan,' I said flatly. 'And I want two things from you. I'm willing to bargain.'

'A sidhe bargain?' She licked her blood-plumped lips, considering my words. 'It has been sixty years since I was last offered one of those. The taste still rankles.'

Whatever. Cards on the table time. 'First, I want the ability to pass into *Between* without using an entrance, for me and one other.' I paused, then added what I hoped would the clincher. 'Specifically, I want to get into the Tower of London.'

'This is not a small thing you ask …' She trailed off, then

reached down and pulled out the bull's horn, which came away with a loud sucking sound. The eel part of her body spasmed, and the wound gushed blood that hissed as it hit the grass. She held her hand out imperiously. 'Give me the milk, little sidhe.'

I hesitated, worried I was giving away a bargaining point.

'Come now; it is not like it can be returned to the cow, is it?'

I unscrewed the cap on the carton and handed it over.

She read the side of the carton and frowned. 'Organic! Hmm, if humans did not scour the earth and deplete its fecundity with their pesticides and chemicals, there would be no need to label this so.' She sniffed it, pulled an 'it will do' face, then poured it over the wound. It healed instantaneously. I briefly wondered if it would have done the same for my throat, but the chance was gone, for the Morrígan kept pouring, an expression of contentment on her face, until the last drops of milk splattered like white tears over the hissing grass.

Just my luck ... Still, the itchy feeling at my throat meant it was healing, even if I did look like a victim at a vamp's bloodfest. Maybe she hadn't nicked a vein after all – or maybe the magic was helping me.

She dropped the empty carton and, smiling, held out her hand again. 'Now the glass.'

This time I didn't hesitate, just handed her the crystal tumbler.

She sniffed it too. Her hand trembled, her acid-yellow eyes widening as she inhaled again, longer and deeper. 'An offering from a fertility fae,' she whispered. 'You are indeed fortunate.' She held the glass above the bull's horn – I had a sudden horrible thought about what she might be asking me next – and she started to tip the glass up.

'No, my lady,' Tavish called, running over to stand between me and the Morrígan, the gold chain uncoiling behind him.

Yes, definitely *no,* even *if I had an idea which fertility fae had made the donation.*

'No?' The Morrígan turned her acid-yellow gaze to Tavish, her voice soft with menace.

'Dinna use the horn, my lady,' Tavish said, just as softly. 'Just the glass. Please.'

Okay, what was he playing at now?

'It is but a drinking horn, kelpie,' she said, in a deliberately casual tone.

'Dinna fool yourself that I havenae recognised it, my lady.' The beads on his dreads flashed from silver to an accusing red. 'For 'tis one of the MacCúailnge's horns.'

The bull's horn belonged to the MacCúailnge, her son? No wonder she'd been fascinated by it. Except he was supposed to have been executed. So was his horn just a grisly memento from the execution – and if so, how was that possible? – or had someone, oh, let's say, like the Lady Meriel been economical with the truth?

'Aye, 'tis one of the MacCúailnge's horns,' she repeated, mimicking his rough burr, 'but tell me, kelpie, how would *you* be in a position to recognise it?'

His gills flared, then snapped back against his throat as he spread his arms and bowed. ''Twas I who removed it from his head, my lady.'

Um, probably not such a good idea to go for the whole truth thing here, Tavish.

Her expression turned predatory. 'You confess to me that you were the one to kill him, then?'

'Nae, I willnae offer you such.' His bead-tipped dreads clicked, the sound suddenly nervous. 'But I will declare I had a part in ... taking the Old Donn's horns.'

She backhanded him and he grunted in pain as he stumbled. He caught himself, and she hit him again, a casual uppercut to the chin that sent him bouncing off the inside of the magical dome and back down, landing heavily at her feet. I flinched as he groaned, and struggled to his knees. She gave the gold chain clamped to his ankle a vicious yank and upended him. 'Stay there,' she ordered. He slumped back, staring defiantly up at her as blood dripped down his pointed chin.

'Now, little sidhe—'

Her voice startled me and I turned back in time to see her tip the contents of the glass into the hollowed-out end of the horn and then spit in it herself. She held it out to me. 'Drink this, and I will grant you the boon you wish ...'

Okay, even without the spit, *eew*! With it? *Double eew!*

'... and the answer to that which you seek,' she finished with a crafty smile.

I narrowed my eyes. 'The answer to what?'

'You seek the answer to the fertility curse, do you not?'

'Yes.' Cautious hope flared inside me.

Her smile widened, her one tooth protruding with triumph. 'Drink then, little sidhe.'

I stared at the bull's horn. All I had to do was drink, and she'd give me the answer. The deal was ... *persuasive*. After all, it wasn't like I hadn't before; it wasn't poison, and no doubt it was as organic as the milk had been. And what was a bit of spit between – two people not friends, one of whom was a goddess of fertility, among other things? And there it was: the problem. It was one of those magic/symbolic things, and drinking it was going to somehow end up with me up the duff. Not only did I *not* want that, but if Tavish's objection was a clue, drinking from the bull's horn instead of the glass meant Finn might be the donor, but it wasn't his kid I'd end up with, but the Morrígan's— What? *Son? Grandson?*

My hand shook as I reached out and took the bull's horn from her. It felt heavier, or maybe that was just my imagination.

'Dinna drink it, doll,' Tavish said, his voice low.

337

I shot him an incredulous look. 'First, I'm not supposed to trust you, and now I am?'

'Remember the vision, the one she' – he jutted his head at the Morrígan – 'showed you—'

'How could I forget?' I snorted. The memory of the horn and hooves that had poked out of my pregnant belly when she'd treated me to her alien baby show was burned into my mind. 'But it can't happen, can it, not since you sicced me with a Chastity spell. So why should it matter whether I drink it or not?'

'The Chastity spell was her idea,' he murmured. 'I hadnae choice, doll.'

Okay, so definitely going with '*not drinking*' here, since his words confirmed one of my suspicions: she'd been the one who'd decided to keep me chaste, probably for just this reason. But I still wanted her boon, and the answer to the curse. Somehow I needed to come up with a way to get both – without drinking – and try and free Tavish at the same time.

I glared at him. 'What about adding cinnamon to the spell; was that her idea too?' I shouted angrily.

His eyes flashed black in shock.

'You have made her barren!' The Morrígan's shout eclipsed mine for anger. She pulled on the gold chain until Tavish was pressed up against the eel part of her body, then coiled herself round him like a boa constrictor and started squeezing. 'You have attempted to block me at every turn, kelpie, interfering and meddling in matters which are beyond your ken, and I will tolerate it no more!'

'Which is sort of what I was thinking,' I said loudly to attract her attention over Tavish's muffled yells of pain. Tavish might be wylde fae, and like all fae he might be hard to kill, but 'hard to kill' doesn't count for much when a goddess decides to end your existence.

I repeated my shout. And this time her head swung up and she fixed me with a venomous stare.

'Squeezing the life out of him is really too quick an end for him, Morrígan,' I said, putting disdain into my voice. 'He did de-horn your son, after all. How do you feel about a counter-offer?'

Chapter Forty-Seven

She regarded me with curiosity. 'What would this counter-offer be?'

'An extension of his pain, both mental and physical,' I stated, 'as due recompense for his interference in your business and mine.'

She swayed down towards me, relaxing her grip on Tavish. 'Tell me.'

'Agree to grant me my boon first, and I'll do better than tell you, I'll show you. If my actions give you pleasure, you'll tell me how to break the fertility curse; if not I'll drink whatever is contained in this' – I held up the bull's horn – 'either now, or at sunset tomorrow.' It was win/win for her, and might just buy me – and Tavish – some time.

Tavish's shout of denial cut off sharply as a loop of the eel's body tightened around his neck.

'Done, little sidhe.' She opened her mouth and gave a loud croaking caw. The dome filled with the sound of wings flapping and a huge raven appeared. He landed on her shoulder, his long talons digging into her flesh for purchase.

Was it Jack? It was difficult to tell— No, this bird's eyes were black; Jack's were blue. So if Jack wasn't working for the Morrígan, why had he been stalking me?

The Morrígan turned and made a low crooning noise to the raven. He rubbed his head affectionately against her cheek, and two of his glossy black feathers floated to the ground, then he flapped his wings, took off and vanished.

She indicated the feathers. 'Your boon, little sidhe.'

I picked them up. They felt like ordinary feathers; there was nothing magical about them that I could discern. 'How do they work?'

'You will know when the time comes,' she said dismissively. 'But remember, the boon will only work for this one night. Now' – she squeezed Tavish more in excitement than anything else, eliciting another muffled groan from him – 'show me.'

I tucked the feathers safely in my back jeans pocket. 'You need to let him go,' I said, pointing at Tavish.

She obligingly lifted him up above her head height, then threw him down as if she wanted to drive him into the ground. There was a loud cracking noise and he let out an agonised yell. She released him and he collapsed, panting, onto his side, his legs bent at odd angles. Damn. She'd shattered his shins.

I gritted my teeth and told myself he'd heal, and that broken bones were still better than dead. Then, my stomach roiling with nausea, I gave him a hard kick that shoved him onto his back. From the corner of my eye, I saw the Morrígan lick her lips in delight.

I crouched next to him, mentally crossing my fingers that I was right, that the reason Tavish didn't want me pregnant, whatever it was, was powerful enough to make him go along with me. 'Okay,' I said, gripping his face so he could see mine. His eyes were muddy-grey with pain. 'This is how it's going to go. If you stop me, or alter in any way what I do, or allow it to be altered by anyone other than myself or the Morrígan before sunset tomorrow, I give my word it will be as if I have already drunk this.'

'Doll! You mustnae drink—'

'Up to you, Tavish,' I interrupted him. Then keeping my eyes fixed on his, I lifted the bull's horn two-handed and slammed it down into his gut. He roared, the sound filling the blood-dome, his face contorting in agony. I clamped my lips together, desperately swallowing back the bile that rose in my throat. Then using my will and brute force, and ignoring the sickening squelching sounds, I twisted the horn until it was firmly embedded into the ground beneath him, pinning him in place. It wouldn't hold for ever, but maybe just long enough to stop her dragging him off. Another wave of dizziness blurred my vision, and I forced myself to look up at the Morrígan.

She wasn't looking quite as happy as I'd hoped. 'You present me with a conundrum, little sidhe. If I say I am not pleased, you or I will have to remove my son's horn for you to drink. But I cannot deny the truth of the matter; I do feel some satisfaction at the kelpie's discomfort, even more so by how you have caused it.'

Behind my back, I crossed my fingers, for real this time.

'Because of that, we will conclude our bargain tomorrow at sunset. I will leave you to your business now.' She bent over Tavish. Shoving her arms under his shoulders and thighs, she tried to pick him up.

Shit. I'd expected her to drag him by the chain, which would've given me some time.

She smiled at me, a smile that said I should know better than to try and fool a goddess, and she kept on pulling at him, the muscles straining in her slender arms. He struggled against her, screaming, and kept on screaming and struggling as the horn embedded itself further in his body to keep from being torn from the ground. I clenched my fists, trying not to heave. She lowered her mouth to his in a kiss and thankfully, he fell limp and silent. This time when she lifted him, the horn slid easily from the ground.

Fuck. That wasn't what I wanted to happen.

'Until sunset tomorrow, little sidhe,' she said, and slithered quickly towards the bronze pool.

The gold chain trailed after her, then tautened.

I staggered to my feet and shambled frantically as fast as I could after them.

She coiled herself round into the pool.

I shambled faster. I had to reach him before she took him into the water.

Her head and torso began shrinking, the pale green colour darkening to match the eel part of her body.

My vision blurred; there were two Tavishes in her arms now.

The pool erupted into a geyser of water and they disappeared.

The water smoothed out into stillness.

Desperate, I fell to my hands and knees next to the silver knife pinning the gold chain to the ground. *Please let me be right.* Gripping the chain with my left hand on one side of the knife, I cupped my right as I delved inside myself. The small gold key that I'd found after the Morrígan's visit popped into my right palm. *I had to be right.* I carefully scooped up the chain from underneath and closed my fingers round it. I pushed my magic out through my skin ... *please let it work* ... and the link around the knife shivered, then as I held my breath, it split and broke.

'Yes!' I shouted.

I looked at the broken ends of the gold chain, one end in each hand. One linked to Tavish ... the other to the Morrígan.

I pulled the left one, the one nearest my heart.

A strong wind buffeted me whipping my hair into my eyes, a thundering noise filled my ears and darkness descended around me. Sharp talons closed around my arms, piercing my skin and then I was lifted, dangling, into the air. Yelping with shock and fear, I looked up. A huge raven had me by the wrists.

The Morrígan's boon.

And my trip to the Tower – but I didn't want to go yet, not without Malik.

It flapped its wings, and as we started to ascend, I looked down at the grassy ground and bronze pool receding into the distance. A long black figure was now lying half-in, half-out of the pool. Was it the eel? Or—?

The figure flung its arms out.

It was Tavish.

Heartfelt relief and guilt filled me. He was free – if you could call being stuck in a blood-circle in the middle of nowhere in *Between* freedom. Now all I had to do was hope he'd leave the Old Donn's horn where it was, or I'd be the one with something I didn't want thrust inside me. My stomach curdled, a combination of that thought and what I'd done to Tavish.

Space wavered as the raven flew us out of the blood-circle.

Nothingness closed round me, leaching into my eyes, drifting up my nose, crawling down my throat. Unseen hands with odd-shaped fingers and claws grabbed at me, pinching, pulling and yanking. Something jerked at my legs, and one of the bird's talons ripped through the skin of my left wrist, its grip loosening— Then I was hanging by only one arm and I screamed, the sound muffled in my own ears as fleshy, muddy-tasting lips stole the scream out of my mouth. Above me the raven gave a loud croaking caw, half warning, half desperation …

Space wavered again.

And we flew into the night sky over London, the heavy feeling in my bones telling me this was the humans' world. Stars glittered in the sky above, rain splattered my face, and the cold spring wind cut through me, raising goosebumps over my body.

Beneath me the Tower of London came into view.

My throat constricted with trepidation. It was where I wanted to go … but the boon had been for two trips, one for me, the other for Malik. Without him, I had no back-up.

The raven sped towards the Tower, its talons digging pain-fully into my wrist as the noisy downdraught from its wings buffeted me, and sent me twisting in its grip.

Briefly closing my eyes against the vertigo, I shoved my hand in my jeans pocket, clutching for the feathers. There was only one left.

I peered down. We were over the grassy moat.

I rubbed the feather over my bloody neck and dropped it, shouting out with my mind for Malik to find it, to use it.

The thick grey stone of the Tower's curtain wall flashed beneath us, then we were above the open space of the inter-ior.

I shouted for Malik again.

The raven flew straight at the bluey-grey walls of the White Tower, the oldest part of the castle, and I swallowed, half-wanting to close my eyes, as the solid stone filled my vision—

—and as we passed through the wall as if it didn't exist, the sudden lightness of my body told me we'd once again left the humans' world and were now back in *Between*.

The raven dropped me.

The stone flagged floor hurtled up to meet me, too fast. I tried to tuck myself into a ball and roll, but instead landed hard on my shoulder. Pain shot down my arm and across my back, the breath whooshed out of my lungs, and a whole Milky Way of stars spun in my vision.

A hand touched my face—

And the memory rushed into me.

Chapter Forty-Eight

'**H**ere's your little man, dear,' Witch Harrier smiled. 'All bathed and ready for his new mummy.'

Behind Witch Harrier came Dr Craig, his bald patch shining pale as a fish's belly in the overhead lights, and his messy brown curls crowding his jug-handled ears.

She squirmed lower in the bed, the memory of Old Big Ears doing it to her as disgusting as ever – but for once she was tired and desperate enough that she almost didn't care that he was here, didn't care that his face held that same suspicious expression it had ever since she'd told him she was expecting after that one time. She'd put up with him if it meant keeping her baby. Nothing was going to stop her keeping her baby.

She took him carefully, nerves and excitement making her tremble. What if she dropped him, or held him too tight? Then as he settled in her arms, her nerves turned to happy eagerness. She gently pushed back the blanket and traced his little scrunched-up face, still flushed from the birth. Her heart stuttered with awe. He was beautiful, perfect, incredible. His nose was hers, and his chin looked like his father's, and his ears were neat and flat to his head – not like Old Big Ears' monstrosities – and his eyes were screwed tight shut . . . but she knew they'd be blue.

She pressed a gentle kiss to his forehead, breathing in his soft baby scent with a deep-felt joy. He wriggled, and she loosened the blanket some more, tucking her finger inside his tiny hand as he waved it. The baby's own fingers tightened, clutching at her with a strength that surprised her, his little mouth puckering up with a quiet whimper.

'He needs feeding, dear,' Witch Harrier told her encouragingly. 'Just point him in the right direction and you'll be fine.' She sent an indulgent smile Old Big Ears' way. 'I was with my two boys.'

She glanced from one to the other in embarrassment. It didn't matter that they'd both watched avidly as she'd given birth, or that Old Big Ears had done it to her. She didn't want them watching now. She rocked the baby, too fearful to ask them to leave, but hoping they'd get the hint and go anyway.

But deep down, she knew they wouldn't. Witch Harrier wasn't going to be denied any moment of her new 'grandson', and Old Big Ears was the school doctor. All the girls in her class knew what he was like, they'd all commiserated with her when he'd bought her Bride-Price, and gossiped with relief behind her back. Of course, she'd always known someone would buy it; she was a ninth-generation witch, the most powerful in her year. She hadn't worried about it much, not after her mother had told her what to do so they wouldn't have to give the money back if she didn't get pregnant within the year, like a lot of the girls had to; wizards were more infertile than witches a lot of the time. But why did it have to be Old Big Ears, that disgusting pervert? When she'd found out, she'd decided to put her mother's alternative into action straight away. She hadn't wanted Old Big Ears doing it to her more than was necessary. He was even worse than the other girls knew, too; he'd spent the last week 'instructing' her with hands-on demos; pinching and squeezing, until she'd wanted to cry. She hadn't, though, but now she hunched her shoulders at the memory. With that and the awful sickly-sweet fenugreek tea Witch Harrier had made her drink to bring her milk on, her breasts were like two aching, swollen boulders sitting on her chest.

The baby whimpered again, more demanding.

347

She shushed him.

'Did you want some help, dear?' Witch Harrier leaned forward, her face solicitous. 'Breastfeeding is so important, not just for his health, but it will make the magic come much more easily to him.'

She knew that, she'd been told it often enough: wizards weren't just born, they were breastfed.

'Maybe, I should help you this first time, Helen?' Old Big Ears said with a lascivious look.

She shook her head, then quickly tugged at the bow on her nightdress, trying not to let them see. Witch Harrier was right, the baby knew what to do; he latched on straight away, no hesitating. She flinched at the slight sting, then the small pain and the soreness and aching dissolved in relief, her worries disappeared and love flooded out of her into her son. She didn't care about the audience any more, this was just perfect. He was her baby. Her wonderful beautiful baby son.

Tired and exhausted, she fell asleep holding him.

Soft singing jerked her awake, and, panicked, she looked at the baby. He was cuddled safely in her arms. He'd fallen asleep as he'd fed, and his little mouth hung open. Now she could see his tiny, sharp fangs, not just feel them: the minuscule specks of white glistened against the soft pink of his baby gums. And two tiny beads of blood trembled on her still leaking nipple. Heart fluttering fast and anxious, she surreptitiously tried to wipe them away as she covered herself with the thin white nightdress.

'Dear?' Witch Harrier's disapproving voice made her look up.

Her heart stopped.

They were all there.

Witch Harrier, Old Big Ears, the kelpie ... and next to him was a young girl, hardly any older than herself.

The girl was the one singing, a soft sad lullaby, swaying from side to side as she twirled her long silver-gilt hair around her finger— Beside her stood the Irish wolfhound.

'No,' she screamed, clutching at her son and staring at the dog in abject horror. 'You said I could keep him! You promised!'

'It's for the best, dear,' Witch Harrier said, her face hard.

The sidhe girl stopped singing and danced over to her. She leaned down and kissed the baby's head, then looked at her with the wide, guileless gaze of a young child.

The pendant was hanging round her neck.

'Don't be sad, pretty girl,' the sidhe whispered, and took her son from her arms.

Chapter Forty-Nine

'**D**id you have to drop her?' Helen Crane's familiar patrician voice, along with the reek of ammonia, pulled me out of the despair of her memory. 'She was already injured, and now you've made it worse. She really needs to have most of her faculties about her for this, otherwise it won't work. It's important; we won't get another chance.'

Looked like I'd found Helen, or rather, she'd found me. And she wanted something, which really wasn't headline news. I pushed her desperately sad memory to the back of my mind and played dead as I tried to assess my injuries through the pain radiating out from my shoulder, down my arm and across my back. The verdict came back: not good. I was pretty sure my collarbone and shoulder blade were broken, and quite possibly my humerus too. My left arm was useless. On a lesser scale of discomfort, the flagged stone floor I was lying on was cold and hard, and the temperature was near-freezing. The icy chill made the police-issue gem- and spell-studded silver cuffs shackled around my wrists and ankles burn like super-heated brands.

'I know it's important, my lady,' an apologetic male voice said. 'I tried my best, but we were attacked and I almost lost her. I ask your forgiveness, my lady.'

I peered out from under my lashes. Jack the raven in his blond, indigo-eyed sidhe guise was crouching by my hip. He was wearing jeans, topped with a thick purple jumper, so his ability to get himself changed from feathers into clothes had either improved, or I'd been lying unconscious for some time. He was looking worriedly at Helen, kneeling next to him.

She looked the most casual I'd ever seen her. Her blonde hair was scraped back in a utilitarian ponytail and she was wearing pressed jeans with a pink tailored shirt and a navy cardigan, all of which looked out of place with her usual jewellery-shop-display of spell-carrying bling. She was treating Jack to an exasperated frown, while absently wafting a small brown bottle under my nose: smelling salts – which accounted for the ammonia. I almost laughed. Did she think I'd fainted or something?

'I told you to stop calling me my lady, Jack,' she snapped at him. 'I'm your mother, not one of your fancy sidhe females you have to flatter and flirt with. Call me Mum, Mother or Helen, I don't care which one, but most definitely *not* my lady!'

So looked like I'd found Helen's changeling son, too, and if her memory was correct, he was also Mad Max's long-lost little boy, and Jack had to be the dog's offspring she was protecting. Part of me was surprised I hadn't put it together before, even if Helen was a witch and Mad Max was a vamp and ne'er the twain shall meet, let alone get down and dirty and produce a bouncing baby boy complete with tiny vamp fangs.

But while mentally playing Happy Families with Helen, Jack and Mad Max was entertaining, it wasn't going to help me escape from my evil witch nemesis, or help me save Nicky and the missing faelings. Hoping for inspiration, I scanned around. We were in a large, dimly lit mediaeval-looking room the size of a tennis court, judging by the ceiling, which was all I could see from my prone position. The walls were irregular grey stone, and the thick wooden beams and pillars were darkened with age. Huge circular wooden chandeliers, stuck with half-melted candles, marched down the centre of the room. The room didn't look too different from the pictures Hugh had shown me of the interior of the White Tower itself – but then, it's always easier to base *Between* on something real; if you rely on imagination too much, there's a chance you'll end up with a pic'n'mix nightmare of whatever the magic decides to winkle out of your mind.

And speaking of nightmares …

'Alternatively, you could always call her Witch-bitch,' I said, my voice sounding as croaky as a raven's caw. 'That works for me,' I finished as they both turned.

Helen's mouth pinched sourly. 'At least you're awake.' She took the smelling salts away and I took a decidedly more pleasant breath.

'Hello, my lady.' Jack gave me a tentative smile; it held the same apology as his voice. 'I'm sorry I dropped you. I wasn't planning on it, you just sort of slipped.'

'Hey, no hard feelings, Jack.' I hit him with my best glare. 'So how's the Morrígan and the mother thing working out for you then? Or am I wrong in thinking you're one of the god-dess' messengers?'

'Um, the Morrígan wanted you here, and so did my la— my mother,' he said sheepishly.

'Ri-*ight*. You do know that pissing off a goddess isn't the healthiest thing you can do, don't you?'

'Ms Taylor,' Helen spoke briskly, 'the Morrígan didn't say how, or where she wanted you once you got here, so Jack has fulfilled the task set for him. Please stop trying to intimidate him.'

'I'm not *trying*,' I said, keeping my eyes on Jack, 'I'm telling it like it is. And I bought *two* tickets for this "Tour the Magical Tower" trip, so, no, he hasn't fulfilled his task yet.'

'I'm sorry, my lady,' Jack said, 'but I have to wait until the feather—'

'Jack, be quiet,' Helen said. 'You don't need to tell her any-thing.'

Jack gave me a 'nothing I can do' shrug. *Damn. So much*

for my intimidation skills. And so much for my fanged back-up: with his super-senses, finding a feather with my blood all over it should've been like finding a giant needle without the haystack.

I switched my glare to Helen. 'Oh, and while we're on this whole need-to-know-or-not subject,' I said, 'how about filling me in on all the Tour's gory details. What's my fate this time? Are you going for straight sacrificial victim, or can I look forward to something more creative?'

Helen ignored me and spoke to Jack, who was hovering anxiously at her shoulder. 'I told you to rest, so will you please do so and get your strength back.'

'I'm fine, my la— Mother.'

'Just do as I say, Jack,' she said tiredly.

He sat back with a loud long-suffering sigh.

'Having problems with the kids, Helen?' I said sarcastically. 'I mean, you just get your son back, then you lose your daughter. Very careless of you.'

She flicked her finger at me, a fist of magic punched my injured shoulder and I disappeared into a furnace of pain.

Then the sharp ammonia scent brought me back.

Fuck. Whatever happened to not making my injuries worse? As I shifted away from the pungent smell, another shock of pain ripped through me and I resolved to stay still. If I didn't move, it didn't hurt. Of course, if she didn't spell-punch me, it wouldn't hurt either.

'Ms Taylor.' Helen clenched her hands, her multitude of rings chinking in anger. 'There are no friendly trolls, inquisitive media or *my* ex-husband here to protect you this time, and my patience is wearing thin. I suggest you keep your mouth shut until I ask—'

A clock struck, sounding like the Westminster chimes of Big Ben. Helen and Jack started chanting under their breath and turned their backs to me. Magic shivered over us like a light snowfall, illuminating the dome of the ten-foot circle enclosing us and melting like cool kisses against my cheeks. I lay there counting the sixteen notes of the hour, waiting for the deeper gongs at the end to tell me how long I'd been here: one, two ... ten, elev—

The eleventh gong cut out halfway through.

Four hours, give or take. Shit, that was a long time. *C'mon, Malik, find the damn feather; the night's not getting any younger.*

In the silence that followed, I could hear the quiet rustling of people moving, the muted cry of a baby, quickly hushed, and the scrape of metal on stone.

The cold round me increased, and my breath fogged into the air as my teeth started chattering.

My stomach heaved as a spell rolled over us like an air pressure wave following an explosion.

Jack moaned and collapsed against Helen; she wrapped her arms round him and gently lowered him to the floor. As she stroked his hair back from his face, sadness and longing crossed hers, and I relived the memory of her grief as he'd been taken from her by Angel.

I scowled; I so didn't want to feel sorry for her.

Then her sadness was gone and she fixed me with an irritated look. 'You're shivering, Ms Taylor.'

I didn't bother to answer. One, it was obvious, and two, my teeth were going at it like they were one of those joke wind-up sets that clatter around until they run out of power and die. A not-so-cheerful thought.

She pulled her cardigan off and laid it on top of me, tucking it under my chin. 'It will warm up in a minute,' she said absently. 'It's just the after-effect of keeping this circle tuned to *Between* so we don't go out of Time-sync.'

'Time-sync?' I asked, then braced myself for another magical shoulder-punch as her attention focused on me instead of her internal thoughts.

After a moment, she said. 'Yes, Time-sync, Ms Taylor. Time here runs slow, around a day for every hour in the normal world. Until the clock finishes the chime we can't get out, and no one can get in. The place is cut off until this time tomorrow.'

I digested that. Time in *Between* – like space and form – was malleable, of course. Not that I had much of a clue where to start with any of that, but that was less important than how long … in other words, how long before Malik, my superpowerful fangy back-up found the bloody Morrígan's feather and caught a raven-powered flight to my (and everyone else's) rescue. Still, the good news was I probably hadn't been out of it for as long as I thought. The bad news— If it took Malik an hour, I could end up trapped here for twenty-four of them—

Panic bubbled inside me and I slammed a lid on it, hard. I'd been in worse situations; I could find a way out of this, I wasn't dead yet – and to be honest, I was pretty sure me dead wasn't part of Helen's immediate game plan, so—

'You have to pick your moment.' Helen interrupted my thoughts. 'It's why it took us so long to get in without him knowing.'

'Without who knowing?' I asked cautiously.

'Dr Craig, of course.' She regarded me as if I was simple. 'This is all his doing – although he had to force Ana – she's his sister-in-law – to pull this patch of *Between* into being, he's not powerful enough to *cast* this sort of magic.'

Ri-*ight*. Dr Craig was The Mother's killer, so the 'horned god' in Her photofit *was* symbolic, as I'd thought. Someone really did need to buy Her a digital camera. I fervently hoped Hugh had already discovered that Dr Craig was the main perpetrator, and that he'd got him locked up in one of Old Scotland Yard's cells, but part of me knew I couldn't get that lucky. And my glee at Helen being a crooked cop wasn't quite as satisfying now she'd got me in her shackles, only— Helen didn't appear to be on the same baddie team as Dr Craig any more, not if she was hiding out in a circle. Plus she wanted something from me, something I needed to agree to if I was supposed to have all my faculties ... and her daughter was missing. I took a mental leap and came up with—

'So, Dr Craig's holding Nicky hostage and I'm your ransom.' I gave her a level look. 'Have I got it about right?'

'Spot on, Ms Taylor.' She looked down her patrician nose at me. 'But you can be quite clever, on occasion.'

'So the real question is, since you're not just handing me over now you've got me all trussed up' – I lifted my uninjured arm with its police issue silver shackle – 'what is it you want me to agree to before you do the swap?'

Her lip curled in disdain. 'Craig's interested in your child-bearing capabilities.'

Of course he was. Everyone else and their dog was, so why not him? But— 'What exactly does "interested in my child-bearing capabilities" mean?'

'Sit up and have a look.'

'Why don't you just do your magic-punch thing again? It'd be easier,' I said flatly.

Her lips thinned, then she muttered and slapped her hand on my shoulder. I yelped, but the expected pain didn't come; instead everything went warm and numb. 'It's not healed, so don't try and use it,' she said warningly. 'And it won't last long, either.'

Better than nothing. Using my good arm as a lever, I sat up.

Chapter Fifty

In the centre of the large mediaeval-looking room there were around twenty metal hospital beds, all in the half-reclined position and set out in a large circle. The beds were all occupied by young girls. As I studied the faces of those I could see, I realised they all were all wearing the same Doppelgänger spells as the two dead faelings found in Dead Man's Hole. Sitting alternatively round the circle were the pretty 'girl next door' with her brown hair and freckles (Sally Redman's spell) and the beautiful, blue-eyed blonde: Miranda, the teenage witch from Morgan Le Fay College.

'Oka-*aay*,' I muttered, 'creepy or what?' Then I realised something even creepier: they were all pregnant, and most of them looked like it wasn't long to D-Day – or rather, B-Day? Not only that, half a dozen of the beds had small clear plastic cots next to them, complete with sleeping baby. And all the girls were silent and smiling, like this was the best place to be in the whole, wide world, like some sort of weird gathering of Stepford mums-to-be. Had to be some sort of Happy spell; twenty folk just wouldn't sit that quietly. I *looked*, but there was no magic to *see*, not on the Stepfords, anyway.

But there was on the right side of the room. About halfway down was a modern pine grandfather clock dripping with spells. It clashed with the whole mediaeval look – suits of armour would've been more in keeping – but then, the clock had to be what was stopping the time – literally. Next to it was a door. I doubted it was the way out: it didn't look large enough to get the hospital beds through, and they'd definitely been imported from the humans' world—

'You are now looking at the Merlin Foundation's newest initiative to produce the next generation of wizards,' Helen said, interrupting my escape-planning, 'all done through a combination of IVF, magic and surrogate mothers. Craig has developed a method of creating test-tube babies that consistently produces powerful wizards, through sex and gene selection. A lot of wizards, especially those older ones whose chance at marrying a long-lineage witch disappeared when the Bride-Price was abolished, are happy to pay his fees.'

'*Dr Frankenstein Does Designer Babies*, in other words,' I muttered in disgust as I tried to *focus* on the far end of the room ... there was something hidden there, behind a massive, curtain-like Look-Away veil. It had to be the way out, or at the very least, worth investigating ... once I got out of the Witch-bitch's evil clutches. 'What's with the Doppelgänger spells?' I asked, more to keep her talking than any real interest.

'They indicate who the baby's biological mother is,' she said coldly.

I shot her an appalled look. 'Surely the biological mothers haven't agreed to that many babies?'

'Apparently yes.' She stared impassively at the Stepfords. 'The witches are being very well paid for their eggs. He's even paying the faelings for their surrogacy services; they've all signed contracts; they're here by choice.'

I snorted. 'So he's killing them to save himself a bit of money? Nice to know he's got absolutely no ethics at all.'

'He's not killing them *per se*,' she said, turning back to me, her blue eyes as cold as her voice. 'The majority of them just don't have enough fae blood. They die not long after giving birth – incubating baby wizards and then breastfeeding them sucks all the magic and life out of them.'

I stared at her, shocked. 'But he's a doctor; didn't he work that out before he did his test-tube thing?'

'He did trials on Ana. The daughter is hers and her husband's, but the sons are all Craig's, both biologically, and by way of being his experiments. Ana is strong enough to survive the surrogacy because of her sidhe blood, but he wasn't successful with any of the other faelings, until he put together this set-up' – she indicated the large stone-walled room – 'here in *Between*. It keeps them alive just long enough.'

'Fuck,' I said in revulsion, 'I don't know which of you is worse, him for killing them off, or you for covering up their deaths. And all because you didn't want anyone to know that you had a child with a vamp.'

'Despite what you think of me, Ms Taylor, I don't condone the death of innocents. I didn't know the full extent of what was happening until recently, and Jack's birth is only a small part of it.' She cast a poignant look at the still sleeping Jack. 'Did you know vampires are infertile?'

'Well, Maxim isn't, obviously,' I said, 'otherwise your boy wouldn't be here.' Not to mention me. 'But what the hell's that got to do with anything?'

She laughed. 'You really don't know, do you? I always wondered if you were actually that clueless, and now I see you are. But then, you wouldn't have spent all this time looking for a way to *crack* the fertility curse if you'd known the truth ...' She trailed off, giving me a sly look.

I narrowed my eyes suspiciously. 'You've got my full attention. What truth?'

'Jack is Clíona's grandson,' she said, giving me a self-satisfied look. 'His father, Maxim, is Clíona's son – the one the vampires took from her.'

I gaped at her in astonishment for a moment, then it clicked into place. 'Maxim's the reason why she laid the *droch guidhe* curse – but he's supposed to be *dead*?'

'Which is what she and the vamps wanted the rest of the other fae to think.'

'She? *Clíona* knew her son wasn't dead?'

'Not immediately, but by the time she found out the truth, it was too late. She'd already *laid* the *droch guide*.'

I frowned down at the stone-flagged floor, trying to see the whole picture. 'So he was a vamp, and not dead, but why keep it a secret?'

Helen's lips thinned in derision. 'Don't you mean: why didn't she tell the fae that she'd been so blind that she'd fallen in love with a vamp's blood-pet, had a son with him, and then blamed the lesser fae when the vamps took her son from her and made him a vampire? And then cursed them to know the grief in her heart, a curse which made all their faeling children into vampire victims? A curse she could not remove?'

Ok-*aay*, so I could see how Clíona owning up to that *so* wouldn't go down well.

'Instead,' Helen carried on with an air of imparting great news, 'she tried to break the curse by having another child.'

'Yeah, I heard,' I said, remembering what Grianne, my faerie dogmother, had told me during my side-trip to Disney Heaven, why Clíona had given birth to Angel. '*A child for a child.*'

'Oh, so you do know some of the story then.' Helen sniffed. 'Of course, actually producing another child was where Clíona ran into difficulties. The vamps hadn't just given the Gift to Maxim, but they'd given it to his father too, so of course he'd been made infertile.'

'Look,' I said, 'you keep saying that, but you only have to look at your own son to know it's not true.'

Helen's superior expression reached new levels as she shook her head. 'Unlike you, I do know what I'm talking about. Vampires *are* infertile. The only way a vampire can make anyone pregnant, including a sidhe, is by using a lot of concentrated fertility magic. Clíona isn't a fertility fae, so when it came to having a child to break the curse, she entered into a bargain with the Morrígan for a Fertility spell.' She gave me a smug look. 'Where do you think they got the fertility from?'

Horror seeped into me as I realised what she was saying. 'Clíona and the Morrígan stole the fae's fertility?'

'They borrowed it,' she confirmed briskly. 'Clíona was supposed to give it back, but when she sent her daughter Rhiannon to return the Fertility spell, the spell was lost.'

Rhiannon was Angel – and she'd *lost* the spell! Fuck, no wonder London's fae were dying. And everyone was blaming it on the curse – which was sort of at fault – but if they didn't know their fertility had been stolen, they couldn't look for it. That was a huge secret Clíona – and anyone else who knew about it – was keeping. Only why would they? Why not tell everyone and get them searching?

But as I thought about it, the tail-end of Helen's memory replayed itself in my mind: *Angel kissed baby Jack's head ... and a pendant was hanging round her neck ...* The huge sapphire pendant that Helen always wore. The one that was even now shining like a captive star beneath her blouse. Damn. No one who knew about the Fertility spell needed to find it, because they all knew where it was.

So the million-pound question was: why hadn't anyone taken it back?

'You've got the Fertility spell,' I said slowly, itching to reach out and rip the pendant from her neck.

'Yes.' She cradled the sapphire in her hand.

Finn's words came back to me when he'd told me about Helen getting pregnant with Nicky: '*We were just fooling around ...*'

'You used it to trick Finn, didn't you?' I accused, then a disturbing thought hit me. 'He doesn't know about the pendant, does he?'

'No, of course not—' She paused, then sighed. 'I did consider telling him, but I had a baby daughter, a new husband, and status in the Witches' Council at last ... and then Craig demanded to know how I'd had another child. He blackmailed me into telling him. Since then he's been using the Fertility spell in his experiments.'

'You selfish bitch!' Bile rose in my throat. 'London's fae are *dying*. Faelings *have* died, not just the two most recent ones, but all those who ended up as vamp victims. Don't you *care*?'

'Faelings have always died at the hands of the vampires, Ms Taylor,' she said bluntly. 'It's sad, but no one can save them all. But what's more important now is saving my daughter.'

'You do know that there's no way out for you in all this, don't you?' I gave her a frank look. 'It won't be long before the police know all about Dr Craig and his experiments, and your involvement in them. The note you left me indicates you've got some connection to the vamps, so you're finished with the Witches' Council.' And Finn will probably never forgive you for putting his daughter in danger – but I kept that comment to myself. 'But you could make it go easier if you help me. All I need to do is find the entrance, then I can *crack* it open and let the police in to rescue Nicky and all the other faelings.' I waved at the Stepfords. 'Then they can all have their babies with a lot more care than this.'

'No, Ms Taylor,' she said firmly, not even considering my idea. 'The Time-sync spell means it will be another twenty-four hours before any help can get here. By then it will be too late for Nicky. This way you'll end up as Craig's next experiment, and not her. I'd say I'm sorry, but I'd be lying. But I will sweeten the deal for you,' she added. 'If you'll give your word to do what Craig wants, I'll tell Nicky about the pendant, so she can tell her father.'

I did consider her proposition. It would save Nicky, and Finn and the rest of London's fae would know their fertility had been stolen and where it was – and where it had been. And unlike Nicky, Dr Craig's experiment wasn't going to end up with me pregnant, not with the Morrígan's Chastity/Contraceptive spell Tavish had sicced on me. But the spell was also the reason I couldn't agree to Helen's terms, even if I wanted to. I couldn't give my word to let myself be impregnated, or even act as a surrogate, or whatever Dr Craig wanted, not when I knew it to be impossible, and when I couldn't lie.

Damn. It was a no-win either way.

I needed an Option Three.

Helen leaned towards me. 'Oh, and if you're worried about having to have sex with him,' she said, 'don't be. One: you're much too old and flat-chested for his tastes, and two: he's a scientist, and his experiments have to be done just so. So do you agree, Ms Taylor?'

I took a deep breath, looked at Jack, still curled up asleep on the floor—

And I punched Helen, a hard uppercut to the jaw. Her head snapped back and, satisfyingly, she crumpled like yesterday's news.

Spell shackles might stop you using magic (not that I had any), but they don't stop you using your fists.

Yep, Option Three worked for me.

Chapter Fifty-One

'So, has she told you, my lady?' Jack's question startled me and I almost swallowed the key I had between my teeth, the one with which I was trying to unlock the shackle on my uninjured arm. I looked up to find him regarding me gravely out of his indigo-coloured sidhe eyes. Damn.

I spat the key out into my palm. 'I knew I should've clocked you one on the head while you were still asleep.' Trouble was, I'd been worried I'd wake him up, rather than knock him out.

'Glad you didn't, my lady,' he said, casting a concerned look down at Helen, whose head I'd pillowed on her large leather bag (which contained nothing more useful than water, veggie sticks and cereal bars; I'd drunk the water). 'Don't worry, I'm here to help,' he added.

I narrowed my eyes, wondering exactly how helpful he was going to be, and who he was really working for. Only one way to find out. I held out my shackled arm in invitation.

He reached out cautiously and took the key from my palm. I stifled a relieved sigh as he unlocked the shackle. It fell on the stone floor with a clang.

'Proof enough?' he asked. 'Now, has my mother told you?'

'If we're talking about the Fertility spell, then yes.'

He took a deep breath, then asked earnestly, 'Do you have it?'

I went to open my mouth ... and then gave him a horrified look.

'By the goddess.' He raked his hands through his blond

hair in frustration. 'She promised she would tell you if you agreed.'

I grabbed his jumper. 'Tell me *what*?'

'There's a Protection spell on it,' he said, clenching his fists, 'one that ensures anyone who knows about the Fertility spell can never find it, even if they're staring right at it. And they can't use force to get her to give the spell up, otherwise it will destroy the fertility in the spell.'

'Fine, I get the picture,' I interrupted. So that was how the Witch-bitch had managed to keep hold of it all this time: she'd booby-trapped it. And why no one, like the goddesses, or Tavish and Malik, would talk to me (I mentally forgave them both), and why the only clues anyone would give me were as cryptic as Hell's worst crossword.

It also explained the pendant's highly confusing flickering in and out of sight during the dozen tries it'd taken for me to remove it from Helen's own neck – and why I couldn't see – or *see* – the pendant even though it was nestling between my breasts, unless I concentrated on the sad memory of Helen losing the baby Jack. But Jack was Helen's son and the Morrígan's bird, so I kept all that to myself.

'Crap,' I muttered. 'How the hell did she manage to *cast* such a complicated spell? It must have taken her years. But there has to be a way to get it.' I glowered at Helen, lying on the stone floor. 'She has to have at least a hundred spells on her.' Blinging herself up like a goblin queen had no doubt been extra camouflage. 'It'll take days to go through them all. But if you can fly her out' – I looked hopefully at Jack – 'and take her to the police, then—'

'I'm sorry, my lady, I can't. I have to procure my sister's safety first, then I have to answer the Morrígan's call to bring your friend here, as soon as the Time-sync spell runs its course.' He reached out and touched Helen's hand, suddenly looking very young again. 'Why didn't she tell you, when she promised she would?'

'Ah,' I said, grimacing, 'maybe because I didn't agree to do what she wanted.'

'You didn't agree?' His mouth gaped in shock.

'I couldn't give my word,' I said, and told him about the Chastity/Contraceptive spell.

He hunched over and hugged himself as he thought it through. I contemplated *calling* a Stun spell from one of the shackles, but decided he might be more useful awake. So instead I kept a cautious eye on him, in case he decided to regain the upper wing – sorry, hand – and knock me out so he could still swap me for Nicky. Although, to be honest, I had him pegged as more the follow-the-plan sort than a decide-what-to-do-next-when-things-go-wrong type of guy.

'But what about my sister?' he said finally with a plaintive look. 'I gave my word to mother to help her. How am I supposed to get her to safety now if you can't be traded in her place?'

Mentally I heaved a relieved sigh: I'd guessed right about him. 'Okay,' I said to Jack, trying to be reassuring for both of us, 'it's not all bad' – *yet* – 'and I've got a plan worked out' – *hopefully* – 'so here's what we'll do.'

After I'd finished telling him, I made a carry-pack out of Helen's cardigan for the shackles with their Stun spells and tied it round my waist, Jack *tagged* my injured shoulder and arm with another of his mother's Pain-Numbing spells, then I left him with her in the circle. There was nothing he could do until Nicky put in an appearance.

I headed for the far end of the room, hugging close to the stone wall, and skirting round the various suits of armour that had appeared from nowhere (or maybe the magic had picked them out of my head?), until I reached the Look-Away veil.

Behind it was a pair of metal double doors that looked like they'd be more at home on a modern lock-up instead of in the Tower of London. They had a thick wooden beam across them holding them shut, and a large shiny-steel padlock. I *looked*, and *saw* the black bars of a Knock-Back Ward buzzing across their metal surface. Lined up by the side of them were half a dozen empty hospital beds like those the smiling Stepford mums-to-be were happily and quietly lying on.

Relief and hope filled me. I'd found the way out.

Now to sort out the time problem.

I made my way quietly to the grandfather clock. Behind the door next to it came the sound of soft snoring. I cracked the door open to find a rosy-cheeked nurse asleep with her feet up in an easy chair: the duty nurse Jack had told me about. Tiptoeing in, I *called* one of the shackles' Stun spells and tapped it on her head. It flashed green mint-scented lightning, and she jerked, then subsided into unconsciousness, putting her out of it for a good couple of hours.

I turned back to contemplate the grandfather clock. *Cracking* the spells on the doors and the clock was a non-starter with twenty-odd pregnant females and half a dozen babies in the room. It would be like exploding a bomb in the place, and they were too close to ground zero. *Absorbing* the spells was a no-go too; rescuing anyone while you're unconscious is one of those impossible-to-do things. And *teasing* the magic apart was too time-consuming (no pun intended).

But if I could get the clock to finish its chime, get everything back in sync and convince the magic to open the doors somewhere useful in the humans' world, then I could *absorb* the Wards and take the hit. Trouble was, someone, like Dr Craig or one of his minions was going to notice what I was doing sooner or later. So I needed … an emergency bolt hole.

Wincing, I bit into my wrist and *cast* a circle of blood drops on the flagstone floor in front of the clock and smeared them together: my own mini blood-Ward, just large enough for me to kneel in. I opened the clock's long door and pursed my lips at the two hanging weights, neither of which had a handy label. Reaching up I opened the clock face door, then, sending a prayer to both the goddesses who I hoped were listening, I started physically moving the large hand.

As the clock's hands came together at eleven o'clock, I waited for the end of the chime, but it still didn't come. Gritting my teeth, I started rotating the large hand, willing the small hand to move faster around the clock's face. Anxious adrenalin fizzed in me as the magic in the spells started shifting ... and the floor seemed to tip sideways like a ship sliding down a huge wave ... I hit one o' clock: the Stepford mums-to-be started moving restlessly. *Keep turning ... Five o' clock*: the Stepfords were moaning, the babies making small whimpering sounds, and a nauseous feeling roiled in my stomach. *C'mon, c'mon ... Eight o' clock*: my legs were trembling and I was almost out of time. *Turn faster, damn it ... Ten o' clock*: a Stepford screamed, the babies were crying, and spots swam in my vision.

A door slammed open behind me. Someone yelled.

Nearly there.

Green lightning hit the wall next to the clock. A Stun spell.

Eleven o' clock.

I jumped in the circle and collapsed to my knees—

The first chime split the air.

—and I shoved my magic into the blood-Ward—

The dome closed over me, and another Stun spell smashed in a shower of green sparks.

Dizzy, I dropped my head to the floor and gulped a couple of deep breaths.

The second chime sounded.

Safe, and in Time-sync ... I'd done it—

—even if I was trapped.

Chapter Fifty-Two

The third chime cut out halfway through, strangled before it could finish.

Crap. Someone had frozen the spell. Time had stopped again.

I swallowed back my frustration and as the dizziness receded, looked up warily to find three people next to my suddenly very tiny, very fragile-feeling circle.

Dr Craig didn't look much different from the way I normally saw him at HOPE: tweed trousers, white doctor's coat, stethoscope round his neck, yellow notepad under his arm, and his grey curls ringing his fish-belly-pale bald scalp and parting around his jug-handled ears. Of course, that was if I ignored the long furry orange-coloured cape-thing that he was wearing over the doctor's coat. And the thick gold chain that clasped it round his neck. He looked like he was auditioning for Caveman Doctor of the Year, and it wasn't a look that suited him. Not to mention that if he was here, then he wasn't in a silver-lined cell at Old Scotland Yard, and Hugh didn't know he was a baddie. Fuck.

Standing beside him was a thickset witch dressed in an over-tight nurse's uniform. Her cottage-loaf bun of grey hair looked like it had been stapled to her head, and her face didn't look like it had ever cracked a smile.

Good to know he's got his own Nurse Ratched.

Behind them both was a faeling who could only be Nicky. Neat hooves peeped out below the hem of the white frilly nightdress she was wearing. Her features were a softer version of Helen's beautiful patrician ones. Her horns curved to sharp triangular points about six inches above her head, and her hair was truly her proverbial crowning glory: sleek sable tresses fell almost to her waist – the same colour as Finn's in his true guise. Seeing her made my heart ache for Finn. She shouldn't be here; she should be safe with him.

Instead, she was smiling: that same wide, eerie Stepford beam that the rest of the girls in the circle had on their faces. I *looked*, trying to see the spell again, but as with the other girls, I couldn't pinpoint any magic on her.

'Hello, Genny,' Dr Craig said genially, as if I wasn't huddled like a stranded turtle on the floor by his feet. 'I was hoping we'd meet again soon. I was expecting you to visit earlier.'

'Yeah, something came up,' I said drily.

'Craig,' Helen shouted imperiously from the other side of the large, gloomy room, 'I want a word with you. Please.'

Dr Craig turned, regarded her for a few seconds, then said, 'Helen, I'm glad to see you've considered your daughter's health and returned.' As he moved, I caught sight of her glaring from inside her circle. A worried-looking Jack hovered behind her. He caught my eye, and shrugged. I frowned at him: he was supposed to have kept her out of this. Movement in the circle of hospital beds caught my eye: two other nurses were moving from one Stepford mum-to-be to the next, obviously checking up on them. The mums-to-be ignored them; instead they were all craning their necks my way. And they were all still smiling that same blank eerie smile as Nicky.

'I want a trade, Craig,' Helen shouted again. 'The sidhe for my daughter. I've told her what you want to do, and she agrees to it.'

Liar! But I kept that to myself.

But Dr Craig obviously thought Helen was lying too, since he ignored her and turned back to me with a smile just as creepy, if not as bland, as the Stepfords'. 'Genny, why don't you get up and we can have a nice chat about things.' He said it like he expected me to agree.

Odd. Maybe he thought whatever spell he was using on the Stepfords would work on me ... except I still couldn't *see* anything.

He kept on smiling and speaking, and I realised I heard him use that same tone of voice on patients at HOPE. I shut him out, and gauged the distance between me and his legs. His rubber-soled shoes were only about a foot away from my nose. It was too far to reach out ... but if I launched myself at him, I could touch him skin to skin and maybe catch his mind in my Glamour—

—and get zapped by the Stun spell Nurse Ratched was ready to sling my way.

Shit. If only he was nearer, instead of a foot away.

His furry cape suddenly brushed the dome of my small circle. I blinked in surprise.

Neither of us had moved, but his shoe was right there, its rubber sole now an inch away from my blood smeared on the flagstones.

I swallowed, feeling almost sick with exhilaration and cast a thankful glance at the suits of armour: the magic was listening to me. I'd wanted him nearer, and nearer he was. I felt like whooping in delight, but instead I shot my uninjured arm out through the blood-Ward and pushed it under the cuff of his tweed trouser leg. I wrapped my fingers round his ankle, touching bare flesh, and shoved my magic into him. A bolt of gold fire shot up from my hand like a skyrocket and hit the gold chain round his neck; it exploded into a chrysanthemum-head of sun-bright magic—

—and pain sliced through my mind like someone had chopped the top of my skull off with an axe.

And before I could retreat into my tiny circle, he reached

down, grasped my wrist and yanked me out. 'Naughty, naughty,' he said chidingly, as I knelt there, gasping like a landed fish, desperately wondering what the chain was Warded with, and what the hell I was going to do for an encore.

'You've got the sidhe, Craig,' Helen yelled, sounding just as desperate as I felt, 'now let me have my daughter.'

'Very well, Helen.' He turned to the smiling Nicky. 'Nicola, please go to your mother now.'

She started trotting towards Helen, hooves striking off the stone floor, her smile unchanging.

I gaped. Was he really just going to let her go?

Helen evidently thought so, as she *broke* her circle and started hurrying towards Nicky, a big concerned smile on her face.

Unease shifted in me. I craned my head ...

Nicky grabbed the frilly nightdress, bunching it up round her thighs, showing well-muscled, tanned calves and long, lean thighs coated with sleek hair the same sable colour as her head. She started to run towards her smiling mother.

Something was wrong.

Helen's smile dimmed.

'Helen,' I shouted, 'get back in the circle—

Nicky leapt the last few steps, kicking out as she did, and one precisely placed hoof caught her mother in the stomach. Helen doubled over and dropped like a broken broomstick to the stone-flagged floor. Another hoof caught her in the kidneys. Nicky circled round to Helen's front and aimed a dainty hoof at her mother's head—

'Stop her,' I screamed, reaching out and grabbing Dr Craig's orange furry cape—

And everything stopped as if I'd pressed the pause button on a DVD: Nicky with her hoof in mid-air— Nurse Ratched with the Stun spell ready to throw— The Stepfords, all smiling creepily in my direction— Dr Craig standing half turned away from me—

Musty air shivered over me, and the rank scent of charred meat choked in my throat, then a huge translucent figure winked into being, superimposing itself like a badly scratched hologram over Dr Craig.

Chapter Fifty-Three

The figure looked half giant, half long-haired orang-utan, if you discounted his broad, mostly human face with its glowing orange eyes, and the heavy scimitar-like horns that were as long as my arms sweeping to either side of his head above his twitching furry ears. He was naked, apart from the orange hair, the heavy gold chain round his neck and a small brown leather loincloth. Underneath the thick hair his skin was covered in an intricate swirling pattern of red, gold and black ink that shimmered with latent power.

He had to be the Morrígan's son: MacCúailnge, the Old Donn.

He was also the spitting image of The Mother's photofit.

Hmm. Maybe she didn't need a camera after all.

He was also a ghost.

My phobia hit. I pressed my lips together hard, stifling the shriek in my throat. Fae don't leave ghosts – not naturally, anyway – but the Old Donn was definitely a ghost, however impossible that was. Which meant he couldn't harm the living, at least not outside of All Hallows' Eve. Or at least that's the way normal ghosts work. And if he wasn't normal ... well, I'd find out soon enough.

He flicked a long cowlick of paler orange hair out of his eyes and grinned, showing brown stumps of ground-down teeth. 'I'm the MacCúailnge,' he pronounced, 'and I'm afther believin' me darlin' mother, the Morrígan, has delivered you here to do my bidding.'

'Yeah? Well, you can forget that idea,' I said, pleased my words came out dry as dust despite the little phobic-fuelled voices in my head telling me to scream and run and don't stop until I was far, far away. 'I've got one dictatorial male in my life already. No way do I need another. So how about we try doing this the democratic "help-each-other-out" way?'

'"Help" …?' The glow in the MacCúailnge's orange eyes turned crafty. 'I might be afther considerin' it, seeing as I'm wantin' something in return.'

Figured. I pursed my lips at him, wondering just how helpful a non-corporeal ghost could actually be, and if I really needed to ask him what he wanted when no doubt the clip-clop of little bull hooves was going to be the answer. I sighed. 'Go on then, tell me what you want.'

He raised his bushy eyebrows. 'Why, a body and me freedom, me darlin'. Forty years of bein' without them both is quite the trial.'

A body? I narrowed my eyes at him. 'What sort of body?'

'A new one, of course.' He waved a huge hairy arm towards the Stepfords. 'This wee wizard man here's been promisin' me one for a rare long while now, but none o' these wee girlies are strong enough for the MacCúailnge.' A sly expression crossed his face and he crouched down so he could look me in the eyes. 'Unless you'll be willin', pretty sidhe?'

The Morrígan's little fertility mix of spit and Finn's donation that she wanted me to drink made even more horrible sense. She didn't want a grandson; she wanted a new body for her son. Her kidnapper rapist murderer son.

'No,' I said, as rage filled my veins with icy determination, 'no way. You don't deserve a new body, not after what you did to Rhiannon, and not after what you're doing now. You're the reason your wizard pal' – I jerked my head at the 'paused' Dr Craig standing within the Old Donn's ghostly presence – 'has been able to kill these faelings. You should have stopped him.'

His large orange eyes did a slow blink, then his expression turned to dismay. 'The wee lassies have been dyin'?' His shoulders lowered and he shot a bushy browed frown at the Stepfords. 'The wee wizard man ne'r told me that. And you have the right of it, pretty sidhe, I should have been afther stoppin' him from doin' such a foul thing in my ain home.'

Ri-ight. I gave him a suspicious look, not sure whether he was for real or not. 'So, are you going to stop him now?'

'I'm thinkin' there's not much I can do like this, pretty sidhe.' His ears flattened. 'Not while the wizard man here has harnessed what little power I still possessed by wearin' me ain skin.'

Nice! Except— 'That's it: he's used your power to Glamour them,' I muttered. 'Damn; that's why I couldn't catch him with mine.' I looked him over speculatively, then tugged on the orange furry cape. 'Okay, everything stopped when I grabbed your skin here, so does that mean I've got control of your power now?'

'Maybe if you were wearin' my hide, you would.' His wide nostrils flared pensively. 'But mind, once ye leave go of your hold on me, time will all be afther startin' again.'

He's wylde fae, murmured my cautious voice, and they're always tricky, not to mention he gave in way too easily on the whole new body thing. Or that it wasn't a coincidence that he'd appeared right at the opportune time. And where was Jack? I squinted up past the Old Donn to see Jack in his raven form perched on one of the wooden chandeliers. He was the Morrígan's bird, and the Old Donn was the Morrígan's bull.

And I knew what the Morrígan wanted.

Wearing his hide was a definite no.

But it wasn't the only source of juice here.

This was *Between*, after all, malleable if you had enough will and power, and if the magic liked you – I glanced at the suits of armour – which it sort of looked like it did … I closed my eyes, sent a quick prayer to The Mother, and *focused* on what *I* wanted: enough time, plenty of space, and a perfect aim—

Something brushed against me, a shy questing touch of an unfamiliar consciousness. It— No, *she*, offered aid ... power freely given. I took half a second to quell my natural cynical response that whispered about unspoken obligations, then, eager and grateful, I opened the part of me that *absorbs* the magic and accepted. Power flooded into me like a tsunami, filling and stretching and reshaping until the barrier between us dissolved and it settled like a warm weight inside my soul. I took a shaky breath, then another, and with the third a rush of searing heat drenched sweat over my body, my bones vibrated like a magical tuning fork as the stone floor trembled beneath me, and the tart apple taste of cloudberries slipped down my throat and poured steadiness into my limbs.

'Well, pretty sidhe, what say you?' The Old Donn's question held a note of eagerness he couldn't quite hide. He'd been waiting a long time.

I opened my eyes and gave him a wry smile. 'Nice offer, but I've had a better one.' I released my hold on him, and he winked out of sight.

The grandfather clock rattled and squeaked, then resumed chiming.

Thirteen chimes for the hour, then eleven gongs for the time.

Twenty-four seconds.

I held my hand up and caught the Stun spell Nurse Ratched threw at me and zipped it straight at Nicky just before she stuck her hoof in Helen's skull, wincing as Nicky dropped like a Stunned dryad. Luckily Helen was there to cushion her fall.

Twenty-one seconds.

I caught Nurse Ratched's next Stun spell and tossed it straight back, grinning as she too dropped like a Stunned dryad. Sadly, there was nothing soft for her to land on.

Nineteen.

I called a Stun spell from the shackles tied at my waist and, yelling at the nurses there to stay back, flung it gently towards the circle of hospital beds. The spell splashed harmlessly to the floor in a burst of green stars.

Fifteen.

I *focused* on the gold chain around Dr Craig's neck and *cracked* the sun-bright magic, rolling awkwardly to the side as he collapsed almost on top of me.

Thirteen.

I scrambled to my feet, grabbed the Old Donn's furry hide and ran for the empty hospital beds stored next to the double doors.

'Just a short distance,' I muttered, and the distance obligingly shortened, so much so that I hit the metal beds in a bone-jarring skid just as the first deeper chime sounded.

'Okay, a bit too helpful maybe,' I murmured as I shoved myself in among the cover of the beds.

Nine.

I hunkered down and quickly gauged the distance to the circle of Stepfords. They were almost fifty feet away in the far corner now, but still much too close. 'They need to be so far away that they're just tiny, tiny figures,' I murmured.

Seven.

The room started stretching, new wooden beams springing up to support the high ceiling like a line of trees popping out of the ground.

Five.

The room kept growing, and more wooden chandeliers dropped down on ropes from the high roof, their candles springing into flaming light as they did so.

Four.

The figures shrank into the distance.

Three.

I *focused* on the Knock-back Wards on the double doors.

Two.

'Somewhere safe for everyone,' I prayed.

One.

I *cracked* the magic—

—and the world exploded.

Chapter Fifty-Four

Thick, clinging greyness surrounded me.

'Pretty sidhe,' crooned a deep, rough voice next to my ear, 'I will be huffing, and I will be puffing, and I will be blowing your house down, said the vampire to the tasty sidhe.' The voice changed to a high-pitched squeal. 'Oh no you won't, squeaked the tasty sidhe.' The voice sank back into the deep bass. 'Oh yes, I will, said the vamp ...' The voice trailed off, leaving a buzzing in my head.

My eyes were open, but the greyness was too thick to see through. I had a horrifying thought that the ton of power I'd used to crack the doors and Knock-Back Wards had destroyed the Old Donn's place. Terror clutched my heart in a hard fist and I took a deep, calming, and oddly dusty breath. I pressed a hand to my T-shirt to check the pendant was still hidden safely beneath it, then catalogued what I could feel: I was lying on cold stone – the floor; behind me was a wall, also stone; there was something heavy on my legs, which were numb ... I reached out and touched cold metal: I was trapped under one of the hospital beds; and the oddly dusty, gritty taste on my tongue was ... actual dust. Okay, so I hadn't destroyed everything. Just banged the place up a bit.

'I will huff, and I will puff ...'

I felt around until my fingers met with long, wiry hair. An orange glow began to penetrate the fog and the huge furry figure of the Old Donn took shape beside me. He was the one singing.

I squinted up at him. 'What—?' I coughed up a mouthful of dust, gritted my teeth against the stabbing pain in my shoulder – *should've asked Jack for another of the Witch-bitch's Pain-Numbing spells to go* – then managed to croak out, 'What's with the singing?'

He knocked his hairy knuckles on one long horn. 'There is a vampire at the door, tasty sidhe, and he says he's after entering.' He leaned closer and whispered, 'He says he can *smell* you.'

Was it Malik?

'Can you let him in?' I asked, my voice a little less croaky.

'I cannot ask.' He winked. 'For he cannot see—'

A loud rumbling noise cut him off. It sounded like thunder directly overhead ... or falling masonry. My pulse sped. Maybe I'd been a bit hasty in assuming I hadn't destroyed the place. 'What was that?' I said, struggling up onto my good elbow.

'You have huffed and puffed and now my house is blowing down,' the Old Donn said sadly.

Fuck. The Stepfords!

'But you can keep the place stable, can't you?' I asked urgently, almost sure he could, otherwise why sing in my ear? 'And let the vamp in?'

His orange eyes glinted slyly. 'I might be doing that, if you'd be agreeing to get me a new body and my freedom back?'

Damn aggravating tricky fae, always wanting to bargain when the chips, or rather bricks are down.

'Let the vamp in and keep the place stable until everyone's out,' I said decisively, 'and I'll do a deal on the freedom.' I paused, then added, 'My terms, not yours.'

'Not good enough,' he bellowed.

'All you're going to get,' I said flatly, mentally crossing my fingers. 'But remember, if the place truly collapses and I *fade*, then you've lost your chance. You might not get another one for ... oh, centuries, at least. So take it or leave it.'

'Obstinate pretty sidhe.' He stood and stamped his foot, and the floor shook. 'Very well, then. I invite you in, vampire,' he finished on a loud roar.

For a second nothing happened, then the bed on my legs went flying and a tawny-haired blur loomed out of the grey fog above me. 'Genny, are you okay?' the vamp said, wiping at my face. 'Your head's all gashed and I can smell your blood, like, *everywhere*.' He sniffed his fingers and wrinkled his nose. 'Though this isn't all yours, is it?'

Darius. My fang-pet.

'How did you get here?' I asked, bemused.

'This big hole just exploded in the Coffin Club's wall,' he said, his excited grin showcasing all four of his fangs. 'We all crowded round, and as soon as I got near it I caught your scent.'

Somewhere safe. The magic had an odd sense of humour at times – although, with Malik's protection … well, a faeling possibly couldn't get safer than a vamp club in Sucker Town just now. Not to mention there'd be no one faster, stronger, or more able to sniff out the Stepfords in the dust than a load of vamps with super-senses.

'Thank you,' I murmured, sending my gratitude to the magic.

I told Darius what I needed. 'So get them all in here, get them hunting, but tell them no fangs, otherwise they'll be begging for Malik to rip their heads off before I've finished with them.'

'Sure thing, Genny,' he said cheerfully.

The hospital beds were made of iron, which thankfully meant the numbness in my legs was temporary, but also meant moving was out of the question, not to mention that my shoulder felt like a dwarf was using it as an anvil, and bouncing hammers off it, so Darius left me propped against the wall amidst the rubble of the entrance I'd made between the Tower and the Coffin Club. The big hole in the wall opened into the inner hallway of the club, and going by the heaps of coffin-shaped and decorated tat lying around the place, my magical explosion had extensively rearranged the gift shop; in particular the shop's window display of DVDs, which was now a three-foot-high volcano of melted plastic and shattered glass.

I shrugged – the DVDs had been on sale, so they obviously weren't hot ticket items – and watched with beady-eyed anxiety as the club's vamps disappeared into the dust, and sighed with heartfelt relief as the first reappeared carefully pushing a Stepford mum-to-be in her wheeled bed, then lifting it over the rubble like the bed weighed nothing more than a tea tray. I relaxed into a weary, pain-filled stupor as more complaining Stepfords, crying babies and sullen nurses were rescued, and waited for Hugh to arrive with his boys in blue. The Old Donn sat with me, humming happily while he polished his horns with his loincloth.

After about ten minutes Darius walked out of the grey dust of *Between* with a white-coated body tucked under one arm and something dangling from his other hand.

'Think he got caught up in the explosion,' he said with a frown, as he held up Dr Craig's head by one jug-handled ear. The neck was still dripping. 'What do you want me to do with him?'

The Old Donn's polishing stilled.

'Probably better put him on ice until the police get here,' I said blandly.

Darius grinned, saluted me with the head and strode off.

'You seem to be havin' a wee bit of a problem controlling your magic, pretty sidhe,' the Old Donn said mildly.

He was right. I'd only meant to *crack* the gold chain fastening the Old Donn's cape across Dr Craig's shoulders, so as to break the Glamour hold he had over the Stepfords, but the power-boost I'd been given had to go somewhere. Not that I was going to lose any sleep over Dr Craig's demise, or that the Old Donn needed to know any of that.

I gave him a wide beam of a smile. 'Nah, the magic did just what I needed.' Which wasn't a lie. I had needed Dr Craig out of action, albeit not quite so bloodily.

The Old Donn's broad nostrils flared, then he nodded and went back to his polishing. A couple of rescued Stepfords later, he said in a conversational tone, 'The vamps were afther comin' afore, into my home. Two o' them, along with the kelpie and the watery man.' His orange eyes glowed with malice. 'Relatives of hers, if you're for believin' that. They were the ones took her and her little girlie away.'

'Took who away?' I asked, keeping my voice casual. Not that I needed to ask: he meant Angel, or Rhiannon, as he'd known her, and Brigitta her daughter: Ana's mother.

'She was always one for singing.' He hummed a few notes in a soft, sad baritone that sounded like 'Rock-a-Bye-Baby'.

'She still is,' I said in the same casual tone as my hand clenched in his orange hairy hide.

'She was happy here.' His massive head dipped in apology. 'We were never afther forcing her, pretty sidhe, not even with the curse as our reason. She agreed to all we asked.'

'She didn't know what it was all about,' I said, only just keeping my fury in check. 'How could she when she's not in her right mind?'

'You're right, of course,' he said gently. 'But then, you're a fine daughter to her.'

My hand spasmed open and I shoved his furry cape away. He winked out of sight.

Angel was *my mother*.

I dropped my head back against the wall as the thought ripped my heart into tiny bloody, painful pieces. In some shadowed corner of my mind I'd known she was ... Not right away, even though seeing her that first time had been like looking into a mirror, but ever since then, the knowing had been dripping into me, as inexorable and unstoppable as Chinese water torture. I'd ignored it. I hadn't wanted to admit it was real. I'd wanted to cling to my belief that my mother was a sidhe called Nataliya, that she'd died when I was born, and that she hadn't abandoned me. And I hadn't wanted to know that my part in the curse wasn't happenstance, hadn't wanted to know that I was just another sacrificial child in a family full of them: a child abandoned to the vampires so she could break a mislaid curse.

No wonder Clíona – my *grandmother* – had been so determined to kill me when I'd run away from the suckers at fourteen and turned up in London. I was her proverbial bloody, tainted laundry.

My throat constricted and tears stung my eyes. But at least now I had the pendant with its Fertility spell and the means to put everything to rights, hopefully without ending up with a sacrificial child of my own.

Jack, in his raven guise, soared out of the grey dust carrying a limp Nicky in his talons, her white frilly nightdress flapping in his slipstream; he didn't stop, but flew straight through the club's wall as if it wasn't there and disappeared. I hoped he was taking her to Finn. Moments later he was followed by a tall, stretched-thin vamp with an equally limp Helen slung over his shoulder. He lowered her to the carpet in the club, and for a second I thought she was dead, she lay so still.

The vamp wrung his hands and gave me a grovelling look. 'Sorry, Ms Taylor, I had to put her out. She kept struggling, and it was making me hungry.' He bent and touched his finger to her forehead and stepped quickly back.

She sprang up like a jack-in-the-box, fists clenched, eyes wild and angry, a purple bruise blooming down the side of her face where I'd hit her. Evidently Nicky hadn't put her hoof in as hard as I'd thought. Seeing me sitting there, she strode over.

'I want it back,' she shouted, and before I realised what she meant to do, she flicked her finger at my injured shoulder.

Pain exploded though my body. *Fucking Witch-bitch*—

And I fell into the blackness.

Chapter Fifty-Five

I woke up in a coffin with the dark spice-and-copper taste of Malik's blood in my mouth. He'd healed me. Part of me was disappointed that I hadn't been around to enjoy it. The coffin was glass, cushioned with plush white velvet, and was in the middle of the Room of Remembrance. A hard knot of worry twisted in my gut. I hoped the coffin was nothing more than someone's black sense of humour, and not some symbolic fairytale portent telling me I'd missed my sunset appointment with the Morrígan.

I jerked up to find the room empty apart from Mad Max, who was watching me with a quizzical expression on his face. He was leaning, arms crossed, against the blood-smeared coffin displayed on the raised dais at the end of the room. He was dressed in his red Hussar uniform, with his long platinum-blond hair pulled back in a ponytail ... and his shiny black knee-boots were firmly planted on the Old Donn's furry orange hide.

'I need to know how long it is 'til sunset,' I said, trying to keep my voice calm.

Mad Max gave me a lazy smile. 'Sun's not going down for a couple of hours yet, love.'

I blew out a relieved sigh. There was still time. 'What happened while I was out?'

'The police troll chappy turned up with all bells ringing and a parade of ambulances,' he said nonchalantly. 'Everyone got carted off to HOPE, or to the nick at Old Scotland Yard.'

'Oh good.' Sounded like Hugh had it all under control.

I hopped out of the coffin, pulled a face at the dirty, bloodstained velvet I left behind, and scowled at the dirty, blood-stained jeans and ripped T-shirt I was still wearing. For some reason my clothes had suffered worse than I'd thought in the magical explosion. I had a brief, wistful thought about a hot shower, ice-cold vodka and clean clothes. Unfortunately, there wasn't going to be enough time for all that.

I still had a couple more problems to sort out as well as the Morrígan.

And Problem Number One, Mad Max, was standing in front of me.

'So,' Mad Max said casually, 'how're you diddling, Cousin? All your aches and pains gone?'

I gave my first problem a neutral look. '"Cousin"? Or should it be "niece"?'

He raised his brows. 'Cat's out of the bag, is it?'

'Yep.'

He flung his arms wide, and bowed. 'Cousin whatever-it-is-removed on your dad's side' – he smacked the coffin he was leaning against: inside it was Fyodor, still lying staked in his diamond- and blood-strewn white clothes – 'and this here is not just *my* Dear Old Dad, but your mum's too, which makes your mum my nutty little sister, and me your uncle. But family are downright hard to keep track of unless you keep them in their place' – he smacked the coffin again with evident glee – 'so don't take my word for it; have a butcher's at that instead.' He pointed to a book propped up against one of the glass coffins opposite me.

I strode across the aisle and snatched it up.

'Watch it, love,' Mad Max snapped out sharply, 'you damage that and I'll take it out of your hide.'

I shot him a frown, then studied the book. It was tooled black leather with each corner protected by silver, and an ornate silver lock and clasp keeping it closed. *Mad Max's diary, maybe?* The silver burned my fingers as I undid the clasp, and as the book fell open where it had been bookmarked by a black silk ribbon, the faint perfume of roses rose like an ethereal ghost.

On the left-hand page was another family tree; a small hiccough of hysteria lodged in my throat that this was the second family tree I'd seen in two days. But it was the page opposite the tree that truly captured my attention. It was dated: 18th June, twenty-six years ago, and written at the top in large, almost childish script was: *Brigitta's fifteenth birthday*.

Below the heading was a faded, pressed pink rose, and next to the pressed flower was a strip of four small photographs, from one of those 'instant photo' booths. The first three photos were headshots of two giggling girls with a silver-haired Irish wolfhound sitting proudly between them – Mad Max in his doggy persona, presumably. The dog was holding a pink rose in his teeth. The last one showed the same two girls, with Mad Max in his human shape, still with the rose in his fangs, looking like some platinum-blond vampire Valentino.

One of the girls was obviously Helen, a much younger version. The other one I'd never seen, but if her hair had been less strawberry blonde and more my own blood-amber colour, and if the pale gold colour of her sidhe eyes had been darker, she could've been my twin sister. She had to be Brigitta.

All three of them looked young and happy, and like they were having a great time.

I looked at the family tree on the page opposite.

I stared at the photos and the handwritten family tree, trying to take it in.

I wasn't my mother's only child.

She'd had another daughter, Brigitta ... who was twenty-six years older than me and looked like my twin—

But Brigitta was dead, killed by the vamps, and I'd never even met her. Rage, and an odd grief for the sister I'd never known, rose like a surging tide in my chest and I wanted to smash something—

'Of course,' Mad Max's loud drawl broke me out of my thoughts and I swallowed my anger back as I turned to glare at his cheerful, smiling face, 'your batty mother – Angel, as she likes to be called now – kept changing her name' – he pointed at the book in my hands – 'which rather makes a mess of the whole thing, love.'

My fingers clenched on his book. With all the family skeletons coming out of the bloody cupboard, maybe he'd tell me about one more. 'So how did my sidhe mother end up in possession of a long-lost Fertility spell right at the time when she met my vamp father?'

'Ah. I'm afraid the blame for that is mine.'

I dug my nails into my palms to stop from screaming at him. 'Tell me.'

'Well.' He crossed his arms again. 'When my barmy sister was returning the Fertility spell to this nasty moth-eaten old thing here'– he dug his heel viciously into the Old Donn's hide – 'she stopped off for a little romantic holiday with the equally crazy fossegrim. But the rub of it was, once she'd finished playing about in his fountains, the spell was missing. Fast-forward a few years, and Brigitta – that's her kid with the old fossy – happened upon the spell on one of her visits to the old man.'

'At which point *you* decided to test it out – on Helen!' I

looked down at the diary in my hands. 'And on Brigitta—' I stopped, appalled. 'Brigitta was *your niece*! My half-sister!'

'What can I say' – he grinned widely, flashing fang, but his eyes were a cold, hard blue – 'other than the girls were great friends, they both had pressing problems they wanted solved with the miracle of a bouncing little baby, and despite being a cad and a really quite terrible uncle, I obliged them. Anyway, the next thing happens, my wacky sister turns up and demands the spell. Of course I handed it straight over. You don't want to get on the wrong side of her, 'specially not when she's got her "goddess" thing going on.' He gave a dramatic shudder. 'But old Andrei – that's "Daddy" to you – was visiting, and my fruitcake of a little sister took a fancy to him, slapped the old boy with enough Glamour he didn't know which way was up, and then, hey presto, nine months later out *you* pop.'

'So my father didn't rape her?' I said, feeling oddly numb that I'd spent the last eleven years believing something about my parents' relationship – and my birth – that wasn't true. And after all this time, if there was a baddie in all that, it wasn't my father, but Clíona and The Mother.

'Good God no!' He shot me a horrified look. 'More like the other way round, if you think of it – not that he objected, no, he was quite the strutting peacock with it all.'

So why did she leave me with him? But I didn't ask. I was pretty sure the curse and The Mother had something to do with the answer. Instead, I carefully closed the diary and put it back next to the glass coffin. I'd had as much of my family history as I could cope with for now. I dropped the grief and pain and anger away into a dark hole in my mind to deal with later. I needed my wits about me for my sunset appointment with the Morrígan.

'Right, miles to go,' I said briskly, since there was still Problem Number Two – the Old Donn – to sort out before my meet up with the Morrígan. 'So I'll take my furry orange hide from under your boots, thanks.' I shot the furry orange hide in question a pointed look.

'You're not thinking about resurrecting him, are you?' Mad Max asked in an offhand drawl.

'No.'

'All yours then, niece.' He tipped an imaginary hat to me and started sauntering to the doors. 'I'm off to see if I can resurrect the shambles you've made of the business. Have fun, kiddo.'

'Wait—'

He turned and flashed me a knowing, fang-filled grin. 'Mr Inscrutable's gone back to spend some quality time with His Royal Brattiness. After all, none of us want Him putting in an appearance, do we? And old Malik's the best man to keep him occupied, what with all that True Gift immortality thing he's got going on—'

Fear, panic and anger that Malik had gone back to the Autarch hit me like a sucker punch right under my heart. Stupid, idiotic vamp.

'—but he's bound to turn up like the bad penny he is, sooner or later.' Mad Max shot his finger at me. 'Told you, Malik never forgets, and he keeps coming after you once he's got you in his sights.' He turned to go.

'He's not another long-lost uncle, cousin or whatever, is he?' I blurted out. Any of which would be like a major *ick*, I added silently.

Mad Max gave a barking laugh. 'Worried he's into incestuous relationships like the rest of our dysfunctional family, are you, niece?'

'Yes.'

'Not his thing at all, love.'

Relief slammed into me like a high wind in a hurricane and I let out the breath I'd been holding.

'Oh,' he added, 'and speaking of dysfunctional families, if

you see my little bitch of a daughter, tell her she'll have to deal with you direct for your blood from now on. It appears my middleman's gone walkabout.'

His daughter—? Oh right, Ana, who I now clicked was another relation … my cousin, or niece, or both … Mentally I shook my head, not sure I wanted to work out exactly how all the family connections fitted together. It was icky enough just knowing they did. But why would she want my blood? And more worryingly— 'What's happened to Darius?'

'Your little fang-pet? Nothing as far as I'm aware. Perhaps I should've said my middlewitch, since it's the beautiful Helena who's done the old disappearing trick.'

Surprise winged through me. 'Helen Crane's gone missing?'

'That's what I said, love,' he said bitterly, his Happy-as-Larry mask slipping momentarily, 'and if you're interested in finding her, you'll have to chase up my black-feathered son.' Then he did his own disappearing trick and vanished, leaving a sad-sounding plea in my mind. *When you see Ana, tell her to stay away … and stay safe.'*

Chapter Fifty-Six

Sunset painted the sky with red, orange and yellow as I walked into the Tower Hill Memorial Garden. A thirty-foot-high fountain shot straight up from the bronze pool in the centre, and the place was crowded with folk: the buzz of their conversation sounded like the overloud birthing-hum of a goblin queen's nest. Surreally, everyone seemed to be holding a glass or tankard, as if they were at some sort of celebratory party. I clocked some dryads from their assorted hats and swaying bodies, and here and there a naiad headcrest stuck up above the crush, while what looked like the whole herd of satyrs were laughing next to an impromptu bar in one corner. And in among them all a horde of about twenty Gatherer goblins were stomping about, the lights in their trainers flashing as they alternatively picked up rubbish and offered nibbles, all while trying to avoid the large, fluffy green-haired puppy who was having fun nipping at their heels.

I stopped in shock, hardly noticing Hugh until he appeared in front of me and blocked my view.

'What the hell's going on, Hugh?' I said, anxiety tightening my gut. 'I've got an appointment with the Morrígan, I need to—'

'You don't need to do anything, Genny.' His ruddy face creased in a wide smile as he pressed a glass into my hand. Bemused, I took it. 'The Morrígan has been and gone, the fae are celebrating the faelings' rescue, and everything is on its way to being settled.'

I knocked the drink back – vodka, I discovered, pleased – and half a dozen others handed to me by an attentive goblin while Hugh explained. After the Stepfords had been rescued, Hugh's anonymous tipster had come forward to reveal that the Morrígan was taking the Stepfords to the Fair Lands until they and their babies were out of danger. The tipster had also delivered details of the biological wizard fathers, many of whom had already offered their future sons' surrogate mothers a place alongside their children, as the boys' nannies.

'That's great news,' I said. 'So who's the anonymous tipster?'

'Ana,' Hugh said, confirming my suspicion. 'She's claiming Craig was blackmailing her into complying with his plans, but now he's dead from an … unfortunate … accident that occurred during your explosive exit from the Tower's *Between*' – Hugh gave me a searching look, which I ignored – 'she's come forward openly. We're still investigating, but if she's telling the truth, that will go some way to mitigating any charges brought against her. She says Craig had Witch Harrier and the faelings under some sort of mind-compulsion.'

'He did,' I confirmed, and told Hugh all about the Old Donn, ending with how I'd taken his furry orange hide to the ravens at the Tower: they were going to peck apart the hide with its glyphs and destroy the magic trapping his spirit, giving him the freedom I'd promised him. On my terms.

After we'd finished talking, Hugh pointed me towards the bronze pool at the centre of the garden. I made my way through the crowd to find a woman waiting next to the thirty-foot-high fountain.

She smiled shyly as I joined her, and I didn't need her hip-length waterfall of pale blonde hair or the baby-bump beneath the long silver evening dress to know she was Ana, my niece/cousin. And I realised it had been she who had freely given me her power when I'd needed it inside the Tower: the connection still jumped between us like barely contained lightning.

395

'Thanks for the help, Ana,' I said, truly grateful and also, suddenly, unaccountably, awkward in the face of yet more family I hadn't known about – and also feeling ridiculously underdressed in the plain black T-shirt and jeans I'd borrowed from a helpful vamp at the Coffin Club.

'No. Thank you,' she said softly as she smoothed her hands over her bump. 'I couldn't stop Craig on my own, so I prayed to The Mother to help all of them, and us too, and she sent you.'

The Disney Heaven penny finally dropped: *Ana* was the one who wanted a new life. But who was— 'Us?'

Her face brightened with love and she gave a soft whistle. The green fluff-ball puppy pricked up its ears and bounded over to us with a sharp-toothed doggy grin. 'Say hello to your Aunty Genny,' Ana said.

Aunty Genny? My stomach flip-flopped with nervous excitement. Damn, I'd never been an aunty before.

The puppy shook like it was shedding water, magic prickled over my skin, and then a stick-thin girl of about eight dressed in jeans and a 'Hello Kitty' top and sporting a spiky green Mohican appeared. 'Hello, Aunthy Genny, I'm Andy,' she lisped, then grinned the same sharp-toothed grin as her doggy shape. And I saw that along with her long white canines, she had two tiny venom incisors – vamp fangs. 'Fanthy a bite, Aunthy?' she added cheekily.

'Andrea!' Her mother gave a shocked gasp, and a large watery hand whipped out of the fountain and swatted Andy on the backside.

Andy jumped and stuck her tongue out at the fountain. 'Watch it, Great-Grandpops,' she said, 'otherwithe I'll cock my leg—'

Ana clapped a mortified hand over Andy's mouth and whispered frantically in her ear, during which the kid treated me to an exaggerated eye-roll.

I pressed my lips together to stop from laughing and shot Andy my best 'not-impressed' look, which earned me another eye-roll, and then she shimmered back into the large green fluff-ball puppy, squirmed out of her mother's hold and went back to tormenting the goblins.

So that was who Mad Max had been giving my blood to.

'I'm so sorry, Genevieve,' Ana said, her cheeks flushed with embarrassment. 'She's going through a difficult stage.'

I smiled. 'Hey, no worries—'

'Clíona says we're tainted,' Ana rushed on, driving all the laughter out of me. 'When she found out about me and Andy, she wanted to …' She stopped and took a deep breath, and I filled in her unspoken words: *kill us*. Which was Clíona's original plan for me too, of course. So it looked like my sidhe grandmother really was the bigoted wicked faerie queen. Ana gestured at the partying fae around us with a slightly awed look. 'I thought they would feel the same as Clíona. It's why I've hidden us away all these years, and why I did what Craig wanted—' Her hands clutched at her bump. 'He said he wouldn't protect us if I didn't comply, not just from the Autarch, but from the rest of them. But then I heard your father was also a vamp, and that the fae had accepted you, so I hoped they'd accept me and Andy now too.'

I knew how she must've felt, all those years of hiding out, thinking the fae would reject her for her tainted blood, since I'd thought exactly the same thing … except I'd only had myself to worry about.

'I'm sure they'll accept you both,' I said, swallowing back the angry lump in my throat. And if they didn't, I'd make them. 'Oh, and don't worry about Andy's blood problem,' I said, 'we'll sort it out.'

She gave a tremulous smile. 'Thank you, Genevieve.'

'Oh, call me Genny.' I smiled back, 'And, er, I was wondering what Andy is?'

'Oh, she's a Norwegian Elkhound,' Ana said happily.

I blinked. 'Sorry?'

'Oh!' More embarrassed heat rose in Ana's cheeks. 'Sorry, I get so used to people asking me when I take her for walks.' She laughed nervously. 'I don't know what she is exactly. The nearest I've been able to work out is she's a dhampir, but I'm not sure if that's entirely right.' She gave another tremulous smile.

But before we could talk more, loud barking cut through the air, and we both turned to see Andy's green fur disappear beneath half a dozen goblins. A stream of water shot out of the fountain, drenching the tussle. No one was hurt, just wet and bedraggled, and I bit back a grin as Ana hurried over to impose efficient motherly order.

Then Finn found me.

Chapter Fifty-Seven

Finn led me to a quiet bench. His moss-green eyes were solemn as pulled me into a hug. 'Thank you, Gen,' he murmured, 'for getting Nicky back.' I wrapped my arms round him and breathed in his familiar warm berry scent and listened as he told me about Nicky. She was pregnant – nearly four months gone, so sadly, Helen's plan to swap me for Nicky wouldn't have saved her, even if I had been able to agree to it – and now Nicky was going with the Stepfords to stay with the Morrígan. Worryingly, the records Ana had given to Hugh didn't say whether Nicky's pregnancy was a surrogacy or not. My heart broke for them both and I held him for a long time as his angry, anxious tears dampened the curve of my neck. And desperately wished things could've been different.

'I have to get back to Nicky,' he said once the storm had passed. 'Walk out to the car with me?' We stopped before we reached the road and its rumble of traffic, and with the party buzz behind us, we were left in an oasis of quiet. He cupped my face with his warm gentle hands and kissed me. A hot, gentle touch of his lips on mine that sent my pulse tripping and thrilled me down to my toes.

After a while, he said quietly, 'I'm going with Nicky, Gen.' He paused, and gave me an echo of his old smile. 'Come with us?'

For a long, heart-searching moment I imagined it … but much as I wanted to find out what was between Finn and me now there wasn't a matchmaking curse hanging about, and much as I knew I'd miss him, Nicky needed her dad without any other complications or distractions.

I stood there long after his car pulled away, staring up at the lighted walkways of Tower Bridge, thinking of Finn and what the future might hold ... and Malik's pale, perfect face slipped into my mind ... they both attracted me in different ways ... and they both touched my heart—

'Och, doll,' Tavish's soft burr came out of the darkness, 'dinna fash yerself, the kid'll be back.' I turned cautiously to find him watching me, an indecipherable glint in his pewter eyes. 'And so will the vampire, more's the pity.'

He walked forward and took hold of my left wrist. I felt a pulse of warmth, and the beaded Charm spell bracelet appeared. The telephone box and the London bus were gone, removed by Ricou when Hugh and I had been plotting our master plan at Dead Man's Hole, but the other charms remained, and glinting back among them was Malik's platinum ring.

He'd given it back to me. But was it just a failsafe for if I was in trouble and needed to contact him, or something more? Part of me, a part I didn't want to examine too closely just now, wanted it to be something more.

I frowned at Tavish. 'You don't sound like you want Malik to come back. But he tells me you're his ally?'

'Aye, so I am,' his expression hardened, 'until I've disposed of his Master for him, and then maebe we'll see.'

Malik wanted Tavish to kill the Autarch? Now *that* was an idea I could get behind a million per cent— Except, troublingly, Tavish didn't look like he could swat a kitten right now. Still, he looked way better than when I'd left him with a bull's horn spearing his stomach. Hopefully he'd forgiven me ...

'Um, about what happened with the Morrígan,' I said anxiously, 'did you find a way to remove the protection from the Fertility spell and *crack* the curse?'

'Aye, doll,' he said, his beaded dreads clicking firmly, 'Ana came to an agreement with her, so dinna fash yoursel' about it.'

'Oh, good,' I said, both grateful to Ana for whatever she'd agreed, and determined to find out what it was. 'Um … what about the Chastity spell you *tagged* me with?'

'It'll wear off in time, doll.' He gave an unconcerned wave that didn't convince me one bit.

I frowned. 'You do know the "horn in the stomach" bit wasn't personal … ?'

'Aye, and 'twas a guid trick you played on the Morrígan, and it's all worked out for the best in the end' – he grinned, serrated teeth white against his green-black skin, and I flinched: maybe I wasn't quite forgiven yet – 'but nae doubt you can think of a way tae make it up tae me?'

Then again, he was a tricky wylde fae, so forgiveness was going to come at a price. I narrowed my eyes. 'What does "make it up to you" mean?'

Just as he was about to tell me, Sylvia rushed up, her pink cycle helmet askew, and enveloped me in a cherry-blossom-scented hug. 'Gosh, Genny, you'll never guess what?' Her eyes shone with joy. 'I'm with child. The first full-blood fae in eighty years. That's why we're all having the party.' Ricou stood behind her, his mouth open in his wide yawn-grin, and his headcrest proudly erect.

'Wow,' I said, stunned, and returned her beaming smile with one of my own, then had a weird nauseous moment as Helen's 'baby memory' kicked back in, and the sapphire pendant with its Fertility spell appeared in Sylvia's 'Hello, Boys!' cleavage, tucked next to Grace's gold pentacle. 'Congratulations' – I hugged her again – 'that's amazing news, and really, *really* superfast!'

'I kno-*ow*!' Sylvia squealed in delight. 'The baby's going to be a Christmas seedling; isn't that totally wonderful?'

It was utterly and unbelievably wonderful. And Sylvia's

news lifted a thousand-ton weight off my shoulders. Now the fae's fertility was returned, and working, I wasn't the one who had to have a child to break the curse. Relief overwhelmed me, and I made my excuses, then found a quiet corner to try and take it all in.

Tavish joined me, leaning his shoulder against the bronze-plaque wall, his expression curious. 'I heard tell the witch knocked you out, then almost stripped you in her efforts to retrieve the spell?'

Well, that explained why my clothes had been trashed. 'Good job I gave it to one of the vamps' – *Darius, my fang-pet* – 'to give to Sylvia then.' I shot him a wry smile. 'I wasn't sure who else was after it, or for what.'

He traced the neckline of my T-shirt. 'And I'm joyful tae see you nae wearing your friend's pentacle, doll. It wasnae right tae hold her soul so long after its time.'

Tears stung my eyes – my own, this time. It had taken me a while to realise that it was Grace who was the one upset and causing me to cry, and that until I'd given the pentacle to Sylvia, Grace couldn't move on. 'I hope she's happy,' I murmured, 'wherever she is.'

'Well, doll, I'm thinking this will maebe cheer you up.' He touched his hand to my forehead and muttered something under his breath, then pointed at Sylvia. 'Look quickly now, for my loan of the *sight* 'twill nae last long.'

Sylvia was surrounded by a soft sheen of magic, and within it was a beautiful, shifting pattern, like glossy leaves dappled with sun and shadow – her soul, protected by her aura, I realised in wonder. But the truly breathtaking sight was the radiant star of hot-gold light that graced her throat and trailed a stream of pure fire to the almost imperceptible glow flickering to life in her womb.

I stared in stunned amazement until the lights and colours

round Sylvia dimmed and she was back to looking like her usual self, and a feeling of peace settled in me.

'Och, doll, there's nae need for tears,' Tavish's soft burr came beside me. ''Tis the way of life for souls to take up with a new shell, and now you'll ken where your friend will be.'

I brushed my hand over my face, wiping away the wetness there and smiled. 'Thank you,' I said, and kissed his cheek.

'A kiss is fine thanks, but 'tis more than that I'm wanting.' His mouth curved in a sly smile as he handed me a letter.

I shot him a puzzled look, then opened it. I read it and looked up in shock. 'This says that I'm the new owner of Spellcrackers?' I checked the date. 'Since two days ago?'

'Aye, apparently you dinna like to be telt what's what by your boss.'

'I can't take this,' I said, holding it out to him. 'Spellcrackers belongs to Finn.'

'Och, doll, if you dinna take it, then the kid will nae have a thing to come back to.' He pulled a disgusted face. 'The herd will give it tae one of his prissy brothers.'

That didn't sound good. 'Well, in that case—' I folded it up and slipped it in my pocket. 'I'll keep it for now.'

Tavish picked me up and swung me round, then planted a much-too-happy kiss on my mouth. 'So, now you're the new boss, I'm thinking you're about tae give me a job and make things up t'me.'

'You don't need a job,' I said drily, wondering what he was up to.

He chuckled. 'What's need got to do wi' it, when you've a Chastity spell that needs *cracking*, and I've always had a hankering to be the fae's Sam Spade.' He flung an arm round my shoulders and winked. 'But that's for tomorrow, doll, for now, come and join in the celebrations.'

**Read more about Genny's
adventures in**

THE SHIFTING PRICE OF PREY

Coming soon from Gollancz

Acknowledgements

Writing a book is part fun, part challenge, part tearing-out-of-hair and all hard work, and this book turned out to be harder work than most. But any book isn't just hard work for the author, but for all those folk who encourage and support it on its way from shiny new idea, through pounding of keyboards, those bad hair days and on to publication. My deepest thanks and appreciation to everyone who have helped this book on that journey; any errors are all my own.

Thanks to John Jarrold, my intrepid agent, for his belief in me, to the Gollancz crew for their support and commitment, and especially to Jo Fletcher, editor extraordinaire, for her patience and excellent work in continuing to make my books so much better; and for buying three more of Genny's adventures. Yay!

Thanks to David (*Eagle Rising*) Devereux for letting me bend his ear about 'dead bodies'; to Gareth Wilson (*Falcata Times*) for kindly lending his name to one of my characters; and a special shout-out to the wonderful Mardel (*Rabid Reader*) for all her epic emails, and for loving Genny & Co.

Thanks to Jaye (the *Sabina Kane* vampire series) Wells for not only being a stellar crit partner, and a brilliant, funny writer (go buy her books!), but for letting me 'steal' – *an apple a day keeps the vampires away*. Thanks to my superb, superfast beta readers: Hasna Saadani (The Book Pushers) and Amanda Rutter (Floor to Ceiling Books), you ladies rock! And to Karen

Duvall, to whom I owe thanks to for her insightful help with *The Cold Kiss of Death* (mea culpa).

Thanks to the Thursday Writers, a truly inspiring bunch for all their help and encouragement: Malcolm Angel, Alison Aquilina, Judy Monckton, and Doreen Cory, who have travelled this amazing journey with me from the start. And massive thanks to BFF Fiona Mackenzie for her endless suffering through many drafts, her dedication to Genny & Co., and her masterful debunking of the paranoia goblins when the muse deserts me.

To Norman, my love, my best friend, and the light in my life, without you the dreams would not be possible, or mean as much – thank you, now and always.

And last, but not least, to all those readers who have read, enjoyed, and taken my books into their hearts – I hope you enjoy this one, and a huge, huge 'thank you' to you all.

Suzanne McLeod
Dorset
August 2010

THE CARHULLAN ARMY

ah Hall lives and works in Cumbria. Her first novel,
weswater, won the Commonwealth Writer's Prize; her sec-
d, *The Electric Michelangelo*, was shortlisted for the Man
oker Prize. Her work is translated into ten languages.